Azalin's Last Stand

Azalin's Last Stand

The Nivaka Chronicles: Book 3

Leslie E. Heath

ELIZABETH CITY, NC

Cover Design: matthillbookdesign.com

Editor: Elizabeth Prybylski

Printed in the United States of America

Dedication

This book is dedicated to all the people who said I couldn't do it.

Without the naysayers, I'm not positive I could have pushed through those miserable days when I couldn't see the end. Thank you all for pushing me to accomplish my greatest artistic feat — a finished series.

Contents

The Nivaka Chronicles: The Full Series

Freeing Nivaka: A Nivaka Chronicles Novella

Book 1: The Last Mayor's Son

Book 2: The Tsari's Last Hope

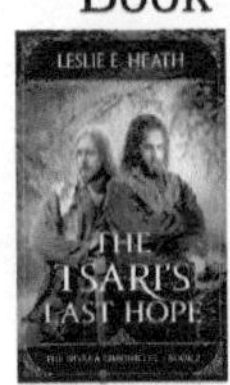

Book 3: Azalin's Last Stand

Journey to Nivaka

The threat is real.

The options are limited.

Could leaving keep his family safe?

Serik has always been different. He's known since childhood that his days in the mountain town were short. But knowing it and living it are two very different things.

Somewhere in the darkness, an enemy watches and waits. Can Serik find safety in the southern forest? Or will his troubles begin anew when he steps into the trees' protected shadow?

Read Journey to Nivaka: A Nivaka Chronicles Short Story, FREE when you sign up for updates on my adventures at BookHip.com/QMLBBC

Acknowledgements

I have to give huge thanks to my editor, Elizabeth Prybylski, and my team of amazing beta readers, Marie DeJarnett, Kelley Lynne, Marlett Pines, Kat Davis, Autumn Araujo, and Lola Steel. You all helped make this book so much better. I couldn't have finished it without your help.

I'm also eternally indebted to Damien Baldwin for his help with the rhyme that Serik used to summon the ancient magic. I'm skilled at many things, but poetry isn't one of them.

And finally, I have to acknowledge my dog, Bear, who wiggled himself between me and the computer any time I got frustrated, upset, or into the suspenseful scenes. Thank you for keeping me safe from all villains both real and imagined.

1.

Betrayed

After an eternity of muffled cries, thumps, and crashes, silence fell in the dark corridor. Ahren eased her door open a crack, careful not to make a sound. Peering out into the hall, she strained her eyes into the blackness and searched for any sign of movement. Nothing. The lamp that had lit the hallway earlier had been extinguished at some point, and now only the faintest blush of light from the lobby illuminated the scene. Halfway between her room and the dining hall, a crumpled form lay unmoving on the floor.

Ahren gasped, rushing out into the hall toward the figure. It had to be Aibek; the brothers wouldn't have left one of their own like that. Broken glass crunched under her slippers, and she slowed, unwilling to risk the glass cutting through the soft fabric into her feet. When she was sure she had cleared the worst of the debris, she paused and brushed a few stubborn shards from the soles of her slippers. Her fingers lingered on the tiny tears in the fabric. She'd just bought these shoes last week, and now they were ruined.

Sighing, she set her foot back on the floor and stepped toward Aibek. From there, she could see his chest rise and fall. Good. He was breathing. That meant he wasn't dead. She couldn't handle another funeral this soon, though he hadn't really been dead the last time.

She knelt beside his still form and placed a hand on his shoulder. He was bleeding from a cut on his cheek, and more blood dribbled from his open mouth. Should she roll him over? No, she wasn't sure how badly he was hurt. Besides, she wasn't strong enough to move him on her own.

"What's happened here?" Wayra's voice echoed in the silence, startling Ahren.

She stood up quickly, lost her balance, and stumbled until her shoulder connected with the wall.

"Wayra! It's Aibek. Help me get him back into your room."

Wayra crept through the broken glass and rushed to Ahren's side, then bent over and examined Aibek's bruised face.

"What happened? Gods! He looks awful. Do you think it's safe to move him?"

Shaking her head, Ahren positioned herself on Aibek's other side. "I don't think we have a choice. The other guests will wake soon. We can't have him lying in the hall when they all come out for breakfast. I'll explain once we have him settled."

They worked together to roll Aibek to his back, then braced his shoulders between them and lifted him off the floor. His feet dragged through the shards of glass as they maneuvered him into the room he shared with Wayra.

Once Aibek was safely settled in his bed, Ahren rushed off in search of the nearest healer. She found Ira in the dining hall, and the young innkeeper directed her to the stone home across from the ferry dock.

Ahren pulled her cloak tighter against the chill and tried to ignore the sense of betrayal that had hung over her all evening. She'd waited up for Aibek, thinking she'd be able to talk to him before he returned to his room. She'd only wanted to apologize for the way she'd treated him before, but she'd been crushed when that other woman had drawn him into her room. Who was she? Aibek had acted like he knew her at dinner and had danced with her twice, but Ahren hadn't recognized her.

The stone house the innkeeper had described loomed out of the darkness on her left, and Ahren stopped abruptly, nearly stumbling into the bushes as her thoughts broke off. Lifting her skirt, she scuttled across the damp stone walkway leading to the door, raised her hand, and rapped on the wood as hard as she could.

The river churned against the dock behind her, its noise both foreign and unnerving to Ahren as she waited for the healer in the faint blue light of dawn. She didn't have to wait long before a stooped, graying man opened the door.

"I need your help! My friend is hurt," she blurted out before he could speak.

"Let me get my supplies." He snapped the door closed in her face, and tears welled up in her eyes.

She blinked against the tide of emotion and breathed in the crisp morning air. Turning, she let her eyes journey over the massive hull of the ferry docked across from the healer's home. In the dim light, it moved gently on its moorings, heaving up and down like the breath of a great beast.

Behind her, the door creaked open. Ahren turned, nodded to the gentleman on the stoop, and stepped down onto the pebbled walk. She didn't speak as she hurried down the footpath, leading him into the inn and straight to Aibek's door. Wayra answered her knock before she'd lowered her hand, ushering Ahren and the healer into the room and snapping the door shut behind them.

The unmoving man on the bed drew her attention, and she pushed past Wayra and knelt beside Aibek. His face had swollen more since she'd been gone, but the bleeding had stopped. Wayra had apparently removed his clothes, because his bare shoulders showed above the heavy blanket covering him.

"Perhaps the lady should step out in the hall while I examine the patient," the healer said.

Color rushed into Ahren's cheeks as she realized the healer would need to see all of Aibek to determine the extent of his injuries.

"Of course," she murmured.

Turning, she ducked her head and retreated into the hall. She paused there for a breath, returned to her room and dressed for the day in a daze. As she dressed, she struggled to keep from waking Zyanna. She could hardly contain her embarrassment when she realized she had made the trip to the healer's home in her nightclothes. Oh, well. She tied the satin sash around the waist of her new day dress. There was nothing she could do about it now. At least none of the other mayors had been out to see her in such a state.

~ * ~

The curtains couldn't block enough of the midmorning light to keep it from shooting knives through Aibek's skull, so he rolled over and pulled the blankets over his head. He stayed that way only a breath before the pain in his ribs forced him onto his back, and the heavy down blanket settled over his face, threatening to suffocate him. With a groan, he pulled the covers down to his chest and flung an arm over his eyes to block some of the excruciating light. The movement tugged at the bandage around his chest but was less painful than laying on his side.

With a creak and a thump, t he door flew open. Aibek groaned and burrowed under the blanket.

"Well, good morning! I thought you'd be up and about by now." The healer's voice echoed through the small room, and daggers of pain shot through Aibek's head.

Why did he have to be so loud? What was the man's name? Aibek closed his eyes, unable to think through the pain.

"How are those ribs doing? I think they're about the worst of your injuries."

Aibek curled his lip at the obnoxious cheer in the healer's voice. He felt like he'd been trampled by an ox and this man wanted to chatter like a squirrel? "Hmph." Ignoring the pain in his side, Aibek rolled to his stomach and tugged the pillow over his head.

"Ahh. You have a bit of a headache today? I'm not surprised. You took at least one good hit to the head." The voice was muffled now, but still seared Aibek's head like an iron from his uncle's forge.

The chair creaked as the healer seated himself, then the covers flew back and Aibek squeezed his eyes shut against the brutal light.

"I have something that will help."

Did he have to be so loud? A rancid odor wafted over him and Aibek retched, rolling to his side to empty his stomach of the broth he'd choked down that morning.

When he'd wiped his face and steeled himself against the stench, he opened his mouth to speak. He gagged again as the disgusting air filled his mouth, then forced his question out in a hoarse croak. "What is that? Tell me you don't expect me to drink it."

The healer laughed. "No, it's not something you drink. Turn your head. I'm going to apply this to that lump on the side of your head."

Frowning, Aibek turned his head toward the healer, presenting the uninjured side of his face. The healer – Androu! That was his name.

Androu chuckled. "Don't worry. The stink doesn't last long. Turn your head so I can see the wound."

Aibek did as he was told, but he still wasn't convinced that this "treatment" would work. How was he supposed to believe that something that smelled so bad could relieve him of anything but his breakfast? Regardless, he held still and winced as the cold liquid ran down his scalp and pooled on the pillow. He fought the urge to retch again as the odor engulfed him.

Focused as he was on not soiling his bed with stomach contents, Aibek didn't hear the door open behind him.

"So, how's the patient?"

Wayra's voice startled Aibek and he flipped to face his friend, inadvertently flinging the rancid concoction from his hair all over Wayra and Androu. Wayra gagged and vomited into the bucket beside the bed, while Androu merely wiped his face with his handkerchief.

Somehow Aibek could still see clearly after the sudden movement, and he smiled. "I think it's starting to work. It doesn't hurt so bad to talk now."

"Wonderful. Take it easy today and eat as much as your stomach can handle. You'll need plenty of meat to heal. I'll be back tomorrow morning to see how you're doing." Androu moved toward the door but stopped before he reached it and turned back to face Aibek. "Oh, um… You should probably keep to your room for a few days until the swelling on your face goes down a bit. You're not exactly pretty to look at."

Chagrined, Aibek stood and positioned himself before the looking glass, then shook his head at the reflection. His face was a mass of bruises and lumps, though the swelling over his eye had gone down enough that he could at least open it now.

"Those men messed up your pretty face," Wayra said, walking up behind him. "You think your girl will mind?"

Startled, Aibek spun to face his friend, the sudden movement pulling at his ribs and shooting pain through his chest. "What rumors have you heard? Whatever they are, they're not true."

Wayra threw his hands up. "Woah. Slow down. It's not a rumor. Someone saw you come out of the girl's room and get jumped by her brothers, that's all."

Aibek lowered himself into a chair by the fire and cradled his head in his hands. He had hoped no one had seen anything. Her reputation would be ruined.

"It's not that bad. I've been able to keep it quiet," Wayra said. "As far as I can tell, everyone believes that you've fallen ill and are staying in your room so you don't spread your illness."

Silence fell. Aibek worried about how the mayors and their guests would react to his bruised and battered face. He'd have to come up with some story about falling in the dark or something. Anything to keep suspicions off of Marah.

Oh, no. Marah! How was she taking his absence? What if she thought he was avoiding her after their one stolen night?

"We'll have to come up with a story for your face, though." Wayra's words brought Aibek back to the present and closely echoed Aibek's own concern. "What if we tell them you got dizzy and fell into the table or something. That works with you being sick. Plus, the healer's been here every day so that works, too."

Leaning back in the chair, Aibek closed his eyes groaned.

"You'll have to do something about that stench, though," Wayra said with a laugh. "No one will believe that's supposed to heal an illness."

They laughed together until lunchtime, enjoyed their meal, and Aibek settled in for a nap until dinner.

Aibek hid in his room for the next three days, thankful his friends brought him food and kept him company. By the fourth day, the walls closed in, and he couldn't bear the thought of another day in the tiny space. Besides, he needed to know if word had gotten out. How was Marah doing after everything that had happened? Did she regret their night together? His mind had gone in endless circles for days, and he needed answers.

When the sun had reached midway to its peak, he bathed and   dressed, determined to find Marah and make sure he hadn't made her life more difficult. The Grand Council meeting would be the next day, so he had very little time to make sure she was all right.

He kept his head low as he emerged from his room and made his way to the tavern. Inside the large room, he spotted Wayra, Zyanna, and Ahren at a table in the far corner and made his way to them. Ahren smiled as he approached, and Aibek straightened his spine.

"It's good to see you out and about," Ahren said with a huge grin. "You had us worried for a while."

Grinning back despite himself, Aibek replied, "Thanks. I think I had myself worried, too."

"You're looking much better," Wayra said. "Much less likely to scare the children, now."

Laughter filled the air as Aibek seated himself at the table.

"I'm starving. What's for lunch?" Aibek laid his napkin on his lap and looked around for the innkeeper or his wife so he could order.

"We ordered for you; I hope that's all right," Zyanna said, a soft smile on her face. "Wayra thought you'd be hungry."

Returning her smile, Aibek nodded. "That's very thoughtful of you. Thank you."

He hadn't gotten to know Zyanna as much as he would have liked over the past year, but she'd been busy having a baby and learning to be a mother. The girl had learned to crawl, making her more difficult to corral, and had stayed with her grandparents while Zyanna made the trip to Kainga.

"Are you enjoying the city?" Aibek asked. "You haven't been able to come as often as Ahren and her friends."

Zyanna smiled. "Yes. It's been lovely. I've bought some new dresses and some clothes for Calloli. There's so many different people here. It's a very interesting place."

She gestured to a table behind him filled with bushy-haired men in stained woolen clothes. Their shirts were so heavily soiled, he couldn't tell what color they had originally been.

"I'd stay away from them if I were you. I think they're Helak's men. They look an awful lot like the ones who attacked us when we got off the ferry last week." Aibek turned back to his group, his face set in a grim mask.

He met Wayra's eyes. "Have you been able to convince any of the guests to guard the doors and keep anyone who doesn't belong in the meeting away?"

"Yes. About twenty men have volunteered, so we have enough that they can take turns and keep five men on watch at all times."

Aibek moved his hands out of the way when plump older serving woman plunked food-laden platters down on the table. He thanked the woman and scooped a forkful of the pheasant into his mouth. The rest of the meal passed in relative quiet with only an occasional comment on the food.

When he had finished his meal, Aibek mustered his courage and went looking for Marah. He needed to be sure she was all right and didn't think he had been avoiding her for the past several days.

He searched both the The Lazy Shepherd, where he and Marah were both staying, and Bard Tavern across the street. The other guests made his search more difficult as they stopped him every few steps to inquire about his health and exclaim over the bruises on his face.

As the sky turned red with the sunset, Aibek gave up and returned to his room to regroup. Marah couldn't avoid him forever; they were both mayors and would be in the Grand Council meetings together. He'd catch her before or after the meetings to make sure she was all right.

His shoulders drooped as he crossed the road. He paused and fixed his posture before entering the inn. He couldn't be seen moping about on the night before the big meeting. Instead, he pasted on a smile and strode into the gathered crowd with his head held high.

2.

Dragons

After a hasty breakfast alone in his room, Aibek strode across the road and opened the meeting room door with trembling hands. This was his last chance to win over the mayors and ensure Nivaka wouldn't have to face Helak's armies alone.

He slipped into the packed room and frowned. Every member of the Grand Council stared back at him. "Am I late?"

"Nah, we all got here early," Vayna said, grinning. He hitched a thumb toward the men and women seated behind him. "They all thought you'd give up and leave after yesterday's meeting, but I knew better, so I made sure I was here to win the bet. Pay up Bartel. Iriz?"

"What? Now?" Bartel's fair skin flushed crimson.

Iriz sputtered and fidgeted. "I would never!"

"All right, since we're all here, let's get started," Aibek said, shaking off his stunned reaction and stepping into the center of the room. "I realize that what I said yesterday shocked some of you—all of you," he corrected when Vayna rolled his eyes. "But, in all honesty, I spoke the truth." Murmurs rose in the room and Aibek raised his voice to make sure they all heard. "I can prove it."

The room grew quiet.

"I can prove it," Aibek repeated, softer. "Come with me to the forest. The Bokinna's protectors have agreed to meet us at the stream to verify that I've met her and that she's willing to help us. I'll even pay the crossing fare for anyone who's willing to give me one more chance."

Silence stretched. Mayors glanced nervously around the room, but none met Aibek's worried gaze. Aibek's heart pounded in his ears and sweat beaded on his upper lip. His mind spun frantically. What would he do if no one agreed to go? The dragons were his only real option to prove he'd been to the Heart of the Forest.

Vayna stood. "I'll go. I want to see what you've got up your sleeve."

Dizzy relief flooded Aibek, and he braced himself on the back of a chair to keep from falling.

"I'll go, too." Marah stood and stepped up beside Vayna.

Six others volunteered, one at a time.

When no one else spoke, Aibek asked, "Anyone else?" A few people shook their heads, while others kept their eyes glued to the floor. "All right, then. Can we meet again this afternoon to discuss our trip and get back to talking about Helak's army?"

"You're awfully confident, Mayor," Kaskin spat. "What makes you think anyone will want to hear more from you after your blasphemy and lies?"

"I have no doubt that the ones who travel with me to the forest will vouch for me after our trip. It's early yet, but we'll adjourn for the day and meet again tomorrow morning. If I'm lying, you'll all hear about it at supper, all right?"

Three people nodded, and Aibek decided that was all the answer he would get. "Okay, well, let's go. I think it's early enough that we can still catch the first ferry." He hurried through the door without checking to see if anyone followed.

"Hey! Wait up! There's no need to run," Vayna trotted up beside him.

Aibek slowed his pace so the mayors rushing in his wake could catch him. "Sorry."

Vayna laughed. "I would have run for it if I were you. They're a tough crowd."

"You could say that again," Aibek said, laughing along. Remembering Kaskin's angry outburst, he shook his head. "Thank you for saving me back there."

"What else could I do? Like I said, I'm dying to see what you've got up your sleeve." Vayna grabbed Aibek's arm and dragged him the last few steps to the ticket booth. "We need nine tickets for that boat," he said to the woman in the shack.

The ferry ride passed in silence as Aibek worried that even the dragons wouldn't be enough to convince the rest of the mayors. What would he do if they wouldn't believe him after this? The others chatted nearby, but he couldn't bring himself to join in.

He waited until they'd left the ferry and found the

road to the forest before he whispered, "We're almost there. Please be there."

Anticipation clutched at his stomach, but he shoved the feeling aside and tried to join the easy banter the others shared.

"I've found that each village has its own unique feel, its own quirks, you know?" Bartel said. "Like Nivaka has all those crazy carvings everywhere, and Bekuz has different colored roofs for people with different occupations: red for the healers, orange for the carpenters, green for hunters, and so on. What about your villages? What are their quirks?" He smiled at Marah, and Aibek's gut twisted again.

Marah grinned back at the handsome mayor. "I don't know." Her voice took on a wistful tone. "I guess the paintings. Instead of stone or wood mosaics like I've seen in Nivaka and a few other villages, we paint murals on the outside of our homes. My father's house has a painting of dragonflies circling above a waterfall. It's so peaceful and welcoming."

A look of sadness crossed her delicate features, and Aibek fought the urge to put a comforting arm around her shoulders.

He tore his eyes away from her lovely features. The tree-line growing on the horizon had grown much closer than he'd expected. His heart hammered against his ribs as he slowed his steps, allowing the others to outpace him.

When he was certain his companions couldn't hear, he whispered, "We'll be in the forest in a few minutes. Are the dragons close?"

He kept his eyes open so he wouldn't trip but focused all his energy on listening to the wind, the trees, and the life around him. A few heartbeats later, the Bokinna replied, "They'll be there, but they'll circle above until the mayors are at the stream. Gworsad worried the dragons waiting would make the others run away, and they could accuse you of leading them into a trap. Have you told them who awaits them?"

Hot shame flushed his cheeks, though Aibek wasn't sure why. "No, I haven't told them. I didn't know how. You're very wise to wait until they're already there to have the dragons land. I hadn't considered that angle."

"I must rest now. They are already above the stream."

The light breeze died, and Aibek fought the sense of loneliness.

"What are you doing?"

Aibek jumped at the sound of Marah's voice so close beside him. Had she heard him whispering? "N-Nothing," he stammered. "Just making sure I'm ready."

"Ready for what?" She placed a hand on his arm, and he lost himself in her amber gaze. "What are you leading us into?"

"Nothing dangerous," he said. The words sounded rushed to his own ears. "The forest's protectors will meet us at the stream."

At her uncertain expression, he added, "If we were facing anything dangerous, don't you think I would've brought my sword?" He gestured to his unadorned waist and she laughed.

"Good point."

They stepped into the dim coolness of the forest, and Aibek's apprehension returned, multiplied by the Bokinna's words.

What if they think it's a trap? He fretted. *What ifs won't help you. You have to deal with what is.*

His uncle's lesson rang in his ears, as clearly as if the man were standing beside him. Aibek dragged in a deep breath, exhaled, and sniffed the air. The musty, sickly odor that had permeated the forest for months had faded in the days he'd been in the city.

He distracted himself from his worries by focusing on the signs of improvement in the forest. The trees had lost their grayish cast, and the green slime had receded. Some trees didn't have any slime patches at all.

A smile stretched across Aibek's face, and he tipped his head back to look up into the treetops. No leaves adorned the trees, but that was expected in the late autumn. Patches of blue sky shone between tangles of high branches.

Nearby, water burbled over the rocky stream bed. The sound brought Aibek's mind back to the present task, and he hurried to catch up with the others.

"Before they arrive, I need everyone to sit down and make sure you're calm." Aibek's voice echoed through the quiet forest. "They're afraid you won't want to meet them."

"Who?" Bartel spread his cloak on the ground and

settled onto it. "Who's coming? And why would they think we wouldn't want to meet them?

"You'll find out soon enough. Is everyone ready?" Aibek forced a smile to hide his nervousness and checked that the mayors were settled. Everyone had seated themselves against the trees, forming a circle around the open area the stream bisected.

"We're ready," Marah said. "Where is the proof you promised us?"

"All right, then. We're all ready." Aibek's stomach fluttered, and he fought the urge to look up.

A great rumbling shook the treetops followed by a strong gust of wind. Gworsad swooped down into the clearing and alighted upon the rocky soil beside the stream.

Marah gasped, and Aibek worried that the mayors weren't taking the surprise very well.

"You've brought us here to feed us to dragons?" Bartel shouted.

Aibek laughed and approached the enormous beast. "Of course not."

Before he could say more, Tukanli dropped out of the sky and rested beside Gworsad, her thorny collar crackling with the movement.

"Everyone, I'd like you to meet the Bokinna's protectors. This is Gworsad." The beast rumbled and ducked his head in an awkward bow. "And this is Tukanli."

"Hello," Tukanli said, her voice soft. "I hope you not… what is word?" She looked to Gworsad with a frustrated expression in her deep green eyes.

"I— I mean *we*… hope you not scared," Gworsad rumbled.

Tukanli made a soft clicking sound. "Yes, of course. That is it."

Aibek smiled, and this time it was genuine. "You've been practicing. Very well done."

More rumbling echoed through the clearing, the sound reminiscent of a cat's purr, only deeper and louder.

Another gust of wind rustled the dried leaves on the ground, and Aibek tipped his head back. Four more dragons circled above.

He lowered his eyes and met the stunned gazes of the other mayors. "Are you all right if the others land? Or would that be too much for you? I'll send them home if they'll make you nervous, but we shouldn't leave them up there all morning."

A shrill, honking laugh pierced the wind. "Bring them down! I'd love to meet them all." Iriz laughed again and met Aibek's eyes. "You really did meet her, didn't you?"

"I did." Aibek sighed and the worry and stress lifted off his back like a garment. "My friend found the medicine that could cure the forest's illness, and we took it to her together. She's offered to help us fight Helak in a couple of different ways. First, these fine friends will help by carrying us to and from the battle and allowing us to fight from their backs."

"What? You mean we can fly? On a dragon?" Bartel's face had gone pale, and his eyes widened further than Aibek thought possible.

"Yes, but you don't have to if they make you nervous. You have to relax and give the dragon the freedom to fly."

"Who wouldn't want to fly?" Marah said, her voice higher-pitched than normal. "This is incredible!"

"So, does that mean the others can land?" Aibek shaded his eyes, and a large green dragon folded its wings and dropped out of the sky.

"Oh!" Marah breathed. "How lovely."

Three more dragons landed in the clearing, one right after the other, and soon the wide space felt small and cramped.

When the wind had died down, Bartel cocked his head. "No offense intended, Aibek, but is there any way we can hear from one of the dragons what they expect of us? And... and could they maybe... I'm sorry, there's no way to say this without sounding awful." He drew a breath and tried again. "Could one of them confirm what you've said? That you met the Bokinna? That they're her protectors?" He coughed once and dropped his eyes to the leaf-covered ground. "That they won't eat us if we try to ride them?"

Aibek couldn't help himself. His shoulders shook, and he coughed once, trying to suppress the mirth bubbling up within his chest. He couldn't contain it long, and it burst from him in a loud, snuffling laugh. Gworsad rumbled along, and within a breath all the mayors and dragons were laughing together.

Once the laughter had subsided, Aibek wiped his

eyes and nodded to the dragons. "Well? Gworsad, can you answer his questions?"

The dragon stretched his moss-covered neck across the clearing, setting his head on the ground in front of Bartel. The top of his nose reached to Aibek's waist, and the horns stretched high above his head. The great beast sniffed and rumbled once. "I am Gworsad. I protect Bokinna with my friends. Aibek helped her, and we help him. We help you if you help him. We not eat you if you his friend."

Marah's eyes widened. "What about those who aren't his friends?"

Gworsad twisted to stare at her with one orange eye. "We might eat men who fight him. Are you friend? Or foe?"

"Friend!" Marah shouted. "I'm his friend. I... I was thinking of... of someone else."

"We not eat anyone until battle, unless they too close to Bokinna," Tukanli said. She shifted so her back leg touched Gworsad and wrapped her tail close around him. "That is right, yes?"

Aibek stroked a hand along her smooth neck, below the thorny collar. "Yes, that's perfect."

"Can— can I..." Iriz stared at Aibek's hand on Tukanli's neck and tried again. "Is it all right if I touch one? Like you're doing?"

"Is that all right?" Aibek looked to Gworsad, where the great beast still rested his head on the ground.

"I think is great idea." Gworsad rumbled. "They need get used to us if we carry them."

Iriz, Marah, and Bartel leapt to their feet. Vayna and Dorrel eased themselves to a stand, but Avatta, Olarel, and Parora leaned back against their respective trees. Aibek didn't push them but watched to make sure they weren't going to run away.

They spent the rest of the morning mingling, talking, and getting to know the dragons. Even the more reserved mayors stood and joined in the conversations once they saw how friendly the dragons were.

When the sun reached its peak in the sky, Gworsad called an end to the meeting, saying it was his turn to patrol around the Bokinna. The dragons flew off in a flurry of wind and rumbles, and the mayors gathered their belongings and headed back to the city.

~ * ~

Eddrick stood between Agommi and Kiri before the ancients in the otherwise-empty chamber. The same paper-thin spirits hovered on the raised dais at the front of the court room, all staring at Eddrick and his family.

"We have decided that your spying can provide us with useful information. You may resume your spying activities, but with a few restrictions."

Eddrick's heart leapt, then dropped as the ancient one spoke.

"You will take Glesni with you wherever you go from now on. We will build an army of our own here to oppose this Helak's spirit force when the time for fighting arrives. But be warned, this is dangerous work. If you are destroyed during this kind of battle, you cease to exist. There is no redemption from that death."

"Thank you, your eminence." Eddrick bowed low and kept his head down. "May we tell our son what we learn in these activities?"

"You may reveal the enemy's location and movements, but nothing more. You may not disclose our proposed role in the coming battle." The spirit's voice carried like a whisper on the wind.

Eddrick frowned, still bent in his bow. "Please excuse my ignorance, your eminence. I'm afraid you've lost me. What is our role in the coming battle?"

"We plan to thwart the enemy by removing his spirits from the humans' battle. Without their interference, the living can fight a fair battle and the best army may win."

Kiri shifted beside him, and he grabbed her hand to still her. Her voice echoed in the empty space, sweet and clear. "May I warn my son that we will not be there to offer him advice or support during the fight?"

"You may tell him that but nothing more."

"Thank you." Kiri slumped, and Eddrick squeezed her hand.

"You may leave us. Glesni will meet you in the grand atrium at dawn and will stay with you until this conflict ends one way or the other."

Eddrick leaned against the wooden door to their suite, struggling to figure out his emotions.

"I can't believe they're letting us keep spying." Kiri threw herself face-down on the bed. "And, they're letting us give Aibek information. That's something, at least."

"I'm not sure how I feel about Glesni going everywhere we go indefinitely. He's the ancients' eyes and ears. Whatever he sees, they see. We'll have to be careful what we say around him."

Kiri nodded without lifting her head out of the pile of pillows. "It's probably for the best. I don't know if I could keep from telling him everything without a chaperon."

"We don't need a nanny to keep watch over us every moment. How will we have any time for us if he's there for everything we say and do?" Eddrick sat on the bed beside his wife and rubbed a hand up her back.

Kiri rolled over and smiled up at him. "We'll be all right, I'm sure, but just to be certain…" She ran a hand up his leg and he leaned over to kiss her.

"Ahem." Agommi's voice startled Eddrick, and he dropped Kiri and leapt to the floor beside the bed.

"It's nice to know how easily you forget my presence." Agommi grinned and drifted to the window.

"Why don't I ever see you and Mother together?" Eddrick cocked his head, studying his father.

"Ours was an arranged marriage." Agommi turned to meet Eddrick's curious gaze. "We got along well enough, but when she died, she went back to her family line. She spends most of her time with her sisters, I believe."

Considering that, Eddrick silently thanked the ancients and the trees for his good fortune. He'd met Kiri at a picnic and fallen for her instantly. He'd learned much later that her father had been the mayor of their village, and a marriage to her would be advantageous for both of them. He'd courted her for a summer and winter, and they'd married the following spring.

The long, cold months when he couldn't see her had been the longest of his life. They'd spent nearly every day together since their marriage, and he'd never questioned spending the afterlife with her. It was a good thing she hadn't wanted to return to her family as his mother had. He wouldn't have been able to bear the pain and disappointment of such a loss.

Kiri hovered above the bed, her clothes and hair as perfect as when she'd thrown herself onto the plush gold quilt.

"Let's go explore the city while we can." Eddrick headed for the door and the others followed him into the bright morning sun.

3.

High Hopes

"That was amazing!" Marah bounced down the trail ahead of Aibek. "When can we try flying? How many of them are there?"

Aibek grinned at her unrestrained enthusiasm. "There are thirty who have agreed to take riders. Ten people have volunteered so far, including me and Faruz. We'll talk to the others tomorrow morning. Maybe some of them will want to fly. If not, we'll ask the army for volunteers."

"Who wouldn't want to?" Bartel stepped up beside Aibek and pressed a hand on his shoulder. "This changes everything! I am sorry I didn't believe you yesterday. You've never given us any reason to doubt your honesty."

"Oh, me, too," Iriz said. "I'm so sorry. That was an awful scene yesterday."

Aibek's smile faded at the memory of the angry accusations of heresy. His gut squeezed, and he wondered if the other mayors would believe they'd visited with the dragons during the outing. *I should've gotten some kind of trinket or something as proof. Aibek thought. Like the one Faruz wore to the swamp. Would they have believed me then?*

Vayna clapped Aibek on the shoulder, pressing himself between Aibek and Bartel. "I never doubted you for a second. Why would anyone make up a story like that? Besides, the forest is getting better. Just look around. Everything smells fresher and the slime is receding."

As they neared the forest's edge, Aibek slowed, putting some distance between himself and the others. "Thank you," he whispered.

"I hope it is enough," the wind answered back.

"Me, too," Aibek said.

"You too, what?"

The nearby voice startled Aibek and he leaped backward on the path.

Marah laughed and grabbed his arm. "Who are you talking to?"

"No one." Aibek flushed and tried again. "I guess it isn't really a secret. I was thanking the Bokinna for her help today."

"She really talks to you, doesn't she." Curiosity shone in Marah's amber eyes and Aibek glanced away. Her scrutiny made him want to squirm like a schoolboy.

"Yes, she does," he answered after a long pause.

"I haven't heard of her talking to anyone but the Gadonus in generations, and my Gadonu says she's only talked to him twice." She cocked her head and regarded him.

"Oh. I didn't know that." He couldn't think of anything else to say, and an awkward silence fell between them.

"I'm sorry about my brothers," she blurted out. "I didn't know they'd be watching my room, honest. I feel simply awful about what they did to you." Tears welled in her eyes and Aibek grabbed her hand.

He wanted to set her mind at ease, so he said, "I'm all right. There's really nothing to get upset about."

"But there is," she whispered. A tear rolled down her cheek. "They could have killed you. I worried myself sick when you didn't come out of your room."

"I—" Aibek began.

"I hope you know you have my support," she interrupted. "I'm trying to get my brothers to go home early so we can spend some time together."

Aibek shook his head to hide his furious blush but couldn't think of anything to say.

"Oh, the others are waiting for us," Marah said. "We should hurry up."

They picked up their pace and caught up to the others, and they continued on to the river as a group.

When the ferry was in sight, Aibek stopped and faced the group. "I know I probably don't have to say this, but I'm going to, anyway. We can't talk about today's trip out in the open in Kainga. Helak has spies all over the city. We'll talk about it in the meeting, and in our rooms, but we need to be careful to keep the secret for now."

He started to turn back to the river, reconsidered, and added, "And thank you." He met each gaze in turn. "Thank you all for giving me the chance to prove myself."

When Aibek returned to his room after a quick lunch, he discovered a sealed note on the floor. He picked it up and shut the door behind him before he broke the seal and read its contents.

Aibek,

I hope this reaches you in time. You must be careful what you say about your work to save the forest. The Bokinna doesn't make a habit of talking to people in the forest, and she hasn't allowed a visitor that I know of in at least six generations. The mayors are likely to take it poorly if you announce your dealings with her in open discussion. Good luck in convincing them to work with you. I fear it won't be an easy task.

Valasa

Aibek folded the note and shoved it into his pack. That information would have been helpful if he'd received it a day sooner. Still, he had high hopes for the remaining council meetings. The morning with the dragons had gone well, and he hoped the mayors would discuss it at length during the evening.

The next morning dawned rainy and cold, the howling wind whipping the icy droplets against the window. The noise woke Aibek early, and he dressed and headed to the tavern for breakfast. He'd eaten supper in his room with Wayra so the otherss could talk without the awkwardness of his presence, but he couldn't wait any longer. He had to know what they were saying. He took his bowl of porridge and mug of famanc to the meeting room across the street, determined to be the first to arrive.

He lit the lamps in the cavernous room and moved aside so the innkeeper could lay a fire on the hearth. When the rotund man had left the room, Aibek settled into his chair and ate his breakfast, enjoying the crackling fire and the quiet solitude. When he'd finished his food, he tucked the empty bowl and mug under his chair. He'd return them to the kitchen after the meeting.

The time passed quickly, and soon the room filled with people. Excited chatter echoed off the bare walls, growing louder with each moment. When everyone had arrived, Aibek stood and stepped into the middle of the circle.

"I'm sure by now you've all heard about our trip to the forest yesterday, right?" Heads nodded, but no one spoke. "Does anyone have any questions?"

To Aibek's chagrin, Kaskin stood. "I do. You'd have us believe that you—*you* of all people— are working with the Bokinna? How do we know you're not just gathering people to feed to her dragons?"

Aibek fought the urge to roll his eyes. Instead, he took a deep breath and met the angry man's gaze. "Yes, I'm working with the Bokinna. If the dragons had wanted to eat us don't you think they would have done so yesterday?" He paused, giving Kaskin time to answer. When the man said nothing, Aibek continued. "Nine of us walked into the forest, and only six dragons landed. We would have made a satisfying meal if that had been their plan, right?"

"Why should they settle for nine if you're going to deliver a whole crowd?"

Dropping his gaze to the empty chair, Aibek sighed. "If they just wanted people to eat, what would stop them from raiding our villages? There are thousands of tasty crunchy people right there in the treetops."

Shock and incredulity showed in Kaskin's face. "Why, of course they won't do that. The Bokinna herself protects us."

"Exactly. Why would she allow her protectors to harm her people?" Aibek swallowed hard and hoped Kaskin wasn't putting questions into the other mayors' minds.

"I—I don't know, but I don't think I trust you." Kaskin flopped into his chair, signaling an end to his interrogation.

Aibek inhaled deeply. "Anyone else?" Silence. "Look, I know this is unusual. I know it hasn't happened in hundreds, perhaps thousands of years. But the Bokinna knows the forest is in danger. The sickness that's been killing the trees is there because Helak's men poisoned the soil. She's willing to help us save the forest—and our homes."

Breathless silence hung in the room.

Finally, someone shouted, "So, what do we have to do to ride a dragon?"

Several people chuckled, and Aibek smiled. "We'll take names today. There are thirty dragons willing to take riders, so if there's more people than that, we'll have to find a way to decide who gets to fly."

The murmur of voices grew as the mayors turned to talk to their neighbors.

"But first," Aibek shouted over the growing din. "We have one more thing to discuss." The group quieted and turned to look at Aibek. "We need a final count. Will you help defend the Tsari from Helak's army? If your village will join our forces, please raise your hand."

Every hand in the room went up except one. Kaskin slumped further down into his chair and crossed his arms over his chest. "I told you we're waiting this thing out," he grumbled. His manner reminded Aibek of the toddlers he'd seen matching wits with their mothers at the market.

"Wonderful," Aibek said. His heart soared with relief and elation. "We should have enough people to win this war, then."

"Does anyone have any questions about riding the dragons before we start taking down names?"

Bartel's hand went up like a child in a classroom.

"Yes, Bartel?" Aibek nodded to the shy young man.

"Has anyone ever tried it before? How do we know it's possible?"

"I have. I've ridden on the dragons' backs three times now. It's… breathtaking at first, but amazing once you get used to it."

"How do you hold on?"

Aibek couldn't tell who had spoken, so he answered to the room. "I've held onto their collars, but I'm thinking about having the leather-workers design some sort of reigns, like what horse riders use."

"Let's do this! Where do I sign up?" Iemes jumped to his feet.

"Form a line over here if you want to ride the dragons. I've got some paper and pens ready." Aibek stepped over to the tables lining the wall to his left and several others followed.

Those who didn't have an interest in the dragons helped themselves to the ale and finger foods the workers had set up on the other side of the room. In half an hour, the line had dissipated, and Aibek had eighteen names on his paper.

He glanced around the room at the restless mayors. "Let's take an hour for lunch, and when we return we'll discuss details of how we'll train for this battle, both with and without the dragons."

The luncheon passed in a blur of conversation as all the interested dragon riders surrounded Aibek and asked question after question about the animals, their behaviors, and how to ride them. They hung on Aibek's every word as he regaled them with the story of his first dragon encounter and how the dragons had gotten him home on the day the villagers had assembled to replace him.

When the allotted time was up, Aibek called the meeting back to order. Everyone filed back to their seats, but one chair remained empty. Aibek searched the mayors' faces, trying to determine who hadn't returned. The realization hit him all at once.

"Has anyone seen Kaskin?" Aibek asked the group.

No one had, and none seemed concerned by that fact. Dread built in Aibek's stomach, though he couldn't say why. He only knew that he needed to find the missing man.

"Let's spread out. Check his room. Check the taverns. He's got to be here somewhere."

"Why?" Bartel said, reclining in his chair. "Let him go. He's been nothing but trouble and he hates us all. Why do we need him here?"

A chorus of "Yeah," and "Let him go," filled the room.

Aibek shook his head. "Let's just make sure he's all right. He's not the kind of person that takes well to being overruled."

More grumbles followed, but men and women stood and followed him from the meeting hall.

"Where's he staying?" Vayna asked as they stepped into the hall.

"He's just down the hall from me. Room eighteen, I think. I'll check the tavern if you check his room." Aibek turned toward the dining area and strode off in search of the petulant mayor.

After checking the taverns in both inns, the common areas, and the meeting room one more time, Aibek asked one of the women at the desk in the Lazy Shepherd.

The petite blonde woman nodded and smiled when

Aibek described Kaskin. "Yes, he left about two hours ago. Said he was homesick for the forest and ready to leave the city behind."

Aibek cursed under his breath, even though part of him hoped the man really had gone home. It just felt wrong. Kaskin wasn't one to give up and slink off. Well, Aibek didn't think so, anyway. He didn't really know the man that well.

Hunched down into his cloak to ward off the bitter wind, Aibek scurried along the rain-slicked street until he reached the ferry. The ticket booth was closed, its shutters clacking in the howling wind. The ship itself looked deserted, so Aibek turned back to the inn. He ducked into the Bard Tavern, stomping to knock the mud off his boots before he continued on to the meeting room.

"I don't know where he's gone," Aibek announced to the assembled mayors, "but the ferry's not running due to the weather, and he's checked out of his room. I guess there are more inns in town. He must have gotten a room somewhere else to wait out the storm."

"Good riddance," Vayna said, laughing. "I don't know why you wasted your time chasing after him."

Aibek wished he had a good answer. Instead, he said, "Let's discuss a training schedule so we can wrap this up. Winter's blowing in early this year, and I don't want to be stuck traveling home in knee-deep snow."

"Good point." Vayna sat down and folded his hands in his lap.

"This will be an interesting winter. While we're

training, the Bokinna will be moving her Shadow Trees into clusters at the outer borders of the forest to hopefully form enough of a wall to keep Helak's men out. That means the villages themselves may move, so make sure you check for new landmarks each day. Once I let the Bokinna know who's training with the dragons and which villages you're from, the dragons will land outside your villages twice a week to practice with you."

"Whoa, slow down." Iemes held his hands up. "What do you mean the villages might move? I don't remember agreeing to a change in location."

"Well, it's sort of unavoidable," Aibek said, trying to make his voice sound soothing. "The Bokinna thinks Helak's men are trying to get to her directly, and the best way to keep her safe is to keep them out of the forest. A wall of trees will keep them from slipping behind our defenses."

"What about the boardwalks? The cisterns? How can the villages move without destroying our homes?" Marah's brows pulled down in a puzzled expression.

"The Bokinna says she can keep the villages intact. They won't be moving fast, maybe a hundred paces a day, at least at first." Aibek smiled and hoped he'd sounded convincing.

"All right." Iemes dropped his hands to his knees. "I guess that makes sense. We'll go back to our regular homes after this is all over though, right?"

"That's the plan." Aibek gazed out the window at the swirling mist. He dropped his voice and muttered, "Of course, that's assuming we win and Helak doesn't destroy us all."

Turning back to the assembled mayors, he raised his voice again. "As I said, the dragons will come twice a week, or every three days. We'll alternate between a day to train together as a group and a day to train one on one with our dragons. We need to get to know and trust them, and they need to trust us if we're all going to fight together without getting in each other's way."

Aibek paused to allow time for questions or comments. When no one spoke, he continued, "I thought we'd wait a couple of weeks to let everyone get home and spend some time with their families. Then we'll start training. Is that all right with you all?"

Heads nodded and several people murmured, "Sounds good," and "That'll work."

"All right, then. We'll have our first group practice two weeks from tomorrow. I can't wait to get started. In the meantime, we should get ready to head home, but I'd love to have one more night of food, music, and dancing before we all go our separate ways."

A cheer went up in the group, and everyone stood and filed out of the room, their voices raised in excitement.

4.

Home

"Are you all right?"

Aibek jumped and pulled his attention back to his table mates. He smiled at the woman beside him—the one he thought had spoken. "Of course. I'm just reflecting on the weeks we've spent here. It's been… interesting."

He hoped the woman—he couldn't think of her name—hadn't followed his gaze to where Marah sat, smiling at her brothers and laughing with her table mates. He shot one last glance in Marah's direction before he shifted in his seat, putting his back to the beautiful blonde.

Vayna laughed as if Aibek had made the funniest joke of the night. "It has been interesting; I'll give you that. I can't believe you managed it. You got everyone to agree to work together. Well done."

Lifting his glass, he shouted, "A toast!"

The room went quiet.

"A toast to Aibek, for risking everything to bring us all together, even when we hated him for it." Vayna winked at Aibek, clinked his glass together with everyone else's, and guzzled his wine.

A cheer rose as mayors and guests tapped their

glasses together and drank to the successful meet. Aibek stuffed his embarrassment down and laughed along with his tablemates as others in the room stood to toast the Grand Council's efforts, singling out Aibek's leadership more often than not.

After about the tenth toast, the cheer began to wear thin, and Aibek stood. "How about some dancing?" Another cheer. People stood and moved tables and chairs, creating a wide circle in the center of the room.

The musicians struck a chord, and dancers paired up and pushed onto the dance floor.

Satisfied with the evening's progress, Aibek stood and stepped toward the door. His head ached from the noise and he longed for the quiet and solitude of his room. Before he made it past his table, someone clamped a hand on his shoulder.

"Well done, Aibek. Well done," Vayna said.

Aibek met his friend's gaze, then dropped his eyes to the floor. "Thank you, my friend, but I don't deserve all the credit. You and Marah saved me more than once this week."

"True enough. I'm happy to share the credit, then." Vayna laughed again and pressed a full wineglass into Aibek's hand. "Let's celebrate. You're not sneaking off early tonight."

Desperate to escape the clamor and heat of the party, Aibek pressed a hand to his head. "Really, I—"

"I don't know how you managed this, Aibek." Bartel stepped up beside Vayna. "But I'm glad you did. I still don't love the idea of battle, but our new friends will change things quite a lot."

"I certainly didn't do it alone, but you're right about our forest friends." Aibek set the still-full wineglass on the table. "They should tip the scales in our favor. Now, if you'll excuse me—"

"Hey! There's the man of the hour!" Several more mayors strolled up and surrounded Aibek.

Defeated, Aibek pasted on a smile and forced himself to interact with the others. He allowed Vayna to hand him his wineglass once more and settled into an empty chair nearby. The rest of the group scooted chairs in close and chattered on about the Grand Council's success.

It didn't take long for his attention to wander to the dancers moving gracefully around the room. He watched closely, hoping for a glimpse of Marah before they said their goodbyes the next morning.

"What're you staring so hard at?"

Startled, Aibek jumped back, his hand gripped the table and knocked his wineglass to the side. It tipped and before he could grab it, it spilled its contents onto the table. He watched, helpless, as the brilliant red liquid raced toward him and dripped over the edge and onto his pale blue pants.

"Oh, I'm so sorry! I didn't mean to startle you!" Marah produced a rag and mopped at the mess on the table.

Coldwine oozed down his leg and settled in his boot, but Aibek kept his face neutral. "Do you have another one of those?" He pointed at the rag in Marah's hand.

"Oh… umm… yes. There's one here." She grabbed one off a nearby table and handed it to Aibek.

He dabbed at the bright stain, trying to dry it without spreading the wine.

"Those may be ruined." Marah leaned over to watch his efforts. When he'd cleaned as much as possible, she touched him on the shoulder. "Dance with me?"

Panicked, he glanced around, searching for her brothers.

She laughed, leaned close, and murmured, "Don't worry. They're busy with a couple of tavern wenches for the night. They'll never know."

"Just dance with her," Vayna said, laughing. "What's the worst that could happen? You've already spilled your drink."

Laughter erupted from everyone at their table, along with a few others within earshot. Aibek's ears burned, but he pushed himself out of the chair. Struggling to ignore the cold, wet spot on the front of his pants, he held out an arm for Marah and led her to the dance floor.

They moved together through the steps of the dance, though he couldn't help plucking at the place where his pants stuck to his legs from time to time. As they moved, he reveled in the soft skin at her wrist beneath his thumb, the pulse at the base of her neck, the sweat beading on her upper lip. After the second song, Marah grabbed his hand and led him out into the darkened corridor.

Before he could object, she pressed her finger to his lips. "I know. I won't do anything to risk bringing my brothers down on you again. I just wanted a minute alone with you before we all leave here tomorrow."

Aibek managed a weak smile but couldn't resist the urge to glance into the shadows down the hall.

"Don't worry, they're not here." Her face flushed, and Aibek wondered at the reason. "Look, I just wanted to ask…" She licked her lips and started again. "I wanted to ask if I can stay near you when we're training with the dragons… and afterward. I'm a bit nervous about where all this is going, but you were so relaxed with them. It would make me feel better to have you nearby."

A wave of relief and embarrassment rolled over him, and Aibek fought back an uncomfortable laugh. "We can try to stick close together on the group days, if you want. I could probably arrange to be there for the first couple of one-on-one practices, too, but you'll need to spend some time alone with your dragon."

"That would help so much." She grabbed his arm, and his heart skipped a beat. "I know I'll have to be alone with the dragons eventually, but I don't think I'm ready for that yet."

"All right. Consider it done." Aibek grinned and nodded as he'd seen his uncle do hundreds of times at the end of complicated negotiations.

Without warning, Marah leaned in and kissed him. Her soft, warm lips moved over his, and his heart skipped then raced. He wrapped an arm around her waist and held her close for a moment. He swept a stray curl away from her cheek, kissed her once, quickly, and stepped to the side.

"Anyone could follow us out here," he whispered.

Her nervous titter echoed down the hall. "I know, but I needed one more kiss. I'm going to miss you when we all go home."

"I'll miss you, too, but we'll see each other twice a week for a bit, right?" He brushed a hand along her delicate cheek.

"I guess. It won't be enough, though."

The door flung open and Aibek dropped his hand.

"What's this all about?" Vayna stood in the doorway, the light spilling past him and filling the hall.

Aibek blinked against the sudden light. "Nothing. She just had a few more questions about our forest friends, that's all."

Vayna bellowed a laugh. "Of course she did. Now, come back in here before people start to talk. Iriz has been looking for you. She wants a dance before this party ends."

"Of course." Aibek shot one final glance at Marah and hurried back into the brightly lit ballroom.

The throbbing in his head returned full-force, and he stumbled through a couple more dances before he made his excuses and strolled across the pitch-dark boulevard and into his room.

Welcome silence enveloped him, and he fell asleep without changing from his wine-stained clothes.

The wind howling outside his window woke Aibek before the sun. Stabbing pain shot through his head. He eased himself upright, poured a glass of water from the pitcher on the washstand, and gulped it down. When the headache lifted a bit, he quickly washed and dressed. He tossed his belongings into his pack, flung it over his shoulder, and headed down to the tavern for breakfast and famanc.

The clinking of dishes filled the empty dining room, and Aibek seated himself at the table closest to the door.

While he waited for the rest of the guests to awaken and the breakfast service to begin, he thought back over the past few weeks. So much had happened since he'd left Faruz in Nivaka. He couldn't wait to get home and tell his friends about the successes he'd had, though he wasn't sure whether he'd tell Faruz about Marah. Somehow, that felt private, like he should keep it between himself and the lovely woman.

A crash shocked Aibek out of his thought, and he sat up straighter in his chair. A heartbeat later, the wide door leading to the kitchen swung open and the dumpy innkeeper stepped into the dining area. Something yellow streaked across his reddened forehead, and Aibek wondered what mishap the innkeeper had dealt with in the kitchen.

The older man bustled through the room, lighting lamps and wiping tables, apparently oblivious to

Aibek's presence. Aibek watched until he'd lit all the lamps, leaned back, and cleared his throat. He stifled a smile when the innkeeper startled.

"Oh! I'm so sorry." The man's thick hand pressed against his wide belly. "I didn't realize anyone was up yet. Good morning, good sir. Can I get you some famanc to start your day?"

Aibek smiled and stood. "That would be wonderful. Thank you so much for your hospitality these past two weeks. I'm afraid you'll be happy to be rid of all of us." He pressed a small pouch of coins into the man's palm.

"Not at all! I hope you don't think it's been anything but a pleasure to have you here." He eyed the pouch, and his ears turned red. "I can't accept this, sir. You've kept my inn filled when it would have been empty. The merchants won't be back until spring, and the farmers are done now that it's frozen." He tried to pass the coins back to Aibek, but Aibek shook his head.

"Keep it anyway. You've done more for us than we expected." When the innkeeper looked ready to object again, Aibek cut him off, saying, "And besides, I never thanked you properly for all your help after my... er... mishap."

The innkeeper laughed, and some of the ruddy color drained from his face. "I guess I could use it to replace that lamp. Thank you, sir. Now, let me see to that famanc." He scurried through the door to the kitchen, and Aibek returned to his seat.

One of the twins brought out his famanc a few

minutes later, and before he'd finished the first cup, Wayra, Zyana, and Ahren joined him at the table.

Aibek did a double take when Ahren sat beside him. *How did I forget she was here? I haven't seen her all week. I wonder what she's been up to.* He worked to keep his shock off his face, though and gave what he hoped was a welcoming smile.

"Don't look at me like that." Ahren beamed up at him. "I haven't been socializing with your enemies, if that's what you're thinking."

His smile twisted a little, though he tried not to display his suspicion. She did have a history of befriending the wrong people.

"Are you actually going home today?" Wayra plopped down on Aibek's other side, leaving Zyana to manage her own chair. "I figured you'd stay until all the others had gone."

Aibek grinned, grateful for the interruption. "I'm ready to get home. It's been a long two weeks. Besides, I need to let the council know what we decided and start working on organizing the group practices with our new friends."

"Sounds good to me." Wayra waved the innkeeper over and ordered his usual breakfast of famanc and porridge. He ordered the same for Zyana and continued, "I'm ready for some of Aunt Breda's cooking. The food here hasn't been bad, but nothing beats my aunt's food."

Zyana smiled her agreement and the meal progressed with a great deal of happy chatter. The group members had each made dozens of purchases during their stay in the city and getting it all home would take some coordinated effort, especially since Zyana's rounded belly meant she couldn't carry much.

After breakfast, they met in the hallway and divvied up the packages. Aibek's shoulders slumped under the excessive weight, and he wondered how he would carry it all the way home. While they walked to the ferry, Aibek toyed with the idea of calling the dragons to meet them at the forest's edge and carry them home.

No, I shouldn't abuse their charity like that, Aibek thought, shaking his head. He glanced around at the other mayors strolling down the street along with his group. Besides, we're not the only ones with heavy packs. It wouldn't be right to accept a ride and leave everyone else to walk.

The mayors and their friends filled the top of the ferry so full there wasn't room for another soul, and the workers had to squeeze between them to set the boat free from its mooring.

Old friends and new talked and laughed as the cool autumn wind whipped across the deck. Aibek took up his usual spot at the far rail and watched for the pier to come into view. His thoughts drifted once more to the week's events and—inevitably—to Marah. He yearned to search for her on the over-crowded vessel, but she was traveling with her broth-ers. Their presence was an effective repellent. He heaved a great, sad sigh and leaned further over the rail, staring down at the churning gray water.

He watched the waves wash over the ship's grayed wood hull and listened to the hum of voices behind him. He let his mind go blank to everything but the relaxing sounds of water and conversation. Closing his eyes, he focused on the sounds and scents around him.

Keep your eyes to your back.

The whispered warning brought goosebumps to Aibek's arms, and he straightened. He turned a breath before a broad, muscular man with a riotous beard barreled into the rail. The man stood there, staring over the side for a long while, and Aibek wondered if he wasn't ill from the ferry's movement.

"Are you all right?"

The man spun and glared up at Aibek. Without a word, he stalked away into the middle of the crowded deck. Aibek froze, stunned. The man was one of Helak's henchmen and had been part of the group that had attacked Aibek and Faruz two weeks before.

Vayna stepped closer and frowned. "What was that about?"

"I'm not sure," Aibek lied. "I think he may have been sick."

"Well, he seems to be feeling better now." Vayna pointed to the open area near the mast, where the man stood talking animatedly with several others.

Aibek shrugged but said nothing. He wanted to talk to Valasa and the rest of Nivaka's council before he told anyone about that previous attack.

Determined to stay alert, he leaned back against the rail and scanned the crowd. Denizens of the wood stood in clusters. Bits of their conversations drifted to him on the cold autumn breeze. A group of the short, heavily bearded men stood off to one side, near the stairs that led to the lower deck. Aibek focused on them, straining to hear their words. He'd once heard of a man who could tell what someone across the room said by the way they moved their mouths, so he stared at one man's lips as he spoke, but quickly gave up. That kind of thing required practice and skill, and he doubted he'd be able to pick it up without a great deal of effort.

Aibek turned his attention elsewhere, frustrated by his fruitless attempt. He glanced over the travelers' faces and let his mind wander.

The ferry docked without fanfare, and the passengers climbed off the vessel and swarmed over the pier. Aibek kept his eyes open, looking for any sign of trouble, but he relaxed when they'd made it halfway to the forest without incident.

The wind blew colder as the day passed, and dark clouds billowed in the sky above. Winter wouldn't wait much longer. Aibek shrugged deeper into his heavy wool cloak and picked up the pace. He wanted to be back in Nivaka before the building storm hit.

Several hundred yards before they reached the forest's border, Marah stepped up beside Aibek. In his surprise, he set his right foot in a hole and nearly fell, his weakened leg unable to support him.

"Be careful!" She laughed and grabbed his arm, helping him keep his balance.

Heat flooded his face, but Aibek laughed along.

Remembering her brothers, he glanced over his shoulder.

"Don't worry," she said, reading his worry. "They're making plans to meet up with some new friends. We can talk for a few minutes."

A space of a dozen paces or so separated them from the nearest travelers, so Aibek relaxed and allowed himself to bask in the beauty of her smile. Warmth spread in his chest, and he couldn't help smiling back.

"I'm not sure how to say this without sounding dumb," she said, dropping her gaze to the ground. "I know you said you'll come with me for the first few training sessions with the dragons, but is there any way we can plan to stay together? Through the battle and everything? It'll make me feel better to be close to you."

Aibek's smile faded, his mind whirling. How could he keep her safe and still participate in the fight? The silence stretched, and he finally said, "I'm not sure how easy that'll be, but I'd love to try."

"I don't expect you to protect me—I can hold my own. I just think it'll make me feel better if you're close by."

Aibek nodded, but said nothing else.

"We're starting training in two weeks, right?"

"Yes." Aibek glanced over at her. "I want everyone to have a little time at home before we start."

"All right. That's a good idea." She chewed on her bottom lip, and Aibek fought the urge to kiss away her worries.

"What's wrong?" He prodded gently.

"You said the dragons will choose their riders, right? What if none of them pick me?"

"Impossible. But maybe Tukanli will pick you. That would be ideal. She's Gworsad's mate, so she'll stay near him—and me—through the training and fighting."

"Oooh, that would be perfect," Marah cooed.

"I can talk to him and suggest it, if it would make you feel better."

A brilliant smile lit Marah's features. "Would you? That would make this all so much easier."

"I can't promise she'll agree, but I'll mention you."

She grabbed his arm and beamed up at him. "Thank you. My brothers don't want anything to do with the dragons, so it'll make me feel so much better to be able to stay near you."

"Marah!" A woman's voice called from behind them. Marah turned, waved, and dashed away, leaving Aibek to contemplate their discussion and fret over whether Tukanli would agree to carry her. He needed a few days away from her to clear his mind, but he wanted nothing more than to spend hours upon hours with her.

He'd have to tell Faruz about her, after all, especially if she would be close during group trainings.

His mind circled around the beautiful woman and the problems she presented, and he didn't notice his surroundings again until he stood at the bottom of Nivaka's stairs. Several mayors called out their goodbyes as they continued on, and Aibek waved to them before climbing to the high boardwalks.

5.

Kasanto

Aibek didn't take long to unpack and rest from the trip. The very next day, he called a council meeting to discuss the Grand Council's decisions. The friends gathered in the small sitting room on the third floor of Valasa's home where they had held their not-so-secret meetings in the past.

Valasa called the meeting to order in his usual, booming voice. "Welcome home Aibek, Wayra, and Ahren! We've missed you. How did it go?"

Several pairs of curious eyes turned to Aibek, and he stood. He met Valasa's gaze first. "I didn't get your note until too late—"

The others gasped, and Zifa leaned forward, but Aibek cut her off before she could speak. "—But, I managed to convince them all that I was telling the truth. They all believe I met the Bokinna, and she's agreed to help us win this battle."

Valasa shook his head, disbelief and confusion warring on his face. Confusion won. "How did you manage it?"

"I showed them the dragons."

Kai leapt to his feet. "You already gave away our secrets? How could you?"

"Only the mayors know. I was very careful to keep the others out when we were talking." When Kai's stance didn't relax, Aibek sighed. "I didn't have any other choice. They were ready to toss me out of the whole meeting for heresy. How else could I prove I was telling the truth?"

Silence fell. Aibek gave the others time to think through his quandary and—hopefully—realize he'd had no choice.

After a long moment, Kai huffed and sat down. "I guess you're right. I wish you hadn't said anything to begin with, though."

Aibek grinned. "So do I. We set our first group training with the dragons for two weeks from now. We'll have to put out the call for a few more riders, though."

"The men would love that!" Faruz perked up. "I'll ask some of the division leaders if they're interested."

Valasa stepped forward, away from the snacks he'd been arranging while the others talked. "I hate to dampen such enthusiasm, but has anyone thought to include the groundfolk? They may want a few of their warriors on the dragons, too."

"Why would we care what they want?" Ahren's pale face flushed red. "What would we gain by having them in on all of our secrets?"

"We need their help. They have knowledge of this forest that we can't even fathom. And they already know about the dragons, remember? Aylen was with Aibek when the dragons agreed to help us, so he knows the basic plan." He paused and stroked his graying beard. "No, I think you'll make permanent enemies of them if we try to leave them out. There's no way to pretend we aren't working with the Bokinna's protectors."

"All right, then, I'll plan a trip to Kasanto within the next week. They'll need time to select their warriors." Aibek paused and added. "I'd like Faruz to accompany me this time. Our army's captain needs to be able to negotiate with the groundfolk."

A panicked look crossed Faruz's face. "I guess that makes sense. Will Serik be going with us?"

"I'll ask him this afternoon."

Something moved outside the window, drawing Aibek's attention. He watched for several breaths, but the movement didn't repeat. He positioned himself so he could see the window and continued. "We also need to warn the villagers. The Bokinna has agreed to move the Shadow Trees to form a wall at the forest's edge, which means our familiar landmarks may be changing soon. I'm not completely sure, but the village itself may move."

"We'll have to make sure hunting parties have some way to find our way back to the village, then," Faruz said. "We shouldn't have any trouble after our practice sessions because the dragons can see for miles, but anyone wandering in the forest is in danger of getting lost."

"That's a good point." Wayra stared out the window, a pensive expression on his face. "How can they find their way back if the village is moving? They can't even mark a track."

Aibek chuckled. "It won't move fast. I'd guess no more than a hundred yards a day. If they can get back to the general vicinity, they should be able to get home."

"Well, it sounds like we've covered everything." Zifa gazed longingly at the trays of food. "Can we eat now?"

Laughter erupted in the room. When it quieted, Aibek said, "Let's take a break, but we're not quite done. I want to hear how things went in Nivaka while we were gone."

Zifa leapt toward the snacks before he'd finished talking, and Faruz smiled. "She's been hungrier than normal since her headaches went away. I think it's because she couldn't eat much for so many weeks."

"That could be," Aibek answered, though he wasn't convinced.

The meeting reconvened, and the rest of the day passed in an endless parade of mundane tasks and problems.

The next morning, Serik carried the usual tray of cakes and famanc into Aibek's sitting room. Aibek had been up and dressed for nearly an hour and had spent the time in meditation and talking to the forest.

When the door opened, Aibek rushed over and met his friend. He took the tray and set it on the table in front of the fireplace. Serik settled into his favorite chair, and Aibek poured them each a mug of famanc before sitting.

They chatted about the weather, their friends, and the forest's recovery until the blue light of dawn streamed through the window.

When it was finally late enough to leave, they made their way to the east entrance where they met Faruz. The three of them strolled down the path. Aibek reveled in the signs of health in the barren forest.

The green patches had almost completely vanished. The once-dead trees had less of a gray cast to them, the sickly gray replaced by a warm, healthy brown. The sun shone down from above, illuminating the leaf-strewn path and warming him in spite of the cold breeze.

As they approached the normal meeting place, Aibek paid more attention to his immediate surroundings. In the desolate grays and browns of approaching winter, it wasn't hard to pick out the slight color differences that marked the hiding elves and dwarves.

When they were completely surrounded, Aibek shouted, "I need to speak with your king and queen."

A heartbeat later, a slender young elf appeared on the walk. "Come. They've been expecting you."

Aibek nodded and led the way onto the parallel trail. There he stopped and allowed the heavily armed elves and dwarves to take the lead.

They passed through the village, and this time faces peeked around buildings at the passing tree-dwellers though no one was brave enough to sit on the benches and watch the short procession.

Anxiety knotted in Aibek's stomach as he walked, remembering his last visit with the rulers. He hoped they had truly accepted that his people were not to blame for the forest's illness, especially once Aylen had returned and told his story.

They crossed through the miniature village and into the forest beyond, pausing at the entrance to the underground cavern.

Aibek tucked a hand in his pocket, ready to cover his face with a fresh handkerchief if the rancid odor hadn't improved. As he stepped into the earthen darkness below, he took a shallow, hesitant breath. The forest's normal, fresh scent greeted him, and he relaxed as much as the narrow passageway allowed.

When they stepped into the wide cavern where they'd always met with Turan and Idril. A little sigh escaped as Aibek spotted the low, comfortable chairs they'd enjoyed on visits before the last one.

Good, Serik won't have to stand the whole time. He refused to acknowledge—even to himself—the fact that he probably wouldn't have been able to stay on his feet through a prolonged meeting. The walk from Nivaka had made his leg throb and ache. He relished the idea of sinking into one of the plush chairs, even though it would put him beneath the rulers and thus at a strategic disadvantage. He'd been there before.

He was so focused on the plush seats, he didn't realize the rulers' seats were empty until a flute sounded from the far end of the cavern.

King Turin and Queen Idril paraded into the room

and settled themselves into their chairs without a glance toward the visitors. Several elves and dwarves fussed about them, arranging Queen Idril's bright yellow skirts, removing King Turin's tall hat covered in autumn leaves, and filling intricately-carved cups for each of the rulers.

Aylen gestured for Aibek, Serik, and Faruz to sit in the chairs below the raised stage that held the tall-backed chairs Idril and Turan sat upon.

When they were settled, Idril glanced down her nose at the visitors. "I suppose you have something more to ask of us?"

Aibek fought back a smile. "Not exactly."

"Have you come to gloat over your victorious return atop the forest's protectors, then?" Idril sneered.

"No." Aibek gave a tiny shake of his head to punctuate the word.

Idril narrowed her eyes and regarded Aibek. Her voice dripped ice when she replied, "Then why have you come here?"

Aibek leaned forward, folding his hands on his knees. "We're building a force of warriors who can fight on the dragons' backs. I thought you would want some of your fighters to learn with us. We have ten dragons without riders, and I would offer them to your warriors."

A tense, breathless silence fell in the cavern. Long moments passed before Turan answered. "We would certainly want our people included in such a force, but we cannot name anyone on such short notice."

"Of course not," Faruz said, smiling. "We won't begin training for eight days, so you only need have names by then. Aibek and I will meet the chosen warriors at the lake on the first training day, if that is acceptable." He added the last bit after a brief pause, as if he'd forgotten the protocol for a moment.

"This would be a great honor for any chosen warriors," Queen Idril said slowly. "We may need more than a week to choose only ten. How many tree-dwellers will be in this force?"

Aibek stood, unable to remain sitting any longer despite the pain in his leg. "The number is not open to negotiation. We have a very limited number of dragons willing and able to carry warriors into battle. Ten do not currently have riders. If you don't want to put your warriors on them, I will offer the positions to my soldiers."

"That is not what I said." Idril's voice snapped, echoing against the walls of the cavern.

Aibek glanced around while he waited for her next move. The pool in the center of the space had shrunk to a fourth of its previous size, but the waterfall had begun trickling water again and the stench of rotting vegetation had vanished. Green streaks marked the edges of the waterfall's normal path.

"If you are to limit us to ten warriors, what concessions are you willing to offer?" Turan stared down at the travelers.

"None." Aibek responded without a second thought. "We are not required to offer you any positions in this force. My agreement was with the Bokinna herself and did not include you." A gasp went through the assembled warriors, and Aibek waited until the murmurs quieted before continuing. "I made this offer because I respect your power and position within this forest, not because I had to."

Aibek could feel Serik's eyes on him, but he kept his attention on the rulers. He needed to read their reactions. Shock and outrage flashed across both of their faces before they regained their strict control.

Turan and Idril leaned close together, and Aibek couldn't make out what they whispered to each other. When they straightened, Turan wore a resigned expression, but Idril's face was as cold and unreadable as ever.

"You have our attention. State your demands." Idril's voice mirrored the coldness in her features.

"I have no demands, only a request," he paused when Idril whispered something to Turan. "and a warning," he added when she'd turned back to him.

The dwarf queen drew herself up as straight as she could without standing, anger flashing in her eyes. "You dare speak to me of a warning? What kind of meeting did you suppose this would be? Three of you—unarmed—surrounded by my guards?"

Aibek smiled. "I did not threaten you, fair queen. My warning is not of any danger from me or my warriors. The Bokinna has agreed to move the shadow trees—"

"What?" Turan's sharp exclamation echoed within

the chamber. "She hasn't moved in over a thousand years!"

Aibek continued as if he hadn't spoken, "To the perimeter of the forest to strengthen our defenses and make it harder for the enemy soldiers to enter the forest."

The guards pointed their spears and axes at Aibek, as if to ward off the surprise of his words.

"That means landmarks will be changing, and creatures that rarely come near our villages may become a threat. That is my warning to you.

"My request is leniency. Because of the very things I just said, I'm afraid my hunters may get lost and wind up wandering close to sunset. If that happens, I ask that you point them in the right direction rather than attacking outright. Any who refuse your aid will be fair game for your warriors."

Silence grew in the chamber as the rulers took in Aibek's words. After a long pause, Turan leaned close to Idril and murmured something in her ear. She replied immediately, her clipped tones betraying her irritation. Aibek kept his face carefully blank. If the queen detected any hint of emotion in him, it could lead to disaster.

While the rulers conferred, Aibek settled back into the plush chair. He feared he'd pay for his impulsivity in giving up the seat when he had to walk the trails back to Nivaka without sufficient rest.

Idril and Turan spat whispered retorts between themselves for a long while, and Aibek's anxiety increased with each passing moment. When he couldn't stand it any longer, he glanced over at Serik, who smiled and nodded in encouragement. Aibek took a deep, calming breath and settled back to wait out the agitated rulers. Every few seconds, Serik cleared his throat or coughed, and Aibek worried about his friend's health.

"Excuse me," he interjected after what had to have been an hour of deliberation.

Simmering rage shone in the queen's eyes when she directed her glare at him. "What more could you possibly want?"

Aibek tipped his head in Serik's direction. "My companion isn't as young as the rest of us. Would it be possible for him to get some water while we wait for your decision?" He bowed low as he finished his request, and act of deference he had resisted up to this point in the meeting.

The queen nodded to a guard and continued her heated conversation with the king. A heartbeat later, the guard appeared with a pitcher of water and three unadorned stone cups. Aibek gratefully gulped down the tepid liquid and handed back the cup. The soldier didn't offer to refill it but placed it atop the pitcher and waited for Serik and Faruz to finish their drinks.

When the guard disappeared through the entrance the rulers had used earlier, Aibek sat back and fought the urge to fidget while he waited.

An eternity passed in the windowless cavern, but eventually the king and queen leaned forward and turned their attention back to Aibek.

"We've discussed your... ahh... request." The

faintest hint of pink colored Turan's cheeks. "I do apologize for the long delay."

Aibek sat up straighter, eager to hear their decision.

"Your demands are unusual," Idril said, fluffing her daffodil-colored skirts. "But that is due to the extremely rare circumstances that require them. We will do as you ask and allow some leniency in the deadline for your hunters to be back in the trees, but we will not hesitate to capture or kill any who refuse our aid. These coming months may prove very trying, indeed."

Turan raised a hand, and Idril fell silent. "We will accept your offer to put ten of our warriors into the division of dragon riders you're building. As you pointed out, you did not have to offer us any such positions, and ten is a generous number. We will have a list of names to you before the week is out."

With that, the king and queen stood and exited the cavern, leaving Aibek, Serik, and Faruz to make their way through the earthen corridor. Aibek held his silence until the friends had ascended the stairs into Nivaka.

"I can't believe that worked!" He grinned, weak with joy and relief and hunger. Noon had come and gone while they'd waited below ground for the rulers' decision.

"That was perfect," Faruz said, clapping Aibek on the shoulder. He stepped away, moving quickly toward his house before Aibek could respond.

Serik said nothing until they'd entered their home.

"Well done," the old man said softly. "But be careful not to treat them so casually again for quite some time. You rattled them. They won't respond kindly if you do it again."

"Thank you. I don't think I'll need to be so bold with them again. I was terrified it would blow up in my face like the black powder we studied at the Academy."

Once they'd traded their boots for the slippers they wore in the treetops, they went straight to the kitchen for an early supper.

6.

Training

Water hissed and steamed, spitting against the glowing metal. Noral dunked the new cart axle again, cooling and tempering the iron. He stood and stretched, pulled the iron out of the water, and set it on his worktable. He went through the motions of cleaning up his shop, but his mind wandered. The recent visit to Nivaka had left him homesick for the village of his youth, and the city felt more cramped and crowded than ever.

Distracted and sad, he stepped out into the afternoon sun and made his way to the market. He'd been searching for a gift for Ira, something to cheer her up a bit. She'd been tearful and quiet since they'd returned from their trip.

"Maybe she's right," he muttered, ducking into a shop with colorful baubles lining the shelves.

His wife had been pushing him to sell his shop and move back to the forest in the south, where they could be close to the young man they'd raised for twenty years. Before their visit, she'd assured him she'd be content with regular trips to see Aibek, but since their return she'd talked of nothing but the lush forest and the friendly villagers.

He chose a bright green pendant shaped like a leaf, then selected a fine silver chain that would shimmer against Ira's golden skin. He paid for the gift. While he waited for the shopkeeper to wrap it up, he scanned the crowd bustling through the streets outside.

His eyebrows drew together at the sight of so many mountain tribesmen. With their long, tangled beards and worn leather clothing they stood out amongst Xona's clean, linen-clad citizens.

"What do you think all these travelers are doing here, Owein?" Noral gestured to the window and accepted the freshly wrapped package.

"I don't know. They're certainly strange, but they haven't done any harm, far's I know. I say leave 'em be. They'll probably move on once the mountain snow melts away." The shopkeeper turned his attention to a pair of earrings he was mending, and Noral stepped out into the street.

He kept his head down but focused his attention on the snippets of conversation around him as he strolled toward home.

"…almost time…"

"…new city…"

"…a little longer…"

"…Helak…"

The words and phrases chilled him to the bone, and Noral picked up his pace. He sighed when he stepped through the door to the little home he shared with Ira. He leaned back against the door and smiled at Ira's flour-dusted face when she rushed in from the kitchen.

"You've been harassing the cook again?" He brushed a white streak away from her eye with his thumb.

She smiled up at him, and his heart swelled. "I'm not harassing anyone. I thought I'd teach her how to make those lovely cakes we had in Nivaka. I made sure to get the recipe from Aibek's cook before we left."

He squeezed her tighter, then pulled back and drew the package from the pocket of his linen shirt.

"What's this?"

"I saw this in Owein's shop and thought you'd like it. Go ahead. Open it."

She untied the string and delicately peeled back the layers of brown fabric. He fought the urge to take the gift from her and rip it open.

When she finally reached the pendant, her eyes went wide. Noral lifted the delicate chain and fastened it around her neck.

"It's beautiful." Confusion shone in her eyes. "But what's the occasion?"

"I've decided you're right. When winter breaks in the south, we'll move down to Nivaka to be close to Aibek."

The smile that lit her face took his breath away. "Oh, that will be perfect! There's so much to do! Will we have enough time? Spring's only a few months away."

With that, she kissed him on the lips and rushed

off into the kitchen, presumably to tell the cook and maid they were all moving to the forest.

Ira chattered like a schoolgirl throughout supper, her joy contagious. Noral listened and smiled but said very little. When they'd finished eating and clearing the dishes, he donned his jacket. "I have a quick errand to run," he told Ira. "I'll be home soon."

Huddled forms lined the darkened streets, a sign that the travelers had overflowed all the inns in the area and had spilled out into the alleys and onto porches.

Noral kept his eyes on the uneven cobblestones, dimly lit by occasional lamps along the roadside. He hurried along the familiar path to the army academy where Aibek had spent so many years as a student.

Self-consciousness nearly overwhelmed him as he approached the family entrance, and he turned toward the large, pillared porch. He tugged on the two-story doors, opening one just enough for him to slip inside and pulling it closed behind him.

His heels clacked against the marble floor, the sound echoing through the abandoned entryway. The residents would be either in the dorms or the dining hall at that hour. Ignoring the press of memories that threatened to overwhelm him, Noral strode toward the administrative offices at the rear of the entry hall.

A head poked out of a door, and Noral picked up his pace. "Noral? Is that you? What are you doing here so late? Come in, come in. How's Aibek doing?"

Noral shook his friend's hand and stepped into the

cluttered office. Stacks of papers lined the heavy iron desk, and a half-filled page sat in front of the abandoned chair. Bright tapestries lined the stone walls, dulling the sound within the narrow room.

"It's great to see you again, Cadwy. Aibek's doing well. The people in Nivaka love him."

"You're looking well. How's the wife?" Cadwy settled into his chair and waved Noral into an empty seat across from him. The silver streaks lining his temples had grown in the months since Noral had seen him last, but his yellow officer's uniform was as crisp as ever.

"Ira's doing well," Noral answered. "But I didn't come just to catch up. We've got a problem."

Cadwy's weathered brow wrinkled. "What kind of problem?"

"I don't know how much you've been out in the city recently—"

"Not much. The new students just started a few weeks ago."

Noral nodded. "Well, in the past several weeks, hundreds, maybe thousands, of mountain tribesmen have moved into the city. They're coming in groups of three or four, so they're not being stopped at the gates, but I'm concerned."

"Is that all?" Cadwy laughed. "They've been mentioned in every meeting for at least a month. The king is sure we have nothing to fear from a group of mountain hunters escaping the winter freeze, and, for what it's worth, I agree with him."

"I'm not so certain. I've been listening to their

conversations." Noral raised his head and met Cadwy's eyes. "They work for Helak, the same man who ordered the attack on my son's village and who has threatened to overthrow all of Azalin."

"What harm could they do? We have a fully trained army in the city, and eight more battalions within a day's march. They don't stand a chance here!"

"They're coordinating somehow." Noral stood, desperate to make his friend understand the danger. "If they have several thousand men inside the city walls, closing the gates won't save us. And most of Xona's army is camped outside the city right now."

"All right. I'll give you that. We're not prepared for an inside attack." Cadwy pressed his palms flat against his desk and leaned forward. "I'll pass along your concerns. You've never been one to overreact or exaggerate a warning. We should at least be keeping tabs on these travelers while they're here."

Relief flowed over Noral, weakening his legs, and he sank into the chair. "Thank you. It might not be a bad idea to call the army back from their training outside the city, too."

"That's above my station, but I'll pass along your concerns. Since I took the position here, I don't seem to have as much pull in the army as I used to."

Noral nodded. "So, how's your daughter doing? She must be getting close to old enough to begin courting soon, right?"

The two old friends spent the next half hour catching up on each other's lives, and finally Noral made his way home, satisfied that his worries would hadn't fallen on deaf ears.

~ * ~

"Are you ready?" Faruz grinned, poking Aibek in the arm. "Let's go, already!"

Aibek swung his pack over his shoulder and worked to hide his nervousness. "I'm ready."

In his years of military training, nothing had prepared him to fight on a dragon's back. This would be his first training session both with the dragon and with the tincture Valasa had made from the Saethem's seeds. The Bokinna had given very specific instructions on how to grind and mix the seeds with fairy wine and shadow tree sap to make a thick, oily tincture, but she hadn't said what it would do. Instead, she'd instructed Aibek to bring the mixture to her, so she could teach him how to use it. She'd agreed to allow Faruz to participate only on Aibek's continued pleading.

He tucked the precious vials into his pocket and stood.

Side by side, Aibek, Faruz, and Serik left the village. "Are you sure you want to go?" Aibek asked Serik as they descended the broad stairs at the east entrance.

"I wouldn't miss it." Serik smiled and patted Aibek's arm. "I'll just sit with the Bokinna while you train with the dragons. I'm too old for your potion or battle. When the time comes, I'll stay with Valasa and help with the injured, instead."

Aibek nodded and strolled with his friends to the clearing nearby where they'd agreed to meet the dragons. His leg throbbed from the previous day's activity. A large storm had blown down several large branches, and he had joined the party that had prepared the wood for storage in the low warehouses near the edge of the village.

Deep down, he hoped the tincture would heal his leg, though he was trying not to get his hopes up too high. The stories Ira had read him as a child had spoken of magical potions that could cure all manner of illnesses and injuries, though those stories had proven somewhat unreliable in the past year. Yes, fairies and emrialks and dragons were real, but they were nothing like the stories had made them sound.

Rumbling and chirps rang through the forest. Aibek picked up his pace, eager to see the friendly dragons again. The stories had been wrong about them, too. They were nothing like the bloodthirsty beasts he'd expected.

They kept their greetings short and climbed onto the dragons' backs for the trip to the Heart of the Forest.

This time, Aibek kept his eyes open and his head down as they flew, watching the trees, streams, villages, and lakes drift past below Gworsad's leathery wings.

A mixture of excitement and anxiety fluttered in his belly. He had no idea what kind of magic to expect from the potion but knew it must be powerful for Helak to want it so badly.

The flight lasted only a few minutes, and soon Gworsad tucked his wings and dove into the forest. Aibek's heart lurched into his throat, and he clung to the dragon's neck with all his might, smashing Serik between his chest and the dragon's mossy frill. He relaxed when Gworsad pulled up and set himself gently on the ground. Aibek climbed down and helped Serik to the soft earth.

Faruz whooped as his dragon dove through the trees. Aibek and Serik stepped into the space between two large Shadow Trees so they'd be out of the way for Gamne and Faruz to land.

When all the friends were on the ground, they stepped together into the Bokinna's inner sanctum.

"Ahh, you have come," the great tree whispered. "I must thank you for helping me heal myself and my shadows."

When no one moved into the clearing, she added, "You may approach."

Aibek and Faruz did as they were told, but Serik sat against a tree at the edge of the clearing to watch.

Clear green eyes stared down at them from the middle of the great tree's trunk, and Aibek dropped to a knee under her watchful gaze. Beside him, Faruz lowered himself to his knees.

"You have brought the seed powder?" The Bokinna's voice carried on the wind and vibrated through Aibek's chest.

"Yes, I have it. Valasa prepared it exactly as you ordered." Aibek pulled the tiny vials out of his pocket and held them up for the Bokinna to see.

"Excellent. They will give you no abilities you do not already possess but will increase the abilities you have. You must be careful not to harm yourself or others while you're learning to control the power."

Disappointment flared in Aibek's chest, but he stuffed it down. He still didn't know exactly what the seed potion would do.

"Go ahead and drink one."

Aibek handed a vial to Faruz, and they each downed the contents with a quick gulp. Bitterness exploded in Aibek's mouth and slithered down his throat. He fought the urge to gag and reached for his water skin. Eyes watering, he washed down the disgusting concoction and swiped a hand across his mouth.

Within a few heartbeats, Aibek felt power pounding through his whole body. Strength grew in his arms and legs, and his vision sharpened.

"What do you feel?" the Bokinna asked, peering down at him.

Aibek raised his head. "Everything." He hesitated, but gave in and asked, "Madam tree, will this heal my leg? And Faruz's?"

A gentle smile lit the Bokinna's face. "It will help, though not right away, and perhaps not completely. Your injuries are old, and the scarring makes it harder to heal."

He struggled to define the sensations and emotions warring within. Relief, certainly, at the hope for healing. Worry that he may end up with a permanent limp despite the tincture. His vision sharpened, drawing his mind away from the injury. The pain in his leg faded, and the sounds of scurrying insects carried to his ears.

"Very well," the ancient tree said. "Lay down your sword, and we shall begin. You won't need a weapon at first."

Moving slowly, unsure of how to use his arms and legs with this new strength, Aibek did as he was told. Beside him, Faruz did the same.

Aibek's leg didn't hurt, but he could feel the weakness in it when he stood.

"Now, do you see those logs over there?" A long branch reached out and gestured to a neat stack of logs at the edge of the clearing. They didn't have the smooth edges of wood that had been cut with a saw or an axe, but looked splintered and jagged, as if the dragons had snapped whole trees into smaller pieces.

"Yes," Aibek said hesitantly.

"Bring them to me."

Aibek frowned, confused, but moved to comply. His legs moved faster than they ever had before, the speed blurring movements around him. In a blink he and Faruz arrived at the logs.

Wondering how much he could do, Aibek lifted a log in one hand. He moved it easily, but struggled to control the speed and trajectory. Before he knew it, the log flew through the air.

"Look out!" Aibek shouted at Serik.

The old man scurried away a breath before the log flew over the spot where he'd been sitting.

"I'm so sorry!" Aibek stepped away from the logs.

Faruz met Aibek's worried gaze and glanced down at the pile of logs in front of him. Hesitantly, he reached down and lifted one with both hands. Like Aibek, he flung it upwards, but his second hand shifted the load backwards over his head where it landed harmlessly in a pile of brush.

"So you see," the ancient tree said, "this will not be easy. You must practice regularly, or you will be unable to control the power when you need it."

"But how do we learn to control it?" Aibek stepped closer to the tree, his hands outstretched.

"Come, sit in front of me. I shall tell you what I know. And then you will have to practice on your own."

Aibek settled onto the mossy ground and waited breathlessly for her to begin.

"It has been more than a hundred years since I have met anyone I believed could handle the power. It takes a great deal of inner strength to control. Without that strength and discipline, you will be a danger to yourself and everyone around you. When the seed powder is in use, you must consider every movement. You must think about what you want to do with any object you pick up, and you must plan for how you will set things down." She stared down at them with gentle green eyes. "I have no doubt you can handle this. But it will not be easy. You do not have much time to learn."

When she said nothing more, Aibek raised his eyes and stared up at her. "Surely there's more to it than that."

"No, child. It is just as simple and just as difficult as concentrating on your every movement. Now, bring the rest of those logs over here." She gestured with a branch to an empty place on her right.

Aibek eased himself to standing, focusing on his every movement as she had instructed. In a few steps, he crossed the clearing and stood in front of the logs once more.

Gingerly, he cupped a hand underneath a log. He held his breath, worried that he would toss this one too. To steady it, he placed the other hand on top and lifted it a hair's breadth at a time until it was clear of the other logs.

Concentrating on every step, he moved across the clearing and set the log down where the Bokinna had indicated. As soon as his hands were free of the log, Aibek whooped in exultation.

Still grinning, he turned his attention to Faruz. His friend copied his technique and carried his log across the clearing. He set it beside the first and gave a cheer.

"If that's all you're going to have them do," Serik interjected, "I have some chores for them back in Nivaka."

Aibek, Faruz, and the Bokinna laughed.

They spent the rest of the day moving items small and large through the forest. They ran, they leapt, and they focused on picking up the tiniest seeds without crushing them. By the time the sky darkened with the sunset, Aibek was exhausted. His arms and legs were as heavy as the logs they had moved in the morning.

He didn't have the strength left to climb onto Gworsad's back, so he swallowed his pride and allowed Gworsad's mate, Tukanli, to lift him off the ground and set him between Gworsad's wings.

The rhythmic beating of the dragon's wings nearly lulled Aibek to sleep, but he awoke as the dragon tucked his wings and dove for the village.

They landed in the clearing where they had met the dragons earlier that morning. As soon as Faruz climbed down, he ran over to Aibek, excitement shining in his eyes.

"I think I've figured out a way to keep us on the dragons so we can free up our hands for battle."

"Well let's hear it." Aibek couldn't help grinning at Faruz's excitement.

"What if —" Faurz patted Tukanli on the neck. "What if we use a leather strap to make a sort of harness to keep us on their backs?"

"Like farmers' horses and oxes?" Gworsad asked, frowning. "That not sound comfortable."

Faruz shook his head. "No. Nothing like that. Just a couple of straps around our legs to keep us from falling off of your back."

"Oh, yes that good idea." The dragon said.

"Do you think it has to be leather? We don't have very much leather available, and we have more than two dozen people who want to learn to ride the dragons." Aibek's mind spun through the possibilities. "What if we use the heavy zontrec that we use for the armor?"

Excitement lit Faruz's features. "That would work,

too, and we could make it whatever color we want. Zifa would love that!"

Aibek laughed. "Come on, the sun's setting. We'd better get home."

They trudged up the broad steps just as the sun's final rays painted a spectacular vista across the sky. Faruz headed for home and his new bride, but Aibek turned toward Valasa's home. He needed to update the Gadonu on the day's events.

He examined the soothing pattern on the outer wall before he opened the door and strode inside without knocking.

Dalan, Valasa, and Ayja sat in the den, reclining in the plush furniture and chatting amongst themselves. Only Valasa stood when Aibek walked into the room.

"Well? How did it go? Come into my study and we'll discuss your day. You look exhausted."

The enormous healer didn't give Aibek a chance to answer between questions but held open the door and waited for Aibek to enter his protected inner sanctum. Aibek kept his eyes down when he entered the narrow room. The rows of vials and books made him uncomfortable, so he didn't look closer. Somehow this room watched him, judged him, and found him wanting.

The heavy door clicked behind him, and Valasa dropped into the closest chair. "So? How was it? I take it the tincture worked?"

Aibek settled into a chair beside the broad healer. "It worked," he said. "It's going to take some work to learn to use, though."

"I wouldn't expect anything less from the Bokinna." Valasa laughed and poured them each a cup of water from a pitcher on the table.

Aibek gulped the water down and waited for Valasa to refill his cup. When he'd finished the second cup, he wiped his face with his sleeve. "Is there anything we can do about how tired the potion makes me? It's great while it lasts, but when it wears off I have no energy left at all."

"I'll have to ask the forest about that one. I don't know how the seeds react with other tinctures." The large man leaned close and Aibek stared blankly at the droplets of water trapped in his long white beard. "How was it? What did it feel like?" Valasa whispered.

Aibek couldn't contain a grin. "It was amazing. I was stronger than I've ever been before, and faster, too."

"Is it hard? The few scrolls I've found say it's next to impossible to use because the power takes over everything."

A harsh laugh escaped Aibek's lips. "Yes, it's hard. I nearly crushed poor Serik with a log before the Bokinna told me how to work the magic. I don't know how I'll manage that kind of concentration in battle. I'll just have to keep practicing, I guess." Aibek paused and cocked his head, considering. "How much of the powder do we have?"

"How many of the vials did you use today?"

Aibek turned out his pockets and counted the empty vials. He placed three full ampules on the table. "Only two each. It lasts pretty long, but four vials a day will use it up in a hurry."

A long, low whistle escaped Valasa's lips. "Well, at that rate, you'll run out within a month of practice. We'll have to ask the Bokinna if she can make us any more, but winter's coming up fast, so I don't know if she can."

~ * ~

Eddrick hid in a scrubby tree at the camp's border. Kiri, Agommi, and Glesni had stayed low, concealed by the scrubby bushes that defined the landscape. They hadn't found the army in the desert, where it had been for so many months before, but in the tall grasses of the plain south of Xona. The camp against the mountain had been abandoned, the tents gone, the buildings knocked down. The passage into the mountain sat wide open, a gaping, exposed sore on the sheer wall of rock.

Eddrick tried to mimic the birds' movement, flitting from branch to branch, as he watched the camp below. He hadn't seen Helak or any of the higher officers among this group, so he worried the army had split. He and Kiri had to stay together, so a divided army would present new challenges.

The guards strolled through their oval patrol, and when they'd passed his position, Eddrick dropped to the ground beside Kiri. Careful to stay out of sight, he motioned the others away from the camp. They formed a circle and held on to each other, closed their eyes, and appeared in the suite of rooms where Eddrick and Kiri spent most of their time.

"Well?" Eddrick asked as soon as they arrived. "Did you see Helak?"

Kiri shook her head, and Agommi murmured a quiet, "No. I haven't seen him or any of his advisers. Have you?"

Silence was Eddrick's only answer. Rain lashed against the windows, and Eddrick drifted over to watch the storm.

"Where is he?" he muttered.

"What?" Kiri's hand tapped his shoulder.

Frustration colored Eddrick's voice, but he didn't turn to her. "Why can't I find him?"

"Well, let's see if we can think through his strategy." Kiri hovered near the fireplace, a few paces behind her husband. "Part of his army is heading north along the plains. Towards what? What could they be going after? My guess is the rest of the army's heading south to the forest."

Eddrick stopped and spun on his heel, turning to face Glesni. "We need to split up. Is there anyone else who could come with us? Or could my father serve as a chaperon to make sure I stay out of trouble?" Bitterness laced his voice at the admission that the ancients didn't trust him, but he didn't stop. "We're no longer watching one army. We're watching *two*."

"Let me consult the others." Glesni floated to the sofa and hovered above a cushion, closed his eyes, and went completely still.

Eddrick strolled over to Agommi, leaving a wide space around the sofa to avoid disturbing Glesni. "I hope you don't mind that I offered you up as a nanny. I didn't think first."

To Eddrick's relief, Agommi smiled and pressed a hand on his arm. "Of course not. I'd be happy to tag along with one of you if they approve it."

"Thank you."

Silence fell, and Eddrick settled in to wait. Sometimes, Glesni would get an answer from the ancients right away. Other times, they could take days. Either way, he wouldn't move until they responded to the petition.

7.

Group Practice

Two days later, Aibek stood at the center of the broad clearing by the river. The day had turned unseasonably warm, and a gentle breeze carried the river's mist over the pebbled clearing. Mayors, elves, dwarves, and dragons crowded around, filling the space between the forest's edge and the swirling water. He stepped up onto a fallen tree and cupped his hands over his mouth so the furthest members of the group could hear him.

"All right." His voice cracked at the strain of shouting over the river, but he continued. "We'll spend today doing a series of challenges to see which person fits best with which dragon. Each of you, choose a dragon for the first challenge."

"How do we choose if we don't know what the challenge is?" Bartel asked, frowning.

"You'll need to be able to do anything and everything with your partner dragon, so it shouldn't matter what the first challenge is," Aibek shouted back.

Several individuals nodded and they all spread out, each choosing a dragon. Aibek stepped up beside Gworsad. The elves and dwarves moved opposite Aibek's expectations and each chose one of the largest dragons. He'd sworn to treat them no differently than the other riders, so he resisted the urge to acknowledge their choices.

When each dragon had a person, he climbed onto Gworsad's back and cupped his hands around his mouth once more.

"Now, when I count to ten, you'll each need to mount your dragon, fly to the river's bend, and retrieve a log without landing. Bring the logs back here as quickly as you can. I warn you; this isn't as simple as it sounds."

Aibek counted to ten, and he and Gworsad stayed in the clearing as the others flew off into the distance. The Bokinna had given him a series of tasks to make sure the dragons and riders could work together, and he and Gworsad had done each one the day before. Faruz and Gamne waited at the southern bend and would make sure none of the others cheated on this task.

Exhausted from the previous day's activities, Aibek laid his head on Gworsad's neck and dozed while he waited for the others to return.

A gust of wind awakened him, and he glanced up to see Marah and Tukanli hovering over the clearing, a huge log clutched in Tukanli's massive claws.

"Set it at the end of the clearing. We'll make a pile there."

They did as directed and landed beside him, Tukanli's long, narrow feet leaving strange divots in the pebbled ground.

"That's amazing!" Marah laughed. "I almost

fainted when she dove for the log. I thought she would throw me for sure, but then she grabbed it and pulled up and I had to hold onto her collar and I thought I'd lose my breakfast. Where are the others?"

Aibek raised his eyes to the southern sky, where at least a dozen dragons darkened the horizon. "They're coming. Tukanli's a bit faster than most."

A deep rumbling sounded from Gworsad's throat as the great dragon rubbed his chin along Tukanli's neck.

"She's amazing." Marah patted Tukanli's front leg, an expression of awe on her face.

The others arrived in a flurry of activity and wind, the dragons' wings stirring the air into wild currents.

When everyone had dismounted, Aibek shouted over the river's noise. "Now, each of you must confer with your dragon and decide together whether you'll do this next challenge with the same dragon or try a different pairing."

"How can we decide that if we don't know what the task is?" Someone yelled from the back.

"The task is unimportant. The team is the point here. Discuss with your dragon. Did you work well together? Or would you work better in a different team?"

The murmur of many voices complimented the rushing of the river. Aibek sat on his log and waited for the others to make their decisions.

During a lull in conversations, he cupped his hands over his mouth. "When you've paired up with a dragon for the next task, come get a drink of water and a snack."

Half the assembled riders rushed close, pouring water from the skins Aibek had brought along and filling their hands with nuts.

The dragons drifted to the river and drank from the swirling pools near the bank.

When everyone had a dragon and had finished their snacks, Aibek gave them their next task.

"This time, you'll fly to the southern clearing, dismount, knock the 'head' off your assigned enemy, climb back onto your dragon, and return here. Each dragon has a colored tag. Your enemy will have a matching tag. Everyone, on your dragons!"

The riders scrambled to their dragons and Aibek wished he could participate. This had been his favorite task when he'd done them with Gworsad.

The day passed in a flurry of activity as the riders and dragons performed increasingly difficult tasks together. The groundfolk blended seamlessly into the new division, laughing and joking with the others as if they'd been friends for years. Before the end of the day, the dragons and riders were paired to everyone's satisfaction.

The dragons took their riders home, each aware that real training would begin the next day.

Soon after sunrise, the group assembled in the clearing once more, and the groundfolk mingled within the groups of villagers. It would be another warm, breezy autumn day.

Aibek inhaled the fresh, earthen scent of the forest and reveled in the river's gentle mist on his face.

"All right," Aibek shouted.

The group gathered close.

"Today we're going to see what we can do. Our practice enemies are set up in the clearing again. I trust you all brought your weapons?"

Steel flashed in the growing sunlight as the fighters drew swords and held bows aloft.

"Excellent. Use the weapon you're most comfortable with. Kill your assigned enemy only. Work on communicating with your dragon. This is harder than it sounds, since you'll be shouting over the rushing wind. The woodsmiths are working on speaking trumpets to make this easier, but they won't be ready for at least a week."

Several riders groaned. Aibek continued as if he hadn't heard them. "And Faruz has been working on a way to keep us on the dragons so we'll have our hands free, and he's going to show us all how it works now."

Faruz grinned and held a long, undyed zontrec rope up over his head. "I have enough rope here for each of us. Come get one so you can do as I do."

When everyone had a rope, he walked them through the steps of winding it over and around the dragon's front legs so they would have something to attach their legs to the dragon without impeding the dragon's movement.

Aibek watched with pride as his friend demonstrated his idea. He'd spent hours working with

Gamne, his dragon. Together, they'd come up with a solution that worked for both members of the team.

Some of the riders were still extremely timid around their dragons, but Aibek hoped the day's exercises would put them at ease. He tied his own rope onto Gworsad and climbed onto the dragon's back.

He watched and waited while the others all did the same. As soon as the last rider was mounted, Gworsad spread his great wings and lifted off, the pressure creating a giddy rush in Aibek's chest.

Marah and Tukanli lifted off next and flew beside Aibek to the clearing. There, when Aibek and Gworsad swooped in to attack his practice enemy, Marah pulled out a lightweight bow and loosed several arrows in quick succession. Each one struck its mark, and arrows protruded from the dummy's chest and head in seconds.

Distracted by Marah's marksmanship, Aibek forgot to follow through on his swing and nearly dropped his sword. Gworsad circled around again so he could try again, and that time he didn't miss. His sword sliced easily through the dummy's wooden neck and sent its stuffed head rolling down the hill.

They'd outpaced the other dragons again, so Gworsad and Tukanli landed at the north end of the clearing to wait for the rest of the teams.

"That was amazing!" Aibek grinned at Marah as soon as she'd dismounted. "I had no idea you could do that!"

Pink color heated her cheeks, and Marah smiled.

"My father taught me. He was one of our village's best hunters. I used to love going with him to find food when I was little."

"Well, I'm certainly glad he taught you. I've never seen anyone shoot like that before."

Aibek tossed caution to the wind, grabbed her, and pressed his lips to hers.

The warm welcome of her kiss heated him within, and his hand tangled in her hair. He nudged her lips apart and delved deeply into the heat of her mouth, exploring the velvet secrets within.

Her arms wrapped around his waist, holding him close as she kissed him back.

His breath came in shallow gasps when he broke off the kiss. At her confused look, he pointed to the treetops. "Sorry. The other's'll be here any second. I shouldn't have done that."

She only shook her head and smoothed a hand over the curls that had escaped her braids.

The pairs arrived in clusters and groups. Some wielded their weapons easily and dispatched their pretend foes, while others struggled to stay upright on their dragons' backs. Several looked as if they'd passed out during the flight.

When all the foes had been vanquished, Aibek mounted Gworsad. "Again! There's another practice army in the northern clearing."

Without another word, he and Gworsad took off, leaving the others to follow.

The day passed in a flurry of flights, weapons, and teamwork. By the time the dragons deposited their riders at their respective villages, Aibek thought even the shyest riders had become more comfortable with their enormous fire-breathing friends.

Aibek longed to spend time in his meditation room with his parents, but the week's activities had left him completely drained. Instead, he devoured every morsel of the roast foul and root vegetables his cook prepared and fell into bed at the first opportunity.

~ * ~

Ahren kept her eyes on the target in front of her. All the other archers had run to see the dragons when they'd heard the rumblings overhead, but she didn't have any interest in the beasts. If she were honest, she'd rather stay as far away from them as she could. She'd heard too many stories of people being attacked by dragons, and dozens of Tavan's soldiers had returned with deadly burns that could only have come from the forest's protectors.

The bowstring creaked under her pull, and another arrow flew into the forest. The wind carried it further right than she expected, and she completely missed the target. Booted feet clomped up the stairs behind her, but she didn't turn her head. The dragon riders had returned, and the archers would soon get back to their practice.

Ahren waited until the dragons' rumbling faded into the distance before she pulled out another arrow and took aim. Again, the wind took it, and it landed in the moss beside the target.

"Would you like some help?" A kind, feminine voice asked from behind her.

Ahren twisted, keeping her feet planted toward the rail. A tall woman stood watching her, with blonde curls in a riot around her head. A handkerchief hung limply around her neck. Dust and grime covered her brown zontrec pants and matching shirt. She looked friendly enough, and she had to be good if she was shooting arrows from a dragon's back. The thought made Ahren shudder.

The woman cleared her throat, and Ahren realized she hadn't answered and was staring at the woman like a fool.

"Oh, um. I guess. I don't know how to keep the wind from carrying them off. I'm pretty new at this."

"That's all right. We all have to start somewhere." The blonde held out her hand. "I'm Marah."

"Ahren." She shook Marah's hand once and grabbed an arrow. She suddenly remembered where she knew this woman from. "You're one of the mayors, right?"

Marah smiled and nodded. "Now, you have to figure out where the wind is coming from first, and how hard it's blowing."

Ahren tried to focus, but all she could see in her mind was this woman luring Aibek into her dark room in Kainga, and her brothers nearly beating him to death a few hours later. Of course, no one was supposed to know about that, so Ahren pushed the images out of her mind and focused on what Marah said. Her tips made sense, and Ahren's next arrow hit the center of the target.

"Great! One more time." Marah grinned and watched Ahren nock another arrow. Again, it struck the center, just beside the first.

Ahren couldn't fight a grin. "Thanks!"

Marah smiled back and ran a hand over her wild curls. "I'm supposed to be meeting with Aibek and Faruz and a few other dragon riders to talk about strategy. If you're all right here, I'll head over to the meeting. They're probably wondering what's happened to me."

"Thanks again," Ahren said. "I'm going to shoot a few more rounds and call it a day."

~ * ~

Noral stepped over a bearded mountain man sleeping in the walkway in front of his house. He made a face at the man and continued into his home. He dropped onto the comfortable sofa and pulled off his boots. An instant after the second boot hit the floor, Ira swept into the room from the kitchen. Her hair was a riot of silver-streaked chestnut curls and something brown smudged across her cheek.

"You're home early." She dropped onto the couch beside him, wiping her hands in her apron. It had once been the purest white, but years of use had stained it red in patches, blue in others. He'd offered to replace it several times, but she'd always laughed and said it still worked just fine.

"I finished the new cart axle for that farmer a bit ahead of schedule, but it's too late in the day to start anything new, so I came on home. How was your day?"

"Quiet. I've almost finished the quilt for Aibek. It certainly does get cold there, doesn't it?" She twisted in her seat, gazing up at him with soft brown eyes. "Do you think the cook and housekeeper will want to go with us? I haven't asked them yet. I'm not quite sure how to broach the subject."

"Go with you where?" The housekeeper picked up Noral's boots and set them on the mat by the door. "Are you planning another trip?"

"Well, yes. And no." Ira frowned.

"Which is it? Are ye takin' a trip er not?"

The housekeeper's diction only slipped when she was irritated, so Noral decided to step in. "We're planning to move south when the winter breaks down in the forest. Would you like to come with us?"

"Really?" A huge grin spread across the older woman's face. "I've heard it's lovely in the forest, but I've never left the city. I'd love to go. I don't have any family left to keep me here."

"Then it's settled." Ira stood and put an arm around her favorite servant's shoulders. "You'll have to come with us. Aibek has an enormous house there, though we'll only stay with him until we have our own place."

"That sounds wonderful! I'll have to start going through my things. Oh, how exciting!" The housekeeper bustled out through the hall door and Ira smiled up at Noral.

Glancing out the front window, Noral startled and turned back to his wife. "Before I forget, I don't want you going to the market alone until these mountain men leave the city."

She laughed. "Whyever not? I've been going to the market by myself since before we married."

"I know. I just don't trust them. I think they're planning something." He grabbed her arms and stared into her wide eyes. "Promise me you'll stay away from them. Promise you'll lock yourself in the house if fighting starts outside."

"All right. I promise. You've never steered me wrong before." She leaned up and kissed him lightly on the lips. "Now, I need to check on our dinner."

Noral watched until she disappeared around the corner, then flopped back into the plush sofa. He considered the previous week's meeting with Cadwy and hoped the army would be back in the city in time to fight whenever the time came.

Worried, he crossed to the hearth and grabbed his sword. He hadn't sharpened it in months. Grabbing a whetstone and cloth, he settled back onto the sofa and ground a razor's edge onto the blade.

~ * ~

A night and a day passed before Glesni moved. When his eyes opened, Eddrick sat up straight and leaned close, eager to learn the ancients' decision.

"They have denied your petition. You have enough time to move between the two camps and watch both, while keeping everyone together in a group."

Eddrick's shoulders slumped under the weight of his disappointment, but he knew better than to argue. "Well, we'd better get to work searching for that second army, then. We've wasted almost two days."

Extending both arms to the sides, Eddrick moved to the center of the room and waited for his father and wife to take his hands, and for Glesni to close the circle. When they were all connected, Eddrick searched for the cold spark of intuition that would tell him where to find Helak. Like the other times he'd tried recently, it didn't come. Instead, he thought of a specific soldier, one he hadn't seen in the north group. He was taller than his companions and kept his uniform clean.

There.

He followed that spark, and the world around them vanished. Wind whipped his hair. Eddrick smiled at the strange sensation. He'd been dead for two decades, and the winds on the ground blew straight threw him. The wind stopped. Eddrick opened his eyes.

Disoriented, Eddrick blinked. Tall, leafless trees surrounded them. The ground sloped gently away from him. Late afternoon sun illuminated a rocky path.

"They're close. Keep quiet," he whispered to the others.

Kiri leaned in until her breath tickled his ear. "Where are we?"

A warning shiver traveled up Eddrick's spine, and he shook his head rather than answer. They needed to get off the trail.

He pointed up toward the branches of the broad oak tree beside them, and they floated up off the ground. The new height offered a better view of their surroundings.

At the crest of the next hill, an army milled around a sprawling camp. Eddrick recognized the soldier he'd used as his focus—the tall, clean one. He squatted beside the first embers of a fire. His crisp yellow uniform stood out amongst the dingy mustard colors his companions wore. The fire flared and he stood. Others rushed in with pans and a spit of rabbits, and Eddrick turned his attention elsewhere. He had no interest in watching the soldiers cook their dinner.

Where could Helak be?

He gestured to the others that they needed to move closer but used his arms to signal that they should circle the camp from the treetops. Kiri, Glesni, and Agommi nodded their understanding.

The group moved slowly from tree to tree, keeping behind the trunks as much as possible to avoid being spotted from below.

When they'd traveled a quarter of the way around the sprawling camp, Eddrick stopped. The black entrance to a cave enticed him. Three tents stood near the cave, each triple the size of the soldiers' tents.

This had to be where Helak was hiding. He moved

closer to the largest tent, but halfway down, he hit something solid. He backed away, shaking off the disoriented feeling, and examined the site again. He couldn't see what he'd hit.

Agommi followed him down, tested the barrier with a hand, and shook his head. Without a word, he moved back into the treetops and held out his hands.

Eddrick held his questions as they formed their circle, closed their eyes, and waited for the wind to carry them back home.

The wind dissolved into stillness. The scent of Kiri's perfume filled the room.

Eddrick's lips were moving before he opened his eyes. "What was that? How do we get through it?"

"It's a shield." Glesni gave Eddrick a knowing look. "It's the same sort of magic we plan to use to draw the spirits away from the living during the battle."

"How do we get through it?" Kiri moved to stand beside her husband.

Agommi grunted. "We don't. We'll have to watch them from outside that shield. If we try to break through it or take it down, we might as well wave a banner and announce our entrance."

"All right." Eddrick rolled his shoulders, as if to release the tension gathering there. "Are we allowed to tell Aibek that the army has split in two? I think that's something he should know."

Glesni went still and closed his eyes. A heartbeat later, he said, "No. We know nothing useful yet. We will continue to watch and wait."

8.

Accident

The days flew by, each filled from dawn to dusk with one-on-one battle training with Gworsad, practicing with the tincture, group training sessions with the other riders, and Aibek's usual responsibilities as Nivaka's mayor.

Serik went along for each day of the magic practice, but Aibek suspected the old man was less interested in his mastery of the art the Bokinna called Kurim, and more interested in spending time in the Bokinna's presence. Aibek didn't blame him. As the forest had healed from the poison, the Bokinna's strength, wisdom, and compassion had been more and more evident.

"Are you ready?" Aibek asked Serik. It was a scheduled Kurim day, but the elderly man was still in his dressing gown when he came to Aibek's rooms for breakfast.

"Oh, are we going into the forest today? Yes, that's right. Just give me a minute and I'll be ready."

Aibek watched Serik dash out of the room, then turned his attention to the tray of famanc and heavy cakes the servant had left behind. He wouldn't eat without his friend, but he poured himself a mug of steaming famanc and savored the beverage while he waited.

He'd managed to steal several more moments alone with Marah during the group training sessions, each more intense than the one before. Just the thought of her took his breath away. He was going to have to do something about her, and soon. He needed to either marry her so he could have her close every day or end the relationship so she couldn't distract him at every turn. He didn't know which was the right choice.

Whenever she was near, he got a nagging feeling she was hiding something. He couldn't put his finger on why, but something in her manner hinted at a deep secret she didn't want known.

That worried him, but only when she wasn't around. Her scent clouded his thoughts until he could think of nothing else when she was close.

Serik burst into the room, out of breath and wearing mismatched zontrec clothing. His bright blue shirt and dark red pants would have been comical if he hadn't looked so panicked.

"What's wrong?" Aibek stood and met his mentor at the door.

"Nothing, nothing. I just couldn't find my leather pants, so I had to put on the first thing I found. I thought you might leave without me. The dragons will be waiting."

Aibek sank back down into his chair. "I wouldn't leave you. I know how much you enjoy spending time at the Heart of the Forest. Eat your breakfast, and we'll go out to the dragons together."

Half an hour later, they strolled out together. They headed down the east entrance stairs and met Faruz in the forest below.

Aibek had to re-orient himself each day since the forest had begun to rearrange itself in preparation for battle. That day, the stairs set them down on the banks of the narrow stream they'd had to cross to get to Nivaka from the city. He held Serik's arm as they stepped onto the rocky soil and jumped over the stream. The dragons waited on the other side.

Faruz, Serik, and Aibek stepped into the Bokinna's clearing side-by-side, as they did before each practice session. They dropped to their knees before the ancient being and awaited her instructions.

"Serik, you're looking quite colorful this morning," the tree said, her soft green eyes smiling down at the old man.

"Yes, madam." Serik blushed, and Aibek tried to remember any other occasion where the elderly servant had seemed even a little flustered. He couldn't think of any.

"You may observe from your normal spot."

He eased to his feet and strolled over to his favorite tree. He leaned against it, but didn't sit.

"Aibek. Faruz. You may drink your Kurim."

They did as she commanded, though Aibek still couldn't suppress the grimace the bitter potion caused. He washed the vile liquid down with half a skin of water and waited for the Bokinna's next instructions.

"Move the logs over here." A long branch indicated an empty place beside the tree-god.

Aibek stood, his leg aching, but better than it had been. He was getting stronger; he couldn't deny it.

As they moved through the familiar exercises, Aibek's mind wandered. He thought of Marah, of her intoxicating scent. He pictured the wild blond curls trapped beneath her bonnet. He imagined himself staring into the warm amber of her eyes.

His heart pattered at the warm sensations growing within.

"Aibek! Watch what you're doing!"

Faruz's voice pierced Aibek's musings, and he looked up. The log he'd been moving had broken free of his hands and soared through the air—straight at Serik, who had fallen asleep against his tree.

"Serik!" Aibek and Faruz screamed in unison.

Aibek sprinted for his friend, arriving a heartbeat before the log. He raised an arm to block the impact but wasn't fast enough.

The log crashed into Serik's chest. The crunch of bones made Aibek sick to his stomach.

Serik opened his eyes and gazed up at Aibek. Confusion and pain colored his face, and Aibek dropped to his knees before his mentor.

"No! Serik! Tell me you're all right!"

Eyes wide with shock and pain, Serik just shook his head. "Take me to her," he whispered. Blood spattered his ashen lips as he spoke.

Aibek hesitated, unsure if he should move the injured man.

"Bring him to me." The Bokinna's voice rasped on the wind, the same as it had been when she had been so weak and ill.

Tears filled Aibek's eyes, but he bent to comply. He braced an arm behind Serik's back and slid the other under his knees. The potion gave him strength, and he lifted his mentor as if he weighed no more than a child.

Concentrating on every movement, he eased Serik closer to the ancient being at the center of the clearing. He set his dearest friend down on the mossy ground at the base of her trunk and eased his arms free.

Guilt and helplessness crushed Aibek's chest at the sight of Serik's caved-in chest and gray skin.

"Leave me here," Serik rasped.

Tears streamed down Aibek's face, and he dropped his arms to his sides.

"Leave us," the Bokinna commanded.

Strength and panic pulsed through Aibek's arms and legs, but there was nothing more he could do. He considered offering Serik a vial of the potion, but the Bokinna had already ordered him away.

Dejected and guilt-ridden, he knelt by Serik's side once more and kissed his mentor. The old man's cheek was cold and clammy, and Aibek sobbed at the knowledge that his oldest friend was dying.

Serik coughed and blood speckled his lips.

"Leave us!" This time, the Bokinna's command carried all the force of the wind.

Aibek stood, glanced down at Serik once more, and trudged to the edge of the clearing, where Gworsad waited. The dragon crouched down to allow him to climb onto his back, and Aibek grabbed hold of the rope. As he swung into place, he could see Serik's lips moving.

He focused his potion-enhanced senses on the old man, desperate to hear his friend's last words.

"All that's been and yet to come…"

Gworsad's great, leathery wings stretched out.

"Defend me now from evil's harm."

Wind roared in Aibek's ears as the dragon beat his wings downward.

"Lower 'er the veil of lights true…"

Aibek strained to hear the last part as Gworsad lifted him above the treetops.

"Hand upon me… Now, I ask…"

The trees blurred beneath him as tears burned his eyes. Aibek didn't know if there was more to whatever prayer Serik recited, but what he'd heard squeezed his heart in his chest.

Serik couldn't die. He just couldn't. Aibek needed him. He was the best friend and mentor Aibek had ever known.

Tears flowed freely down his cheeks as Gworsad pulled him closer to home. As the village came into view below, Aibek realized he had another problem.

He still had the potion in his system.

He couldn't go into the village with his crazy strength. He'd already killed Serik because of a moment's distraction. He couldn't even imagine the damage he could do in a village.

The Bokinna had warned him. She'd told him he had to focus on every single movement. Why had he thought he could daydream about Marah instead?

Gworsad set him down in the clearing beside the stream, but Aibek didn't climb down. Instead, he leaned over, buried his face in the mossy fronds around the dragon's neck, and wept.

"Can we just fly for a bit? I'm not ready to go home yet," he whispered.

Aibek caught a glimpse of Faruz's confused face as Gworsad lifted off and flew away. He hoped his friend would understand.

Gworsad flew to the south clearing, where the scattered remains of dozens of practice dummies littered the ground. Aibek climbed down and set to work cleaning up the mess, grateful for the distraction. It didn't help as much as he hoped.

As he worked, his mind replayed an endless stream of memories: Serik at his first sword fighting tournament, Serik cheering him on in the spelling contest, Serik quietly drilling him on his maths, Serik holding him as he cried over the end of his first real romantic relationship.

"I can't do this without you," he screamed into the silent trees.

Gworsad rumbled and nudged him with a gentle

foot, but Aibek turned away. No new friends could possibly replace the one he'd just lost.

He scrubbed at his eyes, trying to wipe away the vision of Serik's broken body laying propped against the Bokinna.

It was his fault. He had let his mind drift. He had forgotten the Bokinna's warning, and his oldest friend had paid with his life.

When the clearing was clean and the dummies reset for the next training day, Aibek climbed onto Gworsad's back and let the dragon take him home. He trudged up the stairs on legs made of lead but couldn't go home. That big, empty house would feel like a tomb without Serik.

Instead, he turned his steps to Valasa's home and pounded on the door.

The housekeeper opened the door, and Aibek asked to see Valasa, his voice wooden and stiff.

"Of course. Come in, Mr. Mayor."

She led him to the den, where he sank onto the plush sofa and fought back the tears that threatened.

"Aibek!" Valasa's booming voice rang through the enclosed space. "I hadn't expected to see you today. What can I help you with?"

The healer must have gotten a good look at Aibek's tear-stained face at that point, because his voice dropped to a whisper. "What's happened?"

Instead of answering, Aibek glanced at the open door to Valasa's study.

"Of course. Come in here and we'll talk about whatever it is."

Valasa pressed a massive hand on Aibek's shoulder and ushered him into the long, narrow room.

Once inside, Aibek dropped into the closest chair and dissolved in tears once more.

A handkerchief landed on the table in front of him, and Aibek took it gratefully. He pressed the thin fabric to his eyes and wiped his nose, then took a deep, steadying breath.

"There's been an accident. Serik…" He could barely choke out the words before the sobs wrenched him again.

Valasa waited patiently, allowing Aibek the space he needed to grieve for his beloved mentor.

When Aibek's tears finally abated, Valasa offered him a cup of water, which he downed in a few quick gulps.

"All right, then. Tell me what's happened." Valasa's voice was gentler than Aibek had ever heard it, and the tears threatened again.

Aibek swallowed against the grief, took a deep breath, and blurted out the whole, awful story. He relayed every detail, including his preoccupation with Marah and his loss of control over the log. He told the healer about leaving Serik slumped against the Bokinna's trunk, about the blood, his crushed-in chest, and the words Serik had spoken as Gworsad had lifted off. When he finished, Valasa regarded him with a compassionate gaze.

"It sounds like the Bokinna has it covered. She'll take care of him, child. If she can't heal his wounds, she'll take away his pain and let him go peacefully."

Aibek nodded, unable to say anything around the lump in his throat.

"I know this is hard, but you have to trust that she'll take care of everything. She takes care of us all every day. She'll take care of Serik in his time of need."

Tears threatened again, but Aibek swallowed them back. He took a deep breath and tried hard to see Valasa's perspective. Maybe the Bokinna could save Serik. The image of his friend's broken body flashed unbidden to Aibek's mind. If the Bokinna couldn't save him, at least she could take away his pain. Valasa was right about that, at least.

"Here, drink this. It'll let you get some sleep tonight, so you can see everything with fresh eyes in the morning." Valasa pressed a small vial into Aibek's hand.

Without thinking, Aibek downed the vial's contents and grimaced at the tincture's rancid taste.

"Here." A fresh cup of water appeared on the table in front of him, and Aibek gulped it down.

"Let me walk you home."

A fog covered Aibek's vision, but he was vaguely aware of the walk to his home, the housekeeper's worried exclamation, and Valasa's soothing voice.

Somehow, his boots came off and a pillow pressed against his head, and he settled deeper into it, grateful for the release of sleep.

~ * ~

Noral hummed a quiet tune, using the rhythm of his hammer to punctuate the song as he worked. They'd made a great deal of progress in getting the house ready to move over the past weeks, and trunks lined the walls in every room. The cook had declined Ira's offer to travel south with them, but she'd recently become engaged to a nearby widower, so her decision didn't come as a surprise. Remembering her happiness when she'd announced the gentleman's proposal, Noral smiled. Her certain happiness eased any guilt he may have felt at leaving her without employment.

A loud crash sounded outside, and Noral set down his hammer, listening for any repeat of the noise. A heartbeat later, a group of mountain tribesmen ran past his shop. They carried spears and improvised weapons, but their numbers worried Noral.

His heart crashed in his chest as he strapped on his sword. He abandoned his work on the anvil and ran out into the streets. Part of the army had returned from their field training, but many would be trapped outside the city if the mountain men closed the gates.

Or, Noral thought, if the city guard thinks this is an attack from outside and closes the gates to prevent more from entering.

Unsure where else to go, Noral raced to the broad stone building that housed the army academy where Aibek had spent so many years. His breath burned in his lungs with each step, but he crossed the half mile to the school in record time.

Noral braced his hands on his knees and struggled

for breath. Slowly, the sounds of combat carried to his ears and broke through his panic. Eyes wild, he raised his head and took in the scene.

Students and professors fought side-by-side against hundreds of armed tribesmen.

Thankfully, the academy's residents were better trained. Noral watched as the officers-in-training cut down enemy after enemy, aided by the battle-hardened professors.

He wasn't needed there. Noral spun on his heel, took a breath, and raced for the south gate. Low shanties inside the wall there served as the city guards' headquarters. Someone there could tell him how he could help.

As he ran, someone crashed into him from the side. Noral stumbled but kept his feet. He unsheathed his sword, searching for the source of the blow. A squat man with a dirt-smeared face and a knotted beard that reached his knees growled up at him from the street. Without missing a beat, Noral swung the sword and parted the grizzled head from its shoulders.

He wiped the blade on his heavy blacksmith's apron, thankful he'd forgotten to remove the garment in spite of its bulk. When he'd caught his breath, he sprinted toward the gate once more. All around him, Xona's citizens engaged this new threat, fighting with whatever weapons they could find on such short notice.

Ira's face swam in his thoughts, and he hoped she'd stayed inside. Aibek had reinforced the doors and windows in the home as part of his training, so Noral was certain she'd be safe there. This enemy had no siege weapons. In fact, very few had proper weapons at all. Only one in a hundred wielded a sword. The rest had knives strapped onto broom handles— sometimes with the broom still attached to the other end.

There are so many. They may have us by sheer numbers. Noral fought off the worried thought and slowed to a walk as he approached the guard station. He had to fight back a relieved smile when he grew closer. The man standing in the doorway had been Aibek's opponent in the last tournament he'd fought in the Academy.

What's his name? Noral wracked his mind for the strapping young man's name even as he approached and waved.

"Intza!" Noral shouted the name as soon as it popped into his thoughts. "Is that you? Thank the trees you're all right! How can I help?"

"They need more men at the east entrance," the young officer yelled back, straining his voice to be heard over the clanging of metal and the screams of the injured and dying. "I can't leave my post, but you know the way!"

Noral nodded, turned, and hurried off in the direction Intza had indicated. The fighting at the east gate was fierce. Mountain tribesmen pressed forward, trying to force the guard to close the gate, while Xona's soldiers ran toward the city in the distance.

Without stopping to check in with the commander,

Noral unsheathed his sword and joined the fray. He stepped into a gap in the guards' line and earned relieved glances from men on both sides. He cast one more glance at the army outside the gate, raised his sword, and thrust at an advancing mountain man. The enemy impaled himself on Noral's sword, and Noral had to yank to free the weapon. He didn't have time to clean it before the next enemy rushed for him.

A scream pierced the air beside his head, and Noral looked over in time to see his neighbor fall. He regretted he hadn't learned the soldier's name but couldn't give the man more than a passing thought. They had to hold. They had to save the city. These were Helak's men. If they took Xona, they'd have access to power, money, and weapons enough to crush Aibek's tiny force like dust beneath their heels.

9.

Message

The force rolled over Xona like a wave taking the shore, and Eddrick could do nothing but watch. Horror filled him at the death and destruction Helak's men wrought within the city's glittering walls.

Frantic, he closed his eyes and searched for Noral. The spark beckoned from the west gate, so Eddrick grabbed the others, closed his eyes, and transported them to that location.

Chaos reigned. The screams of wounded and dying warriors filled the air, and Eddrick searched for Noral among the fighting.

Helak's men outnumbered the city guards in that ward nearly four to one. All around, small pockets of Xona's best warriors fought against groups of mountain tribesmen wielding hastily constructed weapons.

Eddrick's mouth fell open when two city guards struck what should have been lethal blows, but the men they fought didn't falter. Instead, their eyes glowed green for an instant and they fought back with a new, frightening strength.

"Should we get the others and make the barrier?" Eddrick asked Glesni.

The youngest ancient closed his eyes the way he

did when he wanted to consult with his superiors. At last, he opened his eyes and shook his head. "This is not the battle we prepare for. This is a test for Helak's men. We will let them think their tactics will work."

"But these men are dying! That's my brother! I have to do something," As he spoke, Eddrick spotted Noral. He fought back to back with another Xona citizen.

Both wore the heavy aprons commonly seen in blacksmith's shops over stained linen work clothes. Sweat dripped into their eyes as they parried and blocked the mountain men's jabs and swings.

"Come," Glesni said, his voice grave. "We need to see what is happening in the rest of the city."

"No," Eddrick roared. "I will not leave my brother!"

"You can do nothing for him now," Glesni placed a hand on Eddrick's shoulder, compassion shining in his rich brown eyes. "But we can let your son and his army know what has happened here today. We need to give him all the information he needs which means we must investigate how the rest of the city has fared."

His shoulders slumped against the weight of grief and disappointment, but Eddrick nodded. Glesni was right. If the ancients wouldn't allow them to interfere, he could do nothing to help his brother. He cast a final glance over his shoulder, hoping it wouldn't be the last time he saw Noral alive, grabbed hold of the others, and whisked away to the south gate.

The clanging of steel and the cries of the wounded

filled the air. Bodies lay everywhere, forgotten where they'd fallen in the fury of battle. The stench of blood and death made Eddrick retch, and he gave silent thanks to the trees he couldn't eat anymore. None of the faces stood out in the crowd. Eddrick didn't know these people, but his heart ached for them.

They fought their invaders with desperate energy, but a heavy sense of resignation hung over the scene. They couldn't overcome these men whose eyes glowed green, who fought harder and stronger when they should have fallen, and they knew it.

A messenger wearing a stained white shirt and pale green pants splattered with blood ran through the throng. Eddrick strained to hear the words he screamed over and over.

"The king is dead! We have fallen! The new lord says surrender or die!"

"No." Eddrick grabbed Kiri and Glesni, closed his eyes, and transported them to the great marble palace at the center of the city.

Corpses littered the ground near the wide steps. Blood and excrement ran down the usually majestic entry.

Helak's men stood guard at the door. The few remaining city guards knelt before their captors, allowing the mountain men to tie their arms behind their backs.

"There's nothing more to see here." Glesni grasped Eddrick's arm, but Eddrick couldn't meet his eyes.

Instead, he gazed at the faded beige hair atop the spirit's pale face. "Let's go."

They held each other's hands and flew back to Eddrick and Kiri's home. The cheerful decor wrenched Eddrick's heart as his mind lingered on the last glimpse he'd had of his brother.

Glesni broke the silence. "We need to tell your son what's happened."

"All right. Let's go." Eddrick hung his head but held out his hands. The wind ruffled his hair as the magic took them to Nivaka.

Aibek stood with a group staring up at the crumbling supports at the south cistern, debating the best way to repair them with the forest's gentle movement. The trees had arranged their roots to move the earth beneath the cisterns along with the village, but that slight shift had worsened the cracks in the supports.

Eddrick floated above the crowd, between Aibek and the supports, trying desperately to get his son's attention. When the young mayor finally looked up, his eyes widened. Eddrick mouthed the words, "We need to talk. Now."

He waited impatiently as Aibek excused himself and hurried back into the village. Eddrick and Kiri waited for him in the meditation room—which had once been their bedroom. Glesni and Agommi hovered nearby, invisible to the living.

Time crept by. Eddrick watched the shadows of

the barren branches dance across the window and rehearsed his warning in his mind.

At last, the door swung open and Aibek stepped in. Faruz followed him, and Eddrick smiled. He couldn't have chosen a better friend for his son if he'd tried.

"Father? Are you here?" Aibek lit the lamps and settled into a carved wooden chair before the bare table.

Eddrick concentrated on making his substance more visible in the afternoon light. "I'm here. And so is your mother."

"What's wrong? You've never called me away from a meeting before. You look worried."

Eddrick sighed. "There's no easy way to say this. Xona has fallen."

A chair clattered against the floor, forgotten, as Faruz leapt to his feet. Aibek sucked in an audible breath and leaned closer across the table. "And my uncle?" Aibek whispered.

Eddrick shook his head. "I don't know. We were called away before I could see how he fared."

"Who did this?" Faruz paced the floor, grabbing for his absent sword every few steps.

"It's Helak, isn't it? That's why you saw what happened." Fear, fury, and grief warred in Aibek's eyes, and Eddrick wished he could offer words of comfort.

"Of course it is," Kiri cried. "It was horrible. The ancients wouldn't let us help them." Her face screwed up as if in a sob, but her immortal spirit couldn't produce tears.

"We need to gather the council." Faruz stepped toward the door. "We have to send help to Xona."

"Please be careful." Kiri floated to her son and pressed a kiss to his cheek. "I know you have to go, but please stay as safe as you can."

"I promise," Aibek said gravely. He followed Faruz into the hall and out of the house, and Eddrick closed his eyes.

He concentrated hard on his brother, searching for that familiar spark. Only emptiness echoed back.

~ * ~

Aibek paced in Valasa's upstairs sitting room and waited for the rest of the council members to arrive.

"Of course, we won't be able to keep this a secret for long," Faruz blurted out.

"I know. But the council needs to discuss it and make some decisions before we let everyone else know."

Long minutes passed as they waited. Aibek worried about his aunt and uncle and assumed Faruz was thinking about his own family. Long moments passed, the only sound the crackling of the fire on the hearth and the clicking of boots against the wood floor. Neither man had stopped to change into the normal zontrec slippers when they'd left the forest floor. Some small corner of Aibek's mind registered the concern that he might scuff the floor, but bigger concerns kept his attention.

The door banged open, and Aibek jerked his head toward the sound. Valasa strode into the room, and the rest of the council members followed. Aibek hadn't told Valasa what they'd learned. He'd just asked the Gadonu to gather the council for an emergency meeting. Now all eyes focused on Aibek, mingled worry and curiosity shining in their expressions.

Aibek didn't wait for Valasa to open the meeting. Instead, he began before the others had taken their seats.

"I've gotten some distressing news, and we need to agree on how best to react before the word gets out." No one spoke, so he continued. "Helak's army has attacked Xona."

A chorus of gasps filled the room, but Aibek didn't give them a chance to recover. "Xona's army couldn't hold, and the king is dead. Helak now holds the most important city in the land."

Silence stretched until Zifa stood. "Clearly, we have to do something. We can't just sit here and wait to be next."

"She's right," Dalan said from his spot on the worn, green sofa. "We should gather a division to send to help Xona."

Faruz shook his head. "Were you paying attention last month when I told you about Xona's history? It's impossible to take the city from outside those walls. Helak had to have snuck his men inside before they attacked. An army isn't the answer."

"Then what? Zifa's right." Ahren slapped her palms on her purple-clad knees. Her white hair hung loose, strands sticking to her sweaty face. "We can't just wait for them to show up here next."

"I've given this some thought, and I asked the forest while I waited." Aibek took a deep breath. "I think we should send a few of the stronger dragon riders north to see what's happening. They can get there faster than an army division, anyway. If I go with them, I can communicate with you through the trees and Valasa.

"And there's plenty of caves and hollows to hide the dragons in while we travel. I've spent years in that area. We can do this.

Wayra made a face and shook his head. "But we need the dragons here to protect the forest! What if Helak's trying to pull our army away so he can take the forest unopposed?"

"You're right, of course," Aibek said. "I'm not suggesting we take the entire force. Just a handful of dragon riders who can get there quickly and assess the situation."

Faruz nodded. "We can get a ground division together to follow you, so you'll have backup if fighting breaks out. Maybe about half the army? Or is that too much?"

A great debate ensued, and the council spent the rest of the afternoon discussing exactly how many fighters they should send north. On the one hand, they had to make sure they had enough people to defend the forest. On the other, Xona was the government seat for Azalin, and the center of the land's infrastructure. They couldn't leave it in Helak's hands.

At the end of it all, they agreed to send half the

dragons and half the army to Xona, though worries about the weather couldn't be completely ignored.

When the meeting ended, Aibek turned to Faruz. "I'll do my best to find out about your parents and send word as soon as I get there."

Faruz nodded but said nothing.

With the first blush of dawn, Aibek climbed onto Gworsad's back and flew to the Heart of the Forest to consult with the Bokinna—and to find Serik. The heavy weight of grief nearly crushed him, even as the dragon lifted him into the sky. Serik couldn't possibly still be alive, not with the injuries he'd sustained. And his aunt and uncle were likely dead as well, since they wouldn't have hidden in their home when the fighting erupted. He swallowed the lump in his throat and tried to convince himself the tears on his cheeks were due to the cold wind in his eyes.

Gworsad set him down gently in the Bokinna's clearing, and Aibek kept his eyes closed.

He sat like that for a long while, until a cold wind blew across him. He shivered.

"Are you well, child?" The Bokinna's voice drifted to him on the breeze.

Finally, Aibek opened his eyes and scanned the clearing. It was empty. No leaves littered the ground. No logs stacked beside the great tree. No Serik.

"Wh— Where is he?"

"He is where he belongs. Worry no more about him."

Aibek took a breath, prepared to argue for more information. He thought better of it and released the breath in a huff. He couldn't deny a sense of relief at not having to transport Serik's body back to the village.

"Madam Bokinna." His voice quavered. He cleared his throat and tried again. "Madam Tree, we need your help. Our enemies have taken the city in the north, where all the land's infrastructure and armies are centered."

"And now you wish to take my protectors north to fight for this foreign city."

"Not all of them." Aibek knelt before the ancient being. "I ask your permission to take half of the dragons who have been training with our fighters. The other half and all the unpartnered dragons would remain here to keep you and the forest safe from the enemy's other army."

"What will you do to protect my loved ones in the barren north?"

"I've thought about that at length, Madam." Aibek tugged at a stray blade of grass. "I would keep them hidden by traveling only at night and hide them in the mines and quarries north of the city. There's ample food there for them, and they'll be out of sight of any people there."

"And how will they communicate with me? My strength does not reach that far."

"I had hoped to be able to reach either you or the Saethem from outside the city, but if that's impossible, I will send my father's spirit to Valasa to give you messages." Aibek frowned. "Or can you talk to him directly? I'm not sure how that works."

"I can speak with spirits, if they appear to me, though it has been many hundreds of years since any have. The ones who are here are certainly welcome to speak to me."

Aibek's eyes opened wide as his father, his mother, and two other spirits materialized from the morning mist.

"I beg your pardon, Madam," Eddrick said. "We meant no disrespect. I am Eddrick, Aibek's father, and this is my wife, Kiri."

"I know who you are, my child. I know all of the mayors of my villages. But who is the other young man?"

Glesni blinked, clearly astounded to be addressed as a young man. "I am Glesni, representative of the Council of the Ancients. I am honored to be in your presence. My superiors are telling me I should kneel before one as great as yourself." He shrunk, hovering an inch above the low grass.

"What say you to Aibek's plan to travel to the city?"

No one answered. The spirits looked to each other and back to the great tree.

"Eddrick, answer please." The Bokinna's voice had a sharper edge than Aibek had ever heard from her.

"I think it is wise, Madam. The supplies available in the city could be used to destroy this forest."

"Very well. My protectors will go with you. Time is short. You must leave as soon as darkness falls."

Aibek bowed low. "Thank you. May I—" He

broke off, unsure, then tried once more. "Is Serik alive, Madam Tree? I— I need to know."

"I told you already, he is where he needs to be. Now, be off. I need rest, and you must prepare for a long journey."

The spirits evaporated, and Aibek stood. He wished she would at least tell him if Serik was dead or alive but pushing for more information didn't seem wise. Instead, he climbed onto Gworsad's back, tied the straps around his legs, and let the dragon carry him home.

Once inside the village, he had Valasa send messages to the other villages. Half the dragon riders needed to be ready to leave at twilight. That done, he hurried home to pack for the trip and rest before what was sure to be an arduous night.

Faruz hovered nearby as he tossed his linen and leather travel clothes into his knapsack. "I wish I could go with you, but I think one of us needs to stay to help the others train with the dragons."

"Of course, you're right." Aibek kept his eyes on the extra blanket he was folding. "And they respect you after all the work you've done building and training armies for Nivaka and the other villages. You'll send a ground division within the week?"

"They'll leave within the next two days," Faruz said, nodding. "A few dragons will give you an edge, but they won't be enough to take or hold the city."

"I'll send word as soon as I know anything about our families, good or bad."

Faruz nodded again but said nothing. His friend's

uncharacteristic silence worried Aibek, but there wasn't time to press the matter. When he'd finished packing, he said a final farewell, knowing full well it may be the last time he ever saw his best friend. Battles couldn't be predicted, and this one didn't look good for the villagers.

Queen Idril answered Aibek's note within an hour. She expressed gratitude for the offer but declined to send any of the groundfolk along on the journey north. Aibek had hoped for exactly that response, and he smiled as he read the missive.

Grief, loss, and fear weighed on Aibek, and he finally gave in and drank Valasa's vile sleeping potion. He would need rest if he was to stay on the dragon through the night.

Just before sunset, the dragons gathered their riders in the clearing by the stream. Several additional dragons had volunteered to carry riders after the first practice, so they now had nearly forty. Twelve dragons drank from the stream while their riders wound the zontrec straps around them. Nervous chatter filled the air.

Marah sidled up beside Aibek. "I hope you don't mind, I volunteered to come along."

Overwhelmed with the details of traveling with such a large group of dragons, Aibek didn't answer.

"I've never been outside the forest besides the trip to Kainga for the Grand Council."

A tiny quiver in her voice made Aibek look up from his notes. "I'd love to have you along, but you don't have to come." He hoped his voice sounded gentle.

"No, I want to. I'm just…" She trailed off, the rest of the sentence hanging between them.

Aibek turned to face her. Unbidden, thoughts of her kisses filled his mind, followed by the image of a broken and bleeding Serik. "Look, I—" He bit his tongue. It wasn't her fault he'd let her distract him during practice. He tried again. "I can't promise to be able to keep you safe. You're the best sniper we've got, but I don't want you to feel pressured into coming."

"No one's pressured me, or even asked." She paused, tugging at the scarf covering her wild blond curls. "I just want to be able to stay close to you. Would that be all right?"

A tiny smile tugged at the edges of Aibek's mouth. "Yes," he said without thinking. "I think I'd like that."

Apparently satisfied, she turned back to her dragon and worked at securing her pack to the straps. Aibek did the same, shoving aside the stab of guilt. Serik wouldn't want him to turn away from her, right? He wouldn't make the same mistake twice. He'd keep his mind on his work whether she was nearby or not.

Dozens of elves and dwarves emerged from the forest when the sun set, but none moved to attack the preparing force. They kept their weapons sheathed and strapped to their backs, but never took their eyes from the villagers and their dragons.

Aibek waited until it was almost completely dark and Koviom's pale light hovered at the treetops before he gave the command to mount up. Moments later, twelve dragons took to the skies. They flew northeast, away from the villages that dotted the river and far from the many eyes in Kainga. The dragons chirped and rumbled to each other until they passed the forest's edge. Their sudden silence sent a chill through Aibek, though he had worried they'd alert anyone below with their conversation.

Plains, fields, pastures, and rivers passed below them, illuminated by the moons' watery light. Aibek watched it all, remembering the walk south from Xona and wondering what he'd find when he arrived. Memories of Ira, Noral, and Serik filled his mind, and he wept out the grief of their likely deaths.

They flew without stopping for several hours until one of the smaller dragons signaled for a break. They landed in a narrow valley between hills, where a pebbled stream would provide water and perhaps a snack for the dragons.

Aibek stretched, yawned, and pulled off his heavy gloves. He bent to refill his water skin in the frigid water. The night had grown cold, and the icy stream flowing over his hands took his breath away.

He avoided talking to anyone, afraid his hoarse voice and tear-reddened eyes would betray the depth of his emotion. Thankfully, no one came near. Each rider stretched, walked, ate, and drank without speaking to the others. Aibek climbed the tallest hill so he could watch the others and see if any bandits approached. He glanced up at the untold numbers of stars in the sky and watched the three moons make their journey toward the horizon.

When fatigue threatened to overtake him, he stood and waved for the others to mount up. They had several more hours of travel left before daybreak.

The night grew colder, and the icy wind rendered Aibek's face numb beneath the leather mask he'd pulled down. Only the smallest slits let him see out into the night, but it was enough to allow the bitter cold in. He shivered in his cloak, tightened his grip on the thick straps, and watched the pale landscape below. As the faintest hint of light touched the edge of the sky, Aibek spotted the welcoming darkness of the Saethem's swamp. They'd spend the daylight hours hidden within her borders and continue on when the sun's revealing light had vanished.

He signaled to Gworsad, who led the force down into the trees' shelter. Gags, groans, and complaints greeted Aibek's numb ears when he climbed down. The wintry weather had frozen the top layer of the mud, so they had firm ground to stand upon, but the swamp's odor hadn't diminished. The stink of rotting vegetation, animal excrement, and stagnant water brought tears to Aibek's exhausted eyes.

"We'll climb into the trees to sleep," he shouted. "We'll be warmer there, where we can stay dry."

Aibek expected complaints, but the others only grunted and nodded.

"You sleep. We be back before night." Gworsad

stepped back and unfolded his wings, readying for flight.

"Wait," Aibek called. "Where are you going? What if we need you?"

"You safe here. I can feel it. I talk to Bokinna's sister before we fly tonight."

"Give her my thanks for sheltering us."

Gworsad rumbled, flapped his great wings, and vanished, and Aibek climbed the nearest tree. He nibbled a bit of jerky and tucked his blanket close around him. He really was grateful for the Bokinna's protection. It meant they had no need to post a watch, so all the riders could rest from the night's flight.

Aibek's legs and back ached from spending so many hours atop the dragon, but he ignored the pain, settled back against the tree trunk, and fell quickly to sleep.

10.

Leadership

Faruz's mind whirled as he watched the dragons vanish into the night sky, taking his friends with them. They would fight before he saw them again. Some he may never see again. When the last of the dragons disappeared over the trees, he turned and hurried back into the safety of the village.

What would've become of me if I hadn't come to Nivaka? Would I have been killed when Xona fell? That thought led to others: of his friends, his favorite opponents in the sparring circle, and his family. He let his mind linger there for a breath then blew away the worry. He had other problems to focus on. There was nothing he could do to help the people in the city.

"Are you all right?" Zifa asked the instant he stepped through the door.

Instead of answering, he folded her in a tight embrace and pressed his cheek into the top of her head.

Faint morning light streamed through the glass and streaked across Faruz's face. He stretched and rolled over, reaching for Zifa, but the other side of the bed was empty and cold. Disappointed, he pushed himself out of bed, washed, and dressed for the day.

Half an hour later, he strode out into the Square. Men and women filled the space, some wearing weapons and others trailing after them. The roar of conversation couldn't quite drown out the tears of those who would be left behind.

Faruz stepped onto the dais in the Pavilion and stomped his feet to get the crowd's attention.

"There's the captain!" Someone shouted. "Be quiet!"

"Thank you." Faruz laughed, and silence fell. Booted feet shuffled on the wooden floor, the noise distracting Faruz for an instant.

Faruz cleared his throat and spread his arms. "A new day has dawned. Helak may hold the city of Xona for the day, but we will not let him keep her. You've proven your skill and bravery. Now, let's show Helak and his half-trained army what we think of them! Are we going to let them take control of our government, our armies, and our weapons?"

The crowd screamed out their answer. "No!"

"And are we going to let them think this victory in Xona means they've won the war?"

Louder this time, the crowd shouted, "No!"

"You're all that stands between our enemy and your freedom. You must stand strong. You must prevail. The consequences of failure aren't even worthy of consideration.

"Nay. You must fight the enemy. And you must

win. *You will win.* Helak's half-trained force can't stop you!"

A cheer rose from the crowd, but Faruz kept going.

"Look around you. Failure means death to all you hold dear. You will not let that happen!"

Another cheer, louder than the first, rattled the windows in the nearby houses.

"You'll head west along the forest's edge to Imah and take the bridge there. We cannot risk Helak's men in Kainga seeing so many of you take the ferry.

"Aibek and the dragons will await your arrival and will help you win the city. Your enemy doesn't have dragons. You have dragons!"

A deafening cheer rattled the timbers of the Pavilion. Faruz waited until his voice would carry above the noise.

"And you have the fight of men and women who know their families depend on them to ensure their freedom.

"Now go! Be swift! And be the warriors I know you are."

A thousand men and women streamed for the village's entrance, the clomping of boots and clatter of weapons making it impossible to say more. Faruz followed the force. He watched with mixed emotions as they separated into smaller divisions on the ground.

Section by section, they headed off into the forest, and Faruz fought back a wave of emotion. He yearned to go with them, to free the home of his birth, to find out for himself whether or not his parents had survived Helak's invasion. Instead, he pulled the lever that activated the stairs and watched as they slowly raised into the recess beneath the village. He locked the safety and turned back to the villagers who had stayed behind.

"All right," he shouted. "Let's get back to training. Only half of Helak's force is in the city. The rest are coming for us. We have to be ready."

He spent the rest of the morning sparring and training with the swordsmen who had stayed behind. He purged his emotions with the swing of the sword, the rhythm of the movements, and the special exercises Valasa had given him to strengthen his wounded leg.

Zifa met him at the Pavilion when they stopped for luncheon. She'd lost more weight, and he worried for her health.

"Won't you eat at least a little of this?" He pushed a slice of cold venison toward her, but the sight of it made her gag.

"I'll just eat this instead." She pulled out a dry muffin and nibbled at the edge. "I'll be fine, really."

Faruz smiled at the shyness in her manner as she kept a hand beneath the muffin to catch any crumbs. "Have you talked to Valasa? Does he know why you've been so sick or how to make you better?"

Zifa flushed and dropped her gaze, and Faruz frowned in confusion. "Is it still the trees' sickness? I thought that was getting better?"

"No, it's something else," Zifa said. She dropped

her gaze to the floor and smiled. "Valasa thinks I'm with child."

The weight of the upcoming battle, the forest's tenuous freedom, the uncertain future with the groundfolk, all passed through Faruz's mind, and he felt the color drain from his face. "Are you sure?" He heard himself ask.

"I'm not certain, but Valasa seems to be. Are you all right? Maybe you should lie down."

Faruz shook his head, and the trees spun around him. A child. A baby. A little tiny Zifa depending on him. *Needing a safe place to grow up.* "I'm all right. Promise me you'll evacuate before the battle." When she didn't answer, he grabbed her shoulders. "Promise! You have to keep yourself safe."

Instead of a response, she leaned in close and wrapped her arms around his waist. He leaned into her warmth, and she pressed her face to his neck. They stayed like that for what felt like hours, until approaching footsteps drew Faruz's attention away.

A very young-looking soldier in Nivaka's bright green messenger uniform stood before him, clutching a bit of parchment in his hands. "I'm sorry to interrupt, Captain, but I've got a message for you."

Faruz took the parchment and instantly recognized Valasa's cramped script. He scanned the note. The council wanted to meet in Valasa's upstairs sitting room immediately, though the note didn't say who had called the meeting.

He leaned back, kissed the top of Zifa's head, and

stood. "We're wanted for a council meeting," he said, holding out a hand for Zifa.

She wobbled a bit and Faruz frowned and pressed an arm around her waist.

"I'm all right." She laughed. "I just stood up too fast."

He didn't release her.

"Really. I'm fine." As if to prove her point, she pulled away and strode off towards Valasa's house without looking to see if Faruz had followed.

He smiled and hurried after his wife, his head still spinning with visions of his budding family. He was going to be a father! He just had to make sure his child would have a safe place to grow up. Zifa walked ahead of him and he examined her skinny frame. Her dress hung loose on her shoulders and draped over her hips. He'd heard stories of women dying from complications of pregnancy and child-birth. He'd have to talk to Valasa about how to keep her well before he left the healer's home.

Ahren, Wayra, and Dalan were already there when Faruz followed his wife into the sitting room. Valasa closed the door behind him and called the meeting to order.

"This is a different situation than we've faced before." Valasa's voice stayed soft, which sent shivers up Faruz's spine. Valasa never spoke softly. "Aibek will likely be gone for the entire winter and may never return. His mission is exceptionally dangerous." The large healer drew a deep breath and squared his shoulders. "It's never been done before, but I think it would be wise to select an interim mayor to be the council's voice with the people until this is all sorted out."

None of the council members spoke. Indeed, Faruz felt as if he'd been punched in the gut. Aibek hadn't even been gone a day. Replacing him felt... wrong somehow.

"I think it would be best for us to choose someone from the council, then present that person to the villagers." Valasa clasped his hands behind his back and faced the council.

Silence.

"Don't just stare at me like that. Tell me what you're thinking." Valasa flushed, and Faruz realized he'd never seen the Gadonu look uncomfortable before that moment.

Faruz hesitated. He had to say something. "Forgive me if I'm wrong, sir, but Aibek and the others just left last night. Shouldn't we wait a bit before we replace them?"

"We're not replacing anyone." Valasa sank down onto the empty chair in front of the window. "We're just making sure there's a clear chain of command for the upcoming battle."

Faruz smiled and a weight lifted from his shoulders. "That does sound like a good idea. But Aibek is still the mayor, right?"

"Of course."

The others sighed and relaxed into their chairs. Faruz leaned back. He glanced from face to face and considered who would be the best leader for Nivaka until Aibek returned.

Dalan. He decided. *He's training to be the Gadonu, and has proven his ability to stand up and take the lead when needed.*

"There are only four of you, so this could go badly, but let's try writing down votes without discussing it, first." Valasa handed out bits of paper, pens, and ink pots.

Each council member wrote on their paper, blew the ink dry, folded it, and handed it back to Valasa, who dropped them into a small bowl.

Without hesitation, Valasa unfolded the first bit of paper. "Faruz."

Faruz felt as if someone had dumped ice water over his head. He wasn't from Nivaka. He had no family there. He didn't deserve to be their mayor—or even their interim mayor.

Valasa pulled another bit of paper out of the bowl and opened it out. "Dalan."

Good. He should be the mayor in Aibek's absence.

Another bit of paper crinkled. "Faruz."

Faruz couldn't raise his head as Valasa opened the last vote. "Faruz. I think that's as close to unanimous as we could get. Do you have anything to say?"

The emotions of the day were too much for Faruz to hold back. He was going to be a father. Now, he was also the acting mayor of Nivaka until Aibek returned. Battle loomed on the horizon. Faruz choked back a lump the size of his fist and stood.

"Thank you." The words came out a hoarse whisper, but he didn't think he could do any better. Zifa reached up and grabbed his hand. The warmth of her palm gave him strength, and he tried again. "Thank you all. Your faith in me means a lot. I'll do my best to be worthy of it."

Dalan's face lifted in a comforting smile. "You already have, friend. You know how to lead better than anyone here—your speech this morning proved that."

"Let's have a bit of refreshment before we announce your decision to the villagers." Valasa gestured to the buffet, which had been laid with water, famanc, and dozens of cakes and pastries.

Faruz watched to make sure Zifa ate. When he was satisfied she'd gotten some nourishment, he pulled the healer into a corner.

"Zifa told me she's with child," he blurted out.

The tension on Valasa's face evaporated into a delighted smile. "Yes, I believe so."

"Why has she been so sick? She's so skinny now. How will she make it through the winter if she can't eat any decent food?" All of Faruz's worries tumbled out, unfiltered.

Valasa pressed a hand down on Faruz's shoulder. "I've seen women much sicker do just fine. This will likely only last another few weeks, and then she'll feel better. For now, let her eat whatever sounds good to her, and encourage her to drink plenty of water."

"Are you sure? I mean…" Faruz stared at his wife where she stood laughing with Ahren. "She's only eating cakes and muffins and breads. Shouldn't she have at least some broth or something?"

"If she feels up to it, that's fine, but don't push it. It's better for her to keep down a cake than to vomit a cup of broth."

"That makes sense, I guess."

Faruz woke before the sun and eased out of bed. Zifa mumbled softly and rolled over, and he smiled. Moving as quietly as he could, Faruz dressed and headed to the kitchen where he ate a hasty breakfast and grabbed a few muffins for his pack.

The training schedule hadn't changed, even though so many other things had. Two weeks had passed since he'd been chosen as the interim mayor, and he'd struggled with balancing all the different responsibilities. He'd had to schedule days to hear concerns from the villagers and mediate disputes—how Aibek did that every day Faruz couldn't fathom—and other days to observe the army's preparations. And, of course, he still had to train with the Kurim twice a week and with the dragons two more days a week. He collapsed into bed each night exhausted. Thankfully, the cook worked hard to make sure Zifa got at least a little sustenance. He didn't think he could have handled everything without knowing Tangwen had Zifa's health in mind.

He closed the front door behind him without a sound, hoping to let Zifa sleep a bit longer, and hurried to the south entrance. There, just a few hundred yards beyond the village's border, his dragon waited.

Gamne wasn't as large as Gworsad or as fast as Tukanli, but he was agile and intelligent and had been a perfect match for Faruz's skills.

"Good morning," he said, approaching the dragon. "What do we have planned for today?"

The dragon chirruped and rumbled. He lowered his head for Faruz to pat and said, "Bokinna say you practice quick attacks today. Says you too slow to get away."

Faruz threw back his head and laughed. "That sounds like a challenge."

He wound the thick blue straps around Gamne's chest and front legs and climbed up onto his back. "Let's go!"

The dragon lifted off the ground and flew him toward the Heart of the Forest. Faruz's chest tightened as they approached, his mind on Serik and his mortal wounds. They landed in the clearing, and again, there was no sign of the elderly servant. Faruz sighed and began to loosen the straps from his legs. Someday, he'd be able to land there without thinking of Aibek's loss of control and Serik's dying words.

"Don't get down." The Bokinna's powerful voice carried on the wind, freezing him in place more effectively than the winter weather could.

"My friends have arranged a practice battlefield for you at the south clearing. You need to work on speed. Strike. Kill the enemy. Get away quickly. There will be consequences if you aren't fast enough. You may not use the seeds today."

Faruz smiled. "I love a challenge. Let's go!"

The dragon bore him into the air and toward the south clearing where they had first set up the dummies several weeks before.

Gamne swooped down into the clearing, and Faruz drew his practice sword. He held his breath as the dragon drew nearer to the first target, then struck out as quickly as he could. The sword made contact, the impact nearly pulling the dull weapon from Faruz's hands, and he drew it back and nudged Gamne to climb.

"Not fast enough." The Bokinna whispered.

A long, willowy tree branch struck out, reaching for Faruz's wrist, but he pulled back at the last second, and Gamne lifted him to safety.

Faruz whooped with the thrill of the game and clutched his sword. Gamne tucked his wings and dove back into the clearing. Faruz positioned himself to strike, focused on the next target.

The dragon shifted. Faruz struck and pulled his arms back in. This time, the tree was quicker. The branch wrapped around his wrist and held.

Faruz dropped the sword. Pain exploded from his weak leg as the straps broke loose. A heartbeat later, he hung by his arms above the clearing. Pain seared his shoulders. The trees lowered him slowly to the ground.

"You must be faster." The words vibrated through the branches binding his arms. "Your enemies are more than human. You must work until you can strike them down without endangering my loved ones."

His feet touched the ground, and the branches released him. "Now, do it again, better this time."

Gamne landed in the clearing, and Faruz pulled a new strap from his pack. Once he'd remounted the dragon, the exercise began again.

The day's cold faded with the day's work, and Faruz concentrated on increasing his speed. He and Gamne made three more passes before the branches caught him again.

"Better, but not good enough," the wind taunted.

Faruz rubbed his arms when the trees set him down. This time, he'd left the straps a bit looser, so he hadn't snapped them when the Bokinna caught him. He climbed back onto Gamne and braced himself for another swipe.

On the next pass, he leaned forward, letting the straps alone hold him on the dragon's back, and pulled his arm back as soon as he'd completed the strike.

"Yes! That's how you do it!"

The Bokinna's enthusiastic encouragement spurred him on, and he did the same thing the next three times.

The branches didn't catch him again.

After an hour, he leaned back and signaled Gamne that he needed a break. The dragon set him down on the pebbled ground beside the river, and Faruz staggered to the swirling eddy at the river's edge. He cupped his hands in the icy water, drank deeply, and lay back on the cool ground. His whole body hurt.

Exhaustion tugged at the edges of his mind, lulling him to sleep under the afternoon sun.

"All right. That's enough of a break. Do it again." The Bokinna's breathy voice broke through the haze of sleep.

The sun had barely moved in the sky. His nap had lasted less than an hour, he'd guess. Faruz sat up, ate a bit of jerky, and climbed back onto his dragon.

He and Gamne made eight more passes, each quicker than the one before. By the time they finished, Faruz's muscles screamed for a rest and his vision blurred from sweat dripping in his eyes. The Bokinna called an end to the day's practice, and Faruz slumped over Gamne's neck and stared down into the forest as the dragon lifted them into the air.

Too numb to think, Faruz just stared at the barren trees in the fading daylight. Below, something orange fluttered in the wind. It didn't behave the way a leaf or a vine would, and its alien-ness drew Faruz's attention. He nudged the dragon downward, drawing on the communication techniques he'd learned. They looped around, circling the orange flutter, until they drew close enough that Faruz could make out a man's shape among the naked limbs of a tall shadow tree.

With a tug on the straps and a nudge of his knees, he signaled Gamne to drop closer to the flapping cloth. They dropped, closer and closer. When they were near enough that Faruz could almost reach out and touch the brilliant orange fabric, Faruz almost fell off the dragon in surprise. There, clinging to a branch in the tallest tree, was Serik. Blood loss had blanched his skin a terrifying white, but he clung to the branch with a desperate strength. Faruz drank a vial of the tincture, certain he would need the seeds' power to get his friend to safety.

Gamne landed beside the tree, and Faruz scrambled up the branches. As he climbed, he considered how to get the elderly servant down safely. When he reached Serik's branch, the old man had his head turned away from him.

"Serik? Are you all right? How did you get all the way up here?" Faruz gently prodded Serik's shoulder.

"I am… not quite well, but better than I was. I don't recall how I got here, and I have no idea how to get down."

"Do you think you have the strength to hold onto me? I can carry us both down if you can hold onto my back."

"I… I don't know." Serik sucked in a noisy breath between his teeth. "I guess I can try."

Faruz shimmied onto Serik's branch and put his back to the old man. Power pulsed through his arms and legs as the tincture took effect.

"I don't think I can hold on," Serik said, his frail voice cracking at the effort.

Faruz focused all his strength on a gentle touch and used one hand to hold Serik's hands. With the other hand and his Kurim-enhanced legs, he could lower them down the tree.

He thought… He strained for the next branch.

He might just be able to… Rough bark peeled the skin from his hands. Sweat beaded on his forehead despite the wintry wind.

He couldn't hold the branches and Serik. Once he'd struggled almost halfway down the tree, he let go.

Serik's hoarse scream pierced Faruz's ears as they fell. The wind rushed past his face, icy on his sweat-soaked skin. Faruz pulled his legs up beneath him and braced for impact.

The tincture strengthened him more than he expected, and Faruz landed softly on the moss-covered ground. He fell to his knees to help soften the blow for Serik. His boots and knees left deep impressions in the soft earth, but he and his passenger were unharmed. Faruz focused on his every movement and swung the old man to the ground. What little color had been in Serik's cheeks had fled in the descent.

"Are you all right? That was a tough drop."

"I… I think so." Serik dropped his watery blue eyes to his hands, examining their wrinkles in the dim light of the forest. "Yes, I think I'm quite fine. Well done."

Relief slumped Faruz's shoulders. "Can you climb onto Gamne?"

Serik sat unmoving, staring up at the massive dragon. His mouth opened and closed several times, but no sound came out.

"That's all right. I'll help." Faruz stood and brushed the leaves and debris from his knees. He helped Serik to his feet, but the elderly servant wobbled alarmingly.

Faruz wrapped an arm around Serik's waist and helped him to the dragon. He paused there, trying to decide on the best way to get Serik onto the animal's back.

"I help?" Gamne rumbled.

"Of course!" Faruz flushed, embarrassed that he hadn't considered asking the dragon for assistance.

Gamne stretched his long neck around and grabbed the back of Serik's shirt between his sharp teeth. He hefted the old man onto his back as if he weighed nothing at all, and Faruz scrambled up after him. Working quickly and silently, Faruz strapped Serik onto the dragon and settled himself behind the old man.

"All right, we're ready," he said when he had hold of the straps.

Serik wobbled throughout the short flight home, but Faruz held him tightly. When Gamne descended toward the stream, Faruz nudged him onward.

"Take us to the village. You can land there." Gamne looked back and rumbled out his concern but followed his partner's instructions.

At least two dozen people stopped to watch the large, thorned dragon land on the Square, but others continued about their daily business.

The moment his feet hit the wooden walkway, Faruz started shouting for Valasa. The Gadonu came running, saw Serik's pale form, and hurried to help Faruz get the old man off the dragon.

Together, Faruz and Valasa half carried, half supported Serik to the Gadonu's house. The housekeeper held open the door and they moved directly to Valasa's study.

They laid Serik on one of the narrow tables lining the windowed wall, and Faruz backed away. Serik had gone deathly pale. His breath came in ragged, shallow gasps. His eyes were closed, and his face was completely relaxed. Valasa moved over the old man, poking and prodding gently but confidently.

"Is he going to be all right?" Faruz whispered.

Valasa pressed his fingers to the inside of Serik's limp wrist and paused there. "I think so. I think he just needs time and rest now." He set down the arm. "Let's get him settled in the hall bedroom where I can keep an eye on him."

Together, they lifted the frail old man and carried him down the hall. When he was tucked into bed and sleeping peacefully, Faruz turned toward home. He needed some quiet time by the fire with his wife to process everything that had happened.

11.

Traveling

At the end of the second night, Aibek struggled to find a safe place to spend the daylight hours. The grassy hills southeast of Xona held few places where he could conceal a single dragon, let alone eighteen of them. Even if they resembled great piles of wood lying on the ground, they'd stand out in a place with no trees. Aibek worried that other travelers might approach to try to take what they thought was firewood.

Aibek and Marah flew ahead of the others, scouting for someplace they could hide. His tired eyes roamed the landscape below, searching for any ravine or depression that could protect them. Tukanli chirped and dove toward the ground, and Gworsad followed at a breakneck pace. They landed beside a tall hill, and Aibek and Marah climbed off their dragons.

"What's that?" Marah's voice quivered, and Aibek followed her gaze.

A narrow cave opened beneath the hill, barely visible in the tall grass.

"Let's check it out. Maybe it's bigger on the

inside." She held up a lamp, and Tukanli breathed a tiny flame onto it.

"Hold on," Aibek drew his sword. "Let's make sure it isn't already occupied. This area used to be known for bandits and thieves."

Aibek lit a torch and tossed it as far into the cave as he could, peering after it to see the broad, empty space it illuminated before it landed and went out.

"It looks empty. I'll go first, though, just to be safe."

"Why, so you can trip in the dark? I'll go first with the light."

Marah held the lantern out to the side and stepped into the cave. Aibek followed a step behind, his sword ready, though he hadn't seen anything dangerous.

The ground fell away, sloping steeply down into the hill. When Marah swept the light in a circle, Aibek grinned. The mouth of the cave concealed a network of long, wide caves that could easily conceal their dragons for the day. They listened for long moments and heard nothing but the faint sound of water dripping somewhere in the distance.

"Let's get the others." Marah turned back to the cave's mouth and froze.

Aibek followed her gaze, stepped in front of her and held his sword up, ready to strike.

At the cave's entrance, blocking their escape, stood six broad men wielding swords and axes. Each wore several heavy pouches on his belt and Aibek wondered how they had approached without his hearing them.

"Bandits," Aibek muttered. "Perfect."

"This is our place," one man announced. "But if you give me whatever you have in that pack, I might be persuaded to let you leave here alive."

"Of course, we'll be keeping her." Another man pointed to Marah and laughed.

"I don't think so." Aibek lowered his sword and watched the shadows moving behind the men. "I think you're going to leave us in peace."

"Really? And what would make us do that?" All the bandits laughed and raised their weapons. "That's enough talk. Give me that pack and get out."

The leader stepped closer, and Aibek raised his sword to defend. In the valley outside, a dragon rumbled and someone shouted.

"Oh, good." Aibek grinned. "The others have arrived." He turned to the men, lowered his sword, and laughed. "I'd say you should probably be going now. This cave is perfect for our needs."

"Others?" The bandit leader shifted his weight and turned to peer out of the cave. He drew in an audible gasp and slapped at the man beside him. Both dropped their weapons and ran out into the night.

The rest of the bandits, clearly confused by their bosses' retreat, strolled to the entrance to see what horrors hid in the night. They, too, dropped their weapons and fled.

The last man out of the cave paused and bowed slightly to Aibek. "Sorry to have bothered you, sir.

I hope there won't be no hard feelings." And he ran away in the direction the others had gone.

Aibek laughed and stepped out of the cave. All twelve dragons had landed in the valley. About half the riders had climbed down, while the other half sat atop their partner dragons and waited for the order to dismount. What a sight they presented to anyone not prepared for them. Aibek imagined the bandits running to a neighboring village and trying to tell someone what they'd seen. No one would believe them. And they'd be arrested on sight if they showed their face in town, so Aibek shrugged. They wouldn't be back.

"All right." Aibek raised his voice over the howling wind. "The sun's coming up. We'll sleep here today. There's room inside for all of us." Snowflakes swirled in the gray light and Aibek led the way back into the cave.

"I don't think we can risk making a fire and risking someone seeing the smoke," Aibek said when they'd all settled in. "But perhaps our friends will warm the place up a bit?"

Gworsad rumbled and dipped his head. The men and women backed away and watched, captivated. None of them had gotten used to seeing the dragons breathe fire, though Aibek was thankful for the heat they could provide.

Three men went with Marah to hunt for some fresh food, and the others stretched and paced about the cave. A handful of warriors took lanterns and headed off to explore the deeper tunnels and caverns. Vayna stepped up beside Aibek at the entrance.

"Do you think we should assign a watch?" The large warrior stroked his beard and watched the swirling snow.

Aibek nodded. "It would be a good idea. I don't think those bandits will come back, but we should be ready just in case. They're not the only ones in the area."

Vayna pulled out a bit of parchment and a pen. He'd devised a way to keep track of watches so no one could claim they stood more than others. "I'll go first, and I'll give Bartel and Dorrel the later watches."

He scrambled away to inform the men of their assignments, and Aibek leaned back against the hill's soft grass. The turbulent air felt almost warm compared to the biting cold wind on the dragon's back. His stomach snarled, and he leaned his head back and gnawed off a chunk of jerky. The dried venison had little flavor, but it would satisfy him until the hunters returned with fresh meat.

Two more nights passed with the dragons traveling in the dark hours and hiding in whatever hollows or caves they could find during the day.

The third night, the city's watch tower lights shone on the horizon. Aibek angled closer. He longed to catch a glimpse of Xona, but he wouldn't risk flying directly overhead. Instead, he kept Gworsad high in the air and flew as close to the wall as he dared, close enough to see the red Xona City Guard uniforms on the men atop the walls.

"It doesn't mean anything," he muttered. "Of course, they wouldn't have killed all the city's men."

They glided past the farms surrounding the city. The air had grown warmer as they traveled north, and Aibek hadn't needed his mask that night at all. He closed his eyes and reveled in the familiar smells of the plains.

When he opened his eyes again, the mines marked the ground below. "Just a little further," he shouted to Gworsad. "The northern mines are abandoned. Have been for years. We can hide there."

They landed a few minutes later at the mouth of a wide cavern. Huts and cabins dotted the valley around the mine's opening. Mismatched stone walls jutted out of the rocky ground, topped by rusted steel roofs. Some had windows in the side and rear walls, but most had only one lookout opening beside the heavy iron doors. After so many months in the forest, the absence of wood felt foreign. Aibek tugged open the door to the largest building. The hinges screamed out their protest. Aibek grimaced. The mines were supposed to be abandoned, but he didn't want to take unnecessary risks.

He stood frozen, listening for any sign that the noise had alerted someone nearby. Nothing happened. The birds chirped, squirrels tittered, and other small creatures rustled in the tall grass.

"This will do," he said at last, stepping into the small hut. A small iron table sat against the far wall, pitted with rust and covered in a thick coating of grime. No other furniture adorned the building's only room.

They explored the five buildings. Sturdy stone walls, rusted roofs with occasional holes, and heavy coats of dust lined each one.

"How will we use these?" Bartel asked, sweeping a stray lock of black hair behind his ear. "There's not enough room inside to make them into barracks."

Aibek nodded. "Have the others returned from exploring the mine shaft?"

"Not yet."

"As long as the shaft is stable, we'll use most of these for storage. I don't know how long we'll be here, and it wouldn't be a bad idea to try to make some extra weapons and stockpile some food."

"And if it isn't? Stable, I mean." Bartel laughed, though it sounded forced to Aibek.

"Then we'll pitch our tents and take turns sleeping in the buildings. I do want to keep one as a meeting space, though. Probably the biggest one. It's the easiest to defend."

"That's smart enough." Bartel pulled the comb from his hair and pressed it back into place, something Aibek had seen him do several times during their journey.

"We'll need to give everyone jobs, too. Some will need to hunt. Others can gather greens and berries. Someone else can go to the stream over there and catch fish. And we'll keep up Vayna's watch schedule."

"I beg your pardon, sir, but won't you take one of the huts as your personal quarters? Our leader should have his own space, I'd think."

Aibek shrugged. "I don't outrank anyone else here. We're all members of the same division of dragon riders. Nearly all of us are mayors in our own villages. I think we're pretty equal."

"I don't think so." Bartel laughed again, and this time it sounded natural and cheerful. "You're the one the Bokinna talks to. You're the one who organized the dragon riders. You introduced the rest of us to those amazing animals, and you have the biggest, strongest dragon out there." Aibek started to protest, but Bartel raised a hand. "And if that wasn't enough, you're the one who knows this part of the land. None of the rest of us have ever left the forest. No, sir, you are definitely the leader."

"I suppose you're right." Aibek sighed. "It's hard to argue when you put it like that." He remembered the stories his aunt had told him of a well-loved king and his round table. Perhaps that kind of equality didn't work in situations like this.

He stepped back and examined the uneven line of buildings. "All right. We'll keep that one for a meeting space." He pointed to the largest hut. "And I'll take that one as my quarters." He moved his arm a tiny bit and gestured to the much smaller building beside the first.

"The mine looks secure enough," someone shouted. Aibek turned to face the voice.

Vayna strode toward him, grinning widely.

"There's even a big open area just inside, where the dragons can sleep, and there are little holes in the roof that'll work well to disperse and hide smoke. We can probably make fires without anyone seeing."

Aibek tried to picture it but failed. "Show me." He strode toward his friend, leaving Bartel staring at the buildings.

The cool darkness enveloped him when Aibek stepped into the mine shaft. He followed Vayna into the cavern. Someone had scattered several lamps around the space, so he could see how wide and open it really was. Iron supports kept the roof from collapsing down into an area the size of Nivaka's largest park. The dragons and all the warriors could stay there and be completely protected. He tipped his head back and saw the faint light of dawn shining down through dozens of air holes the miners had drilled in the roof.

Aibek didn't know much about the business of iron mining, but whoever had built this space had thought of everything. The holes were spaced far enough that men could sleep there without getting wet if it rained, but close enough to safely vent any fire smoke to the outside.

"We'll all sleep in here today, and we'll figure out the rest tomorrow." Aibek smiled. This cavern would be easy enough to defend if trouble showed up, and it would conceal their cook fires from any unwelcome eyes beyond the valley.

They rested, hunted, and ate all day and all night. It took some time for the warriors and dragons to recover from the long journey. The six women in the group banded together and made their beds near each other. As far as Aibek could tell, they'd become fast friends during the trip.

By the next morning, Aibek felt the walls closing in. He had to get away from the mine. He needed to try to get into the city. He chose three men who he hoped wouldn't stand out in a crowd of travelers and set about preparing to walk into Xona.

Aibek appraised their clothes and remembered how he'd stood out on his first day in Nivaka. After a bit of deliberation, he gave Bartel, Dorrel, and Gwynn his extra linen shirts and leather pants, so they could blend into the throng at the gate. At least their cloaks were heavy wool or leather, which wouldn't be remarkable in the prairie city.

Once they'd all changed clothes, Aibek examined them closely. Bartel looked like any other archer, with his hair pulled back on one side and leather bracers on both arms. He would blend into the city's throng easily enough.

Dorrel's coppery beard stood out as a contrast against his dark hair and would be too memorable. "Could you shave it?" Aibek made a face. "I don't want to get people talking about our group."

The tall spearman grumbled but took off for the stream with Bartel's shaving kit. Aibek turned his attention to Gwynn. He was tall, almost the same height as Aibek, and wore his chestnut hair short. His most distinctive feature was his brilliant, emerald-green eyes.

When Dorrel had finished shaving, Aibek led the group out of the cave and stopped in front of his quarters. "We'll leave our weapons here." He set his sword on his blankets.

"We don't want to draw attention to ourselves," he explained when Bartel complained. "Besides, they've always taken weapons at the gate, and I'm sure that hasn't changed."

The men expressed their discomfort but removed their weapons.

Marah clutched his arm before he could leave the camp. "You shouldn't put yourself at risk like this. Let the others go without you. What do we do if you're captured or killed?"

"I'm the only one here that knows my way around that city." He peeled her fingers off his sleeve, squeezed her hand, and let it drop. "Besides, I need to find out if my aunt and uncle survived, and I need to check on Faruz's parents, too. No one else knows where to find them."

He turned his back to her before she could try again. "Are we ready?"

The faint blue light of dawn had brightened into swaths of pink and orange. Aibek breathed in the morning chill and stepped onto the rutted gravel path that had once been a busy road. Bartel, Dorrel, and Gwynn fell in behind him. Tall grasses swayed to either side, seeming to follow their movements on the abandoned trail.

Aibek's leg throbbed before they'd made it halfway to the city, but he pushed onward. His slow pace infuriated him, but he couldn't move any faster. Fear that he'd find his friends and family dead dampened his eagerness to reach his childhood home.

The sun had made it halfway to its peak when Xona's sparkling walls appeared on the horizon. Aibek's strength surged at the sight, and he moved faster than he had all day. Within an hour, they stood shoulder to shoulder with the hundreds of merchants and travelers waiting to be admitted into the city.

As they moved closer to the gates, Aibek hunched deeper into his cloak. He couldn't shake the worry that the city guards might recognize him, though he had no reason to think they would. Why would they remember an academy dropout? Still, he had gained some notoriety during his years there, and many students had challenged him to sparring matches because of his skill with the sword. Still others would remember him for the hours he'd spent tutoring the younger students in swordsmanship and battle tactics.

At last, it was their turn to go through. The guards made them lift their cloaks and show they were unarmed, then waved them through. Relief washed over Aibek, but he steeled himself against it. That had been the easy part.

Aibek let the crowd drag them along toward the grand market on the east side of the city. His aunt and uncle lived a few blocks from there, and that would be his first stop. His heart pounded and his hands shook when they turned off the main streets and onto the quiet neighborhood road. The cool wind dried the sweat on his face, but he kept his hood up. When he reached the simple iron door, he hesitated. It felt strange to knock on the door when he'd grown up in that house, but he didn't think it would be wise to enter unannounced. Nauseous, sweating, and weak from anticipation and fear, he raised his hand and tapped softly on the cold black metal.

He couldn't breathe, couldn't speak, and almost couldn't look up from his shoes when the door finally opened. A firm hand grabbed his arm and pulled him inside. He raised his eyes, braced for the worst, and his knees buckled. He landed hard on the couch. Ira's worried face smiled down at him.

"Aibek?" She held out a hand to help him up, but he stood and wrapped his aunt in a joyful hug.

"You're alive," he whispered again and again.

The housekeeper stepped into the room, squealed, "Oh! Aibek's home!" and ran off into the kitchen.

She returned a heartbeat later carrying a tray of food and tea, which she plunked down onto the side table. Relieved of her burden, she wrested Aibek's cloak off of him, waited for the other men to remove their heavy cloaks and boots, and welcomed them all into the comfortable sitting room.

"Tell me everything," Aibek demanded as soon as they were seated.

Tears filled Ira's soft brown eyes. "I haven't seen or heard from—" her voice caught, and Aibek reached across the narrow space between their chairs and put a hand on her shoulder. "Your uncle since it happened. I don't know if he's..." She trailed off and mopped at her cheeks. "Or if he's joined the faction of the city guard that's trying to organize a revolt against this new governor."

Aibek nodded and clung to that tiny shred of hope. If his uncle had survived the invasion, he would certainly have joined whoever stood in opposition to the invaders. "I promised Faruz I'd find out about his family. Have you heard from them?"

A smile lit Ira's face. "Yes, they're doing well. Vebro took a fever a few days before the invasion and was in bed with the shakes when it all happened. They passed the sickness around, but they're all better now. He's complained constantly about being ill when his skills were needed, but we're all happy to have him here to keep our little corner of Xona safe. Is Faruz with you? Wherever you're staying, I mean?"

"No, he stayed to help prepare the forest for battle."

They chatted and ate as if this were any normal visit, but Aibek knew he couldn't return frequently, so he allowed himself to enjoy his aunt's care and company. After a long conversation about Ira's plan to move to Nivaka in the spring, Aibek glanced out the window. The day had flown by and the sun hung halfway to the western horizon. Koviom's pale light climbed in its wake. Aibek stared at the moon and sighed.

"We have to go if we're going to make it back to the camp tonight." He stood and retrieved his boots, signaling the others to do the same.

Tears shone in Ira's eyes as she bade them farewell, but she didn't try to stop them.

"We'll come back as soon as we can," Aibek promised. The latch clicked behind him, cold and final. He hoped he'd be able to keep his promise.

They hurried back to the camp but took a less direct route. Aibek doubled back several times to cover their tracks, worried that the enemy might have set someone on them to see where they went. The sun had disappeared beyond the horizon, though darkness hadn't completely taken over, when Aibek stepped into the old mine shaft.

The warriors had gathered enough sticks and brush to make a small, smoky fire at one side of the cave, and several birds and rabbits roasted on spits over the diminutive flames.

When Aibek retreated to his quarters, he said a silent thanks to Vayna for pushing him into claiming the hut for himself.

As soon as the door closed behind him, he whispered, "Father? Are you here?"

Eddrick and Kiri materialized beside the bed. "Of course."

"Have you found Uncle Noral yet?" Aibek sank onto the mattress that someone had stuffed with fresh straw while he was gone. "My aunt says she hasn't seen or heard from him since the invasion. Do you think he's joined the opposition?"

"I don't know. I can't find him anywhere. Normally, I can sort of feel where someone is. He's always been to find before now. I'm afraid… he probably didn't survive the invasion."

A sad, faraway look crossed Eddrick's face, and Aibek changed the subject. "How am I going to keep this camp hidden? I think someone followed us out of the city today."

Eddrick hesitated. He whispered something too soft for Aibek to hear. The silence grew heavy and Eddrick waited for some cue that Aibek didn't understand. His voice was stiff and stilted when he replied. "I can tell you only of the army's general movements, not of any individual soldier's behavior."

"All right." Aibek weighed his words. Clearly, someone was watching his parents. He'd never sounded so stiff and cold before. "Can you give me advice on how to train with the seeds here without the forest to hide me or the Bokinna to direct me?"

Irritation flickered on Eddrick's face during the pause that followed Aibek's question.

"Your dragon friend, the one called Gworsad, can communicate with the Bokinna no matter the distance." Eddrick spoke stiffly, as if repeating someone else's words verbatim. "He can be an intermediary between you and the ancient one. You can find a wide open, abandoned space to the north of here, but be careful. Kurim is powerful and takes a great deal of time and practice to master. The ancients do not believe you have enough time to learn to control it before the coming battle."

Aibek nodded, remembering Serik's pale face leaned against the Bokinna. "I have to try." Pain shot through his leg and he propped it up on the bed, massaging the overworked muscle.

Exhaustion weighed him down, and he fell back into the lumpy, dusty straw mattress they'd found in the shack and restuffed with a bit of fresh grass they'd dried in the sun.

"You should rest. You've had a hard few days." Kiri brushed a lock of hair from his forehead, her touch a cold wind across his face.

Sapped of the strength to do more than nod, Aibek closed his eyes and drifted to sleep.

Heavy clouds hid the sun and threatened rain. Aibek and Vayna had spent several hours working out a training schedule so the dragons and riders could continue practicing for battle. Each pair would have at least two hours every other day, but they couldn't come up with a way to safely put all the dragons in the air at once.

Gworsad and Tukanli had scouted the area Eddrick had suggested and found an area large enough to fly without any risk of anyone seeing them.

As soon as the dragons returned, Aibek looped his straps around Gworsad and climbed up. Memories of his last training session flooded his mind, but he blinked them away. He had to learn to focus.

The cool wind whipped his hair and droplets of rain stung his face as they circled higher and higher. Aibek kept his eyes open and peered down at the flat, grassy landscape. Rare, scrubby trees dotted the ground below, the only break in the endless sea of grass. Gworsad landed near a little copse of trees and waited for Aibek to drink the tincture.

Power surged through Aibek's arms and legs. He closed his eyes, turning his attention inward. Slowly, he lowered himself to a crouch and opened his eyes. There, he found a tiny kitten hiding in the grass beneath the squat tree. It cowered at his nearness, but didn't run away.

An idea struck Aibek and he stretched out a hand to the creature. It shrank away but couldn't run. Long tendrils of hunter's twine had tangled around the animal's leg, tying it to the tree. How long had it been there?

His hands shook with mingled power and terror. A moment's distraction would be enough to crush the kitten between his fingers. He concentrated on every movement as he lifted the kitten and cradled it in his palm. Slowly, he unknotted the twine and slipped the loops over the animal's skinny foot. The creature's ribs poked into his hand and he wondered again how long it had been trapped. When he removed the last of the twine, he set the kitten back on the ground beneath the tree. He dug a bit of jerky from his pack, broke it into pieces, and set it in front of the cowering animal. It sniffed, then devoured the jerky. When it had finished, he poured a bit of water into his hand and held it out to the kitten. It lapped at the water gratefully, though it shied away, ready to run at the first hint of danger. It finished the water and peered up at him for a heartbeat before dashing away into the tall grass. He caught a glimpse of what looked like a larger cat hiding nearby and smiled. The kitten was back with its mother. Satisfied that he'd managed to help the tiny creature without crushing it under the weight of the seeds' power, he stood, beaming.

"Bokinna says you do good. Says gentleness is sign of great strength." Gworsad rumbled, sounding pleased.

"I never would have believed that before now. What's next on the agenda?"

He spent the rest of his training time practicing leaping from the dragon's back and climbing back on as quickly as possible. He kept his mind focused stubbornly on the task at hand, though his thoughts tried repeatedly to return to the feel of the fragile kitten cradled in his palm. When the strength dissipated, he directed Gworsad back to the camp, satisfied that he'd finally learned to control the crazy power.

12.

Visitor

The days passed in a blur of training, planning, and dull administrative work that left little time for the things Faruz wanted most, like spending time with Zifa and daydreaming about the son or daughter they'd have in the summer.

An emrialk's screech pierced the air, sounding closer than ever before. Faruz winced and tugged Zifa closer. He wrapped an arm over her shoulders and ushered her to Valasa's house.

"Why won't you take me with you? I'm stronger now. I won't fall off."

Faruz smiled and kissed her forehead. "You're the toughest woman I know. I have no doubt nothing could peel you off the dragon's back."

"Then why?"

Faruz squeezed her shoulders. A cold wind pressed his hair into his face, and he shook his head to clear his vision. He was running out of excuses for why Zifa couldn't or shouldn't ride the dragons or watch his practice with the seed powder, but something held him back.

"I just want to make sure you're safe." He didn't

know what had made Aibek lose control that day when Serik...

He shook his head again, this time to clear his mind of the worry for the elderly servant. He still hadn't woken, though he stirred enough to swallow a few spoonfuls of broth a few times a day.

Faruz stopped and turned to face her. "Look, I won't stop you if you really want to go. It's an amazing feeling, flying above the forest. I just worry. I've heard of awful things happening to women while they... I just don't think we should take any unnecessary risks."

Zifa laughed and stepped past him. She knocked on Valasa's door, eager to get more of the concoction that had stopped her vomiting. "You worry too much. Besides, I'd think it would be better for me to go now, before I start to show."

The door swung open, and Faruz ushered his wife inside, grateful for the opportunity to drop the subject. He hovered nearby while the healer checked Zifa's pulse and looked inside her mouth.

Valasa nodded and grunted, apparently satisfied with whatever he found. He disappeared into his study without a word and emerged holding a dark ceramic bottle stoppered with a chunk of cork.

"A spoonful before bed should be all you need." The healer's booming voice echoed in the large room. "If you start feeling sick again, come see me. And don't forget to let me know a few days before you run out so I can make more."

"I will, and I won't." Zifa smiled and Faruz ushered her to the door.

When the latched clicked behind them, Zifa turned to Faruz and whispered, "I know you mean well, but you have to stop hovering and treating me like I'm going to break." She grabbed his hand and met his worried gaze. "I feel better now, honest. I feel as strong as I ever have."

Faruz considered, closed his eyes, and nodded. He had been treating her as if she were one of his grandmother's fragile baubles instead of the strong-as-iron warrior she was. "I'll try. You might have to remind me, though."

A glance at the sky told him he'd spent too long in Valasa's home. "Come on, we'll be late." He squeezed her hand tighter and rushed toward the south entrance.

They'd made it halfway to the stairs when someone shouted. "Oh, there you are, Captain! We've been looking everywhere. You have a visitor."

Irritated at the interruption, Faruz shouted over his shoulder. "I'll have to meet with them when I return. I'm late for training."

"If you can just point me to where I may find the mayor, I'll leave you alone." The cold voice triggered an unpleasant memory, and Faruz stopped.

"I'm acting mayor until Aibek returns." He paused, waiting for the lookout and the visitor to catch up. "I'm sure Valasa will let you have a room in his house. He keeps a few guest rooms ready all the time."

He inspected the visitor and realized he recognized the short, slender man but struggled to place him. The visitor had short hair the color of the caramels his mother had made in the winter and eyes that were almost the same color.

"That isn't necessary. I don't plan to stay. I just need to meet with the man called Aibek." The visitor's high, nasal voice grated on Faruz's already-frayed nerves.

"Aibek is away." A great gust of wind rustled the branches and Faruz looked up. The dragons flew off into the distance, each carrying a rider. He searched for his dragon but couldn't find him in the rapidly fading team.

The visitor's eyes widened at the sight of the retreating dragons. He watched until they vanished over the treetops and met Faruz's eyes. "Well, now that they're not waiting anymore, let's get back to business. I'm Mayor Kaskin. I have business with Aibek. Where is he?"

Ahh. Recognition hit Faruz like a branch falling from a tree. Of course! The man who had caused so much trouble the week of Faruz and Zifa's wedding. Aibek had said he'd been a nightmare during the meetings in Kainga, too.

"I told you, he's not here. He's traveling north to check on some rumors. I don't know for sure when he'll be back."

The visitor glared with his caramel eyes for a long while. Faruz said nothing, and the silence stretched thin. Finally, Kaskin's shoulders slumped. "Then I shall take you up on your generous offer of a room. I will wait until Aibek returns."

Faruz smiled at the young man who had accompanied Kaskin into the village. "Telor, can you take our guest to Valasa and get him settled in?"

His frozen, terrified posture relaxed, and Telor grinned. "Of course, sir. Right this way, Mister Kaskin." The young watchman led Kaskin off toward the Square.

"Come on. Maybe Gamne waited for me. I didn't see him with the others."

A delighted smile replaced the disappointment on Zifa's face. "Really? You think he's still there?"

"Maybe. Let's at least check." Faruz hoped he wasn't wrong. He didn't know how he'd bear her disappointment if Gamne wasn't there.

They descended the stairs at a run and rushed toward the clearing where the group always met. There, drinking from the stream, stood the dragon.

Zifa whooped with joy and ran over to the creature. Her eyes held none of the fear Faruz had expected. She introduced herself while Faruz tied the straps over the dragon's back, just in front of the spot where the wings connected. He tied the widest strap around the creature's chest and patted Gamne's neck.

He knotted his fingers together and made a sort of stirrup for Zifa to use to climb up. The soft zontrec of her cheerful orange pants brushed his cheek as she made the jump. He still didn't love the idea of her coming along, but at least it was just for the group practice and not the Kurim. He still worried, but this was the better option of the two.

Once Zifa had settled in and wrapped the straps over her legs, Faruz climbed up behind her. It felt strange not to have the strong ropes holding him onto the dragon, but he held on to the second strand in front of Zifa. His arms wrapped around her to reach the straps, and he buried his face in her neck.

"Ready?" He grinned and leaned back. "Let's go!"

Zifa whooped and cheered as the trees rushed past them. The wind whipped her hair into Faruz's face, and he nearly let go of the straps to remove the fragrant ebony tresses from his mouth and nose. Instead, he coughed, swallowed, and gagged when some of her hair went down his throat. Zifa didn't seem to notice his discomfort. Blinded by the whipping strands, Faruz couldn't direct the dragon. Instead, he closed his eyes, tried to breathe through his nose, and trusted Gamne to take them to the clearing by the river where they usually started their training sessions.

At last, they landed. Faruz jumped down, coughing and gagging as the hair pulled loose from his tonsils.

"Are you all right?" Zifa climbed down and set a hand on his back. "That was amazing!"

When he could breathe, Faruz dug in his pocket and found a bit of twine. He handed it to Zifa.

Her eyebrows creased in confusion.

"You have to tie up your hair before we fly again." He pulled out his water skin and took a long drink.

Zifa's eyes went wide. "I'm so sorry. I didn't even think about my hair."

When the water had soothed his throat as much as he thought possible, he recapped the water skin and grinned at her. "I didn't either. I'll never make that mistake again. We'll call it a lesson learned." He glanced around. Men and women had encircled them, the dragons forming a secondary circle behind them.

The practice went smoothly, with Zifa staying on the ground any time Faruz needed to use his sword and riding in front of him while they practiced maneuvers and dismounts.

After Gamne dropped them off in the clearing, Zifa grabbed his arm and stared wistfully at the sky. "Do you think, maybe, after—" she glanced down at her belly. "Maybe next summer I could team up with a dragon, too? That was the most amazing thing ever. You and Gamne move like you're the same person. Well… You know what I mean. I've never seen any-thing like that." The words came out in a rush, and Faruz had to concentrate to catch all of it.

"I don't know." He thought for a moment. "I don't know if any of us will be riding the dragons next summer. This is a special arrangement to protect the forest from Helak's threat."

"Oh." Zifa dropped her arm and trudged toward the stairs.

Her disappointment tore at him, and he added, "But if they still let us, we'll definitely find you a partner dragon." He hoped he'd be able to keep his promise when the time came. *I hope we all live long enough for it to be an issue.*

Shaking off the depressing thought, Faruz picked up his pace until he walked beside his wife. Tears streamed down her face, and she swiped at them. Terror clutched at Faruz's chest. He'd never seen Zifa cry before.

"What's wrong? Are you in pain? Do you need me to carry you home? What can I do?"

She laughed through her tears and threw her arms around his neck. "Nothing's wrong. It was a perfect day. My mother says my condition can make me cry sometimes, and that's normal."

"Try to warn me of things like that next time, all right?" he pulled out a handkerchief and dabbed at her wet cheeks.

She nodded and pulled out of his arms. Holding hands, they strolled toward the village. Somewhere in the forest behind them, an emrialk screamed. The sound pierced the happy haze of Faruz's mind, and he slid his sword loose.

"Hurry. Let's get home."

They ran through the brush and trees, spurred on by the answering call of another emrialk. They didn't stop until they'd climbed the stairs into the village. There, they collapsed onto the wooden benches beside the entrance.

The next morning, Faruz dressed early, eager for the day of training with the seeds. He tiptoed down to the kitchen, letting Zifa sleep. She'd dozed off before the sun had even set, exhausted from the excitement of dragon riding and the terror of their flight through the forest.

He stepped into the cold winter morning and squinted at the sun. Wasn't it supposed to provide warmth? He pulled his heavy cloak tighter and walked toward the south entrance. He didn't even make it across the Square before the sound of a shouting voice caught his attention. He spun in a slow circle, searching for the source of the voice, and finally spotted a crowd in the Pavilion.

Curious, he joined the periphery of the group and stopped to listen.

"And now you know, as well as I do, why my town—for it's far too large to be called a village—cannot and will not work with your heretic mayor, Aibek. If you want Bekuz's warriors to join you in battle, you must denounce this outsider and choose a mayor from the forest."

Stunned silence met this pronouncement, and Faruz saw his opening. He leapt onto the dais beside Kaskin. "Aibek has led us through one battle already, has secured the assistance of the Bokinna herself, has convinced the dragons to help us, and has united nearly all the villages in the Tsari against our common enemy. Why would we turn our backs on him now? Even without your warriors, we have a full, strong army that's getting better and better every day."

The small crowd cheered.

Scarlet suffused Kaskin's face, and the short mayor spun on Faruz. "You! You're not one of us, either! You came here for sport from what I've heard. What makes you think you're good enough to even think of leading our warriors?"

"Hey!" Someone shouted from the front of the crowd. "That's our captain. He fought shoulder to shoulder with us. He nearly died trying to save us. He's as much one of us as any other here."

The crowd cheered, clapped, and stomped.

Faruz grabbed Kaskin's shoulder. "You've tried the wrong approach here. Let's go back to Valasa's and talk about exactly what you think you're trying to accomplish."

"We're not finished!" Kaskin shouted at the crowd. "I'll be back this afternoon, and you'll understand why you must turn out these outsiders."

Faruz kept his hand clamped on Kaskin's shoulder as they left the stage and crossed to Valasa's house. The Gadonu met them at the door.

"I just got a message from Bekuz." Valasa's voice was uncharacteristically soft. "It seems our guest is no longer their mayor."

A sharp yank on the visitor's shoulder spun him to face Faruz. "What game are you playing here?"

"It's your Aibek's fault they revolted!" Kaskin jerked free of Faruz's grasp. "He spread ideas of 'voting' and 'representation' through my people's heads. They were perfectly happy to let me lead them until your mayor's visit."

"So why come here? You didn't really think anyone here would choose you over the man who's already saved them several times, did you?"

Valasa interrupted before Kaskin could answer, his voice deadly quiet. "We should take this inside." He nodded to the circle of villagers gathering behind them.

"You first." Faruz gestured for Kaskin to lead the group into the house.

They settled onto the soft, worn chairs in the healer's den, though Faruz perched on the edge of his chair and leaned toward the visitor.

"All right, now. Why did you come here? What did you think would happen?"

"I..." Kaskin glanced down, then met Faruz's gaze. Defiance and rage shone in his eyes. "I came here to challenge your Aibek to a duel. He has cost me everything. My own family turned their backs on me. It is not to be borne."

"And your little speech? What did you hope to accomplish with that foolishness?" Faruz stood and paced in front of his chair, too incensed to sit still.

"Aibek does not deserve to keep his station when he has taken mine. I seek only justice."

"Justice?" The word came out a shout, and Faruz worked to modulate his voice. "You don't want justice. You want revenge. You never wanted to lead anyone—you wanted unopposed rule. Leaders want to hear from their people. Leaders represent their citizens and allow them a vote. You're angry because your villagers realized you were no leader." Faruz paused for breath, sneered, and added, "You're nothing but a sad imitation of every dictator in history.

How was letting you rule any better than letting Helak's governors stay there?"

Kaskin's face turned from pink to scarlet to purple, and Faruz braced for an assault, relishing the thought of knocking that smug expression off the ex-mayor's face. He didn't care that he was twice Kaskin's size, or that he'd had formal training and his opponent had not.

Without thinking, Faruz stood and fell into a defensive stance, though he kept his hands firmly at his sides.

The visitor cracked his knuckles but didn't stand. Faruz waited, poised and eager. His pulse pounded in his ears and he replayed Kaskin's inflammatory speech back in his mind.

Slowly, Faruz relaxed. Kaskin wouldn't challenge him. The man was foolish and self-centered but not stupid.

Valasa sighed when Faruz settled back onto his chair. "I think you should leave," the healer said. "There are plenty of other villages, and they're closer together than ever before. I'm sure someone will take you in. If you stay, the rest of the men may not be as restrained as our good captain."

Without further comment, Kaskin stood and stalked off to the room he'd stayed in. Moments later, he emerged carrying his pack and stomped past Valasa and Faruz on his way out the door. Faruz followed at a distance, watching until the unwelcome visitor descended the stairs at the east entrance.

"What was that about?" Wayra stepped up beside

Faruz as the stairs clicked into place. "I heard about his little speech this morning. Did you throw him out for badmouthing Aibek?"

Faruz chuckled. "No. I wasn't happy about it, but I don't think Nivakans are that gullible." He hooked the lock into the catch to secure the stairs and settled onto a bench beside the entrance. "No, it turns out that our visitor is no longer the mayor of his village. They ousted him after Aibek's visit. Apparently Kaskin just took over the governor's role and no one thought to question it until a better man came around and asked why they weren't voting."

"Well, I'm sure they're better off without him, but why'd he come here? I would've thought he'd avoid everything to do with Aibek."

Faruz summarized his confrontation with Kaskin and leaned back against the bench. The wind numbed his cheeks and made his nose run, but he tilted his head back, seeking the sun's light and warmth.

"Do you think you should make an announcement? Others are going to think the same thing I did—that you threw him out for badmouthing Aibek. He is your best friend, after all."

A monkey chattered somewhere nearby, and Faruz listened to its playful sound until it fell silent. He sighed. "You're right, of course. I'll make an announcement this morning before I leave for training. I don't want people thinking they're not allowed to speak their minds, even if I happen to disagree with what they say."

Silence stretched again, and Wayra cleared his

throat. "Have you heard from Aibek? He should have arrived by now, right? Do you have a way to keep in touch with him?"

"I… Not yet. I'm hoping he can find a way to contact the Bokinna, and maybe she'll pass on what she knows to Valasa." Faruz leaned forward and opened his eyes.

"Have you…" Wayra hesitated. "I know you spend a lot of time with the Bokinna, now that you're leading the training. Have you tried communicating with her the way Valasa and Aibek do?"

Faruz blinked and frowned. "I hadn't thought to try. You're right, though. I should at least make an effort. I'll ask Valasa to teach me." He paused. "I don't know how fast I can learn, though. Aibek struggled for months before he managed to hear what the Bokinna said."

"When do you leave for practice? Do you have time to come visit with Zyana for a bit? Since the babies have had Usartma and a winter cold, she hasn't been able to get out and socialize as much as she'd like. I think she's been getting lonely. She'd rather die than complain, though."

Faruz smiled. "I have a couple of hours before I have to go. I'd love to come by and visit. I haven't seen the kids in a few weeks at least."

The two friends chatted and laughed and made their way to the Pavilion where a few dozen people lingered. Faruz leapt onto the stage and explained the morning's events as succinctly as he could manage. He stayed to answer a few questions and reassured all the citizens that they did, in fact, have the support of every village within the Tsari, and no, they didn't need to vote Aibek out in order to gain any large, influential supporters. When the villagers trickled out of the Pavilion, Faruz stepped down and followed Wayra into his home.

He spent the rest of the morning with the happy little family, playing with children and doing his best to ignore the runny noses and juicy coughs. He did worry a bit about catching something from them, but not enough to make him leave sooner than he had to.

When the sun reached its peak, he excused himself and made his way to the stream where he'd meet Gamne for the day's training exercises.

The wintry wind bit into Faruz's face as Gamne flew him over the forest. He tried to watch the trees and streams glide by, but tears blurred his vision. Tiny icicles grew from his eyelashes, creating a distracting fringe around his vision. The dragon set him down beside the raging river, and Faruz took a moment to clear his eyes and brush away the flecks of ice.

He climbed down once his face and hands had thawed enough to allow movement. Before he'd made it to the spot where the forest met the pebbled beach, the Bokinna spoke.

"Aibek has arrived safely. He has learned a valuable lesson with the Kurim, and turned a corner in his training. Drink your tincture now, and we will proceed with your training once the seeds take effect."

Faruz did as he was told and waited until the wild power coursed through his body. "I'm ready."

The Bokinna's raspy voice still sent shivers up Faruz's spine, even after working so closely with her for so many weeks.

"Today, you will work on speed and accuracy. You're getting faster, but you must not let speed make you careless."

They worked through hours of drills against the dummy armies, and before lunch, Faruz's arms and legs screamed for rest. He climbed down beside the river and drank from the icy water.

"You are finished for today. You may return home."

Faruz frowned and stood. "Excuse me, Madam Bokinna." Faruz hesitated, unsure whether questioning the ancient tree was allowed or not but decided to give it a try. "You said you know that Aibek has arrived, and that he's learned something important, but do you know whether he's learned anything of my family?"

A knot of tension and worry tightened in his belly. He held his breath and waited for the Bokinna's response, half fearful she'd reprimand him for questioning her, and half terrified she'd tell him his parents were dead.

The wind blew through the treetops, rustling the few dried leaves that hadn't yet fallen. Somewhere nearby, foxes chittered and chirped.

"Your family is well. I do not know specifics,

only that Aibek is relieved that your loved ones are unharmed."

Something in the ancient being's choice of words brought Faruz up short. "Do you know anything of his aunt and uncle?"

A long pause made Faruz's uneasiness grow. "Aibek is less at ease about his own family. Please understand that I cannot speak with him directly, but only through my protectors who are with him. His comments about his own family are mixed. Some are safe, perhaps, and others are missing. He is confused, sad, and relieved all at once."

Faruz swallowed against the sudden tightness in his throat. "Thank you," he whispered. He felt the moment the ancient being turned her attention away from him. Loneliness clutched at his chest, and he became aware of the dozens of animals stalking through the underbrush.

Suddenly cognizant of his solitude, he crept closer to the river. He skipped stones across the churning surface until the wild power faded from his limbs. He climbed onto Gamne's back, tired and relieved. His parents were safe. That knowledge brought him strength. His mother would be ecstatic at becoming a grandmother.

He shook his head, smiling. Zifa would be an amazing mother, too. She'd spent enough time helping Zyana with the babies that he had no doubts at all. He hoped he'd be a passable father. He'd never considered a family when he'd made his grand plans for his life. Of course, his plans had veered wildly off course the day he'd decided to put his education on hold and follow Aibek into the forest.

13.

Secrets

"You're coming over for supper tonight, right?" Ahren shifted the basket of clothes on her hip and picked up the pace. The wind had grown colder during their afternoon's work and now bit into her face.

Tamyr hesitated. "I don't think I'm going to make it after all. Sorry."

"Oh." Ahren stopped and set the basket on a nearby bench. She occupied herself by refolding the shirt on top of the stack. "Is something wrong? You've been avoiding me lately."

"I'm not avoiding you. I've just been really busy, that's all."

"Busy with what?" Ahren fought to keep the suspicion out of her voice. "I know the wash house hasn't had any extra business. We haven't had any visitors in weeks. Well, unless you count that weird one."

"No, not the wash house. I've been helping my father collect and catalog herbs since the trees are moving us into different parts of the forest."

Ahren accepted that and picked up the basket. She'd only gone a few steps before the cold wind bit at her nose and she stopped. "Herbs? It's winter. All the herbs are dead until spring."

"We're gathering roots and seeds. There's plenty of those still around and my father's a genius at spotting the right plants without leaves."

A hint of defensiveness crept into Tamyr's voice, but Ahren pretended not to notice. Instead, she changed the subject and chatted about Zifa's condition and the number of babies at their most recent gathering.

When they parted ways, Ahren walked toward home until she turned the first corner. There, she waited until a couple passed out of sight and scampered up the nearest tree. Tamyr's father had been injured the week before and had been visiting Ahren's house daily so her father could bandage the wound. He wouldn't be making any treks into the forest for at least a few weeks, which meant Tamyr was up to something she didn't want Ahren to know about.

Ahren crept along the branches above the wash house and waited until Tamyr emerged. She followed, keeping out of sight behind tree trunks and heavy branches, and remained high above when Tamyr left the village via the south entrance.

Her hands shook as she climbed out over the ground, but Ahren kept her friend in sight. Visions of falling tugged at the edge of her mind. Her father wasn't nearby to catch her this time. She drew a ragged breath and shoved the memories aside.

Below, Tamyr checked over her shoulder and

ducked through the bushes onto the groundfolk's hidden path. Ahren stifled a gasp. The visitor Faruz had escorted out of the village was there, waiting.

Fragments of their conversation drifted to Ahren on the wind, but she couldn't get close enough to hear better.

"—camp…not far now…"

"…more than expected…"

"…take us in…"

Tamyr checked the path every few seconds, clearly nervous about being caught. Ahren hoped the bits of conversation she heard didn't paint an accurate picture of what the two were planning. If it did—well, Ahren didn't want to get ahead of herself.

Careful not to make a sound, Ahren crept back to the village and climbed down to the boardwalk as soon as she found an empty spot. The climb had unnerved her more than she'd expected, and she wiped her damp palms on her cloak. Upset by her friend's deception, she hurried toward home. She decided not to mention Tamyr's rendezvous to anyone until she'd had a chance to confront her. She didn't think she'd be able to hide her distress, so she told the housekeeper she had a headache and couldn't handle the noise of a family supper.

Alone in the plush surroundings of her room, Ahren dropped her cloak onto the vanity chair and sank onto the chaise.

The next morning, Ahren set out at dawn for the wash house. Since they had collected all the linens from the houses on the Square the day before, the wash women would begin the process of boiling, scrubbing, and rinsing early. The laundry would have to stay hung up for a full day to dry in the wintry weather.

The smell of steam and soap carried on the icy wind, promising warmth in the morning's cold mist. Ahren hesitated at the door, unsure how to proceed. She steeled her will and pressed the door open, letting the cold wind blow into the overly-warm room.

Women crowded around great steaming pots set over wide fire pits in the center of the room. Each held a long staff, which they used to stir the linens in the pots. Ahren searched their faces, waved to those who acknowledged her, and continued on into the house. The second room mirrored the first, and again Ahren found friendly faces—just not the one she was looking for.

Frustrated, Ahren worked to remember what Tamyr had said the day before. She'd mentioned something about a promotion.

Of course! Ahren pulled open the door to the dye room and stood in the doorway, waiting for her eyes to adjust to the blinding light. She blinked twice and squinted until her eyes stopped watering.

"Ahren! You're up early!" Tamyr wiped her hands on the dingy apron at her waist, leaving deep blue streaks where her fingers touched.

The door swung closed as Ahren stepped into the room. The pungent scent of vinegar burned her nose, making her eyes water. She gagged once, coughed, and pulled her cloak over her face.

"Do you have a minute to talk? Maybe outside where I can breathe?" Tears blurred Ahren's vision so she couldn't see Tamyr's reaction.

"Of course. I've gotten used to it, but the smell is pretty intense. Come on." She grabbed Ahren's arm and led her out into the broad spaces where women boiled and rinsed the laundry.

Instead of going back the way Ahren had come, they continued on through the building and exited through the back door and into the little courtyard where the wash women went for their breaks.

"Why does it smell like that?" Ahren asked the first question on her mind. She had time to work into the bigger questions.

Tamyr winced. "The vinegar activates the dye and helps it set in the fabric. It does smell awful, though, doesn't it?" She chuckled, and Ahren joined in.

"It certainly does. You said it's a promotion, though? How do you like it?"

A huge smile lit Tamyr's face. "It's a big step up, and it shows they're starting to trust me again. You have to earn a spot on the dye team, because one mistake could ruin a load of sheets and curtains, which could cost us a fortune."

Ahren wrinkled her nose. "I guess that makes sense, but I don't know if I'd be able to handle that smell for very long."

"You get used to it faster than you'd think." Tamyr dropped onto the nearest bench and patted the spot beside her. "Now, what has you out in the cold so early this morning? I know you didn't come to see what the dye room smells like."

A pit opened in Ahren's gut and her stomach fell through. Ignoring the feeling, she sat beside her friend and swung her feet under the bench. Ahren was the only woman she knew—of course besides her mother—whose feet didn't touch the ground from the seats. She licked her suddenly-dry lips and searched for the best way to ask her question.

"I saw you sneak out yesterday."

Tamyr's head jerked up, but she didn't say anything.

Ahren folded her shaking hands in her lap and pressed on. "I saw you meet with that mayor, too, the one that tried to get everyone to turn against Aibek."

To Ahren's shock, tears flooded Tamyr's eyes. "Yes, I met with him. You have to understand... I have to do whatever I can to avenge Ahni."

Ahren frowned, trying to make the connections to seemingly unrelated events. "How can a disgraced mayor help you avenge her?"

"He can help me convince everyone that a stranger from the city can never lead them as well as someone they've known all their lives." Her features softened, and Tamyr grabbed Ahren's hand. "I know you like him, so I won't try to kill him. I just want him to go back where he came from and leave us in peace."

"I don't understand how Aibek leaving would avenge Ahni. Don't you remember?" Tears brimmed and ran down Ahren's cheeks. "I'm the one that killed her. Not Aibek. Not Faruz. Me."

Tamyr smiled a watery, tearful smile. "You didn't mean to, though. It's still Aibek's fault."

"How? How is it Aibek's fault?" Ahren stood and paced in front of the bench. "He didn't want her dead. Look how he treated you. Even when everyone thought you had stabbed Alija, he made sure you were given food and baths and clean clothes. He didn't have you beaten or executed like Tavan would have."

"That has nothing to do with anything! So what if he made a show of being nice to me. Here, sit down. You make me nervous pacing like that."

Ahren stopped mid-step and returned to the bench. She hopped up and swung her feet beneath her, trying to contain the pent-up energy.

"Anyway, like I was saying, if Aibek hadn't shown up, Alija or Wayra or any of the others could have taken that role. They could have done everything he did and then some, and Ahni would still be alive."

Shocked disbelief clouded Ahren's vision for a breath. "How could any of them teach us how to fight? They had no more training than any of us."

"I don't know. How did they kill all of Tavan's soldiers? They obviously had more skill than you think."

Ahren smiled, realizing that no one had told the villagers the whole story. "Poison! They poisoned the soldiers, Tamyr. They wouldn't have had a chance otherwise, and they knew it."

"That's not the point!"

"Oh, for the trees' sake! What is the point? We

needed Aibek to defeat Helak's men. Without his help, we'd all be dead. Why are you so obsessed with getting rid of Aibek to avenge Ahni? He would have saved her if he'd had a chance. He even tried!"

Tamyr cursed and slapped at the tears streaming down her cheeks. Her voice dropped to a low whisper. "You don't know that. No one could know that. I have to do something to avenge her."

"Then help us defeat this army. You're an expert at moving through the forest without a sound. Help the rest of us learn. Ahni would have wanted us to be free."

"Don't tell me what she would have wanted!"

Ahren recoiled at the sudden shout.

Tamyr lowered her voice and continued. "I knew her better than anyone. I loved her, dammit, and she loved him." Her voice cracked on the last word.

Ahren swallowed a lump in her throat. She'd never expected the amount of pain she heard in Tamyr's voice.

"She came here every day. She told me all about how wonderful he was. How they were going to get married. How her child would be the next governor. What could I do?" Tamyr sniffed. "I helped her any way I could, and I kept anyone from telling her that he slept with at least a dozen other girls in town. That would have destroyed her."

Tamyr trailed off, her eyes staring into the past, and Ahren shifted uncomfortably. What Tamyr had revealed about Ahni was intensely personal, and

Ahren wasn't sure she should be privy to that kind of knowledge.

"But what I regret the most is that I never told her how much I loved her. I never tried to convince her that he was bad for her. Perhaps, if I had convinced her…" Tamyr glanced at the sky and stood. "I need to get back to work."

"Can… Can I help you? I… My family isn't up yet." Ahren sighed and hopped off the bench.

Ahren followed Tamyr through the wash house and back into the dye room. Now that she was prepared for the odor, it didn't seem quite as bad. Still, she wrapped the zontrec scarf she'd used as a sash across her face and gazed around at the bottles and vials littering the counters.

"Where do we start?" Ahren tried to hide her watering eyes. She pulled the cloak up higher and dabbed at the tears the strong vinegar smell had triggered.

"Well, we need to put that stack of sheets in the basin. Then, we'll find the perfect shade of blue. It needs to match this." Tamyr held up a brilliant blue pillow cover.

"What do you want me to do?" Ahren hovered as Tamyr dunked the soft zontrec into the boiling hot water.

Is it water? Ahren wasn't sure. She thought it might be straight vinegar by the odor.

"Can you keep it all moving with this while I find the right dye?" She handed Ahren a long iron pole with a wide paddle at the far end.

Ahren did as she was told, but quickly realized the work took more muscle than she'd expected. She untied her cloak and tucked it behind Tamyr's workbench.

The pole weighed half as much as Ahren, and the soggy fabric clung to the paddle, weighing it down into the vile-smelling liquid.

Struggling under the weight, Ahren craned her neck to see what her friend was doing. "How long does this take?" Ahren shrugged, wiping the sweat from her face with her shoulder.

Tamyr laughed. "I forget you're not used to this." She took the pole and swirled the liquid effortlessly. "Perhaps it would be easier if you could reach better. Would you be against using a stool?"

Heat suffused Ahren's face, but she nodded. "I could at least give it a try." Sometimes being short was an asset. Other times, like now, it was a distinct embarrassment.

Tamyr brought over a small, three-legged stool and placed it beside the large metal cauldron. "Do you think you can keep going a few more minutes? I've almost got this right." She waited until Ahren had climbed onto the stool and handed her the pole.

"I can do it." Ahren wished she'd at least stopped for a quick breakfast before she'd left the house, but she'd been afraid of losing her nerve. Her arms shook under the strain, but she kept stirring the foul liquid and moving the heaps of wet linens.

"Perfect!" Tamyr's shout broke Ahren's concentration and she almost dropped the pole into the hot water. "I think this is exactly right."

Ahren watched, transfixed, as Tamyr poured a series of blue, green, and red dyes into the heated vinegar. The color spread and mixed, and Ahren remembered at once that she was supposed to keep everything moving. She ignored the heat growing in her palms as the hot liquid warmed the metal pole. Instead, she focused on the work of stirring the dye evenly into the linens.

"Here, I'll take it now." Tamyr appeared behind Ahren, wrapped her arms around Ahren's shoulders and grabbed the pole.

Something about the move triggered a rush of anxiety in Ahren's stomach, and she giggled once before she relinquished the paddle.

Ahren tried to turn enough to see Tamyr's face but lost her balance. Her left foot slipped off the narrow stool, and her remaining ankle wobbled beneath her. A thin scream escaped her lips, and she grabbed onto the first thing she could reach —the paddle.

She fell in an unceremonious heap on the wooden floor, and her momentum pulled the paddle out of the vinegar solution, spraying dye everywhere. Tamyr toppled behind her and crashed into something Ahren couldn't see. She came to a stop with a soft grunt, and all fell silent.

"Are you all right? I'm so sorry." Ahren shoved herself to a sitting position and glanced around for Tamyr. She found her friend lying on the floor, covered in bottles of inky dye. Some had cracked open and leaked their contents onto Tamyr's apron and skin. The result was an odd blotchy pattern of yellow, red, and blue. Ahren gasped and crawled over to Tamyr, who wasn't moving.

"Tamyr? Are you all right?"

"I'm fine. How big is the mess? I don't want to look."

Ahren's eyes roamed the room, taking in the blue spatters on the walls, the ceiling, and herself. None of the linens had come out of the basin, which had remained upright. A small puddle of deep blue sat beside the shattered remains of a stool leg. The stool itself lay on its side a few feet away.

"I… I'll stay and help you clean up." Ahren couldn't think of anything else to say. "You won't lose your new position because of this, will you?"

Much to Ahren's surprise, Tamyr laughed. "No. The job is done…and done well. We just made a bit of a mess. You don't have to stay if you don't want to. You have to be starving."

Heat spread up Ahren's neck and into her ears. "I understand. I made quite a mess of things. I hope you don't get in too much trouble."

Tamyr jumped up and pulled Ahren to her feet. She brushed away the small fragments of glass and flecks of dye and placed her stained hands on Ahren's shoulders. "You didn't do anything that nearly every person to get this position hasn't done." Tamyr laughed again. "I swore to myself that I wouldn't drop that blasted thing, and now I'm guaranteed not to. You did it for me."

Unable to resist, Ahren joined in the mirth. Tamyr looked ridiculous with multicolored dye splashed across her face and neck, and the room wouldn't take much to clean up.

They laughed until Ahren's side hurt, erupting into a new torrent of giggles when Ahren's stomach grumbled loudly. Finally, Ahren decided it was time to get some work done. She crossed to the broken stool and bent to pick up the shattered leg but slipped in the puddle of dyed vinegar.

"Be careful!" Tamyr hurried over to help. She lost her footing on the wet floor and slid the last foot or two. "Oh!"

They each grabbed hold of the other, steadying themselves and each other as they wobbled dangerously close to the full, steaming basin.

When they came a stop, Ahren realized she had both arms around her friend, clutching Tamyr's waist. Likewise, Tamyr had a painful grip on Ahren.

Ahren pulled back enough to see Tamyr's face and gasped at the intensity she saw there. Tamyr's eyes were wide, her eyes dilated in the bright morning light. A soft blush showed beneath the spots and colors of dye. She didn't give Ahren time to gain her bearings, instead dropping her face swiftly until her lips met Ahren's in the softest caress. The touch lit a fire inside of Ahren, and she pulled closer. Tamyr responded as Ahren had hoped—by deepening the kiss. Vinegar mingled with sweat and tears, the taste driving Ahren to new heights. Soft curves pressed into Ahren's bonier form, and Ahren pulled her closer still.

Somewhere in the world outside their embrace, a pounding noise started. Ahren ignored it, clinging to Tamyr.

"Is everything all right in there?" a female voice shouted through the closed door.

Tamyr broke the kiss and stared wide-eyed at Ahren. "Yes," the word came out a harsh whisper. She cleared her throat. "Yes, everything's fine. I just dropped the paddle. I'm cleaning it up now."

Outside, laughter erupted from at least a dozen women. Tamyr smiled. "See? They were waiting for it." She caressed Ahren's face, pausing at a smudge on Ahren's jaw and rubbing the spot over and over. "You should go. I need to clean this up, and you need to get some breakfast."

Unable to speak, Ahren nodded. She started toward the door, but Tamyr grabbed her arm. "Don't go that way. Here, I'll show you the back way."

They padded quietly through the door in the side of the room, which Ahren had assumed went to another washing room. Instead, it led to a small, separate outdoor area adjacent to the larger courtyard. Tall plants and potted fruit trees hid the space from view. A narrow gate connected it to the courtyard.

"You know how to get out from here, right?" Tamyr rubbed at the spot on Ahren's jaw again and laughed. "You're a mess. Is there a back way into your place? Your family probably shouldn't see you like this."

For the first time, Ahren smiled. "Yeah."

"All right. Well, I'll see you later. I need to get back to work." Tamyr grabbed Ahren's hand, squeezed it gently, and disappeared back into the dye room.

Ahren stood still, staring at the closed door for a long moment. An owl hooted somewhere nearby, breaking the trance. Ahren turned to leave, slipping quietly out of the courtyard and clambering up the nearest tree. She didn't want anyone to see her like this, especially not if she looked half as silly as Tamyr.

The sounds and smells of breakfast drifted through closed windows, and Ahren let the bitter wind dry her face. She didn't want to face her father, so she climbed slowly toward the cistern at the southern edge of the village. Her mind whirled from the morning's events. Had she convinced Tamyr not to betray the village? She didn't know. She brushed her fingers over her lips, relishing the warmth that spread through her at the thought of Tamyr's kiss. She'd tried to ignore her attraction to her friend for several months, since she hadn't been sure how Tamyr felt about her. She knew now.

Ahren shoved thoughts of the kiss from her mind—or tried to. She had a bigger problem. Tamyr had all but confessed to planning to betray Aibek. Regardless of her feelings for Tamyr, Ahren still thought Aibek had been the best leader they could have hoped for. He'd taken risks a villager would never have considered. He'd risked being ostracized and told everyone he'd traveled to the Heart of the Forest to see the Bokinna.

"What do I do? What do I do?" Ahren muttered softly. She stopped and leaned her head back against a broad tree trunk. She closed her eyes, struggling to hear the forest's whispers. Her father had always told her the forest knew the answers, but she could never hear its voice.

If she tried to build a relationship with Tamyr, did that mean she had to participate in the wash woman's schemes? She tipped her face up to the treetops, hood down, oblivious to the cold, until the sleet stung her face. She pulled her hood up and tucked her cloak close. The wind whipped harder, driving the pellets of ice into her eyes and hands. Finally, she left her perch and crawled away.

With no answers and uncertain emotions, she climbed down into her family's courtyard. She couldn't tell this story to anyone, so she'd have to figure it out on her own. She hopped down onto a bench and raced for the small door in the side of the house.

A rush of warm air greeted her, intensifying the pain of her frozen cheeks and nose. The scent of baking breads and roasted venison made her stomach snarl painfully.

The wind ripped the door out of her hand and slammed it against the wall, and Ahren had to wrestle it closed. She turned to the kitchen, expecting to see the maids and cooks gathered there, but only the housekeeper occupied the room.

"Oh, dear. You look frozen half to death. Come to your room and we'll get you all warmed up." The sweet brunette took Ahren's cloak and shepherded her down the hall.

"Really, I'm fine. I just need a few minutes in front of the fire." Ahren's objections fell on deaf ears.

"I'll get you some famanc and some rabbit. That'll warm you right up." The housekeeper sniffed at the air. "You could use a warm bath, too, I'd wager. Well, come on. I've already got water heating."

Too tired to argue further, Ahren smiled and let the older woman take care of her. Before a half an hour had passed, she'd bathed, dressed in clean clothes, and snuggled down into the chaise, a thick quilt wrapped around her shoulders.

She sat there for ages as the wind howled and hurled pellets of ice against the window, trying to figure out how to approach Tamyr again. She agonized and turned the problem inside out and upside down with no success. After several hours, she let her mind go blank and relished the comfort of meditation. Her eyes drooped, and she laid her head on the arm of the chaise.

Exhausted from the day's emotional turmoil, she slept.

14.

Watching

Aibek waited a few days before he returned to the city. For the return trip, he organized two groups of three to scout out the city's defenses. The selected men gathered at the mouth of the cave before splitting off into their assigned teams.

"All right," he leaned close to the circle of warriors. "Remember. We need to find out where their base of operations is. I suspect they've taken the palace as their center, but we need more than my best guess." He straightened and strolled through the circle, his hands clasped behind his back the way he'd seen generals do in his training. "We need to know how organized they are, how many there are, and what kind of threats they're using to keep the existing city guard and army from revolting."

He reached the edge of the circle and spun on his heel in a crisp about-face. He stood there, searching the faces of the assigned men for any hint of indecision. "Above all else, we have to be careful not to draw attention to ourselves or any member of our group. Any questions?"

"I do."

Aibek froze at the fury in Marah's voice. Instead

of answering, he broke free of the ice holding him still and strode over to her. "We've talked about this. We need people who won't be noticed. Whether we like it or not, people in this part of the land don't travel in mixed company. Let this first group go. Next week, we'll send a couple of all-women groups to see what you can scout out."

"Why wait? Why not let me take a couple of others today?" Marah squared her shoulders.

The brilliant red in her cheeks and the fire in her amber eyes took Aibek's breath away. She was easily the most beautiful woman he'd ever seen. He shook his head to clear it. Thoughts like that had taken Serik from him. He needed to keep a clear head.

"Please, just let us go this time. Let us get an idea what's happening in the city, and in three or four days, we'll try again with different groups and you can go then."

Marah braced her hands on her hips, facing him squarely. "Why? Give me a good reason why and I'll happily stay behind. We both know women are more likely to gossip. We can go to the market and chat with the storekeepers. We can probably get more information in an hour than all your men could get in a week."

Aibek's stomach sank. She had a good point, but he'd committed to the assignments already. giving in would make him look weak in front of his soldiers. He couldn't think of anything to say, so he just shook his head and adjusted his belt.

After a long pause, he dropped his voice to just

above a whisper. "You're right. You can probably get more information than any of us." He gestured to the assembled men. "But if I back down now, I look like a weak leader. Please, will you work with me and wait until the next trip?"

Marah threw back her head and laughed. "Admitting that others have good ideas doesn't make you a weak leader. Clinging to bad ideas and outdated ideas does."

A sickly smile crept onto Aibek's face. "I don't know. I think I should stick to my decisions. In the Academy, they always said we had to present a strong front."

"Did the Academy also tell you how to cope with restless dragons?"

"I… Well… Not exactly." Aibek grinned.

"Because that's another problem you're going to have to address. They're not used to hiding in caves. How long do you plan to keep them cooped up here?"

Aibek's shoulders slumped. "I don't know. We need more information. We just don't know enough about what's happening in the city yet."

"When you went into Xona three days ago, did you see any signs that the city was unsafe for women? How busy was the market? Did all the women have male escorts?"

Aibek strained his memory, searching for details he hadn't considered important at the time. He remembered a group of young women laughing and strolling through the streets. In fact, he remembered several women walking alone close to the center of town.

"No," he said at length. "The women don't seem to have changed their behaviors at all. They were shopping and laughing in groups and alone."

Marah nodded emphatically. "Good. Then there's no reason not to add a group of three women to the team. I'll lead, and I'll take Siani and Cati with me. We'll stay fifty paces or so behind you so it doesn't look like we're all together."

Aibek considered. A thought occurred to him, but he worried she'd take it the wrong way. After a long moment, he asked anyway. "Would you mind staying fifty paces in front of us? That way we can see if you run into any trouble?"

"I… I guess that would be all right." Marah frowned, but nodded. "Do you think they'll allow me to bring my bow into the city? I'll feel better with a few arrows in my quiver."

"When I lived there, they didn't take hunting weapons, only swords and spears and such. If the new leadership kept the same rules, they should let you keep it." The thought pleased him more than it should have, but he'd seen how deadly she could be with her bow.

Satisfied that he'd made the right decision, Aibek strolled over to the waiting men. He assumed the same military posture as before, with his hands behind his back and his shoulders squared.

"Marah's made an excellent point. As a woman, she can carry her bow and arrows into the city." Several soldiers murmured, but Aibek continued without addressing them. "As a sniper, she's unparalleled. She and her chosen teammates will stay fifty paces ahead of us, so they can react to any trouble quickly. The distance will also allow us to make us look like separate groups so we don't draw any undue attention at the gate."

After some quick instructions to the warriors staying behind, Aibek led the expedition to the city. He kept the women in the main group until the city wall came into view on the horizon, then held back and let Marah's group get ahead.

He held his breath as the women went through the inspection process, but they proceeded into the city unmolested. As they'd hoped, the guards allowed Marah to keep her bow and quiver. The men went through just as easily and split into their prearranged teams once inside the city. Aibek led his team to the west, toward the building that had once been the city guard's headquarters. They paused in a narrow alley behind the market to plan. Buckets of refuse and human waste lined the low stone walls, waiting for the street urchins to pick them up and dump them in the river. The stench made Aibek's eyes water, but he couldn't think of a better place to strategize.

"Once we get there, I'll do the talking," he told his team. "I'm hoping one of my schoolmates will be there, or someone I know from the years I spent here, anyway."

"That's a great plan." Bartel nodded and stepped closer. "Should keep us from having to do any fighting. We wouldn't have much of a chance here. There's too many of them."

"Nonsense. We've got help. They wouldn't stand a chance." Kai laughed. "Of course, they have weapons, and we don't, so that could be a problem."

"Weapons or no weapons, don't get cocky. Our 'helpers' aren't here and have no way of knowing if we get into trouble."

Kai's shoulders drooped and his face fell. "Good point. What's the plan?"

"Well, I don't know about you, but my plan is to avoid any kind of fighting. We've got no chance of winning anything here." Bartel smoothed his hands over his shirt. "Aibek's right. No one can help us."

"Right. At least we're agreed on that. I think the best thing will be to hang around near the headquarters and see if I can spot someone I know. That should give us a decent chance, I think."

Bartel and Kai nodded and followed Aibek out of the alley.

They took up a position near the entrance to the headquarters building, which was a nondescript, low-slung rectangle built of the same sparkling marble as the giant city wall it leaned against.

Short, bearded soldiers came and went, and Aibek waited, looking for the taller, slender men and women he'd trained with. he'd almost given up hope, when he finally recognized a friendly face.

"Intza! I'm so glad to see you. Can you tell me what's going on?"

The tall, bulky man squinted at Aibek for a breath,

and Aibek worried his favorite opponent had forgotten him. A cool breeze ruffled Aibek's hair and Intza's features relaxed.

"It's Aibek, right? I thought I'd heard you left town."

"I did. I came back to visit my aunt and uncle, but I can't find either of them. No one will tell me anything. What's happened? Who are they?" He pointed to one of the bearded mountain men.

Intza grabbed his arm and pulled Aibek away from the others. His voice was a low whisper when he spat, "Look, we've been invaded. You should probably leave the city. Everyone who talks about starting any kind of opposition disappears. We haven't figured out how they know everything we talk about, but nothing is safe. You need to go. I'm sorry I don't have better news. I haven't heard anything about your aunt or uncle, but I think your friend's family is safe."

Aibek had to listen closely to catch the nearly-imperceptible words. He'd grown used to the slower diction of the forest-dwellers and had forgotten how quickly the people in Xona talked.

Intza glanced over his shoulder. His deep brown eyes met Aibek's, worry and fear evident. "Look, I have to go. Remember what I said. Get out of the city. They hear everything."

Without another word, Intza jogged back to the line entering the headquarters. Aibek frowned and motioned his friends away. They made a beeline for the city gate. None spoke, though Aibek could see the curiosity burning in his friends' faces.

They made it to the wall without incident, but before they'd passed the guard tower inside the first set of iron gates, someone shouted, "There they are!"

Aibek froze. Surely they hadn't been identified already. Intza's words rang in his mind.

They hear everything. Had someone overheard his conversation with Kai and Bartel?

Before he could react, someone grabbed his arms and wrenched his wrists behind his back. Uneven rope burned his skin as his captor tied it tightly above his hands.

Aibek glanced around the tiny stone cell. Metal bars closed the narrow opening to the corridor. A single guard stood watch at the end of the row of cells. He'd watched as Kai and Bartel had been brought to the same section in front of him, but Aibek didn't dare try to talk to them. Someone had overheard them in the alley, so they would certainly be listening for any conversations in the prison.

Think, think, think.

Somewhere nearby, Bartel grunted. Bars rattled. Kai hadn't made a sound since being tossed into the cold stone cell. That worried Aibek, since Kai always had something to say about everything. Aibek longed to reassure his friends but doing so would tip off the guards. He bit the inside of his cheek to keep himself quiet. The metallic taste of blood filled his mouth and he gagged.

Hinges creaked. Metal clanged. Deep voices murmured something Aibek couldn't quite make out. The lamp flickered. The aroma of honey-sweetened porridge wafted through the space. Aibek's stomach rumbled.

Bars clanged, followed by the sound of metal scraping along stone. An instant later, someone appeared outside Aibek's cell. The small door at the bottom of the door opened, and a bowl filled with a gray, lumpy gelatinous substance slid through the opening. No spoon followed, nor was any silverware in the bowl.

Without hesitating, Aibek lifted the bowl to his lips and slurped it down. It had the bland flavor of stale oats mixed with a tiny bit of honey and cinnamon, but his hunger didn't care. He needed the sustenance the porridge would provide.

When he'd finished licking the bowl clean, he tapped it against the door. As he'd expected, the door opened and the guard removed the bowl. The small door slammed closed with a final clang.

His lips stuck together, and Aibek longed for a sip of water to wash down the thick porridge, but footsteps in the corridor signaled the guards' retreat. Aibek sighed and set his mind back to the task. He needed to escape. He had to get his friends out of the prison before their captors discovered their identities.

He examined the cell closer. Its cold stone walls seemed uniform. No edges showed between the blocks. No rough spots would provide purchase for his hands if he wanted to climb out. The narrow window at the top of the wall was far too small for a man to climb out of, even if he did manage to reach it. Panic welled in his chest, but Aibek pushed it down.

Keep your head, he reminded himself. *You need to think your way out of this.*

He walked slow circles around the cell, paying special attention to the floor. There was a way out of this place, Aibek was certain. He'd had to spend a week here as a first-year academy student. They'd wanted all the officers to know the ins and outs of the prison in case the city was ever invaded—as it had been recently. There was a separate jail at the center of the city designed for officers who broke the laws.

He vividly recalled dropping into the darkness below the cell when he'd been here as a youth. He just had to remember how to find the opening.

15.

Escape

Aibek spent the next three days memorizing his captors' routines. Using a pebble, he scratched tallies into the stone to keep track of the guards' rounding times, meal times, and guard changes. At dawn on the fourth day, he closed his eyes and reached out his senses, stretching for any hint of the Bokinna or Saethem or their power. He longed to know he wasn't completely alone in the cell, or that one of them could let Gworsad know he was trapped. He blanked his mind and expanded his area of awareness out over the city, past the waving amber grasses, over streams and including deer and rabbits and foxes. He attuned himself to every sound, the feel of the land, reaching for a power higher than his own.

Nothing.

The sun rose. The effort left him exhausted and sweating. The broad door at the end of the hall banged open, startling Aibek back to the present. Heavy booted feet clomped on stone floors as the guards moved down the row of cells, banging doors and scraping bowls into the cells.

The noise moved closer, and soon Aibek's bowl grated along the cold stone. He gulped the cold porridge gratefully and tapped the empty bowl against the door.

After breakfast, he waited while the guards collected the rest of the bowls and disappeared for their shift change. This was his moment. He rushed to the back of his cell and pressed the small release set in the floor. One stone shifted a hair to the right, just enough that he could get his fingers between the stones. He pressed his fingers down, and another stone moved. A quiet scraping noise filled the cell. Aibek froze and waited to be certain the guards hadn't heard.

No, they hadn't returned to the cell block from their turnover yet. Aibek moved more quickly. His fingers shook as he moved one small stone at a time, revealing the secret opening in the cell floor. In moments, a gaping hole swallowed the light where the floor should have been. Aibek gulped. The last time he'd done this, there had been a professor at the bottom with a torch for light. This time, he'd have to feel his way through the pitch-dark passageway. He hoped he'd been right about which cells housed his friends. He didn't have time for errors.

Steeling his nerves, Aibek took a deep breath and dropped feet-first into the abyss. Cold air rushed past his face, blowing his hair into his eyes. Blackness swallowed him.

He hit the dirt floor with a grunt, stumbled, and fell against the dusty wall. Blood rushed in his ears. He'd done it. Now, he needed to find the trigger that would cover the hole above. He felt along the wall, wracking his memory for the exact location of the small lever.

Aibek's fingers trailed along the rough-cut walls, knocking dust into the air. His eyes adjusted to the dim light from above and he spun in a slow circle until he found what he was looking for: a small lever set into the stone. He pulled it and felt the gears move beneath it. A puff of dust filled his mouth and nose, and Aibek stifled a cough. Above him, stones scraped and the hole in the cell floor disappeared.

The little light that had come through the opening above vanished. Aibek stood still, waiting for his eyes to adjust to the darkness. If his memory served him, the builders had cut small ventilation holes in the stones above the tunnel. Maybe. If he'd remembered it right, those little openings should let in enough light to see the path out of the city. If not, he'd be stuck in the dark with no way to see how to get out.

While he waited and hoped for his eyes to adjust, he contemplated the idea that there might have been spirits watching his cell. Were they following him in the tunnels? He hoped not, but he couldn't rule out the possibility.

An eternity passed before he could make out the shapes of the rough-hewn stones lining the corridor. Pinpricks of light shone down from above. The holes would allow in enough light to see and ventilate the tunnel, but they would also carry any noise straight to the guards above.

Shoving the worries aside, he followed the walls to

the next lever. He hoped his hearing had been right, and that Kai was in this cell. If he was correct, then Bartel would be in the cell beside Kai, and they could escape quickly and quietly.

His fingers tripped on the small lever, and Aibek froze. His hands shook. If he was wrong, opening that trap door would probably make the prisoner in that cell call out, and he'd be caught. He stretched his memory back to the day of their capture. Had he told the others about the enemy's odd habit of hearing whatever the city guard said? Had they been close enough to hear while Intza talked? It was too late to second guess himself now. He held his breath and pulled the lever. A puff of dust flew out from the wall, and the ceiling opened up.

Kai's bearded head obscured the light for an instant. He didn't hesitate. Aibek stepped aside as his friend dropped into the tunnel. As soon as Kai had cleared the opening, Aibek closed the floor above.

"I'm—"

Aibek shook his head and pressed a hand to his mouth. Kai's eyes went wide and he nodded in understanding.

Together, they moved the few steps to the lever beneath Bartel's cell. Again, Aibek held his breath as the floor above opened. He didn't know Bartel like he knew Kai, so he had to hope his teammate would recognize the rescue attempt for what it was.

He needn't have worried. Bartel barely spared a second to glance into the pit before dropping to his feet on the tunnel floor. Again, Aibek closed the opening as soon as he was certain Bartel was safe. Before Bartel could speak, Aibek placed a hand on his shoulder and pressed a finger to his own lips. Bartel copied the gesture and nodded. Good. Everyone understood.

Now, Aibek just had to remember how to get out of the tunnel system.

Aibek paused to orient himself inside the tunnel. He faced the direction of the cell doors. According to the direction of the light through the windows, that was east. He needed to go south. He turned forty-five degrees to his right. That had to be the way out. Bartel and Kai lined up behind and followed Aibek through the tunnels. No one spoke. The only sounds were the soft crunching of their boots on the dusty floors and their breath echoing off the jagged stone walls.

His heart pounded in his chest, so loud he was sure the others must be able to hear it, until they reached the first juncture. Aibek froze at the intersection and pictured his first-year classroom in his mind. The walls had been papered with dozens of maps. Most were of the city streets and the lands beyond the walls, but one had been the layout of these tunnels. He imagined its lines and mentally traced it to their current location.

When he was as sure as he could be, he continued straight through the intersection. They would be under the jail's courtyard, so he needed to keep going through three more junctions. Then a right turn would take them to a ladder-well where they could escape into a cave outside the city walls. He refused to let his mind wander to any of the things that could stop them from reaching that ladder and the safety it offered.

Instead, he focused on setting one foot in front of the other and breathing evenly in the musty tunnel. He didn't dare cough or sneeze, since either would be loud enough for anyone above to hear.

At the next intersection, a cool breeze ruffled his hair. The fresh air tempted him, but he didn't think they had gone far enough yet. No, better to keep going.

A scraping, scratching noise behind them set Aibek's teeth on edge, but he picked up the pace and moved toward the exit without glancing back. Several steps later, he had to admit the scratching was closing in. Voices and market sounds carried down from the air vents, which Aibek interpreted to mean they'd passed the jail walls and were beneath the city.

More scratching sounds. Even closer.

Aibek chanced a whisper to his friends. "Run."

They sprinted through the tunnels until they reached the third intersection.

"This way," Aibek said, struggling to modulate his voice.

When he turned to make sure the others had followed him around the turn, he froze. Bartel and Kai slammed into him and all three stumbled against the rough-hewn wall.

Behind them, a black and white-striped creature ran into the intersection. It stood on all four legs and came up to Aibek's waist. Aibek watched in horror as it reared up on its hind legs and bared a mouth full of pointed teeth. It hissed, an evil sound that carried the stench of rotten meat to Aibek's dust-filled nose. He backed away, moving slowly down the corridor. That ladder-well had to be close.

Unsure what else to do, Aibek reached into his shirt and pulled out the medallion Valasa had hidden the tincture in. He didn't know how he'd use that strength in such an enclosed space and without weapons, but it was all he had.

The creature's yellow eyes caught and reflected every scrap of light, making them seem to glow in the dimness of the tunnel. It dropped to all fours and stalked closer to the retreating men.

Bartel's whisper pierced the silence. "What is that?"

"Maogir." Aibek couldn't force out more than the thing's name. His hands shook as he uncorked the tiny vial and downed its contents in a single gulp.

"I thought they were scavengers." Kai's voice wasn't any stronger than Aibek's had been.

"Normally, they are." Aibek raked his gaze over the beast's sides, taking in the protruding ribs and ragged coat. "But this one's half-starved. They'll hunt when they're desperate, and it thinks we're dinner."

Aibek hoped the animal's condition meant it would be slower and weaker than a healthy maogir. That, or it meant it would be more desperate and therefore more dangerous. He longed for a weapon—any weapon. He didn't want to get close enough to touch that beast with his bare hands.

He met the animal's furious glare and took another step back. His elbow hit something protruding from the wall, taking his attention away from the maogir for an instant.

The creature leapt towards him, hissing and snarling. In the same heartbeat, the tincture reached his blood, and strength surged in his arms and legs.

Aibek ducked as the maogir lunged. He made contact with a rear leg and extended his arm. Bones crunched. The maogir screamed in fury and pain. It crumpled and Aibek backed away. Something warm and wet dripped from his fingers, and he wiped his hand on his trousers.

In the distance, a clicking, buzzing noise echoed, but Aibek ignored it. He kept his focus on the injured maogir in front of him and backed slowly down the tunnel.

"What's this?" Kai knocked against something and the metallic noise clanged off the walls.

Aibek didn't turn. "Is it a ladder? We need to climb to the escape hatch."

The maogir clawed its way toward them, carrying its injured leg. It hissed again, and Aibek braced himself for its next attack.

"It is! It is a ladder." The sounds of boots on metal rungs filled Aibek with relief. At least his friends were safe. If he turned his back on the maogir, it would tear him to pieces.

The buzzing grew more insistent, and Aibek

inclined an ear. His heart sped to a breakneck pace as realization dawned. In the academy, the professors had warned them never to allow themselves to bleed in the tunnels. Blood attracted the haseriet, which were some sort of insects that could devour a person in seconds. Aibek had never seen one, and he wanted to keep it that way. He glanced down at the dark spot on his pants, then up at the maogir's mangled back leg.

"Did you find the hatch?" He shouted, no longer concerned about being heard from outside. Their enemies were the least of their problems.

"Yes, but it's stuck!" Kai's voice sounded like he was speaking through clenched teeth, so Aibek guessed he must be fighting with the catch.

The maogir dove for him, and Aibek jumped over it. He landed behind the confused animal, grabbed its tail, and swung it into the wall. It staggered, dazed, but didn't take its eyes off him.

The buzzing noise grew. It drowned out the sound of Aibek's blood rushing in his ears.

"We need to get out of here!"

"Together," Kai's voice rang from above. "One, two, three, go!"

Metal clanged and creaked. Light shone down into the tunnel, illuminating the bleeding maogir and the swarm of haseriet flying toward the blood. Aibek froze, stunned by the sight of dozens of yellow crickets the size of a man's head flying in a frenzy. They bounced off each other and the tunnel walls, but didn't slow. Aibek leapt straight up, hoping the maogir would be enough to keep them occupied so he could escape.

At the top of his leap, he reached out and grabbed a ladder rung, but his blood-coated hand slipped free. Panicking, he tried with the other hand. His fingers made contact with cold steel, and he jerked to a stop. His body slammed against the wall, but he was already moving, pushing himself up the ladder towards the light and the safety it promised.

One lone haseriet followed him, and he punched at it as he climbed through the hatch. His swing went wide. It followed him through, but Kai was ready. He grabbed the cricket-like beast by its back legs and swung it into the wall again and again until it ceased buzzing and lay still on the ground.

"Close it!" Aibek croaked, reaching for the heavy iron circle. He and Bartel pushed together. It closed with a creak, a groan, and a bang that triggered a ringing in Aibek's ears.

He leaned back against the closed hatch, closed his eyes, and waited for his breathing to return to normal. When he opened his eyes again, he met Kai's worried stare.

"What now?"

Kai's question echoed Aibek's own worries. "I don't know. Let's rest here for a bit and we'll decide when we've caught our breath, all right?"

Bartel and Kai sank to the ground, and Aibek followed suit.

He lay on his back and considered their plight. He didn't know for sure if the enemy spirits were following them. He didn't even know if their escape had been discovered yet. What he did know was that they'd made a great deal of noise in their exit, and he was covered in blood. They needed to get out of the cave, but he couldn't return to the camp until he knew for certain he wouldn't lead the enemy there.

"What happened back there?" Kai asked after a long break.

"Yeah, how did you—"

"Not here." Aibek's voice had the stony quality of a mother chastising her children, and he winced. "I'll explain everything, but not yet. We need to get out of here."

Picturing the maps in his mind, he led the way out of the cave and onto the south road. They traveled in silence for several hours, until they reached a rushing stream.

Aibek didn't have a chance to announce the stop before his friends rushed to the water and dunked their heads and hands in, drinking deeply of the rushing water. Aibek did the same after rinsing the dried blood from his hands and arms. He dismissed the bloodstains on his shirt. The cool breeze made it impossible to wash his clothes without freezing on the road. When they'd drunk their fill, the friends wiped their faces and stepped back onto the worn dirt path.

"We should be far enough away by now, right? Where are we going?" Kai stopped and crossed his arms over his chest.

Bartel stepped up beside Kai and faced Aibek.

"I promise, I'll tell you everything, but I have to make sure it's safe first." Aibek spread his hands in a gesture of hopelessness. "We need to go a little further."

Kai and Bartel shared a look, but didn't argue. Aibek waited, breathless, but they turned back to the road.

Relief coursed through his veins as Aibek followed his friends south. He longed to speak, to reach out to his father and ask for confirmation that there wasn't an enemy spirit following them, but he didn't dare. Instead, he bit his tongue and ignored the hunger gnawing at his belly. Breakfast had been many hours earlier, and the tincture always made him ready for food.

Birds wheeled overhead and the rustling of water faded with the view of the city's glittering walls. Exhaustion weighed on Aibek like a heavy blanket. He didn't stop. The sun set. He pushed on.

Finally, as Thrimanca, the second of Azalin's three moons, crested the horizon, Kai grabbed his arm. "We have to stop for the night. We can't keep going without sleep."

Too tired to argue, Aibek nodded. "We'll camp here, then. I'll take first watch."

Without another word, Kai and Bartel laid on the bare ground and fell immediately to sleep. The gentle breeze rustled the grasses and buried the snuffling and snoring noises the exhausted warriors made.

Aibek tipped his head back and stared into the sun's fading light as it dipped below the mountainous horizon. Squinting into the gathering darkness, he racked his memory for recollection of that mountain on his initial trip south. As hard as he tried, he couldn't remember whether or not he'd seen it. A pit of anxiety opened in his gut. What if he'd taken the wrong road? As the darkness grew, he longed for the warmth and light of a fire but wasn't sure it would be safe.

Although, he reasoned, *if Helak's spirits are following us, they won't need a fire to find us. They may even be watching me now, or leading Helak's men to us.*

He fought the wave of crippling anxiety that thought triggered and worked to think through his problem. Part of him yearned to call out for his parents, but he knew they'd been watching the enemy armies and were likely many miles away.

"Father? Mother? Are you there?" He couldn't help trying, though he listened without hope for a response.

A heartbeat later, he regretted his impulsive shout. Voices carried on the evening breeze.

"I heard it over here! Come on! They'll get away!"

"So what? I'm hungry. Let's head back and hunt."

Aibek whispered a curse. He glanced over at his friends sleeping on the ground and stepped into the night toward the voices. If they ended up being hostile, he'd have a better chance of fighting them off than Kai or Bartel. His stomach heaved, but he pulled a vial of tincture out from under his shirt and downed it. If he needed the strength and speed it offered, he wouldn't have time to reach for it once the source of the voices arrived.

"What did you say you heard?" The second voice asked.

Aibek crouched into the tall grass, low enough that only his eyes and the top of his head would show above the waving stalks. His breath came in shallow gasps as the tincture took effect. Strength coursed through his muscles, bringing with it the drive to move, to run, and to fight.

"I heard a voice… over there, I'm sure of it… I dunno, but we should at least check. We can't go back without them."

A twig snapped in the distance, and Aibek resisted the urge to turn his head toward the sound. Instead, he listened with heightened senses, waiting for the voices' owners to step out of the darkness. He knelt lower, his knees sinking in the soft earth, his legs tightly coiled springs ready to jump into motion.

The crunching of footsteps carried on the breeze, closer and closer. Unconsciously, Aibek leaned forward. Energy surged through his thighs, but he dropped lower.

A strong hand clamped down on his shoulder, and all the energy in Aibek's legs released at once. He stifled a scream. His legs sank deep into the ground.

What had kept him from leaping from the grass — and the hand on his shoulder? Aibek jerked his head to the side, straining for a view of the hand's owner. He just glimpsed a dimly-lit face, a shake of the head, and the hand pressed him further down into the tall grass.

"Be still! They'll hear you!" Warm breath puffed against his ear and he felt, rather than heard the words.

He stopped struggling and listened to the footsteps crunching softly in the grass nearby.

"I don't see anything. I'm starved. Let's go."

"No, I swear. I heard it right over here." Grass rustled, as if someone were parting the tall stalks and letting them fall back together again.

Footsteps moved away, toward the road, and Aibek started to struggle again. He couldn't let whoever that was find Kai and Bartel. They obviously weren't friendly.

A second hand grabbed his other shoulder and shook. Aibek complied and fell still, listening.

"There's no one here. No footprints, no camp. Let's go."

"Just give me a few more minutes. I'll find them."

"No. I'm going back. Stay here by yourself if you want. There's still enough light to catch a rabbit or two before we get back."

A loud, insolent huff sounded on the breeze, followed by the sound of booted feet stomping through the grass.

The noise faded into the distance, and the hands let go of Aibek's shoulders.

Aibek tugged his legs free of the dirt and stood. Slowly, he turned to see who had been strong enough to stop him even with the seeds' strength coursing through his body. What he saw brought him up short.

A little man stood with his hands on his hips. Tattered, flimsy garments draped over his arms and legs, blowing in the evening breeze. The top of his head came to Aibek's waist, but he was neither elf nor dwarf. Kind eyes stared out of a pointy face, though it was too dark to discern their color. His hair stuck out in odd patches all over his head, the way Serik's had.

A stab of pain shot through Aibek's chest at the thought of his mentor. He hadn't gone back like he'd promised. He'd left his oldest and dearest friend to die alone in the forest like an animal.

Aibek tore his eyes away from the stranger and turned back to his friends. He found them exactly as he'd left them, sleeping soundly on the bare ground.

No sounds followed him, and a wave of disappointment flowed over Aibek. He wouldn't get to thank the odd little man for his help.

Anxious from the tincture's unspent energy and the sudden reminder of his mentor, Aibek dropped to his knees and tore a patch of grass loose. It came up easily and gave him no satisfaction. Frustrated, he tossed the dirt and grass aside and dug his fingers into the hole the roots left.

"Don't you want to know who I am?"

Startled, Aibek leapt to his feet and turned to face the little man, somehow certain that's exactly who had spoken, though he hadn't heard anyone approach.

"How'd you do that? I didn't hear you." Aibek squinted into the darkness, trying to discern more of the man's appearance.

"That's no matter. Why don't you tell me who you are and what you're doing in the mountain's shadow?"

"I…" Aibek wasn't sure whether he could trust this person or not, though he dearly wanted to. There was something warm and comforting in the large eyes set above the small, pointy features. "I'm fleeing the city," he said at last.

"I can see that much. You have nothing but the clothes on your back. Why do you run? You're covered in blood. Are you injured?"

Aibek glanced down at his soiled clothes. "No, I'm not injured. I…" he paused, uncertain. "Who are you? I appreciate your help and all, but why should I trust you?"

"Zirvesi sent me. He said intruders were near our borders and that I should make sure you mean us no harm."

The stranger's stiffly formal accent grated on Aibek as wrong. He didn't sound like he belonged in the mountain tribes, the plains villages, or Xona. A frown crinkled Aibek's forehead. "I'm not sure who that is, or whether that means I should trust you or not."

The little man chuckled softly. The sound eased the ache that Serik's memory had triggered in Aibek's chest.

"I mean you no harm. I may be able to help you.

Indeed, I believe I already have once. Why were those men searching for you?"

Confusion and exhaustion warred in Aibek's mind. He couldn't think clearly on so little rest and no food. As if on cue, his stomach rumbled loudly. The little man cocked his head and stared at Aibek, an expression of concern and curiosity on his sharp features. Neither spoke for a long while.

Finally, Aibek gave in. He dropped his head and gazed at the stony ground. Haltingly, he told the stranger everything that had happened since they entered Xona, though he left out the bit about the tincture. He didn't know enough about the stranger to trust him with that detail.

"Well, what's next? Where are you headed?"

"I'm heading south, I think. Towards the swamp where we'll have the Saethem's protection. We can hide there for a few days until we're sure no one's watching, then head back to camp. I have to do anything and everything to keep from exposing our hideout to the enemy."

"You count on the sisters for protection? You must be very special indeed, child. But you're heading the wrong direction to ever reach the swamp."

Aibek sighed. "I was afraid of that. I don't remember seeing those mountains the first time."

"I could lead you to the South road, if you'd like—" Aibek's stomach growled again. "And I could help you get some supplies for hunting. You'll need to eat if you're going to defeat those… those…" the little man sniffed. "Whatever they are, they're foul. We want them gone. If you're an enemy of theirs, you're a friend of mine. Shall we go?"

With a laugh and a shake of his head, Aibek gestured to his sleeping friends. "No, let's let them sleep. We'll set off in the morning."

The little man nodded solemnly. "Shouldn't you sleep, too?"

"I will. We take turns keeping watch." Aibek glanced up toward the moons. "I'll wake Kai soon so he can have a turn, and I'll lay down."

"For someone who's keeping watch, you're easy to sneak up on."

Aibek stifled a laugh. "You're quieter than any man I've ever seen. What's your secret?" His eyes narrowed and he tried again to make out the finer details of the stranger's face. "And what did you say your name is again?"

"I do apologize. I'm Pagi, servant of Zirvesi and protector of the mountain. Do you wish for me to show you to the south road with the sunrise?"

"Yes. We'd appreciate the help." Aibek's head felt like a weight atop his shoulders. He was running out of strength to stay upright. "If it's all right with you, I'm going to switch out with Kai, now. I need sleep if we're going to make any kind of real progress tomorrow."

"All right." Pagi stood and bowed slightly. "I'll return with the sun to see you on your way."

"Well, shouldn't I introduce you?" Aibek glanced over at his sleeping friends. When he looked back, Pagi had vanished. Too tired to worry about how the stranger moved so silently through the waving grass, Aibek woke Kai and took his place on the soft dirt. Sleep took him an instant later.

16.

Swamp

The smell of meat cooking woke Aibek and he groaned, torn between the need for more sleep and the desire for food. Hunger won. He rolled over, opened his eyes, and grumbled. The sun hadn't yet risen. In fact, Illodus still hovered near the horizon. Sunrise was at least an hour away. His stomach snarled, hunger chasing away the residual sleep.

Every muscle protested as he pushed himself to standing. Nearby, meat sizzled and popped, and Aibek stepped toward the light and warmth of the fire.

Kai and Bartel sat in front of a small cooking fire, each holding a hunk of steaming, dripping meat. Aibek's stomach twisted painfully.

"That smells amazing," he said, stepping closer.

The little man from the night before, Pagi, stepped out of the tall grass and grinned. "Ah, you're awake. Are you hungry? I thought you might be. Here, have a bit to eat, and we'll clean up soon and be on our way south, right?"

Aibek almost missed the last bit, he was so focused on the steaming rabbit haunch Pagi had handed him. He wasted no time sinking his teeth into the meat. He couldn't name the spices that blended with the smoky flavor of the rabbit, but whatever they were, they made the meat burst with flavor and a different kind of heat. His eyes watered from the blistering spices, but he ignored the pain and took another bite. He watched the smoke circling into the predawn sky and willfully ignored the potential danger of starting a fire. They'd be on the move soon, so the smoke and light wouldn't help their enemies find them.

They ate their fill of the rabbit and nuts Pagi had brought, covered the fire with dirt, and set out on their way. Since they'd been on the wrong road, they struck out through the waist-high grass away from the path. Pagi moved much more quickly than Aibek expected, and he had to work to keep up with the little man.

By the time the sun neared the western horizon, they'd left the mountains' shadows far behind them. Aibek didn't expect the wave of relief that washed over him at the sight of the well-traveled south road, but he couldn't deny he was happy to be back on the right track.

Only an hour later, the sunset painted the sky in orange and red streaks, and the group agreed to stop for the night. Cook fires lit up the surrounding hills, so Aibek, Kai, and Bartel spread out in search of firewood.

Pagi stayed close to Aibek as he combed the ground for woody sticks. The little man handed Aibek a twig to add to his growing collection.

"You say you're heading to the Saethem's swamp?"

"Yes. We know the way from here." Aibek tucked the twig into the bundle under his arm. "Thank you so much for your help. I'm sure you'll be wanting to get home soon, right?"

"Well, no one's expecting me any time soon. I thought I'd tag along to the swamp, if that's all right with you. Never seen it, but I've heard stories. Lots of stories. Stories to curl your toes and keep you up nights."

Aibek froze, his hand an inch above another stick. "Why do you want to go there? Most people try to avoid it."

"Well, I was raised on the Sisters' lore, and I'd love to see one of their homes. They're the stuff of legends, they are."

"And where do the other ones live?" Aibek kept his eyes down and picked up a handful of tiny twigs.

A pleased laugh came from Pagi's direction. "Testing me, are you? Yes, I know there are only two, and that the other is reported to live in the southern forest. Tell me, do you know where to find their brother?"

Aibek fought to contain his surprise. No one had ever mentioned a brother within his hearing.

"I suppose not. Most people from the southern forest never heard there is a third. Come, this should be enough to cook a rabbit or squirrel. Let's head back, and I'll tell you the tale while our dinner cooks."

Irritation welled in Aibek's chest, but he took a breath and blew it away. He wasn't sure what the little man knew, but he wasn't going to turn down an opportunity to learn more of the forest's history. He wished Serik could be there to verify or dispute Pagi's story, and pain shot through his chest. Once more, he shoved aside the image of his friend lying broken against the Bokinna's trunk.

Shaking from the mental images, he straightened and followed Pagi back to the spot they'd chosen for their camp. There, he kept himself busy building a sad little fire that smoked more than any he'd ever made before. Once the small flames lapped at the larger sticks, he tossed handfuls of twigs and sticks and brush onto them, building the fire until it was hot enough to cook the squirrels Kai and Bartel had snared.

"If I'd had my bow, we'd have had pheasant instead," Bartel grumbled. "I still can't believe I let you talk me into leaving it behind."

"Oh, stop whining," Kai snapped. "If you *had* brought it to Xona, the guards would have taken it when we were captured."

Bartel harrumphed but said nothing more. Aibek kept his eyes on the food roasting over the fire. He glanced up when Pagi approached and tossed something small and round into the glowing embers. A loud pop startled Aibek to his feet and a brilliant blue light flared over the site.

"Wha—" Aibek stumbled backward several steps, his eyes burning from the light and smoke.

The little man loomed large, amplified by the blue flare.

An instant later, the light died out and Pagi returned to his normal, diminutive size. Confused, blinded, and disoriented, Aibek backed further away.

Pagi advanced in step with Aibek's retreat. "Did you know you're being tracked? Followed by the unseen?"

"I… I suspected." Aibek blinked, trying to clear his vision. "That's why we're heading to the swamp. I hoped the Saethem could help me get rid of them."

The silence stretched, and Aibek hoped Pagi would be the one to break it. When he didn't, Aibek asked, "What did you do? What was that light?"

"Nothing to worry about. I just wanted to see who was after you. There's more than one. Did you know that? Two distinct groups. Very strange. Never seen that before." Pagi cleared his throat. "You say you suspected you were being followed? What made you think so? And do you know who the two groups are?"

"Well," Aibek glanced over at his friends, who sat talking quietly and didn't seem to have noticed the blue flash. "I think… one group might be my parents. The other belongs to the enemy and is trying to track us back to our camp, so they can send their army out to destroy us before we have a chance to fight them."

"That's why you were calling for your mother and father last night, then?"

Heat rushed into Aibek's face at the memory. "Yes. I hoped they could tell me for sure if Helak's spirits were after us."

"Well, now that you have that answer, what is your next step?"

"I need to get to the swamp. I don't think they can follow me there, but I'm not sure."

Pagi nodded sagely. "Not a bad plan. Can I come with you? I think I can help you."

Aibek agreed, and they returned to the camp and the odd burn marks on the ground near the fire.

As they sped south, the temperatures dropped, and the wind whipped their hair and clothes around them. Aibek shivered and struggled but pushed onward except for brief rests at night.

They moved swiftly over the next four days, and before the sun set on the fourth day, they reached the swamp's edge. Remembering the stench and muck, Aibek suggested they spend the night on the dry ground and enter the bog with the morning's light.

Near the swamp, wood for fires was more plentiful, and they had a roaring campfire before darkness fell. Aibek, Kai, and Bartel scooted close to the fire, but Pagi hung back, keeping to the shadows. They snared two rabbits and cooked them over the fire.

A wintry wind blew over the camp, flinging sparks out into the night sky. Aibek shivered and longed for his cloak, which he'd left in the tiny shack beside the abandoned mine.

"Why have you come here, with danger close on your heels?"

The voice carried on the wind and brought the hairs on Aibek's neck to attention. He jerked his head up, searching for the source of the whispered words.

His friends carried on stirring the fire and enjoying their supper. Only the old man had sat up and looked around.

Aibek stood and walked a few steps away from the meager camp.

"Madam Saethem?" He whispered. "We need your help."

"And what makes you think I would help you, even if I could?"

This voice was so much harsher and angrier than the Bokinna had ever been, and Aibek faltered.

"Please, Madam, I beg of you. I cannot lead the spirits back to the camp, or we'll have our enemies on our heads by the end of the day. I didn't know where else to go."

"I despise repeating myself, but I'll ask one more time: why should I help you?"

"I'm so sorry. I didn't introduce myself. I'm Aibek, the one your sister sent to defeat the army that poisoned her. You've met my friend and captain, Faruz."

"How do I know you are who you say you are? What proof do you bring?"

Aibek considered. Faruz had brought the ancient amulet with him into the swamp. Realization dawned, bringing a slight smile with it. "I have this." He pulled the necklace out of his shirt and held it up to the swamp.

"Interesting. What is it?" That wasn't the Saethem.

Aibek spun to face the direction the voice had

come from. Pagi stood a step behind him, his eyes fixed on the locket Aibek held aloft.

Startled, Aibek tucked the necklace back into his shirt. "It's nothing for you to worry about. The Saethem knows what it is, and that's all that matters."

"Indeed, I do. I shall consult with my sister while you sleep. I'll have an answer for you when the sun crests the horizon." The voice faded into the distance, leaving Aibek with the same sense of loneliness he associated with the Bokinna's absence.

Aibek cast a wary glance at the old man and strode back to the camp without another word. He spent an uneasy night, waking frequently to dreams of Pagi and others like him stealing the locket and its precious contents.

At long last, the first blush of dawn lit the horizon, and Aibek sat up and stretched. Bartel sat with his back to the fire, watching the road they'd traveled to the swamp's border. Nearby, Kai snored softly. Aibek didn't see Pagi anywhere.

"Where's the old man?" He asked Bartel.

"I think he was going to fetch us something to eat. Why?"

"I don't know. He seems nice enough, but I'm not sure if I should really trust him or not."

"Well, he's helped us so far, hasn't he?" Bartel turned and dropped another log on the dwindling fire.

Aibek sighed. "He has. I don't know. Maybe I'm being paranoid. I've been jumpy since we left the city."

He wished he could consult with his parents or

Valasa or Serik or anyone with more knowledge and experience than he had. He stared up at the brightening sky. The first and brightest moon, Koviom, hovered at the edge of the sky, ready to end its nightly trek from the eastern horizon to the west. The other two moons lit the western sky. Illodus was close to full, but Thrimanca was only at half-moon. Before all three were full again, the battle—and probably the war—would be over. Nervous anticipation built in Aibek's stomach. He hadn't exactly won the battle for Nivaka. In fact, without his parents' intervention, he would have lost everything. This time, he wouldn't be able to count on anyone else to come to his aid. He hoped all the training and practicing they'd done would be enough.

Finally, the sun crested the eastern horizon, casting the sky into pink and orange light and beginning a new day. Aibek stood and stretched. He nodded to Bartel and walked closer to the swamp, eager to hear the Saethem's decision and hopeful that she'd be less angry with the dawn.

He stood straight-backed, with his feet planted firmly and his hands clasped behind his back in the standard military stance and waited. Birds chirped. Something splashed into the water beyond the swamp's border. Small creatures rustled in the underbrush. Aibek kept his eyes fixed on the trees at his eye level. The sun climbed higher, and he considered calling for the Saethem. The memory of her harsh manner the night before kept him quiet.

"My sister confirms you are on her errand."

With his focus on the forest, the words startled Aibek, and it took a moment before he could respond. "Yes, madam. Will you help us?"

"I will, but I must warn you. When I shield you from the spirits, the ones from which you flee will follow your parents instead. You will be unable to call one without summoning the other."

Disappointment flared in Aibek, but he nodded. "I understand. What do I need to do?"

"Bring your friends to my border, but do not enter the swamp. My waters are nearly frozen, and you are not dressed for winter. I will shield you while my sister summons her servants to retrieve you and take you back to your camp."

"Thank you."

Aibek sprinted back to the camp, where Pagi had strung three squirrels over the fire. "Put it out. We're going now. We need to get back to the others."

Bartel and Kai cast him incredulous looks, but Pagi quietly kicked dirt over the fire. He didn't even attempt to save the partially-cooked meat.

"Am I going with you?" The old man asked when he'd extinguished the flames.

Aibek froze, undecided. "I don't know. I…"

The Saethem answered for him. "You may accompany them. They may well need your peculiar type of assistance."

Well, Aibek thought, at least I know Pagi's trustworthy if the Saethem wants him to go along.

"Come. The day grows bright and you have much

to do." This time, even Kai and Bartel heard the whispers on the wind.

Together, they stepped into the swamp's shadows and stepped carefully onto the bog's frozen path.

"That's far enough. Any further and you'll fall through."

Aibek stopped so abruptly that Kai walked into his back. Bartel chuckled, and Kai spun on him.

Aibek grabbed Kai's arm. "Save it for later."

Kai jerked his arm away from Aibek and straightened his linen shirt. He turned his back on Bartel, though, which was enough for Aibek.

The wind whipped around them as they waited for whatever the Saethem had planned. Aibek shivered and thought again of his warm cloak. He hoped no one had disturbed his little shack. Who had taken over in his absence? He should have appointed a second in command before he went into the city. He'd make that a priority as soon as he got back. The wind whistled through the barren branches overhead.

"They cannot follow you now," the Saethem whispered. "Follow the path to your right until the sun is directly overhead."

Aibek wished the ancient tree had allowed them breakfast but didn't voice a complaint. Instead, he did as she'd ordered and moved quickly and carefully along the trail. His stomach grumbled, but he didn't stop until a familiar rumbling echoed through the trees.

He peered into the sky, searching for Gworsad and the other dragons. When he spotted them, he broke into a sprint, racing toward a clearing large enough for the creatures to land.

The dragons' wings stirred the icy air and blew Aibek's hair into his face. He laughed and pushed it back before he rushed over to Gworsad.

"I've missed you." He patted the dragon's moss-draped shoulder.

"I scared they catch you," Gworsad answered. "Others came back, not you."

"We were captured, but we got away, then we had to come here to lose the trackers Helak set on us."

"I am good to see you." Gworsad rumbled happily and Aibek's smile broadened. "But we go back to camp. Your people scared for you."

Aibek nodded. "You'll have to ride with me," he told Pagi.

He helped Pagi up and climbed onto the dragon's back behind the odd little man. Aibek longed for the straps he and Faruz had fashioned to secure riders onto the dragons, but he'd have to hold on as he had the first few times he'd ridden on Gworsad's back. He leaned forward and showed Pagi to grab a handful of the mossy collar around Gworsad's neck. A heartbeat later, before Aibek had a handhold for himself, the dragon spread his massive wings and lifted them into the air. Aibek wobbled and clutched at the collar beside Pagi. He closed his eyes as the wintry wind bit into his cheeks and whipped his hair out behind him.

17.

Missing

Eddrick's shoulders slumped as his son vanished. "Well, I guess that's it."

"We'll see him again soon enough." Kiri slipped an arm over his shoulder. He drew strength from the determination in her voice. "For now, we have work to do if they're going to have any hope of a fair fight."

With a heavy sigh, Eddrick straightened his shoulders and nodded. "You're right. Let's go." He grabbed Kiri's hand in his right and Agommi's in his left. Glesni linked hands with Agommi and Kiri.

"Let's go home," Eddrick muttered.

The frozen swamp swirled around them, swallowed by the windy darkness that marked the passage of time and distance.

When he opened his eyes, the warm familiarity of home greeted him. A fire crackled on the hearth in the sitting room he'd shared with Kiri in life, though he couldn't feel its warmth. He squeezed Kiri's hand and let go of his father's. He drifted to his favorite chair and dropped into it, weary, but not sleepy. He hadn't slept in twenty years. He missed it. He considered the bed wistfully for a moment and turned back to the spirits filling the room.

"Well, I guess we've got a lot to learn." He met Glesni's eyes. "You said you can teach us to make a barrier—a wall of some sort to keep the spirits away from the living?"

"Yeeeeesssss," Glesni drew the syllable out. "But is this really the best time?"

"If we wait any longer, it'll be too late." Kiri threw her hands up. "Are you going to teach us, or do we have to try to figure it out on our own?"

Glesni closed his eyes and held his breath. Eddrick paced the floor between the fireplace and the chairs. The spirit's silent conversations with the ancients could last for hours.

The sky had turned dark and moonlight streamed through the window when Glesni looked up. "They say it is time. If we don't begin now it will be too late."

Eddrick stopped pacing and faced Glesni. "Well, we've been ready for hours. Let's get to it."

~ * ~

Ahren launched herself into constant target practice—she had become a rather good shot with her bow. When she wasn't at the archery range with the other bowmen, she let her aching muscles relax while she carved more animals from the carpenters' scrap wood. While she'd been in Kainga, an old man had shown her a new technique for working fur and feathers that had vastly increased the level of detail in her projects. She rested her head against the back of the sofa and dropped the half-completed hawk into her lap. Her shoulders burned and her back ached.

But no amount of physical exhaustion could erase that kiss from her mind. The heat of it warred with the strength of Aibek's arms around her that night on the bench outside the Pavilion. How could she want both? How would she ever choose?

She needed to talk to Tamyr. She wished she could see Aibek.

Her muscles burned as she pushed herself off the sofa and tucked the palm-sized hawk into her pants pocket. The soft zontrec folded around it, protecting and concealing the little shape.

She strode out the front door before her nerves could stop her. Ignoring the ache in her legs and back, she marched through the village toward the southern edge, where Tamyr lived in her wash house. The icy wind whipped at her hair and clothes, but Ahren ignored that, too. The cold air brought tears to her eyes, but she refused to wipe them away. They left frozen trails down her cheeks as they fell and dripped onto the boardwalk behind her.

When she spotted the wash house, she paused and smoothed her windblown hair and wiped her palms over her tear-stained cheeks.

The door opened before she stepped close enough to knock, and a group of wash women spilled out into the afternoon sun.

A woman with brilliant red hair smiled at Ahren. "Oh, are you looking for Tamyr?"

"Yes, is she inside?"

"No, we haven't seen her in a few days. Is she expecting you? Maybe she'll show up for your appointment."

"Well, if she does, you tell her she's in a heap of trouble." A woman with dark gray hair and weathered features scowled at Ahren. "She's got some talking to do if she wants her job back this time."

Ahren swallowed against the sinking feeling in her gut. "Yes, ma'am. If I find her, I'll let her know."

She waited until the women had cleared the doorway and made her way up to Tamyr's room. She already knew what she'd find. All of Tamyr's things were gone. Ahren's eyes lingered on the bare mattress, the quilts folded neatly at the end of the bed. Curiosity grabbed her, and she drifted to the chest of drawers beneath the small window. She paused there, her hands on the drawer pull, and watched a little green bird flitting from branch to branch outside the window. What would she do if Tamyr was truly gone? Had she met up with the ousted mayor again? Ahren hoped not.

The bird flew away and Ahren dropped her gaze back to the drawers. She slid the top one open, hoping for a note or... or, something.

Nothing but a small sachet occupied the drawer. Its sweet lavender scent drifted up to Ahren and brought fresh tears to her eyes.

She slammed the drawer closed and yanked open

the next one. Empty. So was the next one. And the last. Unable to help it, Ahren knelt on the bare wooden floor and peered into the dimness beneath the chest. Nothing but a tiny fleck of dust waited there.

Ahren grunted and pulled herself back to her feet. Her back and legs screamed in pain at the unusual movement. Fury, betrayal, and hurt battled in her chest. She crossed the room in a few strides and yanked the door open. She'd have to talk to Tamyr's family. Maybe one of them knew where she was. She ignored the little voice in the back of her mind that whispered she knew exactly where her friend had gone. She didn't want to believe it. She just couldn't.

Her mind reeled as she wandered out of the wash house and down the boardwalk to Tamyr's family's home. Ahren hesitated outside the door, her hand poised to knock. She already knew what they'd tell her. She shook herself and brought her hand down harder than she'd intended, pounding on the thin wooden door. The house wasn't as well-constructed as the ones at the center of town. Gaps showed between the walls and the door that allowed the warm air within to flow out and whisper along Ahren's face.

An older man with a stooped back and graying hair opened the door and glared down at Ahren. She smiled up at him and hoped he'd remember her, though she'd only met him once before.

"I'm sorry to bother you, sir, but I was wondering

if Tamyr was here. I…" she trailed off when the man's face flushed scarlet.

"Why are you looking for her? Why can't you all leave her alone?"

"I… I'm sorry." Ahren stuffed her hands in her pockets to ward off the winter wind and her fingers brushed the hawk. The tiniest spark of an idea grew in her mind. "I was working on something for her, and I wanted to make sure she liked the overall design before I spent any more time on it. Is she around?"

Tamyr's father heaved a great sigh and held the door open. "She's not here, but I can send for her, if need be. What is it you're working on?"

Ahren made a show of searching the room for Tamyr's other family members. When she was certain they weren't home, she pulled the hawk out of her pocket. "It's for her mother's birthday next month. I just wanted to make sure I had the right design, since the feathers take so much work."

He gave a low whistle and took the hawk from her. He examined the half-carved animal and handed it back to her. "I think she'll love that. There's no need to call Tamyr back for that."

Ahren stuffed the hawk back in her pocket. "Do you know where she is? I'm worried about her. She's been upset these last few weeks."

"I do. She'll be home before the battle. You've been a good friend to her." He pulled the door open and waved her through it. "I'll let her know you came by."

Ahren pulled her cloak tight around her shoulders and swept out into the bitter afternoon wind.

Restless and tense, Ahren hurried home to grab her bow. She needed the physical outlet of target practice to settle her whirling mind. Half an hour later, she drew the string back and let the first arrow fly. It hit dead center with a satisfying thwack. She didn't pause to enjoy the perfect shot, but instead nocked another arrow and let it fly. Another perfect shot. She repeated the process until she ran out of arrows and waited for those around her to finish their rounds, too. As a group, they climbed down the stairs and went to retrieve their arrows. One of the leaders followed her to her assigned target and watched her yank all her arrows out of its center. Distracted by the news of Tamyr's disappearance, she didn't look to see who it was.

"You're getting really good," he said when she'd replaced her arrows in her quiver. "Would you be interested in more of a challenge?"

Something akin to excitement pushed against the rage and hurt in her, and Ahren glanced up to see who had spoken.

"Faruz! I…" The sun blinded her when he shifted and she trailed off. She wanted to meet his eyes, but couldn't with the glare. "I didn't realize you were personally overseeing the practices. What kind of challenge?"

"I need another dragon rider. Zifa's convinced me to add her to our flying force, and she needs someone to train with. Do you think you could shoot like that from a dragon's back?"

"I don't know. I hadn't really considered joining the dragon riders. I…" She paused to consider. "You said Zifa's joining? I thought she was ill?"

Faruz swiped a hand over his neck. "Not exactly. She's been feeling better these past couple of weeks."

"Oh, well, I'm glad she's improving. I should come over and see her."

"She'd like that. So what do you think? Will you try flying with her?"

Ahren nodded. "I'll try it, but I'm not promising anything just yet. There's a reason I didn't volunteer in Kainga."

"That's all I'm asking." He glanced over his shoulder. "I think they're waiting for you, and I need to see how the spear-men are doing. You should come by tonight. Zifa'd love to see you now that her headaches are gone. I think she feels bad about pushing everyone away while she felt so bad."

"I'll come over after supper tonight, then." Ahren slung her quiver onto her back and climbed the stairs. She'd stood still too long, and the stiffness had settled back into her legs.

Faruz followed her up but kept walking into the village. Ahren spent another hour practicing before she headed home to rest and eat.

She inhaled the venison and root vegetables for supper without really tasting them. Hunger clawed at her stomach, strengthened by the physical exertion of target practice. She shoveled the food into her mouth without pausing to join the conversation that swirled around her. Nothing mattered but the food.

When she'd finally eaten her fill, she leaned back in her chair and tried to figure out what her family was talking about.

"If he doesn't come back soon, they'll have to rethink their entire strategy," her father said.

Her mother shrugged. "I'm sure he's fine. He knows that city better than anyone else. He's probably just being extra careful to make sure he's not followed."

"I hope so," her father answered.

Silence fell as her family turned their attention to the meal. Ahren struggled to decode the little bit she'd heard. Surely, they weren't talking about Aibek? But of course they were. No one else in that group knew anything about the city. She longed to know how long he'd been gone, but decided she'd ask Faruz when she went to visit her friend.

She cleared her dishes and carried them to the washbasin in the kitchen, complimented the cook, and headed out into the cold night air.

The wind whipped her unbound hair into her eyes. Ahren stopped to tuck it down into her collar before she dashed across the abandoned Square to Faruz's house. Zifa yanked the door open almost the instant Ahren knocked, and the warmth from the fire chased away the evening's chill. Ahren settled onto the couch beside her friend and examined Zifa's pale, skinny face. She'd lost even more weight since Ahren had last seen her.

"Are you well? Faruz said you're feeling better."

Zifa flushed and smiled. "I am. I can finally eat without feeling sick all the time."

"Did you figure out what's causing it? The poison's been gone from the trees for weeks now."

Zifa looked startled. Her eyes darted to Faruz. "He didn't tell you?"

"Tell me what? He just said you were finally feeling up to having visitors."

"I thought I'd let you tell her," Faruz murmured.

"Tell me what?" Ahren repeated, her voice a bit louder this time.

Zifa smiled, her face lighting up with joy. "I'm going to have a baby." She met Faruz's eyes. "We're going to have a baby."

Ahren's smile mirrored Zifa's. "That's wonderful!" She grabbed her friend in a tight hug but pulled back in alarm. Zifa's shoulders had grown so skinny and frail it was hard to believe she'd have the strength to walk, let alone fight from a dragon's back.

"Faruz said you're planning to fight?"

Zifa laughed. "Yes, I am. We've talked about it nearly every day. He tried to convince me to evacuate to Kainga, but I can't. I have to know what's happening to my home and my family. And if I'm going to be here—and I am—then I may as well fight."

Ahren opened her mouth to object, but Zifa cut her off.

"Now that I'm feeling better, I'm getting stronger every day. I even ate all of my supper tonight."

"Are you sure, though?" Ahren didn't want to hurt Zifa's feelings, but she looked so frail.

"I am." Zifa settled back against the cushions. "Really. I'm stronger than I was, and we have some time to train. Faruz said you've agreed to train with me?"

"I said I'll try it," Ahren said, though her convictions against flying were wavering. There was no way she'd let Zifa train or fight alone, not with as weak and skinny as she was. "I'm not convinced those beasts are safe."

"Faruz took me up with him a couple of times. It's magical. Just try it and I'm sure you'll love it. Besides, Faruz said he's got a couple of smaller dragons for us, but he swears they're just as fast as the others."

Ahren smiled again at the excitement in Zifa's voice. If it meant that much to her friend, she'd swallow her fears and learn to fight from the sky.

"Was your father all right with the idea?" Faruz asked.

"Oh, well, I didn't exactly ask. I, uh, missed most of the conversation at supper."

"That's all right. We have a council meeting in the morning, right? We can bring it up then. I'm sure he'll be fine with it."

"Speaking of my father, he said something tonight that had me worried. Is Aibek missing?"

Faruz sighed and leaned back in his chair. "Yes. He never came back from a spying expedition into the city. He has a few of the men with him, but the rest of them are getting nervous. I've told them Aibek knows how to escape the prison, but they're not as confident. If he doesn't turn up in the next few days, I'm afraid they may mutiny and come home."

"How do you know all this? When you were in the swamp, we couldn't get any information about you at all, but you seem to know everything that's happening all the way up at the city."

"When I went to the swamp, I didn't have the Bokinna's protectors with me. She can communicate with the dragons no matter where they are, so they pass messages back and forth between me and the dragon riders."

"But no one's heard anything from Aibek? How long has he been gone?"

"Excuse me just one minute." Zifa stood up and hurried out of the room.

"Is she really all right?" Ahren asked Faruz as soon as Zifa had turned the corner. "She's awfully skinny."

Faruz pressed his lips into a line. "She's doing better, and she is filling out a bit more now that she's eating again, but I worry. I wish she'd agree to evacuate with the others, but I understand why she won't. She'd go crazy sitting there waiting and wondering what's happening here."

"I can see that. Do you think the dragons will be safer than the fighters on the ground, though? What if she falls off?"

"That's why she needs a lot of training. We've designed a strap to keep the riders from falling off, but she needs to learn to handle the strain of flying. You'll stay close to her, right? With you as sniper, you should be able to keep her in the air and out of danger."

Ahren nodded. "I'll stay with her."

"Thank you." He smiled brightly when Zifa strolled back into the room.

"Sorry. What did I miss?"

"Not much. Ahren has agreed to be your training partner, so we'll start tomorrow afternoon if you're feeling well enough."

"Perfect." Zifa sat on the sofa and sank into the cushions. She closed her eyes and her pallor struck Ahren again.

"Well, I'm exhausted." Ahren stood and grabbed her cloak from its hook beside the door. "If I'm going to get near a dragon tomorrow, I need to get some sleep."

"Thank you for coming," Zifa said. "Don't be a stranger, all right? Now that I'm doing better, I want to spend time with my friends again."

Ahren nodded and ducked through the door. The temperature had dropped further, and the wind took her breath away. She ran the distance home and hurried to her room.

The next morning, Ahren headed to the archery range after breakfast. She'd lain awake most of the night, and what sleep she'd managed to steal had been plagued by nightmares of dragons and fire. Her hands shook at the thought of climbing onto the back of one of those giant beasts, but she couldn't back out now.

She drew and nocked an arrow even before she'd taken her place in front of the target. Pushing away the thoughts of dragons and flight, she drew the string taught and focused on the target. Someone had replaced hers with a much smaller one. The center circle was now smaller than a hummingbird's head. Ahren smiled at the challenge, adjusted her grip, and let the arrow fly. It hit a hair to the left of the new, smaller center circle.

Ahren sighed and drew another arrow.

"What do you think? Is it more challenging now?" The low voice sounded close behind her.

Ahren started and lowered her bow. In the same smooth movement, she swung around to see who had spoken.

"Faruz! You startled me. You shouldn't sneak up on people like that." She grinned and glanced around. Several other archers had stopped their practice and were watching her with interest. She slid her arrow back into the quiver and stepped away from the practice line.

Faruz lowered his voice. "Zifa's eager to get started. We have a council meeting this morning, but we can leave after the noon meal if that's all right with you."

"I..." Ahren choked on her answer, cleared her throat, and tried again. "Today? I, I guess that's all right. I didn't expect it to be so soon."

"I don't think we have much time before the

enemy reaches the forest. The sooner you start train-ing, the better."

"You're probably right. Have you found dragons for us already, then?" Ahren worked to keep the quiver out of her voice. Her fear wouldn't keep her friend safe, but training might.

Faruz nodded. "They're young, smaller than most of the others, but quick and agile. I think you'll get along well."

Ahren couldn't think of anything to say that wouldn't betray her terror, so she simply nodded.

"We'll meet at the south entrance after luncheon, then?"

She nodded again.

Faruz strolled off in the direction of the Square, and Ahren turned her attention back to the tiny target. She willed her hands to steady, nocked an arrow, and shot one arrow after another until her quiver sat empty. Every one hit the target. Only one landed out-side the two center rings. When the other archers had finished their round, they all headed down into the forest together to retrieve their arrows and reset their targets. Ahren repeated the exercise until the sun's position in the sky told her it was time for the meet-ing.

The council met in the Meeting Hall for a quick review of the villages' plans for the battle. Every-thing had already been settled, so they finished their business in less than half an hour. Afterward, Ahren returned to the practice field and shot arrow after arrow until her stomach growled.

The cool wind blew across her sweat-soaked face, chilling her and cooling the flushed skin. She unstrung her bow and headed toward home and what she was sure would be her last meal. Maybe she'd live to see supper, but she doubted it. Dragons weren't known for being the friendliest creatures in the forest—at least according to the lore she'd read in her father's library.

She barely tasted the cold rabbit and potatoes. Distracted and worried, she finished her meal and went to her room to change into a warm pair of leather pants and leather cloak. She was sure the wind would be cold, even if the dragon decided to cook her with its fire breath.

Without a word to her family, she left to meet up with Faruz and Zifa. When she reached the village entrance, though, she froze. All the dragon riders in the village had met there, and they stood in a cluster laughing and talking amongst themselves. She tried to find the nerve to stroll up and join them, but her legs refused to move.

Finally, after what felt like hours, Zifa's laugh drifted to her on the afternoon breeze. Ahren spun, searching for her friend, who strolled toward her beside Faruz.

"Are you ready? I can't wait!" Zifa's excited grin and flushed cheeks were almost enough to ease some of Ahren's terror. Almost.

Unable to force a reply, Ahren nodded. She was as ready as she was likely to get.

Faruz walked over to the assembled warriors and

raised his voice. "We've got a couple of new riders to train today. I'm going to have you all show them how to do the drills before you carry on with your own training."

A chorus of cheers and excited babbling followed the announcement, and the group expanded to envelop Ahren and Zifa.

Their smiles and welcoming hugs eased some of Ahren's nerves. These people had spent weeks with the dragons, and none of them had been eaten. She drifted along with the group until they reached the stream. Her fears redoubled at the rumbling sounds above. The dragons had arrived. The experienced riders stood just inside the trees and waited for their dragons to land. Small groups of three or four dragons landed and waited while their riders mounted, then lifted off again and were replaced by the next few dragons. Ahren's knees shook and her breath came in shallow gasps.

At last, all the riders had departed and only Ahren, Zifa, and Faruz waited in the forest. Three more dragons landed, one huge one and two that were about half the size of the big one. Faruz strolled up to the largest, patted it on its great, long neck, and murmured something Ahren couldn't hear. The beast grunted a reply, and Faruz turned back to the women.

"Zifa, this one is Ekys." He walked over to the middle dragon. It had a thorny collar, brilliant green eyes, and an eager expression that set off warning bells in Ahren's mind. "She'll be your partner dragon. She's as eager to join the warriors as you are."

Zifa walked up to the beast and talked to it softly. Ahren hung back, afraid to interfere in their initial bonding.

"Ahren, this one is your partner. Her name is Chyndri. She's a bit afraid of humans, but is eager to learn to work with us. Just be gentle with her, and I'm sure you'll get along well."

Ahren's mind worked to process the warning. How could such an enormous animal be afraid of her? What could she possibly do to threaten it?

"H— hello," the dragon chirped. The shy, hesitant voice made Ahren smile.

"Hello, I'm Ahren."

The dragon named Chyndri lowered her head to the ground and examined Ahren. "You're so tiny," she said at length.

Ahren patted the long, graceful neck extending above the dragon's shoulder and tried to slow her racing heart. Hundreds of leaf-like shapes covered the dragon's shoulders and back, making her look like a walking pile of dried autumn leaves.

"I am. I'm one of the smallest people in my village." Ahren ran her hand over the smooth, cold scales covering the dragon's leg. Each scale was the size of her palm, and each was a slightly different shade of green. The effect was a dazzling, shifting shine that made the dragon fade into the background. "Do your leaves turn green in the summertime? Or do they stay these lovely colors all year round?"

The question slipped out before Ahren could call it back. She held her breath and waited for a response, hoping she hadn't offended the dragon.

"Oh, they change to match the forest. I like them better in the summer. They're so sad and drab like this."

"All right," Faruz interrupted. "We'll have more time to get to know each other later. Let's get you mounted up."

Terror filled her stomach, and Ahren gulped and stared wide-eyed at the dragon's shoulders, more than an arm's length above her head.

"Here, I'll help you." Faruz's voice was soothing, as if he were talking to a frightened child.

The tone crashed over Ahren like a bucket of ice water. She squared her shoulders and brought herself up to her full height. She ran her hands over the dragon's smooth scales, searching for something to grab onto. Nothing. Frustration budded in her mind. She tried stepping up onto a downed log, but that didn't help any at all.

After several eternal moments of searching, she gave up. Her shoulders slumped as she turned to Faruz for help.

His cheerful laugh didn't help her mood any.

"Don't look so put out." He laughed again when she rolled her eyes. "No, really. We all needed a bit of help our first time or two. At least Chyndri's not picking you up by your pack and dropping you into place like Gamne did me."

Ahren cast a glance at the dragon's dagger-like

teeth and silently agreed she'd rather have Faruz's help.

Swallowing the bitter taste that rose in her throat, she turned and stepped into Faruz's cupped hands. He lifted her foot as she reached upwards, and the combined movement was enough to swing her up onto the dragon's back. Or rather, onto Chyndri's neck just in front of her shoulders. If Ahren had sat any further back, she'd have to splay her legs straight out to the sides, and she didn't think she was quite that flexible.

Faruz flipped the end of a long black strap up to her, and she held it tightly while he wound it around Chyndri's chest and shoulders, looping it over Ahren's legs and around her waist as he went. When he'd finished, she tucked her end under the part across her leg and pulled it tight. That finished, she waited while Faruz tested the strap with a series of sharp tugs. She kept her eyes carefully trained on the dragon's neck in front of her. She worried if she looked anywhere else, she'd lose her nerve and run screaming back to the village.

She sat without moving or blinking and waited while Faruz strapped Zifa onto her dragon and climbed onto his own. When he'd finished, he gave a shout and her stomach fell into her toes. Dizziness assailed her as the cold wind buffeted her face. Ahren clenched her eyes shut against the rush of icy air and tried to hold her breath. The dizziness hit her like a wave of misery and she fought against the rising nausea. Worried she was about to either pass out or vomit, she opened her eyes and drew a deep, gasping breath.

The sound and movement drew the dragon's attention, and the creature swung her broad head around to peer at Ahren through one brilliant green eye.

"You all right? Your color... wrong." Chyndri chirped something more, and Ahren had the impression the dragon was trying to convey her concern.

"Yes, I'm fine. Really," she added when the green eye narrowed. Sun glinted off the facets of the lizard-like iris and glowed back from unfathomable depths, pinning Ahren in place. "Really." Ahren dropped her gaze to the black strap cutting across her thighs and hoped the dragon hadn't seen how unnerved she was.

Somewhere nearby, Zifa whooped with joy. The sound drowned out Ahren's discomfort and a fresh wave of shame washed over her. She really hadn't given the dragon or flying a chance.

Slow inch by inch, she pulled her gaze away from the scales around the black strap and raised her head until the horizon came into focus. Her vision swam, and she blinked away the wind-blown tears and tried again.

If she deliberately kept her gaze away from the ground, the beauty of the forest stretching away to the river and beyond took her breath away.

From that moment on, Ahren tried not to blink. Instead, she stared in wonder at the landscape flying past below her, though she couldn't look straight down without experiencing a wave of dizzy nausea. The minutes flew by with the trees, and soon they slowed and circled over a wide clearing on the banks of the churning river. One by one, the dragons folded their wings and dove into the empty space at breakneck speeds. They slowed and adjusted at the last second, so they landed softly instead of crashing into the stony ground.

Ahren gulped and fought to slow her ragged breathing. Blackness edged her vision, and she clung to the straps over her legs.

Chyndri swung her head back to meet Ahren's terrified gaze. "You ready to land?"

Unable to force words out of her dry mouth, Ahren nodded. They had to land eventually and waiting would only make it worse.

The dragon tucked her massive wings and dove. Ahren's vision swam and her stomach lodged firmly in her throat. Ahren couldn't get a breath with the icy wind buffeting her face, but that only kept her from screaming. A heartbeat later, dizziness hit her again as Chyndri spread her wings and set her feet on the ground.

Ahren couldn't move. It was all she could do to breathe. Her hands shook too badly to undo the straps, so she sat motionless atop her dragon and waited for further instructions.

A shout pierced the air, followed by a laughing scream. Zifa's dragon landed beside Ahren an instant later. Zifa's face was flushed, and a joyful smile lit up her features. Ahren worked to hide some of the terror that must have been written on her own face.

Before Ahren could say anything to her friend,

Faruz stepped into the center of the group and shouted his instructions. "We're going to start with some basic drills today, because we have two new archers among us. I need you to show them the drills and how to work with the team."

"Aren't you going to introduce us?" A man shouted. Ahren couldn't tell which rider had interrupted.

"Later. For now, we need to get started. Archers, your targets are set up on the north course. Spearmen and swordsmen, you're going south for now. I'm going with the archers to make sure our new riders catch on."

Right. Archery. Ahren had forgotten about the bow and quiver strapped to her back. She reached back and ran a finger over the bow's smooth wood but didn't pull it from its strap. From what Faruz had said, they'd be flying somewhere else for that.

Small groups of two and three dragons took off side-by-side and vanished over the treetops. They split in two directions, but Ahren kept her eyes on the ones with bows. None of the archers had their bows on their backs like hers. Some had a modified quiver attached to the strap over their legs, while others held theirs across their laps. All had their bows already strung.

Ahren pulled hers loose and wrestled the string into the notch at the end of the wooden limb. It took her several minutes, and by the time she'd finished, only she and Zifa remained beside the river. Chyndri chirruped once and took to the sky, but this time, Ahren was ready. She closed her eyes while the dragon climbed so she wouldn't get dizzy from the trees rushing by. When they leveled out and flew in one direction, Ahren opened her eyes and watched the forest glide by.

The ride ended far too soon when the line of dragons they followed dipped below the barren canopy. Ahren watched the first two dip and cocked her head in confusion when they reappeared above the trees a heartbeat later. The other dragons followed suit, and Ahren strained to see what the challenge was.

Too soon, it was her turn to swoop into the forest. Four targets had been set up around a narrow clearing, each the size of an average man.

Ahren froze. *Are they wearing armor?*

The dragon drew closer and she realized it was only paint, but all the arrows sprung from the unpainted parts of the targets. Those represented the areas a real foe would be vulnerable to an arrow shot from above.

The wind whipped her hair into her eyes, but she brushed it aside. She nocked an arrow and pulled the string back to her cheek in one smooth movement. She released it an instant too late, however, and the arrow landed harmlessly in the brown grass beside the dummy. She scanned the area, searching for any other stray arrows, but saw none and cursed under her breath. Before she could reach for another arrow, Chyndri flapped her great wings and pulled up out of the forest and back into the line of dragons circling above.

Leaning forward, Ahren stretched her arm out and touched Chyndri on the side of her neck. The dragon swung her head around and met Ahren's gaze with her unfathomable gold-flecked eyes.

Before she could lose her nerve, Ahren blurted out, "Could we get closer? I want to see how they do it."

Chyndri rumbled and chirruped, and nearby dragons repeated the sounds. Ahren watched, her head cocked to one side as the dragons conversed—she couldn't think of anything else that could be happening. They had to be discussing her request. They hummed and chirped and rumbled until Ahren's insides vibrated from the noise.

Without warning, Chyndri dipped and dove beneath the treetops, whipping through the branches and back toward the clearing so fast that Ahren had to duck to keep from being slapped by branches. She settled onto the ground a dozen paces from the center target. From that vantage point, Ahren could see all the targets and would be able to tell where the archers were when they let their arrows fly.

The dragons swooped into the clearing at breakneck speed, and their riders shot their arrows with deadly precision. It happened so fast Ahren missed the archers' movements the first two times. She narrowed her eyes and focused hard on the spot the dragons had descended from, waiting impatiently for the next archer to shoot.

That time, she saw the exact moment when the dragon reached the bottom of its descent and the rider loosed her arrow. It flew true and hit the target in the unprotected neck. Ahren settled back and watched the next several archers repeat that technique.

When she was certain she knew when to shoot, she murmured, "Let's give it a try."

Chyndri didn't make a sound, but stretched her wings and lifted Ahren into the sky. She drew an arrow and held it lightly to the bowstring, but her fingers twitched in anticipation. She held her breath and her arm taut until her dragon dropped into the clearing.

The first release point passed before she could react, but she let loose on the second and her arrow hit in the center of the chest. It stuck straight out of the dark brown, painted breastplate. A thrill of excitement shot through her at the same time as a pang of disappointment. Yes, she'd hit the target, but that hit wouldn't have had an impact on a real foe. Faruz had been right. This was much more challenging than target practice from the boardwalk. She ran through the steps in her mind until it was her turn to try again. That time, she hit the dummy in the shoulder.

Better, but not quite up to the others' standard, yet. She tried to remind herself that this was only her first day, but she'd been among the best of the ground archers and she wasn't used to being behind. Frustration mounted as she practiced. She didn't seem to be getting any more accurate at all, though she did hit the target every time.

By the time the dragons left the clearing and headed back to the beach where they'd originally assembled, Ahren's back, legs, and arms ached and shook from the effort of staying on the dragon. The straps helped, for sure, but when Chyndri dove and turned, she felt herself slip a bit to the side and clamped her legs down on the dragon to hold tight.

Faruz waited at the tree line and stepped forward when Chyndri landed. He helped Ahren undo the straps and held her arm while she climbed gingerly off the dragon. After so long astride the dragon, she wobbled when her feet hit the uneven ground. She staggered for a couple of steps before she righted herself and walked three steps to a small boulder. Her knees wouldn't hold her any longer and she collapsed down onto it. Someone chuckled nearby, but Ahren ignored it. Elation finally won the tug of war with frustration and a huge grin split her face. She'd ridden a dragon! And she'd successfully hit a target from a dragon's back in flight! She'd have more time to practice and would get the hang of aiming quickly, she was certain.

18.

Camp

Early the next morning, Gworsad swung far west of the camp and circled back down from the north. Aibek said nothing. He just assumed the dragon knew where the enemy watches were, while he'd been away too long to know anything of the enemy's movements.

While they flew, he worried. What exactly would Pagi's role be in his army? How would he keep the strange little man from getting killed in the approaching combat?

He glanced down at Pagi's face, filled with wonder and split with a wide grin, and turned his attention to what he'd find when he arrived back at the camp. How had his warriors managed with their leader gone for so long? Sure, he had a chain of command in place, but he'd brought his next two leaders with him into Xona. Vayna was strong, both as a man and as a leader, but what if the others wouldn't follow him? He'd have his answers soon enough, he decided. He shoved the worries aside and watched the golden landscape pass beneath him. The tall grasses moved like the sea in the gentle morning breeze.

As they'd flown north, the air had warmed, and he'd stopped shivering for the first time in days. He held on tight when Gworsad dove toward the cave and wished again for the straps that held him in place during tough maneuvers during battle training. His heart fluttered when Gworsad came to rest on the stony ground outside the abandoned mine they'd chosen as their camp.

"Aibek! You're alive!" Vayna's voice boomed from the mouth of the cave a breath before Aibek saw his friend.

Since he didn't want his grand entrance to include falling off the dragon, Aibek didn't answer until he'd dismounted and landed firmly on his feet.

"We're alive." He helped Pagi off Gworsad's back and gestured to the other dragons approaching. "This is Pagi. He's with us now." He paused and added, "Thankfully, my professors at the academy made sure all their students knew how to escape from that prison."

Vayna slapped him hard on the back and laughed. "We're just cooking before we get some training in. Have you eaten?"

The scent of cooking meat wafted out of the cave, and Aibek's stomach rumbled loudly.

"I'll take that as a no." Vayna put an arm around Aibek's shoulders and pushed him into the cave. A glance told him Pagi had followed close behind. Each person they passed shouted a welcome. Several left the cave to welcome Kai and Bartel back to the camp.

Aibek paused just inside and waited for his eyes to adjust to the dim light. As soon as he could see well enough to distinguish faces, he scanned the room, searching for Marah. He checked every shadowed nook but came up empty.

"She's out flying overhead, looking for you," Vayna said.

Aibek tried to mask his disappointment, but he must have failed, because Vayna blurted, "Don't worry. She'll be back soon, since the local farmers are usually getting up right about now."

Heat flushed his face at the realization that he'd been so obvious, and Aibek shifted his attention to the fire. "What's for breakfast? I'm starved." He stared at the skillets sizzling above the fire, and his eyes widened. "Is that fish? What's the occasion?"

With a laugh, Vayna waved him over to the fire and settled down before it. He handed Aibek and Pagi chunks of steaming fish on wooden plates before he answered. "It's easier to fish here than hunt. We've been eating more fish than anything else since you've been gone."

Unable to think of a suitable response, Aibek took another bite of fish. He'd missed this staple of life in the north and wouldn't complain if he had fish all three meals every day until he returned to the forest.

Halfway through his meal, Aibek noticed that Pagi hadn't settled onto the ground, but had instead crouched near the fire. His stance made him look ready to run at the slightest hint of danger.

Aibek shifted closer but kept his voice down. "Are you all right? You don't look very comfortable."

"I can't hear the trees here. There's no Zirvesi, no forest, no whisper on the wind."

"I know." Aibek put an arm out, beckoning the little man closer to the fire. "It makes me uncomfortable, too. The dragons can still hear the Bokinna, though, and they pass messages between us. That helps a bit."

Pagi turned to stare at the enormous dragons that filled most of the cavern.

A commotion at the entrance drew Aibek's attention. Kai's laugh announced that the others had landed. The rest of the warriors drew Kai and Bartel to the fire, where they dropped to sitting and dug into their breakfast of fish with exclamations of surprise. Aibek watched quietly, happy to be back with his friends.

"Aibek! You're back! I knew you'd come back!" Marah's shrill voice brought a wide smile to his face.

Aibek turned in time to see her before she collided with his chest. She clung to him with a strength that surprised him and buried her face in his neck. In that instant, Aibek realized he hadn't bathed in nearly a week, and he gently pulled back.

"It's good to see you, too." He glanced around, heat flushing his face when he saw every face turned to watch their reunion.

"Is the little shack still private?"

Marah's grin hit him like a fist in the gut. "It sure

is. Vayna wouldn't allow anyone in there until you came back."

"As eager as I know you are to welcome him back, Marah," Vayna broke off with a cough that sounded a bit more like a stifled laugh. "Aibek needs to meet with the rest of us first. He needs to know what we've learned since he's been gone, and we need to come up with some plans."

Disappointment surged within him, but Aibek sighed. "He's right." He dropped his voice to a whisper. "We'll have plenty of time later."

His stomach fluttered in anticipation, but he turned back to Vayna and settled back down beside the fire. He tried to hide the little thrill of delight that went through him when Marah followed and sat between him and Kai.

The discussion went longer than Aibek had anticipated. His friends had spent their time wisely and had gained insight into the daily lives of those within the city, but they hadn't managed to learn anything about the enemy's plans or timeline. He spent the rest of the day training with Gworsad, though he stopped at the stream to wash before heading back to camp. He finally dragged himself to his shack as the sun sunk below the horizon. Exhaustion made his legs heavy, and he trudged up the incline from the cave to the shack with his head down.

He sank onto the straw mattress and pulled off his boots, but before he could lie down, all the worries and fears he'd ignored for days assailed him. His friends were counting on him to lead them into battle, but he'd gotten captured on his second attempt to spy in the city. He stood and paced the floor, trying to piece together a plan.

Doubts leaked through, despite his efforts to focus on workable tactics. He longed to talk to Serik, but the thought of his friend ripped an aching wound open in his chest. He sank onto the bed, gasping for breath. He'd give anything to hear Serik's voice telling him what to do, reminding him not to do anything stupid, or just helping him think through a battle plan. Cradling his head in his hands, he struggled to stem the tide of memories flooding his mind. Serik had always had faith in him, even when he hadn't deserved it. And the old man had beamed like a proud father after the battle for Nivaka's freedom, even though Aibek essentially lost that battle. Only the last-minute intervention by the ancestors had kept the villagers from being slaughtered by Helak's army.

A knock on the door brought Aibek out of his memories and off the bed. He drew a shaky breath, attempted to wipe some of the emotion from his face, and crossed the tiny room to the worn wooden door. Marah's blonde curls picked up the orange light of the sunset, making them look like flames dancing around her face. Her amber eyes held concern.

"Are you all right? You look upset."

Aibek held the door open and backed into the room, inviting her in. "I'm all right. Just a bit worried. I wish we had a better plan."

Marah nodded and stepped closer. "I'm so glad

you're back. I was so worried." She wrapped her arms around his middle and pressed her face to his chest. "We'll all get together in the morning and work out the details, but I think we have a pretty solid start. It's going to be tough, though."

He set his cheek on the top of her head and held her close for a long while, letting go only when she pulled away and backed toward the bed.

The morning dawned bright and clear, and the early sun shone right through the window and into Aibek's eyes. He rolled away from the glare and stretched, reaching for Marah, but his arm met only cold blankets. Disappointment and loneliness surged through him. He stretched once more and pushed himself out of bed. The cool morning air brought clarity to his mind, and he inhaled deeply. The faint scent of fish cooking reached his nose.

Grinning at the prospect of fresh fish for breakfast, he stretched again, dressed quickly, and hurried to join his friends in the cave.

Before he ate, he sought out Pagi, and found him huddled in the shadows at the far end of the cave.

"Are you all right?" He crouched beside the odd little man.

"I… I don't like the silence here. Do not worry yourself about me, though. The Saethem said the dragons can communicate with the sister. Is that correct?"

"Yes."

"Do you think it would be too much to ask if I

could pass a message to Zirvesi, the brother, who I follow?"

"I think that's reasonable. I can't see why they'd object, though it's up to the dragons, of course."

At that, Pagi finally raised his eyes from the floor and peered at Aibek. "Do they not obey you?"

Aibek couldn't contain a laugh. "No, they obey the Bokinna, not me. They're only here because she asked them to help us."

"Oh." Pagi went quiet and returned to scratching shapes into the stone floor with a pebble.

"Did you get something to eat?" Aibek asked gently.

"I did. I went with the fishers early this morning to try to reach one of the beings. Of course, it was for naught, but I got to spend some time with your people. They are good people. Good hearts. You have chosen your friends well."

Aibek smiled again. "I know. I couldn't have asked for better." His stomach rumbled, and he stood. "If it's all right with you, I'm going to get some fish and spend the morning developing some solid plans. I'd appreciate any insight you may have."

Pagi grunted, and Aibek wasn't sure if that was an answer or just an acknowledgment of his request.

Once he'd eaten his fish and lamented the absence of famanc, Aibek gathered the other warriors and spent the next several hours working out several battle plans and contingencies. By the time they broke for noon training, Aibek felt much better about the coming battle. The fighters from the Tsari were only a few days away, and the dragon riders would wait for them before they struck. Once the backup warriors had arrived, the dragons would attack the south gate, force it open, and the two segments would work together to take back the city. Aibek still worried—there were so many things that could go wrong—but the awful panicky feeling in his gut had settled.

19.

Trouble

"Captain, I have an urgent report."

Faruz looked up from the note on his desk and waved the young man into his study.

"Sorry to interrupt, but the scouts have found an enemy camp just outside the forest, sir."

A deep sense of foreboding rippled through him, and Faruz set down his pen. "Where? How far?"

"Two miles from the forest on the northern border, sir."

"Thank you. Could you gather the council members for me? We'll need to discuss this. Just have them meet me in here."

The boy's brilliant blonde hair dropped into his face with the force of his nod. "Yes, sir."

Faruz hoped the young man—who couldn't have been more than fifteen—would live to see the end of the coming battle.

With a sigh, he turned back to his letter. He needed to meet with Queen Idril and King Turan one more time before the battle, and he wasn't looking forward to it without Aibek or Serik there to soften relations.

The soft scratch of pen on paper filled the room while he waited for the others. When he'd finished his note, he set it aside to dry and capped his ink bottle. A bird playing on the windowsill caught his attention, and he watched the light shine off its blue and red plumage while it hopped and chased insects flying nearby.

"Why are we meeting here instead of the room in Valasa's house or the Meeting Hall?" Wayra's voice brought Faruz back to the moment.

"The scouts found something. I don't want to alarm everyone until we've had a chance to discuss it and maybe investigate for ourselves." He leaned over to see around Wayra and into the hall. "Are the others with you?"

"They're coming. Ahren just got back from training, and the others are finishing their luncheon."

"Oh, no. I forgot about Zifa's lunch." He grimaced. She wouldn't be happy he'd missed it.

"It was fun. I wish you'd been there. I know you're busy, but it was almost like before, when we could all spend a day together without planning for war."

"I guess I must have missed that. I showed up as part of the war plan, remember?" Faruz chuckled and hoped he'd get to experience that kind of relaxed friendship once this battle was over.

Wayra and the messenger exchanged awkward smiles, but an uncomfortable silence fell.

Voices in the corridor announced the arrival of the other council members, and Faruz stood. Ahren, Zifa, and Dalan strolled into the room, laughing and chatting. He dismissed the messenger and waited until they'd settled into chairs before he spoke.

"The scouts found an enemy camp not far from the northern border. I'm going immediately to investigate. Who's going with me, and who's staying here?"

Everyone chimed in that they'd go along. Irritation scratched at him like a woolen sweater, and he shook his head. "We can't all go. If we're caught, someone has to be here to run things."

"He's right," Zifa's voice was barely audible. "I'll stay."

The others met each other's eyes over the narrow room, but no one else volunteered to stay behind. At length, Ahren let out a sigh. "This isn't working. We should draw straws to see who stays. We need more than one person in the village. I'm the best sniper you've got, so I'm going. Dalan? How would Father react if you got caught?"

Dalan scowled at his sister. His lips pressed to a line, and his blue eyes flashed. Faruz marveled that the young man could keep quiet through the fury evident on his features.

"I'll stay," Wayra said. "Someone has to be here to run things if you screw up and get caught." He laughed, and Faruz smiled back at him.

Dalan huffed and leaned back in his chair. "I guess I'll stay with Wayra. Ahren's right. My father needs me here."

"Well," Faruz let out a sigh and met Ahren's defiant gaze. "I guess it's just the two of us. Meet me back here in an hour."

The council members filed out, and Faruz hoped Ahren wasn't about to put a dagger in his back. She'd made no secret of her animosity toward him and Aibek, though she had been tolerably friendly in the previous few weeks. At least she enjoyed training with the dragons. He considered flying to the enemy camp on the dragons but discarded that idea almost as soon as it occurred to him. He didn't want an enemy to see the dragons yet. He'd save them for a special surprise in battle.

Two hours later, he and Ahren hid behind close-packed trees at the northern edge of the forest, staring out at the enemy camp. He took a silent count of the tents he could see, though the camp stretched over a low hill and disappeared from sight. His gut clenched at the size of the camp. There were far more than he'd expected—perhaps too many for his little army to fight off. He signaled for Ahren to follow him back into the forest.

He didn't speak until he was almost halfway home, out of fear that an enemy scout might hear them. When he was sure they were safe, he stopped and met Ahren's worried gaze.

Ahren spoke first, her words echoing his own thoughts. "We have to do something to weaken their force, or we don't stand a chance."

"What can we do?"

Anxiety creased her features, and she shrugged, her hands raised in a helpless gesture.

"Let's get back and meet with the others. Maybe someone will have an idea."

Faruz led the way back to Nivaka and up the stairs. When he reached his study, he sent a runner to summon Wayra and Dalan, and asked the housekeeper to bring Zifa to him.

They all arrived within minutes of each other, and Faruz explained what they'd seen.

"What if we just ask the dragons to burn them up?" Wayra offered. "That would solve it."

Faruz smiled, but said, "No, we can't ask that of them. The Bokinna said they can help us defend the forest, but that means waiting for them to make the first move."

"Well, Aibek tried giving them usartma," Zifa leaned forward, her eyes intense. "And that helped a little, but what if we gave them something stronger?"

"Like what?" At Wayra's interruption, Zifa glared.

"I was thinking, what if Valasa had some kind of poison we could slip into their food supply? You know they're not feeding an army that size off rabbits and birds."

"I don't think my father would agree to something like that." Dalan stood and stretched. "He wasn't happy when he found out we stole his potion to poison Tavan's guards."

"It wouldn't hurt to ask, though, would it?" Zifa pressed.

"There's no point. It goes directly against everything the Gadonu's post stands for. He heals—never hurts. That's why I haven't officially started my apprenticeship yet; I want to fight, and the Gadonu can't." Dalan's voice held a note of finality that brought an uncomfortable silence to the room.

"Well, what other options do we have?" Faruz asked after a long pause.

Ahren leaned forward. "What about fairy wine? It would be easy to slip into their rain barrels. We've all felt what happens the next day. It doesn't even take much."

"Do we have enough to poison an army, though?" Wayra's eyes shone with interest, but his words sounded doubtful. "That would take a lot of wine."

No one spoke for a long moment.

"Well, we don't, but what about the other villages?" Zifa sounded uncertain. "If each village pitched in a barrel or two, I bet we'd have enough."

Faruz smiled at his wife. "That's a great idea, Zifa. We should send messages to the other villages and see how much they can spare."

Faruz scribbled on the paper in front of him and glanced around the room. "Who has an idea of how we can get that much wine through the forest without detection? Or any other ideas? What other illnesses could knock the soldiers down a notch? The Bokinna tells me the army probably won't have the spirits for help this time."

And neither will we. He kept that last thought to himself. He didn't know if Aibek had explained their bizarre victory to the others.

The rest of the afternoon passed in debate and deliberations as the council members tossed ideas around and tried to come up with a workable plan.

~ * ~

Two days later, Ahren tapped her toe while she waited for Faruz at the northern entrance. She shifted the heavy pack, trying to ease the strain on her shoulders. Fairy wine was heavier than she'd expected.

An eternity passed, and the sun crept over the horizon, painting the sky with pink and orange light. A family of monkeys swung through the trees beyond the boardwalk rail, stealing Ahren's attention from her irritation. She couldn't stifle a laugh when one of the babies tried to run away down the branch and the mother caught the infant by the tail and kept it from getting lost.

"What's so funny?"

Ahren spun, her hand flying to her chest. "Faruz! You shouldn't sneak up on people like that. It's not very nice." She didn't wait for a response but swept past him to the entrance and pulled the lever to lower the stairs.

"Sorry. I didn't mean to scare you. What were you so focused on?"

Heat suffused Ahren's face and she kept her eyes on the stairs as they fell in slow motion towards the mossy forest floor.

"Just a group of monkeys. Nothing that should have kept me from hearing you walk up."

"I still haven't gotten used to the monkeys here. Were there babies? I love watching the babies run and play."

Ahren smiled at the effort he was making. She really had overreacted. She blushed again. "Yeah.

The one baby tried to run off, but the mother caught it by the tail. It was so funny trying to pull loose."

They chatted about monkeys and other wildlife while they walked, and they reached the edge of the forest faster than Ahren expected.

"The villages are so close together now," she commented when they approached the shade of another, smaller village.

"Yes. I think we're almost done moving."

"You mean almost in our battle positions." Ahren's voice fell flat. She didn't want to admit how scared she was of this battle. The last one had terrified her, and it had only involved their one tiny village. This one would include the entire forest, and if they failed, the Bokinna herself would likely perish.

"Well, yeah…" He trailed off as they neared the tree line and bright sunlight filtered through the trees.

They fell silent and crept closer to the forest's border. Ahren's breathing came in raspy breaths, as if she'd been running, and she worked to calm her racing heart.

Faruz stopped near the edge of the forest and waited for her to catch up. When she was close beside him, he whispered, "Stay in this area and see if you can locate a few water barrels. I think they must have them scattered through the camp."

She nodded her understanding.

"I'm going a bit further to see if I can get a better look at the officers' tents."

Apprehension warred with panic in her gut as Ahren watched Faruz slip away through the trees, leaving her alone within earshot of the enemy soldiers.

When he'd vanished into the depths of the forest, she turned her attention back to the camp. A patrol approached her position, and she ducked behind her tree and waited until their footsteps faded. Since she didn't know how often they passed that spot, she decided not to move closer. She wouldn't be of any help to anyone if she got caught.

From her hiding spot, she could see into the camp between a row of tents. While some soldiers busied themselves with mundane tasks such as shining their shoes, others cooked over fires or sharpened an arsenal of weapons. Still others lounged nearby, making conversation with those who worked.

They must be waiting for their turn to patrol, Ahren guessed, thinking back to how Tavan's guards had behaved during their rule in Nivaka.

Distracted by her thoughts and unaware of how much time slipped by, she forgot to listen to what the nearest soldiers said, until someone called out a familiar name.

"Tamyr, are you finished with that washing yet?"

Ahren froze. Surely, it couldn't be the same Tamyr. It wasn't an uncommon name, she reasoned. It had to be someone else.

She leaned forward, unable to stop herself.

In the tent to her right, something clattered to the ground. The flap snapped like a sail as the person inside came dashing out into the sunlight.

Tamyr—her Tamyr—emerged into the narrow space Ahren could see, a basket propped against her hip.

"I'm nearly done folding it, but if you're so impatient, you can do it yourself." She plopped the basket onto the ground beside the soldier, sending up a puff of dust that carried away on the breeze. She vanished back into the tent amid a chorus of raucous laughter and jibes aimed at the abashed soldier.

Weak from the shock of seeing Tamyr amid the enemy, Ahren sank to her knees and pressed her back against the tree, the camp sprawling out behind her. She sat there unmoving, until Faruz returned and tapped her on the shoulder.

"Are you hurt?"

Ahren leapt to her feet, shaken. When she'd regained enough composure to speak, she said, "No, I'm fine. Let's get home."

Concern showed on Faruz's features, but he nodded and grabbed her pack. They hid the bags of fairy wine in the tree branches, where the groundfolk could easily find it, and turned toward home. Ahren had been as surprised as anyone else in the village when King Turin and Queen Idril had agreed to take part in poisoning the enemy, but she was glad they had. It meant she didn't have to sneak into the camp.

Ahren fought the urge to fidget while they walked home, instead forcing her arms to her sides. A knot of anxiety twisted in her gut. She couldn't get Tamyr's face out of her mind. The memory of their one heated embrace burned in her memory, but she shoved it aside. She had to let the others know they'd been betrayed, didn't she?

Betrayed. The word hung in her thoughts and knocked the breath from her lungs. Tamyr had gone to the enemy, knowing it would endanger her family and friends, knowing what it would mean for Ahren, knowing it would end any chance of Ahren taking on the mayoralty—a goal Tamyr had pressed for months, but Ahren had resisted. The more she thought, the less she worried. There really was only one choice to make, no matter how hard it would be.

Without a word, Ahren followed Faruz into the village and to the sitting room on the third floor of her home. The others lounged in chairs, sipping famanc and snacking on small cakes, oblivious to Ahren's inner turmoil.

Faruz took his place at the front of the room, and Ahren slipped past him and settled into a soft chair in the far corner. She knew what she had to do, but she had no idea how to do it without shattering into a thousand pieces. How could Tamyr have betrayed her like that? How was she supposed to tell the others?

When her father had called the meeting to order, he gave Faruz the floor.

"I have some disturbing news from today's trip to the enemy camp. I'm afraid someone has given all our secrets to the enemy."

Ahren gasped, but the exclamations of the others covered the soft sound. Had he seen her, too?

Dalan stood and clenched his fists at his sides.

"How is that possible? Who would've done such a thing?"

"You all remember our visitor from a few weeks back? The mayor who blamed Aibek for his removal from office?" Every head in the room nodded. "Well, I saw him in the camp today. He warned us that was his plan. Perhaps we should have taken him more seriously."

"How much does he know?" Dalan asked quietly. "Do we have any secrets left?"

"I don't know for sure how much he knows. He was in the meetings in Kainga. He was included in all the messages about the dragons and training. I think it's best to assume he's traded our strategic information for clemency with Helak's forces."

Stunned, Ahren sat, frozen. Could she be off the hook? As long as the others knew their plans had been leaked, did she really have to tell them about Tamyr? She bit the inside of her cheek and knotted her fingers in her lap. The beginnings of a plan dawned in her mind, but she sat quietly while the others discussed their options.

Several hours later, the council broke up and headed to their respective homes. Ahren bypassed the kitchen and went straight to her room. She didn't think she'd be able to force any food past the anxious lump in her chest, anyway.

She mumbled incoherent thoughts and bits of plans as she paced her room, too restless to sit still. A soft knock at the door brought her back to the present.

Traitorous tears had broken loose and streamed down her cheeks, and Ahren swiped at them before she swung the door open. Her brother stood in the darkened hall, a worried expression on his pale features.

"Can I come in? I know there was something you wanted to say in the meeting, but you got overshadowed by Faruz's news. Is everything all right? Do you know something more?"

Ahren heaved a sigh and opened the door wider, waving her brother into the room. She settled onto the chaise and let him have the high-backed chair by the window.

The silence stretched, a palpable, painful thing, until Ahren couldn't take anymore. "I saw Tamyr in Helak's camp. I…I caught her sneaking out of the village to see Kaskin before she disappeared, and I didn't say anything because I hoped I was wrong, but I'm not, and now she's told the enemy everything she knows, which is everything because I thought she was my friend and told her all our ideas."

"Well," Dalan stood and handed her a handkerchief, but turned to stare out the window instead of sitting back down. "I can't claim to be surprised, exactly, but I am a bit shocked she would choose the enemy over her family. Why does she hate us so much?"

For a heartbeat, Ahren struggled with how much to reveal. Tamyr's secrets were her own, weren't they? Only, now they put the entire forest at risk. "I think Tamyr was more involved with Ahni than we ever knew. She blames Aibek and Faruz and the new council for Ahni's death and swore to do anything to avenge her friend."

"How long have you known this?"

Ahren sniffed and buried her face in the handkerchief. "I found out the day before Tamyr disappeared. I didn't want to believe she'd really do something so awful."

A hand settled on her shoulder, and the tears erupted from a trickle to a waterfall.

"I know she was your friend, but we have to tell the others all of this. They're thinking we still have some tactical advantages, but if what you're saying is true, then all our secrets now belong to our enemy. We need a new plan and quickly."

Ahren nodded but didn't stand.

"Do you want me to tell them? Or would you rather I let you do the talking?"

"Could you? I'm not sure I can." Deep in her gut, Ahren knew she was taking the coward's way out by letting her brother speak for her, but as long as the council knew the extent of the betrayal, she didn't care.

20.

Attack

From where he sat behind a prickly berry bush, Eddrick could see all the activity in the courtyard below, or lack thereof. The army hadn't done anything of interest in days, and boredom made keeping watch more challenging with every passing hour. He'd become so distracted, Eddrick didn't notice the officers in their brilliant yellow jackets when they strolled into the army's midst. The unexpected flurry of activity — of men running to the center of the clearing, forming ranks, grabbing weapons, donning helmets — drew his eye back to the field.

Alarmed, he tugged at Kiri's arm and drew her close to his side. She followed his gaze and watched the activity below. Her eyes reflected his own panic back at him.

Fear and urgency filled his voice when he spoke. "Go. Watch over Aibek. Help him if you can."

Kiri nodded once and vanished. Eddrick felt her absence but ignored the emptiness and turned to watch the army. He made sure to avoid meeting Glesni's disapproving gaze. In moments, they'd formed neat lines and rows and begun to file out of the city through the southern gate. He glanced back, ready to speak to Glesni, but the ancient spirit had vanished. Eddrick watched the courtyard until the first rows had vanished beyond the sparkling marble wall and flew to the elders to warn them that the battle was imminent. He landed on the hill above the ancient city, ready to run to the hall where the elders waited, but Glesni had beaten him there and waited with six of the paper-thin ancients.

"We have seen," the tall one said before Eddrick could speak. "The battle is upon us. You must go and do what you can to make it a fair fight among the living. My best men and women will go with you." He heaved a sigh and an odd look of longing passed over his faded features. "Once, I would have leapt at the chance to fight in such a grand battle. Alas, I must not. I am not strong enough anymore. Go. Be strong. Be brave. Be victorious."

Before Eddrick could respond, or even react, the elders vanished from the hill, leaving Eddrick and Glesni alone. An eagle screeched overhead, breaking the tense quiet that had fallen. Moments later, spirits appeared one at a time at first, then in groups of two and three, then dozens at once, until the grassy hill was covered with a small army of spirits. None carried weapons—why would they? Their fight wasn't with the living. Their mission would be to keep the enemy's spirits out of the fight so their descendants could fight for rule of the land they all loved. Among the spirits, Eddrick spotted the most recent king of Azalin, who had been mercilessly killed when Helak took Xona a few months before. The shadow of his crown still pressed his hair down. Eddrick bowed low, straightened, and flew to the point of light that represented the enemy soldier he'd followed these past weeks.

There would be no more spying. No more sneaking around. No more secrets. No more training. It was time. Nervous flutters filled his gut, but Eddrick grinned. He was sick to death of skulking in shadows. He had always been a man of action. Now, it was time to fight.

~ * ~

The morning dawned cold and frosty, unusual for that part of the land. Aibek pulled Marah closer and snuggled deeper in the blankets. The softest gray-blue light shone through the shack's window. Marah sighed and pressed her face into his chest, and Aibek pressed a soft kiss to her forehead. He loved her. He wouldn't—couldn't—tell her that, not yet anyway. But soon, the battle would be over, and he'd ask her to marry him. He wouldn't ask until the war was won. He couldn't give her the attention a new bride deserved until then.

A scream pierced the early-morning quiet, followed by the clang of steel. Aibek threw back the covers and dove for his armor. There wasn't time to don it all, but he tossed his heavy, embroidered green zontrec breastplate on, followed it with his chain-mail tunic, and smashed his helmet onto his head before he grabbed his sword and ran for the door. Behind him, Marah stumbled about, tossing clothing and corsets from her pack as she searched for her battle gear. He hoped she'd be close behind him but couldn't wait to make sure. He closed the door behind him and froze.

Enemy soldiers ran through the camp. Dragons circled overhead, rumbling and chirping their displeasure, but unsure where or how to land to gather their riders. Men and women fought for their lives in various stages of dress.

Aibek signaled to the dragons to land. They could help their riders win the day. The dragon riders moved aside when the shadows grew, though most didn't bother to look up. A few managed to position their opponents beneath the dragons' great paws as the beasts landed at the mouth of the cave. The door to the shack flung open and Marah stepped up beside him. Her lips set in a firm line as she surveyed the scene, then she spotted her dragon and sprinted towards him. Aibek found Gworsad and did the same. He pulled the thin strap from the pocket on his belt and flung it over the dragon's back and climbed up. Gworsad took off before he'd secured the straps, but Aibek had practiced enough to be able to fasten himself onto the dragon's back in flight.

Below, several more dragons took to the air, their riders frantically working to strap themselves on. Gworsad circled, knowing that Aibek was the commander and needed to know what happened to his warriors. One by one, the dragons beat their wings against the cold winter air, lifting into the gray skies. Finally, the last dragon lifted off, its back still bare and empty. He screamed with fury and his sides swelled out with breath. A torrent of flame flew out of his mouth, filling the cave and igniting every-thing—and everyone—in his path. The enemy sol-diers scattered, screaming, but few escaped without at least a portion of their clothing in flames.

Aibek's mind circled much faster than the dragons could. The backup warriors were still at least a day and a half away. How had the enemy found their camp? Had they been betrayed? He hadn't seen the old man that morning. Had he escaped? Had he shown the enemy where they were? A stab of guilt shot through his chest at the thought. Pagi had been nothing but kind and helpful since their paths had crossed. And the old man had helped them get rid of the enemy spirits that had been tracking them. No, Aibek wouldn't believe that he'd done anything to hurt the Tsarians' cause.

Then how? How had things gone so very wrong? More importantly, what did they do now? They couldn't storm the gate. That would be the expected move, and they didn't have the backup they needed for that scheme to succeed.

He leaned over Gworsad's mossy neck and tapped the dragon's shoulder. When an orange eye reflected his panicked features back to him, Aibek com-manded, "Take us to the ground fighters. We have to make sure they haven't been attacked."

The dragon rumbled his acknowledgment and

chirruped to the others. Moments later, they sped through the sky toward the spot the fighters had last been seen.

They had only flown for about twenty minutes before Aibek spotted them. They'd been ordered not to march as an army, but to look like a merchants' caravan, and it seemed the guise had kept them safe. They moved north at a pace any real merchant would envy, with smart-looking horses pulling a few wagons. Weapons? Or food? Aibek wasn't sure what the wagons carried, but they completed the 'merchant caravan' look, and so he wouldn't question it.

Instead of landing near the caravan, Aibek led the dragons in a wide arc, searching the area for any enemy troops that might be waiting to spring a trap. After several minutes of circling, he decided it was safe and landed several miles in front of the caravan, near where he thought they'd be by noon. They stayed out of sight of the road, just in case he'd miscalculated and that wasn't the warriors from the Tsari approaching.

Desperate and panicked, Aibek strode away from the dragons and riders over the next hill. He needed alone time to think and come up with a new plan of attack. The tall grasses swallowed him, and he closed his eyes and reached out his senses, as he'd learned to do in the forest.

Somewhere nearby, he felt a comforting presence. "Mother?" he whispered the word, unsure if he would alert nearby enemies with a louder call, as he'd done when fleeing the city guards.

Kiri's slender form and brilliant red hair materialized a few feet from him, though she remained translucent.

"I'm not supposed to give you advice, but don't wait for that caravan. You must attack now. They think they've driven you away. Your only hope is to attack while they celebrate."

His mother rushed to Aibek and squeezed him in a hug of icy wind. She released him and vanished as suddenly as she'd appeared.

Loneliness washed over him at her absence, but he decided to take her advice. Breathless from the encounter, he sprinted back to the other's and relayed his message.

Confusion showed on every dragon rider's face. Marah gave voice to all their questions.

"How do you know this? Who has that kind of knowledge about the enemy's positions? Do you have spies we don't know about?"

"I…" Aibek fidgeted, caught himself, and locked his hands behind his back in a military stance. He pulled his chin up and met her confused gaze with what he hoped was an air of confidence. "I have my ways. We need to attack while the enemy thinks we're retreating. Otherwise, they'll be expecting us, and we won't have a chance."

"It sounds like a good strategy to me. I'm in." Vayna stepped up beside Aibek and mirrored his stance.

"I don't know. How will we ever hold the wall

without backup? There's only twelve… I mean eleven of us. We lost Dorrel at the cave."

Aibek nodded. "I know it sounds crazy. Let's sit down and see if we can come up with a strategy, but we don't have much time. They'll know we're rallying to attack, but we have to defeat them before they expect us."

An hour later, they were no closer to a plan than they had been at the beginning.

"Enough of this." Aibek stood and crossed his arms. "We need to attack now, or we'll lose our opportunity. Can we send Dorrel's dragon to alert the warriors so they can meet us at the city today? They're not so very far away. They can make it if they hurry."

"I can do that," the dragon said, rumbling. "I think I could carry some of them to get them there faster, too."

Aibek smiled at the enormous dragon. He was nearly double Gworsad's size and could likely carry two dozen men at a time. "That's a wonderful idea."

Without another word, the dragon flew off toward the caravan.

"Are we ready, then? Let's do this!" He met each person's gaze, saw and acknowledged the fear he saw there, and hoped he wasn't leading his friends to their deaths.

"Now hold on just a minute." Bartel kept his head bowed over the stick he whittled down to a toothpick, but Aibek recognized his soft voice. "Isn't the wall fortified with archers? They'd be able to bring down even a dragon in broad daylight."

A chorus of worried agreement filled the makeshift camp.

"He may be onto something," Vayna said. "It might be better to wait until nightfall, when we can fly over the walls and take the palace. You know they have most of their fighters on the walls and at the gates. We can bypass them all. It'll be the easiest victory in the history of war!"

The others agreed, but Aibek was less certain. Still, he went along. He couldn't think of any reason to attack the city in broad daylight besides his mother's warning, especially since the morning sun had already burned away the fog that had shrouded the dawn.

"We've already lost the element of surprise we've been counting on." Marah's voice quivered, barely above a whisper. "Wouldn't it be best to hide under cover of darkness, swoop in, and take the palace? You've said the castle itself isn't well protected, and they rely on the walls to keep the king safe. If we wait, we can be over the walls and in the palace courtyard before the enemy can even raise an alarm."

The chorus of agreements reached its loudest pitch yet.

"All right, then let's have an easy, restful day so we're ready for tonight." Aibek released the dragons to hunt and find a good place to rest within earshot, and the dragon riders settled in to a lazy day. Marah took Gwynn with her to shoot a few rabbits for a meal, and Aibek strolled away over the nearest hill to try to calm his own anxieties. He stretched out his senses, searching for any sign of the Bokinna or her sister, but only silence answered his cry. Feelings of loneliness and abandonment made him want to weep, even without thinking of the loss of Dorrel in the morning's attack. His mind turned to the adventures he'd shared with his new friend, and he wished he'd had more time to get to know the personable young man. A tight knot of grief joined the anxiety binding up his insides, and Aibek pushed all thoughts from his mind. He tried again to stretch his mind to reach the Bokinna or the Saethem, but only the soft buzz of insects and the whisper of the wind answered back.

His thoughts wandered back to the battle for Nivaka. It seemed so long ago, yet it had only been a year and a half. His parents and their ancestors had saved the day then, when his plan would have seen all the villagers slaughtered by Helak's advancing force. He hoped this plan was better. His parents couldn't help him this time. They hadn't said as much, but somehow he knew they'd be busy elsewhere.

A lump grew in his throat, but he swallowed it down and took a deep breath. The time for worries and anxiety had passed. Now it was time for war.

~ * ~

The sky shone in shades of red and orange when the camp came to life again. Quiet anxiety turned to soft murmurs and then to excited talking. It was time. No more waiting. No more training. They were ready.

Aibek called the warriors together for a strategy meeting before they flew out. He'd spent the day reviewing the layout of the city and considering various plans of attack. He'd also fought against the waves of self-doubt that reminded him of his failure in the battle for Nivaka. This fight would be different. He knew his enemy. He knew the city. And he had dragons. Surely that counted for something.

"You look nervous, child. What's the matter?" The familiar voice scared Aibek so badly that he had his sword drawn before he realized who had spoken.

"Pagi! How did you find us? I'm so glad you got out this morning. We couldn't find you…" Aibek trailed off, remembering his earlier suspicions. "Where did you go, anyway?"

The little old man met Aibek's gaze with no hint of deception. His few tufts of hair stuck straight up and blew in the evening breeze. "I was at the stream, catching fish for breakfast and trying to find some way to contact my god. The silence in this place is eerie."

A pang of longing shot through Aibek. He missed Serik. Something about Pagi made him think of his mentor and friend, and each memory arrived with an unexpected jolt of pain. He'd killed his friend. Aibek turned to watch the sunset, blinking the moisture from his eyes.

"Did you know there's an army approaching?" Pagi startled Aibek again by appearing at his shoulder. "I don't recognize their banners, but they're try-ing not to look like an army."

"Yes. They're my friends. They're here to help me free the city."

"All right, if you're certain, then I won't worry about them." Pagi sat and drew a pattern of circles in the dirt. "What will you do about the city?"

"I have to attack. I—we—don't have any other choice. My family and friends are trapped inside those walls, along with thousands of other innocent people."

"You must do what you feel in your heart is right. Not what others tell you is right. Not what you think must be done, but what is truly, deeply right. Only you can say what that is. You are the leader here, if I've read the situation correctly."

Something in the old man's words touched Aibek on a level deeper than he'd expected, and a dull ache formed in his chest. "Thank you. I'll try. What will you do?"

"I will wait here. I do not want to involve myself in other mens' wars, but I've come to like your peo-ple and want to see you all safely through this nasty business." Pagi stopped drawing and stood, meeting Aibek's gaze for the first time in the conversation. A deep, unfathomable pain shone through his ancient eyes, and Aibek fought a sudden wave of tears. "Mind you, I understand why you do it. If you do not attack them, they will attack and kill you, as they did this morning. Do not think I judge you harshly. I only wish there could be a better way."

Aibek couldn't think of anything to say. He agreed with the old man. He'd take any nonviolent option if one was available, but the time for peaceful resolution had passed. He only hoped they could take the palace and oust the invaders with as little loss to civilian and friendly lives as possible. He gazed over the bustling camp and wondered which warriors would survive to see the sunrise.

Once the fires had been extinguished and the camp disassembled, the warriors mounted their dragons and took to the skies as the last rays of daylight faded into darkness. Aibek and Gworsad led the way south, toward the army. He wouldn't launch his attack until he knew the army was poised to back him up. The dragons landed beside the road and waited for the army leaders to approach.

When the division leaders' faces came into view, Aibek did a double take and ran to confirm what his eyes told him must be true.

"Alija? How is this possible?"

His friend forced a sad smile. "Yes, I'm here. I can't stay and help, though. I've come only to make sure the army made it this far unmolested, and to let you know that your ancestors will make sure you have a fair fight. This will be a dangerous night for us all."

"I'm afraid it will." Aibek knelt and drew the city's outline in the dirt beside the road. When he'd finished, he beckoned the other dragon riders and the division leaders to form a close circle.

"We'll split the dragons into three groups. Three

or four of us will attack the palace and hopefully oust the standing leader there before the army realizes what's happening. The rest will split into two groups. One group—only two or three dragons, will attack the west gate." Aibek drew an arrow in the dirt pointed to the gate closest to their discovered camp.

"Make it look like we're making room for the army to approach. Draw all the city's resources to that location and away from the South gate. The rest will wait until the city guard has gone to defend the west gate. When most of the soldiers are gone, you'll take the south gate and open the gates to let the army in, then fly directly to the inner wall and open the parade gates there. Once we're in, we should be able to hold the gates and possibly take the wall. All the defenses point out toward the prairie."

"What if they surrender?" The army's leader asked. "Are we taking prisoners? Letting them go? Or killing all who resist?"

"Remember that this is where I grew up. I'd rather not kill indiscriminately. Many of those manning the walls were my friends and classmates, and now have been forced to serve an enemy they despise. No, don't kill any who surrender. They're either free to leave their weapons and leave the city or take up arms beside us. I'm hopeful that many of the city's soldiers will turn on Helak's men once they have another option."

A heavy silence pressed in upon them as the last of the daylight faded to black.

"All three moons are dark tonight. Extinguish the

lamps and the guards will never see us coming. Leave the wagons here. They make too much noise."

The division leaders nodded and whispered to the warriors close behind them, passing along the order.

"One more thing. Are there any warriors who would be willing to ride in on the dragons with us to help take the palace? We need more than four people for that fight, but the dragons won't be much help inside the building. Gworsad and the other dragons will help keep the walls while we're inside, but I have a whistle to call them back if we need them."

Marah grabbed Aibek's arm, her eyes wide and luminous in the fading light. "This isn't how we trained for this."

"I know, but we didn't plan on them finding our camp, either." He squeezed her hand and met her eyes. "I'd love to have your bow to cover my back, if you're all right with that."

"I wouldn't go anywhere else if you ordered me to."

Vayna made a gagging noise.

Grinning, Aibek glanced around the circle. "Vayna, you're responsible for getting those gates opened. We're sitting ducks if the army can't get in."

"I'm on it," Vayna shot back. "They'll be wide open before the enemy even knows we're here."

Aibek was less sure of the last assignment, but called for Bartel, anyway. When the shy young man answered, Aibek assigned him to lead the assault on the western gate. "Is that all right with you?" He added at the end.

"Yes, sir, I can make sure the soldiers stay busy on that front. Do you want me to open the gates, so they think the army's coming that way?"

"I think that's a great idea, if you can. As for the rest," Aibek glanced at the dragon riders. "I'll let you choose which team you want to join, as long as we divide the archers and swordsmen up. We don't want all the archers on one team and swords on another. Neither will succeed without the other."

The warriors stood to carry out his orders, but Aibek called them back. "One more thing. Keep your strafing runs isolated to the walls and only use the fire against the soldiers. We're here to free the city, not burn it to the ground."

The dragon riders formed a clump beside the road to decide teams, and Aibek turned back to the army's leaders.

"You'll find a network of tunnels under the city that lead out beyond the walls. Use them if you must if we get trapped in there, but know that any blood will attract creatures far worse than anything the enemy can throw at you." When the leaders nodded, Aibek added, "Can you find me twenty warriors to ride in with me to take the palace?"

The leaders went to do his bidding, and Aibek stepped away from the milling crowd. His hands shook. His breath came in shallow gasps. How was he supposed to lead these people to victory in a city they'd never seen before that day? Especially when he'd failed to win the battle in their own home village. He clutched at the medallion beneath his shirt and reached out with his senses, straining for any sign of the Saethem or the Bokinna. Only silence answered back. A bat fluttered close above his head, and somewhere far off, a hawk screeched. Aibek sighed and opened his eyes. He was on his own this time.

21.

Gworsad rumbled and nudged his shoulder, and Aibek grinned. "You're right. It's time. Are you ready?"

"I am. I am ready battle to be over so I go home. I miss forest. I miss Bokinna."

Aibek nodded and climbed onto the beast's moss-covered back. "Me, too, but I'm afraid this won't be easy."

"Why not? You planned. We trained and ready." Gworsad bent his long neck around and stared at Aibek with one gleaming orange eye.

"I'm just worried, I think. It's impossible to really plan a battle. Are you ready for the other soldiers? They're not used to flying, so you'll have to avoid any sudden maneuvers."

"I am ready, but dragons should help at gate first, then come for them and take palace? If I leave you at palace, our training wasted. I want to help."

Aibek smiled at his eagerness but stopped short of disagreeing. It wasn't a bad idea.

"Take me over to the other dragons. Let's see what they think."

A gust of wind and dust flew about Aibek's face as Gworsad did as he asked. When he landed, Aibek called out to Vayna, who was closest.

"Gworsad thinks the palace team should help take

the gate before we fly into the city. What do you think? I have to admit, I'm tempted. I don't like leaving others to do such important work—not that I don't think you perfectly capable," he added quickly. "I just feel like I should be there to help."

Vayna shook his head. "I see where you're coming from, but I think we should stick to the plan. Don't give the palace time to prepare, like you said before."

"Vayna's right," Marah cut in. "Stick to the plan. I know you want to personally manage every front, but this time, you just can't. We've all trained. We're all ready. Let the dragons fly back to help with the walls once they drop us off. I have this," she held up a small wooden whistle. "I can call them back if we need them. Tukanli knows the sound and can call the others."

Leaning far out over Gworsad's neck, Aibek murmured, "Is that a good enough compromise?"

"I don't know co… comp… whatever word was, but sounds like good plan to me."

Aibek couldn't quite stifle a grin. "All right, let's get the soldiers up."

The dragons worked quickly, lifting the fighters onto their backs as the trained riders helped get everyone positioned so they wouldn't impede the dragons' wings.

Bartel swept his hair back behind his ear and strung his bow. "We'll go first, so we can draw some of the guards away."

"We'll give you a fifteen-minute head start."

Vayna paused, then asked, "You think that's enough?"

"I'll make sure it is."

Aibek couldn't suppress a surge of pride at Bartel's courage. The young man had been vocal in his attempts to prevent war but had apparently overcome his trauma from the Nivaka battle. That, or he'd simply accepted that this was the only way to keep his friends and family safe. Aibek didn't have time to ponder the issue any more before Bartel's dragon lifted off the ground, followed by the others on his team, and they shot out toward the city at top speed.

~ * ~

"This is it!" Eddrick shouted. Dragon flames lit the sky above the city's western gate, creating a surreal image he wouldn't have believed possible. A giddy excitement rose in his belly. "It's time! They're fighting!"

Glesni drifted over to hover beside him. "I do believe you're right." He closed his eyes, communicating his thoughts to the other ancients.

When he opened his eyes, he tightened his lips into a firm line and nodded. "Let's go."

Eddrick grinned and let himself float up above the plain where the army had gathered. He concentrated hard, joining his energy with that of Glesni and all the other spirits hovering above the city.

All at once, something gave way beneath them,

and spirits floated up from the flickering lights below.

"What do you think you're doing?" a ghost shrieked in Eddrick's face. "We have to help him! Let us go back, he can't win without our help!"

"We can't interfere in the business of the living," Eddrick said between gritted teeth, fighting to keep his concentration and hold up his part of the force-field.

"That's garbage and you know it! That's my son fighting down there!"

"Well, it's my son your son is trying to kill. Let them fight it out. We need to stay out of it." Eddrick glared at the panicked ghost.

The angry spirit threw himself at Eddrick, frantically trying to break the bond between him and the other spirits above the city. Eddrick squeezed his eyes closed, focusing all his energy on repelling the young-looking father.

His energy wavered for the barest moment. He knew exactly what that father was going through. He'd absolutely kill to be able to help Aibek, but his son was well trained, and he had to have faith in his training and in him. He didn't know if this father's son was as well-trained as his or not. Part of him hoped not. If he was, then Aibek would have a hard time winning. Still, it was up to Aibek to win. He'd interfered more than he ought to give him a fair fight. Now, it was up to him.

Pain shot through him as the spirit struggled to

break through, but he redoubled his efforts and repelled the desperate father.

Several more points of pain threatened to tear him apart until Eddrick screamed for help. Immediately, several older, more experienced spirits rushed to his aid. They pressed their energies against the wounded areas and shored up the forcefield until the father and his friends left in search of an easier target.

~ * ~

Dragons pawed the dusty ground and soldiers shifted in their armor as the seconds ticked by. Fifteen minutes was an eternity. After only eight, Aibek signaled to his team.

"We're going. I want to be inside the city before you start fighting for the gate." He met Vayna's eyes and struggled to hide the apprehension in his own. "Here we go!"

He nudged Gworsad's shoulder and held on as the dragon unfurled his leathery wings and propelled them into the darkness. Somewhere to his left, the west, a bell rang once, twice, thrice. The guard had sounded the alarm.

The wall burst to life as Gworsad approached. Without consulting with Aibek, the dragon changed his course and veered right. Aibek let Gworsad make the calls, since his eyesight was so much better. It was the right decision. They flew over a dark, silent portion of the wall. It looked to Aibek like the watch there had abandoned their posts. They'd probably rushed off to help at the western gate.

Brilliant yellow flames lit the night sky at the western end of the city, and Aibek turned his head away. He hoped the dragons wouldn't get carried away and set the city on fire. Still, there was no better way to take the city. The walls were too well-fortified for any traditional siege tactics to have a chance.

Below, the city sprang to life, but no one looked up to see them gliding overhead. Soldiers filled the courtyard around the palace, so Aibek directed Gworsad to land on the wide, flat roof. That entrance would likely be unguarded. A wide stone wall ran the perimeter of the roof, creating an ideal place to gather their force.

Aibek had been on the palace roof once before, when the king had hosted a celebration for the tournament winners several years before. He hoped he could remember how to navigate the winding passageways, but there was no time for second thoughts.

Tukanli circled close behind as Gworsad swooped low and settled onto the roof. No guards raised the alarm or rushed towards them. Relieved at this tiny victory, Aibek leapt down and helped the soldiers off the dragon.

"Here, wait beside the wall," Aibek whispered.

One by one, the dragons landed. The group amassed by the wall grew until they had all twenty-five fighters ready. The soft ring of steel filled the air as they drew their blades.

In the distance, screams sounded and bells rang.

Brilliant orange light filled the night sky. The dragons flew off, racing through the darkness to help their friends take the gate.

Aibek raised his sword. "Let's go."

He pulled open the door nearest their group and stopped cold.

A sentry stood in the doorway, his hand raised to the height of the doorknob.

Before he could sound the alarm, Aibek drew his blade across the man's neck. He dropped the lamp in his hand and fell with a surprised expression and a soft gurgle. The lamp oil flared, creating eerie shadows on the two men standing behind the fallen soldier. They stared in stunned silence at their fallen comrade. Arrows sprouted from each of their bare necks before Aibek could react. The lamp oil burned itself out, casting the roof into darkness once more.

When his eyes had adjusted again to the lack of light, Aibek turned and gave Marah an approving nod before he led the way down the narrow staircase beyond the door.

No torches burned in the sconces, leaving the stairway in complete blackness. Aibek kept his right hand on the wall and felt his way down the steps one at a time. One of the men breathed on his neck, a hand coming up every few steps to feel for Aibek's arm and make sure they stayed close together. Aibek wished he knew who was behind him, but he couldn't tell in the pitch dark of the stairwell. Further back, the scrape of boots on stone and rustle of fabric gave away the rest of the soldiers' movements.

The darkness stretched on endlessly, until Aibek thought he'd lose his mind from the never-ending anticipation and anxiety, which the dark curves of the stairs only heightened. Finally, his right hand bumped against a door, and he paused. The man behind him didn't stop soon enough but rammed his nose into Aibek's shoulder.

If he remembered correctly, Aibek thought the door opened onto a wide ballroom, which would present few places to hide and could leave him and his warriors completely exposed. He rested his hand on the knob but listened intently for any sounds of patrols beyond it.

"What the hell is taking them so long?" Footsteps echoed off the polished floor, and the vaulted ceiling amplified the voice.

Aibek pulled his hand free of the door and pressed himself back against the wall, knowing full well that hiding would be useless. He focused on the sounds of approaching guards, trying to sort out how many sets of boots were crossing the stone floor. It sounded like three or four. Not a large number. He and his men could take them, if they had to. Before he could brace himself for combat, the door swung open and a tall man stood silhouetted in the doorway, his eyes just below Aibek's.

Without giving the man time to sound the alarm, Aibek brought his sword up and slashed at the guard's throat. His elbow crashed painfully into the staircase's stone wall, but Aibek ignored the pain and rushed forward to silence the other two men in the room.

The string of a bow creaked behind him, but the wall would keep Marah from getting any kind of a decent shot. Aibek caught a glimpse of the soldier behind him when the man rushed up to attack the third guard beside him. Aibek felled his man and waved to the door on the opposite wall. They had to hurry. More guards would certainly be coming soon, especially since those last three had been so loud in their movements. Someone had surely heard them fall.

The others crossed the marble floor behind him, each stepping carefully to minimize the sound of their footsteps in the empty hall.

When he reached the far door, Aibek paused only long enough to listen for sounds beyond it. Hearing none, he yanked the door open and rushed into the wide passage. A thick tapestry covered the floor, muffling the sounds of their passing. Aibek led the others through the winding passageways until voices ahead brought him up short. He waved the others into a small room and pressed in close behind them, watching the hall to see who passed.

"We're under attack! Make no mistake, they'll be here to try to take back the palace any minute now. Man the doors. Make sure all the entrances are guarded." The man's voice echoed through the long hall.

"But sir, shouldn't we see what's keeping Brion

and Dairre? They went up to check the roof more than fifteen minutes ago."

Someone sighed and feet shuffled. "Knowing that lot, they're probably having a smoke and a nap. No. Man the doors. Be prepared for an assault. The men are keeping the fighting to the walls so far, but they won't stand long against those dragons. Once the army's through, they'll have this palace in their sights, you can be sure of that."

"Yes, sir. I'll watch the service entrance. You don't think they'll try to come in the front, do you? Those doors are too easy to barricade. If I were an enemy, I'd try the smaller doors on the sides or back."

"You're probably right, but we'll keep all the doors guarded until we know what tactics they'll use."

"Yes, sir."

Footsteps faded down the hall, and Aibek waited several minutes to be sure the guards were truly gone before he moved forward.

They turned down the next hall, moving ever closer to the chambers the king had once occupied. At the end of the hall, a cluster of men in city guard uniforms stood guard. One of them spotted the intruders and called out to his comrades.

Aibek rushed down the hall toward the men. They were deep inside the palace now, and Aibek was fairly certain most of the guards would be out of earshot, but he didn't want to take unnecessary risks. The lead guard met Aibek with his sword raised and thrust it out low at the last second in an attempt to catch his attacker off guard. Aibek dodged right and parried the thrust, and the two moved in a slow circle in the center of the hall. A man fell beside Aibek with a dull thud after an arrow lodged in his neck, and one more followed an instant later.

The hallway erupted in a flurry of activity and metal. Aibek's warriors attacked with all the pent-up energy of men who'd been poised for battle for many days. They quickly overwhelmed the guards' defenses and in minutes all the enemy soldiers lay dead or dying on the plush velvet floor. The heavy wall coverings had muffled most of the sound, but voices called from further down the halls in answer to the guards' initial cries.

"Time's up," Aibek muttered. He planted his shoulder into the door the guards had been protecting and slammed his weight against it. Pain shot through his shoulder, into his arm, and across his chest. At that moment, he realized he had neglected to swallow the tincture. He hesitated but decided the time for secrets had passed.

He stepped aside, rubbing his shoulder, and let one of the soldiers take a turn at the door. Once he was clear, Aibek pulled out the vial and downed its contents in one swift movement. With nothing to wash down the bitter liquid, he gagged and made a face and tried to suppress a shudder when the foul substance slid down his throat.

A gentle hand settled on his arm. "Are you all right?" Marah's lips were so close to his ear, Aibek could feel her breath ruffle his hair.

"I'm fine, I just didn't expect it to be quite so heavy." Aibek tried to force a sheepish grin, but felt his face contort into a grimace instead. His shoulder throbbed, so he rubbed at it and hoped that would convince her.

"Well, we need you strong enough to fight. Don't get hurt on a door." She tossed her long braid over her shoulder and strolled over to where three soldiers worked at forcing open the door.

One heartbeat at a time, strength suffused Aibek's body, spreading like the warmth of a good brandy through his chest and into his arms and legs. He waited until his hands tingled with the tincture's effects, flexed his fists, and took a position close to the spot where the door met the wall.

Aibek timed his movement to match the soldiers surrounding him but didn't attempt to harness the tincture's power. The door creaked, splintered, and crashed inward. He stumbled under the forward momentum and staggered several paces into the room.

~ * ~

Faruz leaned over the rail and surveyed the scene below. The Bokinna had moved the village so close to the forest's edge that he could see the flicker of enemy campfires through the trees. Zifa put her arm around him and set her head on his shoulder.

"How long do you think they'll wait?"

"I don't know. Probably not long, if I were to guess." He put his arm around her waist and pulled her close against his side. She'd refused to stay back away from the fighting when it began. She was carrying his child. The two thoughts warred in his mind, inducing a panic unlike anything he'd ever experienced.

He opened his mouth to beg her—again—to stay with Valasa, but a clamor rose from the enemy camp. Faruz frowned and leaned over the rail, straining to hear the words the soldiers were shouting. An arrow whirred past his head and he jerked back.

"Sound the alarm! They're attacking!" He pulled Zifa away from the rail and pulled her toward the closest house, where they could regroup and make a plan. To his amazement, Zifa didn't stop. She kept running, vanishing into the night's blackness.

Faruz didn't call after her, instead using the time to concentrate on the Bokinna. How fast could the dragons get to them?

He'd just opened his eyes when Zifa sprinted around the corner, holding his armor and the straps they used to keep their seat on the dragons. She'd already donned her armor, and the reinforced zontrec emblazoned with Nivaka's new sigil—a dragon breathing fire above a graceful, smiling tree—fit her well. He wished the sun would come up already so he could see the contrast of the brilliant green dye against her pale skin. He sighed and pulled her close for a quick, hard kiss.

He hadn't even finished pulling his armor over

his clothes when the dragons' rumble first shook the boardwalk.

"They're here! Let's go!" Zifa pulled him along by his sleeve while he finished strapping his sword belt on.

"I've asked some of the dragons to light the camps on fire before they pick up their riders!" Faruz shouted over the clamor of shouting villagers and whirring arrows.

Enemy fighters had already flung grappling claws up onto the railing, and Faruz rushed to help protect the village from the onslaught while the others clambered onto their dragons behind him.

Villagers passed around pots of flame-proof salve that Valasa had made, slathering it over their faces and arms. Brilliant flashes of light illuminated the forest as the dragons made their strafing runs over the enemy's camp, followed immediately by screams of terror and pain.

The man in front of Faruz froze, his eyes wide, his hands still clutching the grappling line. "Dragons?"

Faruz simply nodded and cut the line above the man's hand and watched as the rope and man fell together toward the hard, rocky ground.

"I've got this," a man behind him shouted. "Your dragon's here."

Faruz stepped back and bowed slightly to the villager, though he didn't look up to see who it was. "You can hold them. We've learned a lot since the first time."

He didn't wait for an answer, but sprinted off

toward the Square, the only open area in the village large enough for the dragons to land.

"Gamne!" He grinned at the sight of the dragon that had become one of his dearest friends. "Did you get a chance to light some fires?"

"No," Gamne answered glumly. "Bokinna send me straight here for you while others have all the fun."

Faruz scrambled onto his back. "Don't worry, buddy. You'll get your chance." He pulled the straps tight and glanced around for Zifa. She was almost finished strapping herself onto her dragon.

Gamne swung his head around to glare at Faruz, who stifled a sheepish laugh. "Let's go!" he shouted, loud enough for the people below to hear.

The dragon leapt into the dark night, leaving the shouts and screams to fade into the forest below. He glanced around for Ahren as Gamme lifted him out of the village. He hoped she'd be close enough behind him to keep Zifa safe.

"Let's give the villagers a little more time, shall we?" Faruz shouted to Gamne. The dragon didn't look at him but dove into the forest's cover. The village came back into view, but before Faruz could make out anyone on the rails, the dragon let loose a blast of flame that lit the attackers' ropes, axes, and ladders on fire and left the enemy soldiers burned and screaming. Those who weren't in the direct line of the flames scattered like flies when the dragon pulled up to come around again.

"To the clearing!"

The dragon rumbled a complaint but did as Faruz said.

Heavily armed villagers, elves, and dwarves were already pouring onto the battlefield from the forest, and enemy soldiers met them as they emerged. Neither group bothered with forming into lines.

The night's inky blackness made it hard for Faruz and the other dragons to distinguish friend from foe. Tents and supplies burned bright against the moonless sky, providing the only light for the battle.

Gamne swooped toward the ground for another run at the camps, but this time, something flew at him when they drew near. The flash of light blinded Faruz for a heartbeat, making it difficult to guide the dragon away from the flaming projectile.

"Did you drink your seeds?" Gamne asked as he pulled up. "Can you see what they're doing?"

Right. The tincture. In the rush to prepare and join the fight, Faruz had completely forgotten it. He pulled a vial from beneath his shirt and downed the bitter liquid in a single gulp.

Almost immediately, warm strength flowed through his arms and legs and enhanced his vision and hearing. Below, men stood beside the fires, lighting arrows on fire and aiming up at the dragons. He squinted, searching for a familiar face. Sure enough, he spotted Kaskin standing with a group of soldiers, talking and pointing up at the circling dragons.

Faruz took comfort in the fact that Kaskin hadn't joined them on any training days, so he had no real idea what the dragons could or couldn't do. Still, the fact that he had betrayed them by joining the enemy galled Faruz more than he'd like to admit.

"Can you take them out?" He shouted to Gamne. "Maybe we can come around behind them?"

The dragon bobbed his head once and changed his course. Gamne's sides swelled beneath Faruz's legs as the dragon drew in as much air as he could hold in preparation for the strafing run. They dropped low to the ground and sped closer to the traitor and his companions, but Faruz froze at the scene before him.

The forest's citizens had already reached the camp and were fighting hand to hand against Kaskin and the other soldiers.

"Don't burn them!" Faruz shouted. "Those are our men! Get me close – like we practiced!"

Gamne let out his breath a little at a time, releasing a steady flow of smoke from his nostrils. Instead of using his firebreath to burn the camp, the dragon dropped lower to the ground and allowed Faruz to swing his long blade toward the unprepared enemy. Two men fell in one swing of his longsword. Gamne followed up on the blow with a well-placed swing of his massive tail, taking down the rest of the men gathered around the campfire.

The villagers dodged the dragon easily, but Kaskin and his friends hadn't been so lucky, Faruz saw when he looked back. Kaskin lay bleeding by the fire, and the three men he'd been talking to had all fallen, as well.

Faruz let out a whoop in celebration at the tiny victory, but his spirits fell when the dragon flew higher and he saw the battlefield laid out beneath him.

Everywhere he looked, men and women fought desperately against enemy soldiers who were bigger, stronger, and faster than they were. Several of the enemy fighters stumbled and staggered between combatants. One fell over without a villager even nearby.

"Good, the fairy wine is working." He nodded and twisted on his seat to get a better view of the fighting near the forest. Before he could bring the scene fully into focus, an emrialk's scream split the night.

Everyone on the field below froze in unison. Faruz couldn't remember ever hearing the beasts so close to the forest's edge before. Another shriek announced a second emrialk somewhere further north than the first.

"Oh, this is bad," Faruz told Gamne. "I don't suppose the Bokinna can control them, can she? Or reason with them? Help us somehow?" His voice rose with each question.

Gamne went quiet for a long moment and Faruz waited while he asked his deity for help. An eternity passed before he swung his head around to meet Faruz's gaze with a wide green eye.

"Bokinna say they are creatures of forest, but they not obey her. They obey themselves."

Faruz cursed. His mind drifted back to Aibek's wounds from the emrialk he had encountered on his way to meet the Bokinna the first time. Aibek had assumed that the creature was protecting the

Bokinna, and no one had disagreed with him. Apparently, they'd all been wrong. His stomach sank at the realization that the enormous canines could rip through the battlefield below, and there was nothing he could do to protect his people from them.

Time stood still. Faruz spurred the dragon into motion and swept along the treeline. He couldn't see the dreaded beasts, but their cries persisted. He had to find a way to keep them from leaving the forest and joining the fray.

~ * ~

Brilliant lamplight blinded Aibek, and he stood blinking and struggled to make out the room's contents. The tincture helped his eyes adjust an instant before an axe would have collided with his forehead. He ducked under the strike and brought his sword up, catching his attacker in the gut and nearly cutting the man in two.

Aibek lowered his sword and brought his head up, scanning the room in an instant. His heart sank to somewhere near the soles of his boots. The room was full to bursting with soldiers, most with Helak's insignia on their shirts, rather than the familiar dragon and moons of the Xona guard. He cursed under his breath and stepped further into the room to allow the rest of his team to enter. Only a long, narrow table separated his warriors from the enemy men.

It took a moment for the scene to fully make sense in Aibek's mind. These men were dressed in soldiers' uniforms, but none wore armor. Their hair hung loose to their shoulders, and only a few had weapons close to hand. To his right, a pile of shields, swords, and spears leaned against the wall where they'd be easy to grab on the way out the door.

His sword sagged in his hand. Aibek hesitated, but the men behind him pushed him forward and flooded into the room.

"Wait!" Aibek's voice boomed in the close room, echoing off the bare walls and stone floor.

Kai shouldered his way up to stand beside Aibek. "We need to attack now, while we've got them off-guard. Don't give them time to recover."

"No." He gestured to the weapons piled beside the door. "I won't murder a room full of unarmed men. But I can't leave them to attack us from behind, either."

"What's your plan, then? I don't see a third option." Kai shook his head and raised his sword.

Aibek froze, his gaze landing on a metal ring inset into the floor. "You there," He pointed to a soldier standing beside the ring. "Pull back that rug."

The man did as Aibek instructed, revealing a trap door wide enough for two men to stand atop.

"Open it," Aibek commanded, relief flooding his chest.

The trap door opened in a cloud of dust and creaking hinges. It clearly hadn't been used for many years. Pitch darkness yawned up through the opening.

Aibek suppressed a smile. "Are any of you injured? Bleeding?"

The cornered soldiers glanced around, and the one who had opened the trap door answered, "No, we haven't seen any battle, yet."

"Good. Take a torch. Down you go. This tunnel leads out of the city. You're free, as long as you don't turn and attack us."

The soldier moved to climb down into the tunnel, but Aibek held up a hand. "Be warned. If anyone among you is injured or bleeding, you'll attract creatures you can't outrun. It will mean death to you all."

The man met Aibek's eyes for a long moment before breaking the gaze and descending into the darkness below.

"It's safe," he called. "Come on."

Aibek watched until the last man had cleared the steps, then flung the trap door shut behind them and threw the latch. When he'd pushed a heavy chair over the door, he turned and hurried out of the room and down the still-abandoned hall.

"Weird," Kai whispered. "I thought we'd have an army in our faces by now."

Aibek nodded and continued down the hall, stopping to check for signs of attack at each intersection and opening every door they passed. They reached the front entryway unimpeded and paused to regroup.

"They're either moving ahead of us, or they've gone to help at the gates," Marah offered.

Kai chuckled and stood in front of the broad, intricately wrought iron doors. "I don't think we should go out the front doors. That's just asking for an ambush."

"He's right. We should go back to the roof and call the dragons to take us to the gates."

Aibek didn't know the soldier's name but met his eyes when he answered. "I have a better idea. There's a courtyard through those doors. If I remember it correctly, it's large enough for the dragons to land. The walls should keep us from being ambushed while we're mounting up."

"Even better," the soldier answered and followed Aibek through the narrower doors on the left.

Intermittent blazes lit the night sky, but Aibek ignored the sights and sounds of battle and set about shoving the fine iron furniture off to the sides, so the dragons could land. Marah blew her whistle several times, tucked it into her pocket, and helped with a heavy planter. Within moments, Gworsad swooped into the courtyard, followed by several more dragons.

The soldiers climbed silently aboard, while Marah covered the doors with her bow. Twice, enemy soldiers flung themselves into the courtyard. Both times, Marah's arrows took them down before they could call for help. The band of dragons took flight without a sound and rushed toward the battle raging at the south gate.

Aibek fought waves of apprehension and disappointment as they flew. His expectations for the battle at the palace had fallen flat, but the night was far from over, and more fighting waited at the wall.

22.

Traitor

Ahren struggled to keep her wits in the chaos.

The dragon swooped low over the melee, but Ahren nudged her back to the sky. She'd already lost sight of Zifa in the rush to get out of the village. Flaming projectiles flew between the dragons.

"We have to stay clear of their arrows!" She shouted over the rushing winds and the screams of the injured and dying below.

When they'd reached a safer elevation, she scanned the battlefield and worked to separate the villagers from the enemy soldiers. The enemy's bright yellow uniforms made them stand out on the field, which helped set them apart.

In the area nearest the forest, where the fighting was the most intense, a villager wearing the forest's deep green uniform fought a desperate battle against three enemy soldiers. She notched an arrow and drew the bow taut against her cheek, verified her aim, and loosed the weapon. The arrow sank deep into the side of the soldier's neck and sent blood spraying out to the side. He stumbled once and collapsed. The other soldiers froze and stared toward the sky, but Ahren wasn't about to give them time to recover. She nocked another arrow and let it fly. It lodged in her target's chest. Ahren didn't stop to watch him fall before she drew another arrow, but the villager felled the last soldier without her help.

She turned, searching for another target, but her dragon dove and twisted. A blinding light flew past Ahren's face, and Chyndri righted herself.

"What was that?" Ahren shouted at the dragon. "We're too low!"

Before Chyndri could answer, another flaming projectile flew past, missing the leafy fringe on the dragon's neck by a finger's breadth. Leathery wings folded and the dragon dove and twisted, avoiding two more flaming arrows.

The blood rushed from Ahren's face, and her vision went black. She fought the wave of weakness with everything she had, but it wasn't enough. Her heart raced even as the darkness took her.

Cold wind rushed in her face, cooling the sweat on Ahren's brow. Her eyes fluttered open and she righted herself. Her straps had held her on the dragon's back, though they pressed deep into the flesh of her thighs. Wincing, she righted herself and eased the pressure off her legs. The dragon beat her wings again, pressing more speed into her flight. Treetops blurred beneath them, though Ahren could only see dim shadows in the near-complete darkness.

"Where are we going?" Her voice came out a raspy whisper, and she cleared her throat and tried again. "Chyndri! Where are you taking me? We have to go back!" This time, her voice carried up to the dragon's head.

Chyndri swung her head around to examine her charge. "You not sick? I take you to Bokinna. She know how fix you."

"I'm all right. I just wasn't ready for that twist." Embarrassment flushed her cheeks, and Ahren was glad no one had witnessed her fainting spell. "Remember, I didn't start training with the others. I haven't had as much time to master those kinds of movements."

Chyndri rumbled and sniffed at her. "If you sure, we go back."

Great leathery wings banked, and the dragon tilted and turned back the way they'd come. Within moments, Ahren could see the enemy campfires on the horizon.

~ * ~

Faruz directed Gamne along the treeline, watching closely for the emrialk and keeping an eye on the villagers fighting below. Many of the enemy fighters stumbled and staggered under the influence of the fairy wine the groundfolk had slipped into their water.

Still, frustration built in his chest at the precious little he could do to aid the villagers from his dragon. He'd trained, he'd practiced, and he'd prepared, but he'd given no thought to how darkness would change his battle plan. No, that wasn't quite right. He'd never considered—even for the barest second—that the enemy would risk attacking them at night, so of course he hadn't devised a battle plan for the dark.

A fresh volley of flaming arrows caught his attention, and he pressed Gamne to a higher plane to avoid the weapons. His dragon had just swung around for another pass over the melee when one of the brilliant projectiles punctured a dragon's wing ahead of him. The dragon wheeled in a tight circle, struggling to maintain control with the wound in her wing.

Faruz didn't know what he could do to help, but he hurried Gamne toward the smaller dragon, anyway. They had covered half the distance when the dragon's rider slid from the straps and plummeted to the ground below. Gamne dove toward the spot where the fighter had landed, and Faruz prayed the rider wasn't badly hurt. The injured dragon had lost most of her height in her thrashing, so a tiny sliver of hope lodged in Faruz's gut.

When he drew close enough to identify the dragon, a fresh wave of horror and fear washed over him. The wounded dragon was none other than Ekys, the young female paired with Zifa. Fear for his wife and child nearly paralyzed him, and he struggled to make his fingers work against his strap knots when Gamne finally landed near her. A new scream rent the night, but nothing existed but her unmoving form huddled on the ground. He cried out and fell to his knees beside her. He cradled her head in his lap, brushing the sweat-soaked hair back from her face. A line of blood trickled from her mouth.

"No! No, no, no! You can't die. You can't. I need you." His voice trailed to a whisper, and he hunched over her lifeless body until his forehead rested on her chest. He needed to listen for a heartbeat, but he couldn't bring himself to do it. If he heard nothing—his mind blanked, unwilling or unable to complete the thought.

Gamne nudged Faruz's back, but he ignored the gentle touch. "Your seeds help her."

That brought Faruz's attention to the dragon. "How?"

"As long as heart still beats, the seeds make her stronger, help her heal."

Faruz needed no further encouragement. He pressed his ear to her chest, careful not to press too hard and accidentally hurt her. Her heartbeat was rapid and weak, but it was there.

Elation coursed through him, warring with the mingled grief and horror he'd felt since she'd tumbled from her dragon. He reached under his shirt, grabbed one of the tiny vials, and yanked until the cord holding it snapped.

With shaking hands, he pulled the little stopper out and tossed it aside.

"Please let this work." He didn't know who he was begging, but it didn't matter. He wiped the blood from her lips with a clean corner of his shirt and used his thumb to pull her bottom lip down. The oily liquid dripped into her mouth, and he held the bottle there for a long moment, making sure she received every drop.

A weak cough and grimace gave him hope, though she didn't move or open her eyes.

It takes a few minutes to work, he reminded himself. It never worked as fast as he'd like.

"Faruz," Gamne called, an urgent note in his voice.

Faruz tore his eyes from his injured wife and leapt to his feet. An enemy soldier charged toward him, sword held aloft as he ran. The man screamed, rage and pain evident in the sound.

Light flashed above, one of the dragons letting out a breath of fire that illuminated the entire field, if only for a moment. It was enough for Faruz to identify the man charging toward him.

"Kaskin! What are you doing?"

His words slowed the man's charge but didn't stop it.

Kaskin screamed a curse and swung his blade toward Faruz's chest, though there wasn't much power in the blow.

"Where is he?" Kaskin screamed, madness and rage filling his eyes.

"Who?" Faruz blocked another half-hearted attack and stepped away from Zifa's still-unmoving form. He couldn't risk stepping on her or worse—deflecting Kaskin's blade into her flesh.

"Where is he? Where's Aibek? I've looked everywhere. He's on one of those beasts, isn't he?" Kaskin pointed to the sky.

Another blaze lit the night, and this time, Faruz got a better look at Kaskin. Blisters and open wounds marred his face, his clothes were ripped and scorched, and the arm he wasn't using to hold his blade hung limp at his side, the shoulder protruding at an odd angle. The memory of Kaskin standing by the campfire when Gamne flew overhead flashed through Faruz's mind. Another dragon had torched the camp behind them. Somehow, the man had survived that, likely driven by his need for revenge.

Faruz scowled and backed further away from Zifa. "He's not here. You did all of this for a chance at him, didn't you? You gave away our position. You told the enemy about our dragons, and you helped them come up with a strategy to fight against them—all so you could kill Aibek, didn't you? Well, guess what, he's not here. He's still in Xona, freeing the city from your new master."

Fury filled Kaskin's face again, and he raised his blade in a fresh assault. He rained down swings and jabs so fast, it took all of Faruz's considerable skill to avoid them all.

"I have no master," Kaskin ground out between attacks. "I am the one in charge. I'm always in charge—or at least I was before that no good, meddling foreigner," he spat the word like a curse, "took everything away from me."

Faruz stepped forward, ready to end the fight once and for all, but Kaskin spun on his heel and raced away. He took several long steps before Faruz realized his goal.

"Ekys!" Faruz shouted, but the dragon didn't look up. She kept her head on the ground, watching Zifa as if she were the only thing that mattered.

Before Faruz could get the dragon's attention, Kaskin reached her. He grabbed at the leafy collar around the young dragon's neck and tugged, struggling to pull himself up onto her back. The yanking got Ekys's attention, and she spread her wings and hopped a short way, trying to shake Kaskin off her frill. When that didn't work, she tossed her head and leapt into the air, her injured wing beating weakly and limping into the sky.

An emrialk screamed, silencing the field for a heartbeat. This one sounded close. Faruz had read that emrialk would scavenge if fresh meat was available, and bodies of fallen soldiers on both sides littered the ground near the trees. They must smell the blood. A fresh wave of horror struck him when he realized just how close Zifa was to the forest. He had to get her away, somewhere safe. Safe? Where would she be safe? Enemy soldiers had begun attacking the village even before the dragons had landed. They'd be in the forest, in the clearings. The only safe place he could think of was the Bokinna's clearing, but that was too far from the battle.

While he searched for a solution, Kaskin screamed again, though this time the sound was filled with pain and terror. Ekys gave another shake midair, and Kaskin finally lost his grip on her tender fringe. He toppled through the air, his good arm and legs flailing. An emrialk jumped over the strip of ground between the dragon and the forest and snatched Kaskin from the air. His scream cut off with a sickening gurgle, and a terrified silence fell over the battlefield.

A fresh fervor filled the voices of villagers and enemies alike as each worked to finish the battle and retreat to safety. A few less-disciplined soldiers from both sides scrambled away, running into the blackness of the grassland.

Faruz turned his attention back to his wife. To his relief, she had sat up and had a hand pressed to her chest. She looked pale and dazed and bloody, but she was alive. He fought the urge to crush her against him, instead kneeling and taking her hand.

"We can't stay here. Do you think you can walk? Or should I carry you?"

An emrialk screeched, punctuating his words.

"I'm all right. I can walk. Where's Ekys?" As if called, the dragon landed beside Zifa and lowered her head to Zifa's level.

Zifa pressed her hands to the ground, easing herself up out of the mud. Faruz jumped to his feet and grabbed her elbow to steady her as she stood.

"Can you fly? I go slow. I hurt, too." The dragon held her wing out at an angle, so Zifa could see her wound.

"Hold on." Faruz ran to the dragon's injured wing and pulled a second vial of the tincture from under his shirt. This time, he dumped the contents in his palm, rubbed his hands together, and massaged the oil into the dragon's injured wing.

"Ooh, that much better," she said, laying her head down and lowering the wing so he could reach it better.

He massaged the wound until another piercing shriek told him he'd run out of time. He grabbed Zifa's hand and helped her onto the dragon. He watched while she tightened the straps down completely, anxiety tightening his chest and making it hard to breathe. In moments, the two lifted into the night sky and disappeared into the darkness.

His wife safe, Faruz sprinted back to Gamne and scrambled onto his dragon's back. He yanked the straps tight and urged the dragon into the sky before he'd finished tying it off.

~ * ~

Gworsad led the other dragons beyond the wall, where they dropped their extra warriors off with the waiting army. As soon as the fighters were clear, the dragons leapt into the air and raced to join the fight at the gate.

A dozen dragons circled the gates, occasionally raining fire down on the towers when archers gathered there. Gworsad held back while Aibek searched for Vayna in the melee. A blast of white fire blinded Aibek for an instant, but before darkness fell again, he spotted his friend circling the tower to his right. He pointed him out to Gworsad, who nodded and sped off in that direction.

Vayna spotted them and waved, and Aibek gestured him to the side. The dragons found a spot away from the fighting where the friends could hear each other.

"I didn't expect you so soon! Have we captured the palace?"

Aibek shook his head. "Yes and no. We defeated the few soldiers that had been left to guard it, but no one important was even there. I'm hoping they're here. If not, we may have to search them out in the city."

Vayna nodded. "We've almost got the gates opened. The army's in position to flood the city as soon as we do. They can't fight the dragons. They've tried aiming the trebuchet at us, but Ogarren made short work of them." He patted his dragon's flank. "He's got the longest range of any of the dragons."

"Well done." Aibek fought a grin at his friend's obvious pride. "Where do you need us?"

"Can you help back up the men at the gate? They need some help since we don't have a battering ram."

"Got it." Aibek nudged Gworsad, and the two flew high into the air over the wall.

"Any ideas?" He asked.

The great dragon swung his head around to peer at Aibek with one gleaming orange eye. "You have Bokinna's strength, yes?"

Aibek nodded.

"I pull beside and you shove gate? I swing tail and hit as we fly away. We go again until metal breaks?"

"It's worth a try. Let's go!"

Gworsad flew close to the top latch on the gate, but Aibek couldn't reach the metal over the dragon's wide flank. Gworsad slammed the end of his tail into the lock as they flew away, denting the bars and creating a deafening racket.

"Can you get me any closer?" Aibek shouted over the rush of wind and clang of metal.

The dragon didn't answer; instead, he circled around for another pass.

This time, the metal creaked and groaned under the pressure from Gworsad's flank pressing against it. It gave a final high-pitched scream as the lock and hinges broke away. Below, a cheer rose up from the soldiers waiting to enter the city.

The top half of the gate hung limply from its frame, but the bottom half still held its ground.

"Lower!" Aibek shouted. "We can break it!"

A tiny shiver of regret passed over him at the sight of the ruined gate. This had been his security as a child, and now he was responsible for breaking it to pieces. Still, it had to be done, and no other armies were likely to attack in the near future. The city's blacksmiths could repair the gates before any real threat could challenge them.

The dragon swung close, and this time, Aibek had to use his sword and all his training to keep the enemy soldiers from swarming when Gworsad's body and tail raked the gate. The lock groaned but didn't give way.

Aibek directed Gworsad to give it one more try

and hung on tight when the dragon looped back for another pass.

This time, the dragon's flank pressed against the creaking iron, and Aibek leaned over to give it a mighty shove. The lock sprung loose and the metal groaned as the enormous gate swung loose.

Gworsad pressed high into the air and circled the city. Aibek glanced down, wondering why the dragon had left the battle, and noticed a stream of dark blood oozing from his friend's flank.

"You're hurt!" He screamed to project his voice over the rushing wind.

Gworsad swung around to circle the east side of the city.

Below, Aibek spotted the market his mother had always favored. The broad streets were deserted except for a few individuals rushing toward the gates.

"Over there, that looks safe enough. Can you land there? It looks like enough room. I'll tend your wound and see if I can find anyone I know." His throat burned from shouting, but his voice carried up to the dragon's sensitive ears.

Moments later, the dragon landed in the open area in the center of the market. Aibek shimmied down in a heartbeat and rushed to inspect the gash along the dragon's rear flank. Up close, it didn't look bad. Aibek thought it was just a shallow scrape, though dark red blood still oozed from the wound.

"Aibek?" An excited voice cut through the darkness and interrupted Aibek's inspection. "We heard you were dead! They said you'd been captured. Is this your dragon?"

Aibek's head snapped around, toward the familiar voice. He struggled to place it, then relaxed and grinned.

"Mehribahn? Is that you? I haven't seen you in forever!"

The man chuckled low. "Yeah, not since you beat me in that tournament, right? You always were the best fighter in the academy. Are you here to free us?"

Aibek choked back an awkward laugh and turned his attention back to Gworsad's injury. He pressed a wad of cloth hard into the shallow wound to staunch the bleeding.

"Yes, if I can find the governor that's been ruling here. He's vanished.

"Oh, he's out at the wall. Said he needed to be where the action was." Mehribahn paused. "You know, most of the city guard are people we know from the Academy. They'd fight on your side in a heartbeat if they knew you were the one leading this attack."

A chill swept over Aibek and he froze, his hand covered in sticky dragon blood. "How would we let them know? I mean, how would I make myself known without making myself a target for our enemy?"

"Stay here. I have an idea."

Before Aibek could object, the man disappeared into the shadows of the abandoned market.

"Are you all right?" Aibek whispered to Gworsad

in the sudden silence. "What can I do to make you better?"

The great dragon swept his head around to peer at Aibek in the darkness. "The seeds Bokinna gave you. You have them?"

"Not in pure form, but in the tincture she told Valasa to make, yes."

A great gust of wind rose up, throwing dust in Aibek's eyes and stopping all conversation while another dragon landed beside Gworsad.

Aibek blinked the dust out of his eyes and glanced up to see who had joined him. He stifled a smile at Marah's tense form, her bow drawn tight and her arrow swinging in broad sweeps across the empty market.

"It's all right. We're safe here." His voice echoed against the empty shops.

Instead of relaxing, Marah set out on a circle around the broad market. Aibek sighed and turned his attention back to Gworsad. Without a sound, he pulled out a vial of the tincture and rubbed the oily liquid into the tender, exposed tissue.

His eyes grew wide as the wound puckered and pulled together under his hand.

"That much better. Save rest for later, in case other dragons hurt." The dragon's voice had taken on a happy, rumbling quality. Aibek smiled, glad to hear the strained tones disappear.

The dragon had just settled his head down on the dusty cobblestones to rest when footsteps echoed in a nearby alley. In a heartbeat, Marah drew her bow and slipped up beside him.

"It's all right. It's just us. Hullo, have you got another dragon?" Mehribahn stepped into the faint light provided by the now-constant dragon flares, followed by at least a dozen battle-weary men.

Aibek recognized all of them on sight. They had been schoolmates, if not classmates. Several he had personally tutored.

"These are the city guard division leaders. They're as glad to see you as I am, and they'll tell their men to fight with you instead of against you." Mehribahn's voice rose to be heard over the clamor of greetings.

"Let's hope it doesn't come to that," Aibek said, grinning. "I'd rather avoid as much bloodshed as we can. Let your men know that my fighters have orders not to pursue anyone who isn't actively fighting them. That may be enough to end the battle. We can figure the rest out later."

Without another word, Aibek turned and climbed onto Gworsad's back. Mehribahn and his friends vanished into the abandoned market. Gworsad took to the air, with Tukanli and Marah close behind. They raced to the wall, where Aibek instructed Gworsad to land on one of the round parapets.

"Are you sure? No other dragons close."

Aibek glanced up to confirm Marah's position. "I'm sure. If anyone tries to attack us, Marah will take care of them."

Gworsad shifted and curled his tail closer around himself. There was barely enough space for him to turn around on the narrow wall. "Someone coming… the stairs."

An instant later, Aibek heard it, too. Heavy booted feet running up the wooden stairs inside the tower.

"Stay alert, but don't attack right away. They may be friendly." His heart pounded in his chest, and strength flooded his arms and legs. Somehow, he didn't believe the approaching soldiers would be on his side.

A dozen men flooded the parapet, though they stayed far back from Gworsad. Clearly, they'd seen what the other dragons were capable of, and were in no rush to get too close to this one.

They stood frozen, staring at Aibek and his dragon, unwilling to make the first move.

"Throw down your weapons and leave us in peace, and you won't be pursued," Aibek shouted. The wind carried his voice down to the soldiers below the wall, and several shouted and looked up to watch.

"What do you mean?" The soldier in front asked, his voice filled with fear.

"I mean that we will not attack anyone who is willing to lay down their weapons. We're here only to oust the vile army that killed the king and imprisoned my friends. I have no interest in ruling the city or the land beyond."

"No one will believe that," A deep voice shouted above the throng.

Aibek glanced around, unsure where the voice had come from. "Show yourself, and I'll prove it to you."

No one moved.

Aibek locked gazes with the terrified soldier in front. "I mean it," he whispered. "Lay down your weapons. Go home. I'm not here to cause any more bloodshed."

"Why would you attack with dragons if you wanted to make peace?" The deep voice echoed off the stone walls.

"How else would we have breeched the walls? This city's defenses are legendary. I'm no fool. I'd have had zero chance of winning without the dragons."

"Ah, now that's where you're wrong. You most certainly ARE a fool. Why else would you challenge me without even seeing what I can do?"

"I've seen your army in action. I've seen them flee when we defeated them in Nivaka, and again when we kicked them out of the forest altogether. I've seen your men begging for their lives, and I've let them live to see another day, as long as they were willing to leave us in peace." Aibek raised his voice and shouted for all to hear, "I want no blood. I only want peace."

"You don't think you're the only one with help from the ancient ones, do you? How do you think I know where the others are hiding?"

Aibek frowned, struggling to keep up with the change in subject, but not wanting to give away his surprise.

"What's the matter? Didn't they tell you about their brother? No, I don't suppose they would. They aren't exactly close."

"Where are you?" Aibek shouted. "Show yourself. None of that matters. I just want to free the city."

"I don't recall asking what you wanted. Nor do I care."

Aibek drew his sword. "Show yourself. Face me like a man."

"Do you take me for a fool? Send away your dragon and we'll face each other on equal footing."

"I thought you said you had help, too." Aibek fought a smile.

"I do, but not the same type that you have. Call off your dragon and you'll see what I can do."

Aibek turned in a slow circle, searching for the source of the taunting voice. "I'm not sure I want to do that. Come out and talk to me."

The silence stretched, punctuated by the clanging of metal as the soldiers shifted in their plate armor. In the distance, flashes of dragon fire illuminated the night.

Finally, Aibek waved Gworsad away. A great gust of wind nearly blew the nearest soldiers over as the dragon took to the sky. Above, Tukanli circled. Marah had her bow trained on Aibek, and he knew she would protect him from any sneak attacks.

"Ah, a wise decision at last."

Aibek narrowed his eyes at the derision in the deep voice.

The soldiers blocking the tower door parted and a man dressed in a crisp yellow uniform strode through. Aibek couldn't see his face in the dark.

"You are?" Aibek asked, not raising his sword, but keeping a tight grip on its hilt.

"I'm Helak, of course." The man swept low in a bow. "And you're the infamous Aibek. I've heard your name so much I despise the sound of it."

"I'm afraid the feeling is mutual. Your men killed my parents, my uncle, and far too many of my friends. You've caused more death and destruction than any man should."

The man laughed, the deep sound echoing between the low stone walls at the top of the city wall. "You think so? You want to know something funny? I didn't set out to kill anyone. That wasn't my plan. I certainly couldn't let a bunch of backward forest fools stop me from saving my family, though. Then you made it clear you weren't reasonable to work with me, so I had no choice but to summon you here so my men can finally take that blasted forest for me. I don't honestly care if they burn the whole thing to the ground. I only want the being you call The Bokinna."

"Yes, I know all of this," Aibek said, laughing. "You think she's going to give you her seeds so you can reanimate your dead wife. But you've killed her friends and loved ones. Why would she ever help you?"

"Oh, I don't need her to agree to anything. I just need to get to her without you and your fool friends getting in my way."

"If you think I'm the one who's been stopping you, then you really are a fool."

Helak growled and drew his sword, a long, jagged weapon with a curved blade unlike anything Aibek had seen before.

"Very well, you've had your chance. Now you will die." Helak brought his blade up and charged, moving faster than any man Aibek had ever seen.

Fueled by the Bokinna's tincture, Aibek stepped aside and dodged the attack.

Rage filled Helak's face, and for the first time, Aibek saw the scar running down the side of his enemy's face.

Overhead, Gworsad rumbled and used his fire-breath to light the sky. Helak ducked his head and blinked at the unexpected brilliance, but Aibek pressed the attack, using his enemy's hesitation to his advantage.

Helak ducked left but wasn't quite fast enough. Aibek's blade pierced his leather armor and dug into the flesh of his sword arm.

With a bellow of rage and pain, Helak shoved Aibek away and rushed in close for an attack. Aibek's strength kept the shove from having much effect. He only took one step back. Helak overextended himself, apparently expecting Aibek to stumble further back, and Aibek swept his sword into the opening. His blade found flesh again, this time through the chest plate, though he didn't have enough leverage to mortally wound his opponent.

Helak clutched at the wound and stumbled back, crashing into a catapult fastened to the stone wall.

Aibek rushed in, quick to take advantage before his enemy could regain his feet.

"Where's that kind and gentle ethos now," Helak ground out over the clang of steel as their blades met.

"I meant what I said. Any who throw down their weapons and stop fighting are free to go." He drew back and gave the man time to stand. "Even you."

"Ha! You've caused me too much trouble to walk away now." He took a few steps back toward his men.

Helak raised both arms over his head and dropped them, as Aibek had seen people do at horse races outside the city.

He shouted, "Hymossod!"

Nothing happened.

Helak turned back to the men watching from the ramparts. "What are you doing? I said, hymossod! Attack him!"

They turned to each other and gave a confused shake of their heads, but none drew their blades.

Helak turned back to Aibek. "What have you done?" His face bore an unhealthy purple hue when Gworsad lit the night once more.

"I've done nothing to your men beyond offering them a chance to retreat without pursuit. Maybe they want the freedom instead of more of your lies."

Helak shook his head and repeated his command again. Still nothing happened. He raised his blade in one hand and drew a dagger in the other. "You'll pay for this!"

Aibek shrugged, unsure what he could have done

to anger the enemy leader so much. In the back of his mind, he wondered if his parents had found a way to free the soldiers from the spirits who had previously possessed them. That would explain their confusion and Helak's sudden lack of control.

Before he could contemplate further, Helak was on him with a furious barrage. Aibek parried and blocked the initial attack and waited for his enemy to wear himself out, as his uncle had taught him early in his training. He backed along the corridor, allowing Helak to think he had the upper hand for a short time. When the thrusts and swings finally slowed, Aibek leaped up onto the short wall and ran along it, attempting to get behind his opponent.

Helak recovered before he'd completed the maneuver and thrust his sword past Aibek's side. Aibek jumped back to avoid the blade, but his feet found no purchase and he plummeted through the black night. He cursed, scrambling to catch hold of the slick marble wall.

Panic clutched at his throat. There was nothing to hold on to. He landed hard on something rough and familiar, the impact knocking the breath from his lungs. As soon as he could breathe again, he worked to figure out what had happened. Leathery wings stretched out and drove them higher, and he grinned and patted the dragon's back.

"Thanks!" His voice carried far enough for Gworsad to hear. The dragon peered back at him with a shining orange eye and rumbled deep in his chest.

Then the moment was over and Gworsad lifted him back up over the wall.

Helak's face went from elated to horrified in an instant when Aibek leapt up onto the turret.

"Did ya miss me?" Aibek asked, grinning. "He raised his blade and prepared for another onslaught.

"You can't win," Helak growled. "You might as well give in now."

"And why would I do that? You've yet to show me any spectacular ability." Aibek blocked Helak's swing and stepped in close. "In fact, I do believe I have you outmatched."

He stepped back and waited for Helak to attack again. This time, his enemy left an opening, and Aibek took it. The tip of his sword pressed through Helak's leather armor and deep into his chest.

Helak clutched at the blade, his eyes wide. Aibek pulled his sword free, allowing Helak to stumble backward toward his men. Instead of helping their commander, however, the men stepped back and watched as he struggled to draw his last breath on the cold marble wall.

When he finally fell silent and still, the men on both sides let out a cheer that shook the very ground beneath them.

~ * ~

His assistants left him as suddenly as they'd appeared, and Eddrick opened his eyes, eager for a glimpse of the battle below. It didn't look like the citizens had much of a chance against the dragons. Aibek's army had already breached the gates and were flooding into the city. Eddrick had no idea how much time had passed. Without the moons to mark the passing of time, the battle seemed an endless struggle.

"Hymossod!" The foreign word echoed through the night, igniting a new level of furor among the spirits the ancients had forced out of the city.

Eddrick struggled to hold his part of the energy field together. Fatigue stole some of his resolve, but he pictured his son fighting for his life and squared his shoulders. The battle below had reached a fever pitch, with two men fighting on the wall. One of them had to be Aibek. He knew it as surely as he knew his own name, though he couldn't see exactly what was happening.

Without warning, one of the fighters below stepped up onto the narrow wall protecting the ramparts. Moments later, the man mis-stepped and tumbled from the wall. Eddrick strained to see; he had to see if his son was safe. Who had fallen? A dragon had him now.

Pain shot through Eddrick's back.

"Ha! I've got you now!" The father had returned and had a weapon in his hand. He rammed it again into Eddrick's back, and the pain exploded into a white-hot light.

"No!" Kiri reached Eddrick an instant before he

vanished into the night. She grabbed the spirit by the head and rammed him again and again into the unyielding wall of light her comrades had created. When he finally dropped his weapon, she snatched it from the sky and rammed it into his chest. Blinding light shone from the wound, expanding to swallow the ghost completely.

Kiri stifled her sobs, focusing instead on filling the gap in the field where Eddrick had been. Aibek still fought for his life in the city below, and she had to stay strong for him.

23.

Retreat

Ahren clung to Chyndri's back and struggled to keep from yanking on her sensitive leafy frill. The sights and sounds of the battle faded into the forefront, blocking out everything else. Ahren struggled to make sense of the mass of bodies below. Now that blood and mud tarnished the enemies' brilliant yellow uniforms, she couldn't tell friend from foe.

"Lower!" The wind carried her raspy voice away, and she cleared her throat to try again. "Get me closer!"

Chyndri bobbed her head once and dove toward the grassy field. The flickering light of the burning camp illuminated the bloodlust on the warriors' faces.

An emrialk screamed, and Chyndri lurched away from the forest and the shadows within it. Ahren peered hard into the darkened tree line. Several massive shapes moved just inside, hidden by the trees and protected by how close together the Bokinna had placed the shadow trees. Chyndri flew faster, moving away from the forest and the dangers within.

Ahren nocked an arrow and pulled the bowstring taut. She moved the bow with her head as she scanned the field, searching for villagers who needed her help.

The fire flared higher, and Ahren froze. A figure she'd recognize anywhere stood silhouetted against the blaze, her back to the fire, facing half a dozen warriors.

"There!" Ahren pointed to where Tamyr fought for her life, and Chyndri dove. The rapid loss of altitude brought back the lightheaded weakness, but Ahren fought the feeling and managed to stay conscious.

The dragon brought her low enough to take aim, and she focused in on one of the warriors fighting Tamyr, but the tree on the back of his zontrec armor brought her up short. She was fighting villagers, not enemy soldiers.

Ahren lowered her bow and waved Chyndri lower. She couldn't shoot her comrades in the back, but she had to do something to help Tamyr.

Chyndri couldn't land in the narrow strip of land between Tamyr and the flames, so she swooped low enough for Ahren to jump down.

Ahren stumbled a few steps from the drop, regained her feet, and threw herself between Tamyr and the men.

"Let's go, Tamyr!" Desperation nearly stole Ahren's voice, but she ground the words out. "My dragon will be back in a minute or two."

"Miss Ahren?" One of the soldiers frowned at her and lowered his sword. "This isn't one of your friends, Miss Ahren. This girl has been fighting for Helak's men all night. She killed two of our men."

The man pointed, and Ahren followed his gaze to the crumpled bodies of two Nivakan men.

"I can't go back to Nivaka," Tamyr shouted over the din of battle. "Even if that hadn't happened," she waved toward the fallen soldiers, "I still couldn't go back."

"You have to. You're one of us!" Ahren dropped her voice to a whisper. "I thought we had something special."

Tears welled in Tamyr's eyes, but she shook her head. "You're a good friend, the best I've ever had, but I only ever loved Ahni. I can't go back. I need a fresh start. I was hoping I'd find it here, with them." She pointed to the blazing camp behind her.

"What did you tell them?"

Tamyr shook her head again. "Nothing they don't already know. You have dragons. I don't have any more to give them."

"What am I supposed to do?"

One of the soldiers stepped closer, and Ahren held up a hand to stop him.

"How should I know? You're sweet on the interloper now, aren't you? You could spend more time with him."

Ahren stifled a bitter laugh. "You really don't know what's been going on, do you? Aibek's been courting one of the mayors from another village. They're inseparable."

"Well, that makes your life a bit harder, but it doesn't change mine. I still can't go back." The compassion left Tamyr's face, replaced by a mask of determination.

"Well, then maybe you should leave. Go north. Make a new life. That's what Aibek's uncle did, isn't it?"

Tamyr dropped the six-inch knife she'd been wielding, spun on her heel, and stalked off. She stayed near the flames and skirted the fighting until she'd vanished from Ahren's view.

"Your dragon's coming back, Miss Ahren," the soldier who'd addressed her before said. "You want us to help you on?"

Ahren forced a smile. "No, just clear a little space for her and we'll be back in the air in no time."

The man spread his arms out and pressed the others back several paces. When they'd made enough room, Chyndri dropped to the ground. Ahren scrambled up onto the dragon and tightened her straps. When she was secure, she called to Chyndri. With a great gust of wind, they took to the sky once more. Ahren stared in the direction Tamyr had run, but she couldn't pick any specific person out of the fray. Tears streamed down her cheeks unchecked. She'd lost more than just a potential suitor. She'd lost one of her best friends. Her chest ached from grief, but the battle raged on. Ahren wiped a sleeve over her face, nocked an arrow, and turned her attention back to the fight.

~ * ~

Sobs ripped through Kiri's chest, making it difficult to concentrate. Still, she had to take Eddrick's place and make sure his death hadn't been for nothing. Points of heat and light stabbed at the forcefield, though none were close enough to injure her. The link between the spirits maintaining the shield meant she could feel every attack, which made it even harder to maintain her focus. She hadn't trained for this as intensively as Eddrick had. He was supposed to hold the shield while she kept an eye on Aibek.

She yearned to know what was happening below but didn't dare glance down. It was that instant of distraction that had meant the end of her precious husband.

Another pain shot through her, this one much closer. Her vision blurred from the pain, but she blinked it away and glanced around for the source of the attack. Three enemy spirits had teamed up and focused their attack on Agommi. Horror washed over her as he endured one assault after another. She could do nothing to help him. If she moved to support him, her—Eddrick's—section of the shield would collapse. She screamed for help, but no sound came out.

Somehow, Agommi held strong against the repeated attacks, though each stab of pain shot straight to Kiri's heart. Had this been what Eddrick felt in his last moments? The thought brought on a fresh round of sobs. She wished she could shed tears, but those were impossible without a physical body.

An eternity passed before Glesni showed up with

reinforcements. They drove the enemy spirits back, and Agommi sagged. The spirits on each side held him up until he'd recovered some of his strength. Kiri wanted to lean on those around her, too, but she had to stay strong. The battle wasn't over yet.

An eternity later, the enemy spirits froze in their attack, but they hung millimeters from the forcefield, arms outstretched and hands clenched into deadly claws, ready to resume their assault. She had no idea why they'd stopped, but she welcomed the respite. It didn't last long enough to suit her.

Before Kiri could catch her breath, the enemy spirits attacked with a fury that shocked her to her core.

Pain exploded over every inch of her being as the enemy focused their assault. For a moment, she didn't think she could bear it, but Eddrick's memory flashed through her mind. She wouldn't let him die in vain. She would hold his place.

Her strength renewed, Kiri repelled the attack and waited to see what the enemy would try next. They seemed to realize they couldn't defeat her, and they moved on to the next spirit in line. Glesni repelled them with no visible effort, and they continued on down the line, searching for a weak link in the chain.

Kiri's vision fuzzed when they focused in on Agommi. He repelled their initial attack, but they sensed something in him that made them persist. Perhaps, Kiri thought, they sensed his grief at the loss of his son. He didn't last long under their concentrated assault. His light flickered, and Kiri willed her strength to him. It had no effect. He flickered again, and the light of his spirit shattered into a thousand pieces and faded into the night.

No! Kiri's head fell to her chest, weakness flooding her heart at the loss of her last remaining family member. She was alone: well and truly alone. She could have fallen to the ground and wept for days from sheer, crushing grief, but Agommi's loss left a hole in the shield. All the spirits shifted to cover the empty place, and Kiri adjusted her position and tried to find a new source of strength.

She had only one hope left.

Aibek.

She had to stay strong. Her son still fought the enemy somewhere beneath her. Tears filled her soul, but she kept Eddrick's face in her mind and focused on the shield. She would do everything in her power to make sure her son won the battle on the ground. Everything. Anything.

The night stretched into an endless moment of pain and grief. Nothing existed except for Aibek's struggle below. Nothing else mattered. She would live for him.

~ * ~

From his perch atop Gamne, Faruz struggled to make out the dynamics of the battle below. It wasn't a structured battle like he was taught to oversee. There were no clear lines, no flanks to defend or shore up. It was a jumbled mass of bodies, small pockets of men and women fighting desperately against their foes. Without the signs he'd been taught to watch for, Faruz had no idea if the villagers were winning or losing. The emrialk continued their haunting cries but had only snuck out of the forest far enough to steal the bodies of the dead soldiers beside the tree line.

Much of the training he'd done with the dragons had proved just as useless as his officer training. He couldn't swoop and swing in the dark, when he couldn't tell friend from foe. The archers had been more effective. Their dragons could bring them low enough to shoot an arrow or two, aiding the villagers in their battle against the invading army.

"I give up! Put me down. I need to fight with my friends."

Gamne swung his head around and peered at Faruz but made no argument before he dove for the ground and landed in the center of the melee.

Enemies and friends alike scrambled away from the dragon's descent. Faruz climbed off the dragon and drew his father's longsword.

He waited for Gamne to take flight, but the dragon settled low to the ground and rumbled.

"I help you, if I can."

Faruz smiled and nodded. He put his back to the dragon and waited to see who would challenge him.

For a long moment, none did. The enemy soldiers gaped at the scene and many left in search of easier battles.

Finally, three men faced him. Each held a dripping

sword in one hand and a dagger in the other. They danced back and forth, keeping just outside Faruz's reach.

Adrenaline coursed through his veins, adding to the tincture's power, and Faruz fought a grin. They were trying to goad him into stepping away from the dragon, if he was reading their movements right. And he was pretty sure he was.

Faruz closed his eyes and breathed in the cold night air, calming his nerves and focusing on the sounds of footsteps and heavy breathing his enemy made. The gentle sound of the dragon's strong heartbeat eased his nerves.

A booted foot squelched in the muck in front of him, and Faruz opened his eyes and swung his blade in a calculated counterattack. He bent to the left, easily avoiding the enemy's blade, and his sword cut deep into the soldier's flank. The man screamed and dropped his sword, clutching at his side. A river of dark blood flowed through his fingers. Before the man could either fall or stagger away, the other two stepped in, closing off Faruz's view of the injured soldier.

"You'll regret that," the taller of the two warned. Blood dripped from his sword and covered his once-yellow uniform. A brass button gleamed in the flickering firelight, somehow untainted by the filth coating the rest of his coat.

An officer. And a high-ranking one, based on the amount of brass gleaming at his collar and sleeves. Faruz adjusted his stance, facing the officer more directly, but never letting the other soldier out of his sight.

The short man moved first, jabbing his dagger toward Faruz's side. Between his years of training and the extra speed the tincture gave him, he had no difficulty side-stepping the attack. Before he'd stopped moving, the officer stepped closer in a vicious barrage that pressed Faruz back toward the dragon.

Gamne chirruped in alarm, but Faruz ignored him. His attention focused purely on the two men in front of him.

Again, the shorter man moved to attack, but this time, Faruz anticipated the move and slid his sword under the man's swing and jabbed hard, the tip sinking deep into the soldier's thigh. The man screamed in pain but didn't drop his weapons. The officer pressed his attack again, but this time, Faruz was ready.

Faruz parried the first jab and pressed closer, leaving his own broadsword useless, but also moving inside the officer's reach. The enemy's eyes widened in surprise, but Faruz wouldn't give him time to recover. He sank his dagger deep into the man's chest and immediately yanked it free.

He resumed his fighting stance, planting his feet in the ankle-deep muck and waiting for the officer's next attack.

The man with the gleaming buttons dropped his sword. He grabbed at his chest and coughed. A line of blood ran from the corner of his mouth. He stepped back, but his boot slid in the mud and he fell forward to his knees.

A horrifying scream of terror and rage filled the night, startling Faruz's gaze away from the dying man. The other soldier, the shorter one, ran to the officer's side and wiped the blood from his face with a dingy sleeve.

Faruz stood still, unable to tear his gaze from the two men. After a long moment, the officer gave a final gasp and fell still. The other man stood but didn't face Faruz. Instead, he produced a white rag from a pocket and tied it to an abandoned spear he found on the ground nearby.

The white rag fluttered in the night's wind, echoing the soldier's cry. "Retreat! Lord Kyron has fallen! Retreat!"

At the man's announcement, enemy soldiers within earshot dropped their weapons and turned to flee.

"What do we do?" A villager asked, not even trying to hide the bewilderment on his face and in his voice.

"Let them go."

Another man stepped up beside them. "What if they come back and attack again tomorrow?"

Faruz shrugged. "Then we'll fight them tomorrow. We're not the kind of men to stab a fleeing man in the back, are we?"

No one answered, but several men shifted as if to follow the escaping army.

An endless silence stretched, filled only with the

groans of the dying and moans of pain from the injured.

Gamne finally said what Faruz had been thinking. "What now? We cannot risk the forest with the emrialk so close. But we cannot stay here."

"Gather everyone to the north of the battlefield who can walk." He waved to the dragons circling overhead, and Gamne rumbled as if to echo his meaning.

One by one, the dragons swooped down and landed in the muddy field. The dying fires lent an eerie cast to the scene. Faruz dragged an unsteady breath through his teeth and waved the riders over.

He handed one vial of the tincture to the first five to reach him, which included Ahren and Zifa. "One drop of this should be enough to heal the wounded." He ran a hand through his hair and tried to ignore the dozens of bodies littering the ground near him. "Don't waste it on the dead. Make sure they have a heartbeat."

In the distance, and emrialk screeched.

"Gamne, can you and the other dragons move the dead and the wounded away from the forest?"

Without a word, Gamne spread his wings and took to the air. He and the other dragons went about the grisly business of moving the villagers and the enemies to safety with only an occasional chirp between them.

~ * ~

The fighting ended as abruptly as it had begun. The spirits fighting against the forcefield stopped and drifted away. The battle had ended, but Kiri didn't know—or care— who had won. Her Eddrick was gone. And this time, he was gone forever. How could she face an eternity without him? He'd been with her for at least a dozen lifetimes. How would she ever live again without his face to comfort and guide her?

She hunched in on herself, unable to stop herself from falling toward the black ground below. Every part of her being screamed out for her husband, but he couldn't answer back. He never would. Never seemed like such a long time.

The sun rose, but Kiri didn't notice. Why would she care? Her love was dead.

"Kiri?"

"Go away," she sobbed.

"Your son needs you," the voice said gently. "He's calling for you."

Kiri stifled another wracking sob and pulled herself upright. "My son? He's alive?"

"That's right. Aibek. He won, but he needs you. He needs his mother right now."

This time, Kiri raised her head and met Glesni's gentle brown eyes.

She drew a deep breath, even though she couldn't feel the air in her lungs anymore and squared her shoulders.

"Well, then I'd better go to him." She closed her eyes, focused on the point of light her son created, and let herself fly through space until she stood near him.

24.

Meditation

Aibek wiped his blade on the fallen enemy's sleeve and hurried down the tower stairs. He swept along the lanes, toward the palace at the center of the city.

The first blush of dawn painted the pale stone building blue when Aibek finally arrived. The dragons all landed on the lawn, and the citizens flooded in around them.

Aibek counted the dragons and riders as they landed and gave a sigh of relief when none showed any serious injury. Bartel had a scrape along one hand and a scratch on his right cheek, and several others had minor scrapes and cuts, but all were walking. Including Marah. Relief weakened his knees at the sight of her, unscathed and whole. He fought the urge to sweep her up in a crushing embrace. Twelve dragons, including Gworsad. Ten riders, not counting Aibek. His chest squeezed at the sight of Dorrel's unmanned dragon, and he wondered how many of his friends and classmates had died fighting on the walls. He might never know.

The dragon riders gathered behind him on the palace steps, and Aibek searched for the words to let the gathered citizens know he hadn't come to replace the tyrant who had ruled for the past several weeks.

Midway through the crowd, a familiar face caught his eye, and Aibek smiled.

"High Constable Cadwy, will you join us?"

A crease appeared between the old professor's bushy white eyebrows, but he moved through the throng to the front, where he stood in front of Aibek on the gleaming marble stairs.

Aibek cleared his throat and spoke in a voice that reverberated through the courtyard. "I have not come to take over this city or the kingdom she represents."

A murmur went through the crowd, but Aibek continued. "I've come simply to free you from the force that took you by surprise and has ruled without honor or justice. I have no wish to be your king." He met Marah's confused gaze and pressed on. "No, I'd rather reinstate the government that has ruled for so many hundreds of years. High Constable Cadwy will oversee the army and will take command until elections can be arranged to select a new king."

"What are you about, boy?" Cadwy whispered. "You led the force that freed us; you're the king."

Aibek shook his head. He pitched his voice low enough so only the elderly constable could hear. "No, I don't belong here. I belong in the forest, with the people my father loved so much."

"Maybe you should take the night to sleep on it. I don't know many who'd turn down the chance to be king."

"Do you hate us so much that you'd rather run

away than lead us?" A male voice shouted from the crowd.

"Of course not." Aibek stifled a laugh. "I love this city. I grew up here. I know many of you by name. I love you enough that I want to return you to the prosperity and peace you've had for generations." A cheer went up, and he waited until the crowd quieted. "I'm not sure that I'm the best person to lead you into that peace, so I'll let you choose your leader."

"What if we choose you?" Another voice, this one female, shouted.

"Then I suppose I'll have no choice. But know this— I want the very best for you and for this city, and the lands she rules beyond her walls. I never even graduated from the academy. There are many who are more qualified to lead you than I am. I hope you'll choose one of them."

Before anyone else could voice a plea for him to stay on as their ruler, Aibek turned and strode into the palace. His heart pounded in his ears. He hadn't been prepared for their pleas. He didn't know what else to say to dissuade them. And he could hardly wait to be back in the forest with his friends.

~ * ~

"Merdarou Emrialk! Bokinna emrleri! Bruanna ati dorn!"

Faruz struggled to translate the foreign shouts.

When he failed, he turned his attention to discovering their source.

The words repeated again and again, coming from dozens of points along the forest's border. They continued rhythmically, a growing chant breaking the stillness of the night.

His hand paused, an inch from an injured man's lips, and the last drop of tincture dripped into the soldier's mouth. Faruz barely noticed.

First one, then a dozen, then a hundred elves strolled through the tree line and into the clearing. They continued the chant until they'd all made their way onto the battlefield. Valasa and twenty others in Gadonu robes followed them out of the forest.

Faruz bit back a relieved sigh but couldn't contain it. Valasa made a beeline for Faruz's position and held out a handful of vials of the Bokinna's tincture. A heavy black leather bag hung around the healer's neck, and bottles clinked softly within it when he moved.

"I'm so happy to see you," Faruz said when the old man didn't move away. "I'm guessing the elves drove the emrialk away?"

"They did. They tried before but couldn't overpower the bloodlust while the battle was still going. Once the fighting stopped and you moved the dead and dying away from the forest, it was easier to drive them off."

"You think that was easy?"

It took a moment for the speaker's identity to sink

in, but once he recognized King Turin, Faruz dropped to a knee in the blood-soaked grass.

"Oh, stand up, boy. You're the one who was out here fighting and making sure I still had a forest to rule over."

Faruz forced a smile and stood.

"We weren't idle while you fought, though. Don't think that. We took care of the enemy soldiers who had already entered the forest and the ones who thought they'd poison the Bokinna again."

Faruz considered that and nodded. "I doubt any within the forest have been idle this night." He gestured to the injured soldiers on the ground. "Now that the Emrialk are gone, can we move them into the villages? We need to get them out of the wind and cold."

Valasa nodded. "I've got an idea. We can use the dragons. Stay here." He rushed off without explaining his plan, but Faruz didn't have time to puzzle it out.

He turned his attention back to the hundreds of injured and dying men and women on the field, distributing one drop of tincture to each. He handed the extra bottles to other uninjured warriors and had them do the same.

As a group, they worked their way through the field of blood and death, reviving those they could save and placing sheets the elves provided over those they couldn't. There were far too many sheets.

Light had begun to brighten the horizon before Valasa returned. He carried a stack of blankets so tall he could barely see over them, and several dragons followed behind him. The dragons each carried a long log that had been stripped of all its branches and leaves.

The dragons set their logs down parallel to one another, and Valasa set to work spreading the blankets between them. Faruz gave his last drop of tincture to the man he was tending and stood, examining Valasa's work and trying to discern the old man's plan.

He gave up after a moment and strode over to help and to learn what the healer had planned.

"Here, take this. Fasten this blanket to that log," Valasa ordered as soon as Faruz was in hearing distance. The healer handed Faruz a small hammer and a handful of tacks and turned back to his own work. Faruz did as he was told, though he still hadn't figured out the purpose. He dragged a hand over his eyes, pushing away the weariness and working to complete the task Valasa had given him. He was too tired to even try to figure out why he was doing it. Instead, he swung the hammer in time with the others nearby, keeping to their rhythm and letting the sound cleanse the night's memories from his mind.

When he'd finished, he straightened and looked to Valasa for his next task, more than pleased to relinquish command now that the battle was over.

"All right, now, bring those men over and lay them here on the blanket." Valasa's voice boomed in the pre-dawn quiet.

All at once, the realization dawned on Faruz. Of

course! The blankets and logs were huge litters that the dragons could carry. They could move dozens of injured at once, and cut the morning's work down to a fraction.

Faruz worked with Dalan, lifting and moving one person at a time onto the makeshift litters. When one was full, two dragons worked together to carry it to the villages. Faruz hoped there were enough people left in the villages to move the people off the litters and into houses where they could be taken care of.

The sun rose and bathed the battlefield in light, illuminating the dead, the patches of scorched earth, and the tatters that remained of the tents. Some warriors with only minor injuries had helped load the more dire soldiers into the litters and had stayed behind to help with the cleanup.

Grief and loss squeezed at Faruz's chest at the sight of the rows of bloodstained sheets filling the field. There had to be a better way.

"You have done well, my child."

The Bokinna's voice brought up gooseflesh on his arms, and Faruz paused in his chores. She couldn't hear his thoughts, could she? He worried for a moment, his eyes finding Zifa's tired form where she tended to the wounded who still waited for their turn to be carried to the villages.

"You have led your people to freedom. You have helped those who were injured and given them a chance to recover. And you have saved the one you loved. Why do you still judge yourself so harshly?"

"So many are dead. Too many. Surely there must

be a way to save our homes without such needless losses?"

"Perhaps, someday, there will be. Until then, you will continue to protect my forest and your loved ones."

Faruz bowed his head, unable to keep his eyes on the hundreds of dead. "What do you know of Aibek? Has he won in Xona?"

"He is beyond my reach, but my Dodonni tell me he has won the battle and destroyed the enemy leader."

Relief and exhaustion made Faruz's shoulders sag. Zifa hurried to his side.

"Are you all right?" She pressed a hand to his back and handed him a water skin.

He accepted it gladly, drinking until he emptied it, and handed it back. "I'm fine. I'm just a little tired. And the Bokinna has just told me that Aibek won his battle in Xona."

Zifa whooped in happiness, drawing stares from the ragged soldiers left on the field.

"Helak is dead," Faruz whispered. "This whole nightmare is over."

Zifa smiled and placed an arm around his waist, pulling him close. "And what will you do now, city officer?"

"Stay in Nivaka and raise my family in peace?" He grinned and pressed his forehead to hers, heedless of the sweat and grime that covered them both.

~ * ~

Aibek strode to the rear of the palace through the same winding corridors he'd traversed earlier in the night and found an empty room where he could safely lock the door and attempt to talk to his parents. He needed their guidance more than ever.

Pushing away the anxiety and grief of the day, he focused his mind, searching for the Bokinna or the Saethem or his parents or any other willing and friendly presence.

"Mother? Father? Are you there?" Despite his best efforts, desperation crept into his mind at the prolonged silence that answered back.

A knock at the door drew his attention back to the sitting room, and he turned just in time to see Marah step through the ornately carved wooden door. He frowned and stared at her. He'd thought he'd locked that door.

"I hope this isn't a bad time," she said, closing the door behind her. "I need to talk to you, and it can't really wait any longer. I've put this off too long already."

He'd been poised to tell her it wasn't a good time but changed his mind at the seriousness in her tone. "All right. Have a seat." Aibek gestured to the plush upholstered chairs encircling the fireplace and waited until Marah had seated herself.

Settling into a chair near her, he met her worried gaze. "What's wrong?"

"Well, I…" She dropped her chin to her chest and refused to meet his eyes. "I don't want you to turn down the kingdom for me." Her eyes darted up to his, then back to the fireplace. "Of course, I don't know that you are, but if you are, you shouldn't."

Aibek swallowed hard and tipped his head to one side. "I don't understand what you're trying to say."

"Look, I like you, a lot. And I think you like me," her words came in short bursts, and she still wouldn't meet his eyes. "But there's something you need to know."

She gripped her hands in her lap, squeezing until her knuckles turned white. "I'm sorry. I didn't mean to lead you on, really, I didn't." She paused and took a deep breath.

Aibek froze, terrified of what she had to say next, but unable to stop her.

The rest of her words came out in a rush so fast Aibek had to focus to make sure he caught it all. "I'm with child. I was with child before our night together in Kainga."

Aibek had no words. He could only gape. Tears ran down her cheeks. He'd never seen her cry before. He longed to comfort her but didn't know what to say or how to make her feel better. None of his experience had prepared him for this.

He said the only thing he could think of, "Who is the father? Do you love him? Should I step aside and let him raise his child?"

Loud sobs erupted from Marah's side of the room, and this time, Aibek couldn't contain the urge to comfort her. He crossed the room and settled into the chair beside her. He gathered her in his arms and pressed a hand to the back of her head, letting her spend her tears onto his shoulder.

He let her cry until her sobs dissolved into random, uncoordinated hiccups. When he was sure she'd finished, he pulled back and asked again, "Who's the father?"

"He was killed in the battle for my village. Saham is free, but Cane is dead, and I'm alone."

Marah dissolved in a fresh wave of tears, and a barrage of helplessness more powerful than anything Aibek had ever experienced washed over him. He held her for an interminable moment, then pulled back.

"What would you have me do? I'll raise the child as my own, if that's your wish, but I won't force myself into your life."

"Would you?" She sniffed and hiccuped. "Would you really?"

"I would—I mean, I will. But we don't have to make any solid decisions tonight. We're both worn to the bone. Let's get some rest, and we'll talk more in the morning."

He stood and grabbed her hands, tugging gently until she stood. Unsure whether it was the right thing to do or not, he pulled her into his arms and held her until she sighed and pulled away.

"You're right, of course. Let's get some sleep. We'll talk more tomorrow." She smiled then, a sweet, sad little smile that pulled at his heart and made him more determined than ever to make her his forever.

"I'm going to meditate for a little while. You go

on to bed." Aibek held the door for her and closed it softly behind her.

The fire crackled on the hearth and Aibek sank into the nearest chair, staring hard into the flames. Somehow the coals he'd burned his entire life felt strange and foreign since he'd spent a year in the forest. He missed the comforting scent of a wood fire. He missed more than that, he realized with a sigh.

"Mother? Father?" He scanned the room, hoping to see them appear in one of the corners.

Nothing happened.

He sighed again and stood, rolling his shoulders to ease his sore muscles. Before he managed a step toward the door, a huge yawn took him by surprise. When he could see again, he started and dropped back into his chair. His mother stood between him and the fire, her face drawn and sad, her hair wild, but her clothes as impeccable as always.

"Are you all right? What happened?" The grief in her eyes stabbed fear into his heart.

Kiri wiped a hand over her face and faded to near transparency. "It was horrible," she whispered. The words tumbled over themselves as she told him all that had happened that night and in the months leading up to it. Anguish choked her when she reached the part about Eddrick's demise. She had to try several times to get the words out.

Shaking, Aibek held out a hand to his mother's fading form. Tears streamed down his cheeks, unheeded. "What happens now?"

"I... I don't know. I have to go back to the city

of the ancients to find out. I can't imagine living an eternity alone. It may be time to be reborn. I'd love to feel the dirt between my toes and the wind in my hair. I want to stay in the forest, though. Eddrick loved the forest so much." Her face twisted in grief once more. She spun away from him and leaned on the hearth, her shoulders shaking with the force of her sorrow.

Unsure what else to say or do, Aibek stood and reached out to comfort her, but his hand passed right through her. She didn't acknowledge him, so he sat back down and let her cry.

Slowly, Kiri regained her composure. Her sobs quieted and her shaking slowed. When she was ready, she turned to face Aibek.

"You look so much like him," she whispered. Her misery was a palpable thing, filling the room and almost making Aibek forget his own grief. "Tell me, what's happened here? You look exhausted. I guess you're the new king. Will you rule from here? Or will you travel between Nivaka and Xona?"

Aibek shook his head. "I'm not taking over the kingdom. I've never wanted to be a king." He explained how he'd appointed a stand-in and planned to hold an election within the month. When he'd finished, he drew a deep breath and told her about his conversation with Marah.

"What will you do?" She asked. "Do you love her? Will you make the child your heir?"

After a moment's hesitation, Aibek answered, "I do. I think I'll raise the child as my own—including making him my heir. Give him all the love and the family he deserves…if Marah will have me, that is."

"What if he's a she?" Kiri smiled at the thought of her son raising a daughter.

"Then I'll raise her as my own. She'll learn to fight, to listen to the forest, to hunt and fish and swim." He paused, considering. "—and of course whatever else she wants to learn will be fine, too." He stopped and grinned. "Does this mean I'm going to be a father?"

"Yes, I think it does." Kiri kissed his cheek, and Aibek felt the touch as a breath of icy air. She pulled back and stared hard at his face. "I'm being summoned. If they send me back to the living, I may not be able to come to you anymore, but I'll never forget you, and I'll always be nearby."

Fresh tears stung Aibek's eyes and blurred his vision. He almost couldn't bear the thought of losing both his parents in one night, especially after so many years without them, but he couldn't ask his mother to stay alone and adrift just for him. He had his Aunt Ira. He had Marah. And a baby to plan for. And a whole forest full of friends and neighbors.

"I'll be all right." The words came out harsh and hoarse, but he pressed on. "You shouldn't have to face an eternity alone, and I don't plan to join the spirit realm for a very long time. Be happy. Be loved. I'll never forget you."

Kiri touched him once on the hand and vanished, leaving Aibek utterly alone, perhaps forever.

No. No, he reminded himself again. He wasn't

alone. He didn't try to hide his tears when he left the sitting room and made his way down the hall to the room where Marah slept. He wouldn't wake her, but he needed to be near her.

25.

Cleanup

Aibek woke with a start, his heart pounding, and listened for the sound that had dragged him from sleep.

Metal clanged somewhere nearby. Though the sound was muffled, it wasn't distant. Aibek sat up, struggling to move quietly and keep from waking Marah unless he had to. Soreness had set in while he slept, and his legs burned and ached when he stood. No light shone through the curtains, but whether he'd slept through the day and night had fallen or whether the curtains simply blocked all the light, Aibek couldn't say.

Tap tap tap.

Aibek leapt away from the rug. The noise had come from the floor beneath the plush tapestry.

The tapping came again, louder this time.

His heart slammed against his ribs, and he glanced over to where Marah slept, tucked in among a mountain of quilts on the king's four-poster bed. He might not be a king, but she certainly deserved a room fit for a queen.

Instead of waking her, he pulled the curtains around the bed and grabbed his sword. Careful not to make a sound, he padded, barefoot, around the room and pulled on the rug, moving it to the side wall opposite the door. A wooden trap door in the floor rattled, and the tapping sound came once more.

He debated downing a vial of the Bokinna's tincture, but he only had two left, so he resisted the urge. Moving with all the stealth he could manage, he inched closer to the trap door. The muscles in his back and legs screamed in protest when he knelt and slid the iron latch away.

Metal hinges groaned and squealed, and the door swung upward. Aibek staggered back, bringing his sword up and preparing to face whatever threat invaded his space.

A serpent's head the color of swamp moss squeezed through the too-small opening, and Aibek couldn't contain a shout.

Marah sighed and shifted behind the curtain, and the beast turned its head to stare at the bed with a soft green eye.

"No!" Aibek threw himself between the snake and the bed, sore muscles forgotten in the rush to defend Marah.

The animal drew back, its narrow pupil widening in surprise.

"I mean you no harm." The snake's long tongue made language difficult, and each word was drawn out and the statement ended with a soft hiss. "You are the one the Bokinna has chosen, are you not?"

Again, the snake drew out every word. Irritation rose in Aibek's chest by the end of the question. He wanted to answer before snake finished speaking but couldn't bring himself to interrupt such a beast.

"I don't know about chosen, but I'm helping defend her, yes."

He wondered if this was the same serpent that had killed Amiran only a few months before.

Deadly silence stretched, and Aibek itched to break it. If only he knew what to say that wouldn't get him killed.

The serpent struggled further into the room, stopping when his head brushed the ceiling. Aibek swallowed, trying to will some moisture into his mouth. He decided to use the same authoritative tone he used to solve disputes in Nivaka. He cleared his throat, hoping he'd be able to speak.

"I'm Aibek," he finally croaked. "What can I do for you?"

"I am Nulsha, servant to the great Saethem." His head bobbed in an awkward bow. "I am here to help you."

The snake squirmed further into the room. "Do you know there are men in these tunnels? Many men. Men with swords. Men with spears and bows and arrows. Are they your men?"

Aibek frowned. The Tsari's fighters didn't know the tunnels existed. And if they had, they wouldn't know to be wary of the maogir or how to avoid the haseriet. A shudder ran through Aibek at the memory of fleeing those awful creatures.

"No," he answered after a pause. "They're not

mine. My men wouldn't brave those tunnels, not knowing what's down there."

The serpent's long pupil dilated, shoving the pale green to the side. "What's down here? Surely nothing scarier than me?"

"The only creatures that could threaten you are called haseriet. They're bloodthirsty insects that feed on injured or dying animals. They're drawn by the smell of blood, and they hunt in swarms large enough to overwhelm and kill an ox in seconds."

The snake cocked its head to the side and blinked. Three sets of eyelids covered each beady eye, coming from different directions and meeting in the center. Aibek suppressed another shudder.

"So I only need to make one bleed, and they will all die? That's easier than I expected."

"If you make someone bleed down there, then you'll have to get out of the tunnels in a hurry. They'll come after you just as fast as they'll attack the men."

A soft hiss filled the air as Nulsha considered this. "What should I do? You are in danger. They surround the castle."

"How fast are you? Can you injure one and get away from the city in a hurry?" Unbidden, the image of the tincture vial flashed in Aibek's mind. He only had two left. Surely, this creature needed it more than he did, especially now that the battle was over, right? He didn't wait for the serpent to respond.

Aibek grunted and reached beneath his nightshirt.

"The Saethem gave me this. You need it more than I do now."

Nulsha stared, his head cocked to one side. "Is that made from her seeds?"

"It is. It will give you strength and speed. Here, bend down." Aibek popped the little cork off the vial and held it up. When the snake opened his mouth, Aibek poured the oily liquid into his mouth, careful to avoid the razor-sharp teeth. Faruz had said the snake's venom had killed Amiran in less than an hour. His hands shook when he lowered the vial and waited for the serpent to respond.

"That feels… quite strange. I will get rid of these enemies below the city. You may rest easy. Thank you for taking care of my mistress and her sister."

Aibek searched his mind for an appropriate response, but before he could come up with one, the serpent had contracted on himself and disappeared through the trap door. Terrified of the creatures Nulsha was about to summon, Aibek hurried to close the door and latch it shut.

"Stay safe, friend," he whispered before he pulled the rug back over the trap door. He scurried back to the bed and beneath the covers, but his ears pricked, searching for any hint of the danger below.

When no sound met his ears after a long while, he fell into a fitful sleep. He dreamed of lost friends, of parents he'd known only too briefly, and of dangers he'd faced and survived.

Faint blue light filtered through the windows when

a knock at the door woke Aibek once more. He swung his legs free of the blankets and padded to the door in his bare feet. He pulled the door open a crack and met the eye of the soldiers stationed in the hall.

"Sir, we don't know what's happening, but it's got the whole palace awake."

Aibek cocked his head and listened. Screams echoed through the halls, punctuated by a faint buzzing that made the hairs on his arms and the back of his neck stand on end.

"Whatever you do, don't open those trap doors." He relayed the midnight encounter with the serpent and his own experience with the haseriet. The soldiers eyes widened with every word Aibek spoke.

Courtesy forgotten, the man ran off to spread the word to keep all the trap doors closed and locked against the threat below. Aibek closed the door and eased himself into the chair beside the hearth. He stared into the dying fire and listened to the horror unfolding beneath the palace.

"I hope you got out all right, Nulsha," he whispered.

In the predawn light, he focused his senses and listened to the night, stretching his awareness outward, searching for the familiar, guiding voice of the Bokinna. He needed to know she had survived the night. Deep down, he knew the battle had flared in the Tsari at the same time he'd fought the enemy in Xona.

Minutes stretched into hours, and Aibek's frustration grew. If the dragons and Nulsha could hear the ancient beings from inside the city, he should be able to do the same.

"Hello, boy. I've heard so much about you."

The voice carried on the breeze through the open window, bringing Aibek up short. He searched the room for the source of the voice, and when he saw nothing, he stuck his head through the window and searched his surroundings.

Nothing.

"You have proven yourself worthy. You have defeated my champion, befriended my child, and overcome every obstacle you have faced. Most impressive."

The voice wasn't unlike that of the Bokinna or Saethem, except it had a distinctly masculine quality.

"Who are you?" Aibek whispered into the morning mist.

"Who am I? I am as old as time itself, but still as young as the day I first existed. I am the ruler of the mountains, the lord of the tree sprites and mountain elves. I am the brother of the ones you call Bokinna and Saethem."

Recognition flickered in Aibek's mind. Pagi had spoken of a brother. "How do I know you are who you say you are?"

"You don't. For now. Run back to your forest home. Ask the one you call Bokinna. She will tell you who I am. And that my friendship is not something freely or lightly given."

"Very well. I will talk to you once I've talked to the Bokinna. If you are who you say you are, then I would be most grateful for your friendship." Somewhere in his chest, Aibek knew the voice belonged to the one Pagi had called Zirvesi. No other beings could speak to him on the wind.

"Aibek?" Marah's voice pulled him from the window.

Empty loneliness filled him—the same feeling he'd had when the Bokinna had turned her attention away from him.

"Who are you talking to?" Marah poked her head out between the heavy curtains. "It's so early." She frowned. "Have we slept all day and all night, too? It looks like morning again."

Aibek rushed to her side. "I'm sorry. I didn't mean to wake you. How are you feeling? Are you sore? Can I get you anything?"

A smile brighter than the sun lit her face, rendering Aibek speechless for the moment. "Does that mean you're all right with… with everything?"

He pulled her into his arms. "We'll face whatever today brings together, and tomorrow, too."

~ * ~

As soon as Faruz has managed to sleep, bathe, and eat a meal fit for a king, he summoned the rest of the mayors to meet with him in his home. The Bokinna's handiwork had brought all the villages close enough to shout from one to the next, which had become the preferred method of communication in the previous week. This time, though, Faruz thought it worth the formality of sending out fairies.

The afternoon sun hung high in the cloudless sky when the mayors filed into Nivaka.

"What is this about? Surely you know we have our own dead to mourn and our own damage to repair?" Iriz snapped before she'd even stepped into his home. "We don't have time to be socializing."

Faruz forced himself to keep his tone civil. "Is that what you think this is? A social call?"

A flush filled her round cheeks and she glanced around at the assembled leaders. She sounded meek and tired when she spoke. "No, of course not. I'm sorry. I think we're all a bit on edge."

She hurried to the sofa and settled in beside Zifa without meeting anyone else's eyes.

Several more mayors filed in behind her and settled into open chairs and onto chests around the edge of the room.

When everyone had quieted down, Faruz stood at the center of the group and addressed them.

"Thank you all for coming. Some of you may already be aware that our representatives in Xona fought the enemy at the same time we did last night." A murmur moved through the group. "For those who haven't heard, Aibek and his dragon riders, along with the army we sent, were successful in driving the enemy out of Xona. Even better, he fought and killed Helak. Our struggles with that overlord are finally at an end."

The mayors stood and cheered and clapped each

other on the back and shoulders, completely drowning out the last words Faruz spoke.

He waited until the celebration died down before continuing. "It's likely that Aibek will be crowned the new king of Xona, which means he will be in the city for a while. I've thought about it all morning, and I think it would be best to send a few dragon riders out to meet him there and develop a plan to develop a new, unified government."

"What does that mean, 'unified?'" Iriz's ruddy cheeks turned almost scarlet under her angry flush. "You want us to be ruled by the king all the way up in Xona?"

"No, that's not what I said. I said we need to discuss our options, nothing more." Faruz took a deep breath, searching for the words to make them understand how important this was. "Still, we need to make sure the rulers in the city don't forget about us again. If we'd had their armies twenty years ago, Helak's forces could have been tossed out on their ears before they had the chance to take the forest."

"How do you propose we manage that? If Aibek's the new king, he shouldn't need anyone to remind him of us, right?" The question came from behind him, and Faruz wasn't sure which mayor had spoken.

Zifa answered before he could. "You don't really think Aibek's going to stay there and take the throne, do you?"

"Well, what else would he do? Doesn't everyone dream of being a king someday?" That was Iriz again. Faruz turned to face her, feeling somewhat like a child's top as he spun to answer questions.

"Not Aibek," Faruz said, chuckling. "He wouldn't even be the mayor if he'd have found some way to refuse without hurting everyone's feelings."

"He's right," Zifa chimed in. "Aibek will hand that crown off at the first opportunity—assuming he accepts it in the first place. We need some way to make sure whoever takes the throne doesn't forget us again."

"We can't send everyone. Most of us need to stay here, make sure everything gets back to normal, finish the cleanup, that sort of thing," a short, stocky mayor with receding hairline said.

"You're perfectly right," Faruz answered. "I was thinking three or four would be plenty. I'll stay here, since Aibek's already in the—"

A tapping at the door stopped him short, and he turned again to see who had knocked. He reached for the door, but it swung open and Valasa poked his shaggy silver head through.

"I'm sorry to interrupt, but you should come…" The healer's voice was softer than Faruz had ever heard it, but it left no room to argue.

Outside in the daylight, Faruz blinked up at the old man. "What is it? What's happened?"

"It's Serik. He's finally awake."

"What changed? You've tried everything already." Faruz couldn't contain the joy of knowing his and Aibek's friend would be all right.

"Everything, right. I tried everything except the

tincture. It never crossed my mind until you used it to help all the people injured last night."

A fresh wave of happiness filled Faruz's chest. He couldn't wait to tell Aibek. He probably still thought his mentor was dead, Faruz realized with a start. He'd found Serik after Aibek had already left for the city.

His musings cut short when he walked into the sickroom in Valasa's house and found Serik sitting propped against the pillows and chewing on a big slice of roast venison. The aroma made Faruz's mouth water, but he ignored his own hunger and settled himself on the edge of the bed.

"How are you feeling?"

"I feel…" Serik held his gnarled hands out in front of him and grinned. "I feel strange, but I'm alive, and that's all that matters for now."

"It's so good to see you awake." Faruz couldn't think of anything else to say, so he sat, grinning stupidly and watching his old friend eat.

Serik finished his roast and set down his fork. "Tell me what I've missed. Are we gearing up for battle? How is the training with the dragons going? Has Aibek learned to master the power?"

Faruz laughed. "No, we're not gearing up for anything." He explained everything that had happened while Serik had lain unconscious and ended with the plans to send a group to Xona. "Will you go? Do you think you can? Aibek doesn't know you're alive. He'll be so happy to see you."

"Now, don't you think that's a bit much to put on

him this soon?" Valasa boomed from the open door. "The man just woke up half an hour ago."

"You're taking dragons, you say?" Serik grinned again and guzzled the last of his famanc. "I think a bit of time in the sky would do me just fine. I'd love to go."

26.

Reunion

A soft tapping at the door woke Aibek. A few days had passed since the battle and the horror in the tunnels, but nothing had been settled in the city yet. Judging by the light streaming through the curtains, he guessed it wasn't long after dawn. Careful not to wake Marah, he threw on his clothes and answered the door in his stocking feet. If shoes were required, he'd have to put his boots on in the hall.

"Sorry to wake you, sir," the young man in the red city guard uniform said. "You have visitors, and they said they can't wait until a more decent hour."

Excitement rose in Aibek's chest. He'd seen his aunt a few times since the battle, but still held out hope that his uncle was somewhere inside the city. Perhaps that's who had woken him?

"Very well," he answered, trying to sound more regal than he felt. "Give me a moment to dress and collect my boots."

"Yes, sir." The guard turned his back when Aibek opened the door to his bedchamber.

A few of the officers had voiced concerns about Aibek and Marah sharing a room. Since they weren't married, many felt it wasn't quite proper. Given

Aibek's place as the election director (as he'd named himself), they said it would be best if Aibek either married her or took a different room, perhaps on a different hall. Aibek had thanked them for the advice and made no move to follow it. He'd marry Marah as soon as things settled down, if she'd have him.

He hadn't asked.

The mere thought of her saying no made him feel lightheaded and nauseated.

He'd have to ask her soon, he knew. If he didn't marry her before they returned to Nivaka, her brothers would probably kill him. In fact, he wasn't sure they wouldn't do that anyway, just to finish the job they'd started in Kainga.

These thoughts occupied his mind while he tugged on his boots and laced them up. They kept him worrying the buttons on his sleeves during the walk to the sitting room where his guests waited.

He worried and picked at loose threads until he swung the door open—and froze.

There, sitting in front of a roaring fire in the palace, was Serik. Alive. Breathing.

"Serik! You're alive!" Aibek barely managed the words around a gasp and tears of joy. "I'm so sorry. How did you recover? I thought you were dead." He swept into the room and gathered his mentor in a hug to rival one of Valasa's.

"Faruz found me and Valasa saved me." Serik said when Aibek released him. "I'm not quite as I was, but I'm well enough for now."

"The Bokinna told Gworsad that you won the battle in Nivaka," Aibek said, moving forward and clasping Faruz in a welcoming hug.

"We did. I could use a hot drink. How about some tea? It's awfully cold out there for flying."

Ahren straightened up then and asked, "What about famanc? That would be perfect."

Aibek smiled and pulled the rope to call a maid. "We don't have famanc, but we do have some very good tea. I'll have them bring in a tray."

He stood awkwardly for a moment, unsure how to greet her after the warm hugs he'd shared with Serik and Faruz. She didn't seem eager to embrace him, so he extended a hand and waited until she grasped it.

"It's wonderful to see you again. I trust your family is well?"

"They are, thank you. Father is overseeing the repairs in Nivaka with both you and Faruz away, and Dalan is taking on more of the Gadonu's healing duties."

"I'm happy to hear it." The stilted formality chafed against his friendlier nature, but Aibek decided not to let her unpredictable moods bother him. His friend was alive. The battle had been won on every front. And the love of his life would awaken at any moment. He was going to be a father. He still couldn't quite believe it.

Another woman stood to take his hand as soon as he'd released Ahren's.

"Oh, Koviom it's good to see you looking so well." She used her grip on his hand to pull him into an awkward hug. "You're a touch skinnier than the last time I saw you."

Aibek flushed and searched his memory. "Iriz, right? I'm sorry, it's been too long, and I'm terrible with names."

"Aye. You do know me." She released him and settled onto the sofa beside Faruz.

"What news do you have for us?" Faruz asked after the maid had left to gather the tea tray.

"Well," Aibek glanced over at Ahren, who sat picking at a loose thread on the divan and studiously ignoring him. Why had she come? "I've refused the crown, though they try to shove it at me every day."

"I told you." Faruz nudged Iriz. "Go on. What else have you done that I predicted?"

"I've set myself as the election director, so I've promised to stay in the city until a new king is chosen."

"All right, I might not have predicted that one, but it doesn't surprise me, either."

Aibek couldn't keep his eyes off Serik's face. The time had aged him faster than all the years they'd spent together, but he was alive!

The maid returned and set a tea tray on the sideboard. "Miss Marah is awake, sir. Should I bring her in?"

Aibek grinned. "Yes, I'd appreciate that. Thank you."

The girl left, her blonde curls reflecting the firelight as she swept from the room. Aibek turned back to his friends.

"That's something you might not have predicted. I'm planning to marry Marah."

Faruz squeaked and jumped up. "I knew it! I knew you two had something going on. And she said yes? She's willing to marry you even though you're a complete nutter?"

"Well, that's the thing. I…"

"You haven't asked her yet, have you?" Serik's soft voice cut through the clatter of dishes.

Heat filled his face and Aibek hung his head. "No."

"Asked who what?" Marah's voice rang from the doorway.

Aibek cursed under his breath. "I… It wasn't supposed to happen this way. Oh, well." He stood and reached for her hands. "Marah, I love you. One lifetime's not enough. I want to love you until the end of time. Will you marry me?"

Marah pulled her hands free and clapped them over her open mouth. Tears streamed from her amber eyes, and Aibek thought she was the most beautiful woman he'd ever seen.

"Yes. Yes, I will."

Aibek's chest swelled with excitement, and he wondered how much happiness one man could take before he just exploded from joy. He had to be nearing the threshold. He grabbed her in a gentle embrace and kissed her lightly, aware of his friends' eyes on his back.

"Well." Faruz cleared his throat. "I guess now we have a wedding to plan."

Marah laughed and pulled free, noticing the others in the room for the first time. "I guess we do. Aibek, I'd take some of that tea, if you don't mind."

"Of course." Aibek handed her a freshly poured cup, along with the cream and sugar she liked.

They spent the morning catching up on gossip and the events in Xona and Nivaka, until Aibek called an end to the visit by claiming he had to go to plan the election. And a wedding.

The next morning, Aibek rose at dawn and dressed without a sound. Since Faruz and Serik had arrived in Xona, Aibek had been anxious to talk to them in private. He craved more news of Nivaka and the people there, and he wanted to tell them all that had happened with his parents.

Careful not to wake Marah, he snuck out the door and hurried down the hall to the sitting room Serik and Faruz had shared. Along the way, he stopped a maid and asked for a tea tray to be brought in.

Half an hour later, he grinned at the return to their previous habit. He shared a comfortable sofa with Serik, who still looked pale and drawn, and Faruz sat across from them in an overstuffed leather armchair. The tea tray sat empty and abandoned on the low table between the seats.

They'd spent the time on small talk and had avoided the more difficult subjects, until Faruz leaned back and sighed. "All right come out with it. You're dying to tell us something, I can tell. What is it?"

Serik raised his bushy eyebrows and adjusted his position on the couch so it was easier to maintain eye contact.

"Well, there's a lot more, actually." He hesitated, drew a calming breath, and launched into all that had happened in Xona after the battle, beginning with Marah's revelation. He teared up when he relayed the news of his father's demise and his mother's plan to reincarnate.

"I don't think I'll see her again," he finished.

Faruz sat, stunned and speechless for the first time Aibek could ever remember. Serik gave a sad little smile.

"It looks like I'll get to take care of another generation of Nivaka's mayors, after all. I'm not sure how long I'll be able to stay, though."

Aibek furrowed his brows in confusion. "What do you mean? Where are you going?"

"Ah, child. I'm older than you can fathom. And the injury in the Bokinna's clearing broke me in ways I cannot explain and that can't be healed. No, I will only have a few more years in this body, if that." At the sorrow in Aibek's eyes, Serik placed a gentle hand on his shoulder. "Don't worry. It'll be a while yet."

"I'm so sorry for what I did to you." Aibek whispered. "I never got a chance to tell you how sorry I am."

"Don't be so hard on yourself, boy." Serik handed him a handkerchief. "You did nothing wrong. You introduced me to a being I'd wanted to meet since I arrived in the Tsari. You gave me the chance to fly on dragons. I have no regrets."

Wiping his face, Aibek nodded, but couldn't think of a single word to say.

"So, when's the wedding?" Faruz broke the pained silence. "And do you think you'll need a bodyguard when we get back to Nivaka? How are her brothers going to take your marriage? I heard they didn't take kindly to you courting her."

Aibek laughed, trying not to remember the beating he'd taken in Kainga. The others joined in, and the conversation shifted to lighter subjects. They laughed at the antics of the elderly women in Nivaka, who always managed to keep the council members on their toes with their squabbles and parties. Faruz shared updates on Zifa's condition and relayed the story of how she'd fallen from her dragon during the battle.

Two hours had passed in banter and laughter by the time a maid knocked at the door to inform Aibek that Marah was looking for him. He asked the maid to bring her to him and bring a fresh tea tray.

The next three days passed in a blur of camaraderie as Faruz and Serik got to know the rest of the dragon riders, including Marah. Aibek organized speeches and debates among the few top-tier military officials who had stepped forward as candidates to take over the kingdom, and Marah spent her days planning for their wedding, aided by several of the dragon riders and Aibek's aunt Ira. The mood and attitude of the staff improved drastically when Aibek and Marah announced their intention to marry, and all the maids and footmen greeted them with smiles instead of the scowls that had marred their first days there.

The day of the wedding dawned wet and dreary. Aibek stood in the window for a long while, watching the rain pelt the glass and hoping it would stop soon.

A soft hand on his shoulder dragged his attention away from the storm. "It'll be fine. We can use one of the ballrooms in the palace." Marah pressed her lips to his neck and gathered her things. "I'll see you in a few hours."

A smile crept over Aibek's face as he watched her go. She'd spend the day being pampered by the palace maids. She deserved every bit of it. Excitement bubbled in his belly at the thought of making her his bride. Was this how Faruz had felt? Aibek's mind flashed back to that moment when Faruz had been standing under the arch, looking like a child who'd gotten away with robbing the cookie jar. That certainly fit how Aibek felt that morning.

He strutted down the hall to make sure the maids had moved everything to the main ballroom, feeling like he'd been given the greatest gift in the land. Of course, his aunt had everything well in hand, and Aibek returned to his chambers. The palace maids cut his hair and trimmed his unkempt beard, making him look every bit the military officer. He dressed in his school uniform, the red and gold coat having been freshly pressed the day before.

The hours flew by and soon it was time for Aibek to take his place. It felt strange to stand at the front of the room in the palace, with candles and lamps and gleaming crystals in place of all the leaves and flowers that would have decorated a forest wedding. Faruz winked at him when the musicians struck the chord that announced the bride's arrival, and Aibek couldn't fight back a grin. Soldiers, dragon riders, friends, and citizens filled the cavernous ballroom to capacity, but all fell silent when Marah stepped into the room. Her dress was fitted at the top and a mass of flowing skirts at the bottom, in the color of the forest's canopy in summertime. Gold embroidered leaves decorated the sleeves, hem, and waistline.

He'd spent hours working with the palace priests on vows that mingled the city's traditions and those from the forest, but he couldn't remember speaking a word of them. All he knew was the happiness in her amber eyes lit by the glow of a thousand candles. Without warning, it was over. Aibek bent and kissed her softly, grabbed her hands, and strode toward the smaller ballroom where a reception had been set up.

His aunt caught him up in a surprisingly strong hug as he entered the room, tears in her eyes. "I'm so proud of you," she whispered. "Your uncle never said it enough, but he was, too. You'll always be my little boy."

Aibek hugged her back and a little of the longing

left his heart. His parents weren't there, but he still had his aunt, and now his wife. An idea crept into his mind, but now wasn't the time to bring it up. Perhaps at breakfast tomorrow. Whatever happened next, he knew deep down that he'd never truly be alone again.

27.

Epilogue

Five years later:

"Excuse me, Mayor?"

Aibek set down his pen and twisted in his chair to greet the young messenger boy.

"Yes, Akash?"

"Sorry to bother you, sir, but someone's here to see you. He says you know him, and he won't see anyone else."

Aibek pursed his lips. Everyone he'd expected had already arrived. "Did he give his name? Never mind, I'm coming. Just let me put this away." He corked the ink bottle and blotted his pen dry, leaving the letter unfinished on the desk. He stood and followed the tow-headed boy out of the room.

"I had him wait in your den. I hope that's all right," Akash blurted out.

Torn between amusement at the boy's eagerness to please and a hesitance to have strangers unsupervised in his house, Aibek just nodded.

His heart skipped a beat when he walked into the den. Pagi, the old man who'd helped him before the battle who reminded him so much of Serik, perched on the edge of a plush chaise. He swallowed the lump that sprang up in his throat and held out a hand in greeting.

"Pagi, it's so good to see you again. I didn't expect you." Aibek's words held a question he couldn't disguise. He'd never told the man where he lived.

"Come, sit with me." Pagi held out a hand in invitation, and Aibek settled onto the sofa beside him. "You've lost a dear friend."

Aibek swallowed again. "Yes."

"How much did Serik tell you about his history and what happened when he was so badly injured inside the forest?"

"Not much. He said it broke him, and he aged so fast after that." Aibek couldn't force his voice above a whisper. The loss was just too fresh. He wasn't ready to talk about Serik yet.

"It did. It quite literally broke him in two. It separated his mortal form from his immortal spirit."

The words didn't make sense, and Aibek struggled to understand.

"Serik's father was an immortal being—the son of Zirvesi himself," Pagi explained. "He'd lived for well over a hundred years before that injury. The old magic he called on separated him."

Aibek held up a hand. "What do you mean 'separated' him? I know it changed him, but how can one person become two?"

"You held the pyre for his mortal form today." Pagi continued as if Aibek hadn't spoken. "I am his immortal form. Now that his conscious spirit has been released, I hold all his knowledge and memories. I was drawn to you before, and now I finally understand why."

It took several minutes for Aibek to process what he heard. When he thought he understood, he asked, "So, are you staying, then? If you're any part of Serik, then you're welcome here."

Pagi laughed. "No, child, I can't stay here forever. I have a home in the Raksaso Mountains with my father and grandfather."

"Of course." Aibek tried to hide his disappointment. "Well, will you stay for the evening? We're all gathering to celebrate Serik's life tonight."

"I can stay for a few weeks, if that's all right. And I can come back and visit from time to time."

Aibek nodded. "That's—"

"Papa! Papa help!" A little girl flung herself into the room and into Aibek's lap. Her flame red hair had been secured into neat braids down her back that morning but had come loose during the day and framed her face in a wild disarray.

Aibek picked her up and set her on his knee. "What's wrong, Kiri?"

"Galfrid and Don have a frog, and they're trying to put it on me!" Her lower lip pushed out in a pout and she put her fists on her hips.

Aibek struggled to keep from smiling. Seconds later, the boys in question ran through the door she'd left open. Galfrid, the older of Aibek's two boys, held something enclosed in his hands.

"Leave the frog outside, Gal." The level of patience in Aibek's voice impressed him, and he managed to keep a straight face.

"Aw, Papa, it's really cute, see?" He opened his hands just enough for a tiny green face to peek through.

Kiri screamed and climbed up Aibek's side.

"Outside," Aibek said, his voice firmer this time. The boy disappeared back through the door, and Kiri settled back down onto Aibek's lap.

Kiri noticed Pagi on the other couch and gave him a shy smile. "I'm Kiri." She said. "Galfrid says he's bigger than me, but he acts littler." She crossed her legs and tossed a wind-swept, mostly-undone braid behind her shoulder.

Aibek smiled. "Yes, he's older than you, but only by a few minutes. Kiri, this is Pagi. He's Serik's…" Aibek paused, unsure how to explain the situation to the little girl.

"I'm Serik's brother," Pagi finished. He gave a little bow. "I'm happy to meet you, Kiri."

Two hours later, Aibek stood in the den holding his sons' freshly washed hands and called out for the women. "It's time to go! The food will be cold if we don't go now."

Aunt Ira emerged first in her favorite zontrec dress. She'd returned with Aibek after the battle for Xona and had never left. Marah and little Kiri followed close behind. Both had washed and braided their hair, though Marah's blonde curls still refused to be contained.

"Ready?" He asked.

Rather than answer, Marah led the procession out the front door and across the Square. Pagi strolled beside Aibek toward the brightly lit Pavilion.

Faruz and Zifa pressed through the crowd, and villagers stepped aside with repeated, "Hey, Captain," and "Glad you could make it."

Zifa pressed a hand to her rounded belly and eased herself into the chair beside Marah.

"How are you feeling? Any better?" Marah asked.

Aibek couldn't help noticing Zifa's pallor and weight loss. Each of Zifa's pregnancies had been the same, with several weeks of severe nausea even Valasa's tinctures couldn't cure. This time, the nausea had lasted well into the second half of her pregnancy, and she had only recently been able to start eating regular food again.

"Better. I ate everything cook made last night, and I feel so much stronger today." Zifa busied herself with the three dark-haired little girls who'd followed her in.

"Papa! I can't see!" the smallest girl, Vorana, stood on her tiptoes and strained to see what was happening at the front of the Pavilion.

Faruz lifted the tiny girl onto his shoulders and seated himself beside Zifa. "Is that better?"

Vorana nodded and grinned, and Aibek wondered at how the child could look like an exact copy of Faruz, but with her mother's straight dark hair.

Aibek helped Marah settle their children onto the benches before he climbed the steps to the dais. Villagers crammed into every corner of the Pavilion, and more strolled along the boardwalks outside its peaked roof.

The chatter died as more and more people noticed Aibek standing on the stage, and he waited until he was sure the people in the back could hear him before he spoke.

"Thank you all for coming. Serik lived a long and happy life and made it very clear we were not to mope around after his passing." A chuckle went through the crowd at this. "He loved each and every one of you, and he asked me to host this celebration to ease our transition into a life without his patient guidance. We have all of his favorite foods and we'll have dancing later tonight.

This night is about celebrating the life Serik lived and rejoicing in the years we got to spend with him. Who knows, maybe we'll make this a new tradition to honor our loved ones when they pass into the eternal arms of our ancestors.

Now, I'll open the floor to anyone who has a story to tell or a thought to share."

King Turan stood and rushed onto the stage. He'd replaced his ordinary forest garb for a cloak and matching suit in resplendent purple silks from the city. The fabric shone in the lamplight, drawing Aibek's eyes away from his face.

"Serik risked everything to come to us. He came to ask for safe passage to save Mayor Aibek from the first invasion more than twenty years ago. He returned several times with Aibek to beg for our help in the struggle against those who would have seen this forest destroyed. He worked tirelessly to protect the forest from enemies who meant to kill us all and take the Bokinna's fertile wealth for their own.

His trials will never be forgotten. Not by us. Not by you, up here in the strange treetop villages. Not by those who live in the villages and towns beyond our forest's border. Serik loved this forest as his home, and she loved him in equal measure in return."

The crowd roared its approval, and Turan took his seat beside Queen Idril and turned his attention to his meal. While they ate, the villagers told story after story of Serik's wisdom, patience, and charm. Aibek hadn't fully realized how much his mentor had helped everyone else in the village until then. He leaned back in his chair, watching, listening, and reveling in the loving community that had become his family.

The stories slowly wound down after an hour, and the band struck a chord. Marah took to the dance floor to teach Galfrid her favorite dance, and Ahren settled into the seat his wife had occupied.

"It's so good to see everyone," she said.

"I'm glad you made it in. The weather's been awful." He cringed at the small talk, but couldn't make himself ask more personal questions.

Ahren had moved to Kainga after the battle. She'd said she needed time to figure out who she was away from the forest and her father's presence.

"It has." She smiled. "You can ask. I'm doing all right, though. My carvings earn a good living, and I have a little house near the river."

"I'm glad to hear that. Are you staying in the city for good, then?"

Before Ahren could answer, little Kiri bounced up to the table and grabbed his hand.

"Papa! Dance with me! Mama's dancing with Gal and I want to dance, too." Ahren smiled and waved him away. Before he'd even stood, she scooted closer to Zifa and leaned close.

After a few dances, he led Marah out to one of the benches beyond the Pavilion for a bit of rest and fresh air. He settled onto the polished wood and she leaned back against him.

"How would you feel about another little one?" Marah asked after a long pause.

Aibek grinned and pulled her close. "Really? Another one? How long?" He pressed a hand to her belly, trying to feel the life growing there.

"Probably near the winter solstice." She placed her hand over his and sighed.

Aibek couldn't contain his happiness. He pressed a kiss to her neck and tried to remember the life he'd once dreamed of. He had planned to be an officer, to travel the land with the army. How silly those dreams sounded to him now. He leaned back and stared up at the stars through the tangle of branches overhead. He couldn't imagine a better life.

Free story offer

I hope you've enjoyed this adventure through the land of Azalin. You can receive a free short story detailing Serik's early days in Nivaka, regular updates about my newest projects and book releases, and more free books and stories by signing up for my newsletter.

I also provide short stories and sneak peeks for each book/series I produce. Be the first to know what's coming. Sign up now at BookHip.com/QMLBBC

About the Author

Leslie E. Heath lives in rural North Carolina with her husband, children, and an unsettlingly large number of rescue pets. She enjoys writing, which is important because she plans to do a lot more of it. When she's not writing, she enjoys spending time at the beach, training for and competing in long-distance running events, and working as a registered nurse.